gracefully yours
best friends book club

jennifer chipman

Copyright © 2023 by Jennifer Chipman

All rights reserved.

No part of this book may be reproduced in any form or by any electronic or mechanical means, including information storage and retrieval systems, without written permission from the author, except for the use of brief quotations in a book review.

Cover Art © @alfromnowhere on Instagram

※ Created with Vellum

For everyone who's waiting for their happily ever after.

Playlist

1. Imagination - Shawn Mendes
2. the 1 - Taylor Swift
3. Rain Check - Elias.
4. ceilings - Lizzy McAlpine
5. Lavender Haze - Taylor Swift
6. Anyone Else - Joshua Bassett
7. What If (I Told You I Like You) - Johnny Orlando, kenzie
8. Someday - Michael Buble, Meghan Trainor
9. I'm Only Me When I'm With You - Taylor Swift
10. Light Switch - Charlie Puth
11. Make You Mine - PUBLIC
12. Love Somebody - Alex G, Jon D
13. Two is Better Than One - Boys Like Girls, Taylor Swift
14. Like Real People Do - Hozier
15. Never Get to Hold You - Carly Rae Jepsen
16. Sweater Weather - The Neighborhood
17. Marry Me - Train
18. Today Was a Fairytale - Taylor Swift
19. This Dance - Five for Fighting

20. Marry You - Bruno Mars
21. Turning Page - Sleeping At Last
22. invisible string - Taylor Swift
23. Heaven - DJ Sammy, Yanou, Do
24. Kiss Me - Ed Sheeran
25. Adore You - Harry Styles
26. Dress - Taylor Swift
27. i'm yours - Isabel LaRosa
28. Still Falling For You - Ellie Goulding
29. Nothing - Bruno Major
30. I Want to Write You a Song - One Direction
31. I Think He Knows - Taylor Swift
32. Dandelions - Ruth B.
33. You Are In Love - Taylor Swift
34. Lover Of Mine - Five Seconds of Summer
35. Cornelia Street - Taylor Swift
36. Like I'm Gonna Lose You - Meghan Trainor, John Legend
37. Hesitate - Jonas Brothers
38. Love song - Lana Del Rey
39. Someone to Stay - Vancouver Sleep Clinic
40. To Build A Home - The Cinematic Orchestra, Patrick Watson
41. I Believe - Jonas Brothers
42. Forever Now - Michael Buble

Table of Contents

Prologue	1
1. Charlotte	21
2. Daniel	29
3. Charlotte	38
4. Daniel	48
5. Charlotte	55
6. Daniel	65
7. Charlotte	75
8. Daniel	85
9. Charlotte	95
10. Daniel	107
11. Charlotte	117
12. Daniel	125
13. Charlotte	132
14. Daniel	143
15. Charlotte	156
16. Daniel	167
17. Charlotte	175
18. Daniel	182
19. Charlotte	190
20. Daniel	204
21. Charlotte	212
22. Daniel	220
23. Charlotte	230
24. Daniel	245
25. Charlotte	254
26. Daniel	263
27. Charlotte	277
28. Daniel	285
29. Charlotte	294
30. Daniel	304

31. Charlotte	311
32. Daniel	320
33. Charlotte	324
34. Daniel	330
35. Charlotte	337
36. Charlotte	345
37. Daniel	356
38. Charlotte	365
39. Daniel	373
40. Daniel	377
Epilogue	385
Extended Epilogue	392
Acknowledgements	403
About the Author	405
Also by Jennifer Chipman	407

Prologue
CHARLOTTE

FRESHMAN YEAR

My fingers strummed against the plastic underneath the car window as I stared outside, watching the passing view. There was greenery all around, even in the summer. I loved it. I loved the mass of bridges that we were passing by as we drove up the interstate towards my new home.

Home. I was searching for what that really meant.

Maybe it was because I didn't quite feel at home in California that I'd chosen a small, private school in Oregon. Maybe it was something else pushing me entirely.

"Are you sure this is what you want?" My mother asked me—for the tenth time since that morning—as we'd taken one final car ride from our hotel to my new college campus.

The place where I would spend the next four years of my life.

The place that would be my home, where I could be my own person and make my own choices. That newfound freedom that had me leaping out of my bed each morning on our road trip up.

I looked over, staring at her light blonde hair–the same shade as mine, though she'd long since started dyeing it that shade–and studied the tightness in her jaw. The slight downcurve of her lips.

"I'm sure, Mom," I said, smiling out the window as we pulled onto campus.

There were a thousand reasons she'd given for me staying closer to home, but there was something about this school that called me there.

It was a small university—nestled along the bank of the Willamette river in Portland—but here, I wouldn't be one of a hundred thousand students, just one of four thousand. The average class size was thirty people, instead of three hundred.

On the tour I'd taken last fall, they'd talked about *community*. Each dorm was a community. The residence hall you lived in was so much more than that.

It had everything the giant state schools had not.

Trees lined the drive as we pulled in, towards my dorm and new home: Juniper Hall. I couldn't wait to meet my roommate. Maybe we wouldn't be best friends, but as long as we got along, that would be enough. I'd never shared a room before, but excited jitters ran through me as my mom parked the car and I hopped out, heading towards check-in to get my keys.

The process was quick, and after I'd met my RA, I headed up to my dorm with my key in hand, pulling an enormous suitcase behind me with my duffel swung over one shoulder.

My new roommate was sitting on the floor, her long red hair pulled back into a thick ponytail, folding a turtleneck sweater, when I walked in. Her orange patterned bedspread was already spread out over her lofted mattress, giving her plenty of room underneath for storage.

"Oh my gosh!" she exclaimed, standing up as I walked into the room. "You're here!"

"Hi," I smiled, extending out a hand. "I'm Charlotte."

Not Lottie or Charlie. I'd grown out of those nicknames a long time ago, and now I wanted to figure out who I was on my own. Charlotte seemed like a good start.

Ignoring my hand, she pulled me into a big hug, and I instantly sank into the embrace.

"Noelle," she said, cheeks rosy as she beamed at me. "This is so exciting. What are you studying? I'm an English major, but I'm hoping to work in the book industry one day because I *love* it."

I dropped my duffel on the bed and left my suitcase next to it. Straightening out my pink dress, I got ready to head back out to the car. I had brought very little with me, especially compared to my roommate. We'd gone shopping for the other essentials when we got here.

I focused back on my new redheaded roommate, who was unloading a box onto her desk in the corner, several romance books in her arms. My eyes grew wide, finally connecting the dots with what she had just said. "You like to *read,* too?" There was no containing my smile. "I have to get another load from the car and find my mom, but we're *so* going to be good friends."

Maybe best friends. I hoped.

I needed one.

"Do you need any help?" Noelle asked, but I shook my head.

"I don't have that much more—I'll be quick!"

"Okay. Just let me know if you do!"

I darted out into the hallway, heading for the stairs to head back down to find my mom and get my bedding and the other stuff I'd left in the car.

By the time I'd come back with my mom, and I emptied all the stuff from the car, I closed my door, looking at the little name tags the RA had made for me and Noelle.

Maybe it was the excitement that distracted me from my surroundings, the anticipation of all of it, but I was lost in my own world until a hard body ran into mine.

"Oh!" I gasped, startled by the contact as the guy turned to look at me.

He was tall—over six foot, compared to my five foot four stature, with dark, almost black hair and a pair of brown eyes that seemed to take all of me in.

"Shit. Sorry." He smoothed a hand over his face, messing with his hair. "I should have been looking where I was going."

"Are you okay?" I watched him try to rub at his shoulders. "I was just... staring at my door. It's all sort of surreal still." I pointed at my dorm room.

He gave me a small smile, probably just placating the silly freshman who was just standing in the hallway. "I get it."

I wondered why he was in our hallway—if he'd helped someone move in, who were they to him? The dorm was co-ed, but our floor was girls-only. The question slipped out of my mouth before I could stop it. "Are you helping your girlfriend move in?" I asked.

Why? It wasn't like I was asking because I wanted to date him.

The guy blinked at me. "What? No. Just my sister. Angelina." He looked at the door behind me.

"Oh." I tried to suppress a blush at my embarrassment. "That... makes sense."

"So are you Charlotte?" He looked at my door. "Or Noelle?"

"Charlotte. But my friends call me Char." I felt my cheeks pink. Because it was my first time offering someone my nickname, the one I'd chosen for myself, and that felt... good. "Noelle's my roommate."

"Well, it's very nice to meet you, Charlotte. I'm Daniel." He grinned.

Daniel. That was a nice name. He seemed nice, too. Considering he was standing here and talking with me, even when he didn't have to.

"It's nice to meet you, too, Daniel. I guess we'll probably be seeing a lot of each other?"

He raised an eyebrow, and I was about to kick myself for not explaining why, because it wasn't like I was trying to be some weird creepy stalker. But then—"Right. Because you live right across from my sister."

"Yep." I nodded, a small smile spreading across my face.

I'd met his sister, Angelina, and her roommate Gabbi— earlier, and I was pretty sure that it was the closest thing to love at first sight for me. It might have been cliche, but I could already tell I was going to be friends with them and Noelle. We'd already made plans to walk over to the first Orientation activity together, and then to eat dinner together.

I didn't have a brother, but I kind of liked that he was close with his sister. Me and my sister weren't close, and I wished I had one that cared enough about me to help move me into college. "I promise I'm not normally this much of a klutz." Of course, I'd almost topple onto someone on my very first day on campus.

He chuckled, a sound that I found was calming. "Hey, I go running every morning, and I still trip over my own two feet sometimes."

When I'd decided on moving to a new city for college by myself, I'd resolved myself of two things. One was that I was going to make friends. Besides my roommate Noelle and the girls across the hall, he seemed like a good option, even if I'd only just met him. Plus, he'd been polite enough to check on me instead of just glaring and walking away.

Plus, I liked to run too, to keep in shape because of dance, and if I could have a running buddy, well... "Oh, you like to run? I have to figure out a route myself around here... I moved up from California, so I'm not too familiar with the area, honestly."

"I ran track in high school. So I can probably show you a few routes. You know. Give you some pointers." He stretched his arms behind his head, flexing his muscles, and I tried hard not to show how affected I was. I didn't come to college to date, but to get an education and find my path in life. No matter what happened, I wasn't entertaining those thoughts. Not now, at least.

"I'd like that. I'm a dancer. Running helps me stay in shape." I couldn't keep my grin off my face.

Daniel extended out a hand. "Friends?"

"I'd like that." Placing mine in his, we shook on it, and that was that.

From then on, Daniel Bradford was one of the biggest constants in my life.

And my best friend.

SOPHOMORE YEAR

At nineteen years old, I was perfectly comfortable with the fact that I'd never had a boyfriend. In high school, I'd been too busy with dance practices every day to even think about dating, and now that I was in my second year of college, well...

I was sitting on Daniel's bed in his house, eating marshmallows and staring at my best friend as I procrastinated doing my history paper.

But I wasn't focusing on the screen in front of me, or the taste of the marshmallows on my tongue. I couldn't stop staring at his lips. My best friend's lips. A place where they absolutely should not have been, but I couldn't help it.

Noelle had a boyfriend. Gabbi had another girl had hung around the dorm for a few months before she shared with all of us that she was bi. And Angelina, with her tight ponytails and red lipstick, had more confidence than I could ever muster, and I... still hadn't had my first kiss.

Not that I felt like I was lacking because of it. I just wondered what it would be like, and part of me wanted to get it over with. To not have this feeling dangling over my head. Like people could take one look at me, with my glittery shoes and my pink canvas backpack, and see *virgin* plastered all over my forehead. I didn't want to be some innocent or naive girl, in the same way that I hated it when I got labeled as a dumb blonde.

"Hey." I threw a pillow at Daniel's head, missing him as it fell on the floor.

He perked up from his engineering textbook, looking at me. "What?"

"What's it like to kiss someone?" My cheeks flushed pink, but I didn't care.

He raised an eyebrow. "What do you mean? Isn't this a better question to ask the girls?" Probably. But I didn't want them to make fun of me. And no matter what Daniel would say, he would never laugh at me.

"Well, I... I've never kissed anyone." I swallowed roughly, not able to hold his eye contact.

"What do you mean, you've *never* kissed anyone?"

I could feel his eyes on me, but I shrugged and shook my head, plopping another marshmallow into my mouth.

He had a girlfriend last year—or maybe more than one, I wasn't really sure—but the closer we got, the less I saw of anyone else. Selfishly, I liked it that way. Knowing he preferred to spending his time with me.

"Really?" He asked again.

Slumping back against his pillows so I could stare at his ceiling, I brushed my hair away from me, letting it fan out over his dark gray pillowcases.

"You know I haven't had a boyfriend. Why is *this* so surprising? Of course I haven't kissed anyone. Besides, I spend all my time with you, dummy." I threw a marshmallow at him, because that seemed like the most illogical thing I could do right now.

Deflecting.

What I didn't want to do was explain to my best friend why I'd even asked. Why was I still staring at his lips?

I shouldn't have brought it up in the first place.

Apparently, I wasn't done putting my foot in my mouth, though. "I always wanted it to be with someone special," I whispered. "I didn't want to waste it on someone who wasn't."

Once, in middle school, my friend had told me she wanted to only kiss the person she was going to marry. She thought it was romantic. Even then, back when I still thought kissing boys was gross, I thought it was silly. I didn't have any ridiculous notions or even expectations. I just... wanted to kiss someone I cared about. Not a guy whose name I would forget in ten years, or ten minutes.

7

"How many girls have *you* kissed?" I asked, unable to stop myself.

"Um." He blinked. "A few."

I didn't know why that gave me an unsettling feeling in my gut. This was just Daniel. My best friend. I'd never looked at him like that, and I knew he'd never looked at me that way either. It was why we were so close, why our friendship worked so well.

Sure, I thought he was attractive, but it was an attraction I would never act on. So what did it matter?

"What's it like?"

"What?" He blinked a few times, like he'd been thinking about something else. A girl he'd kissed before, maybe? The thought soured in my mouth.

"*Kissing*. What's it like?"

Could the earth open up and swallow me whole right now? Why did I keep asking him this?

"Well..." He tugged at the collar of his shirt. "I guess it's nice, with the right person."

"And have you found the right person?" I danced my fingers across his bed, still determined not to look him in the eye. What was wrong with me tonight?

Sugar high. I was going to blame it on that. Or maybe someone spiked my marshmallows. That was the only explanation, certainly.

He shook his head. "No. That's why I'm not kissing them right now."

Sitting up, I pushed at him playfully.

We fell back into an awkward silence as I kept eating my marshmallows, letting my mouth be full so I didn't keep saying stupid things.

I was going to say them anyway. I couldn't help it.

"Daniel?"

"Hmm?"

"What if..." My cheeks turned hot, and finally, I turned to face him. "What if *you* kiss me?"

"What?" He sounded shocked. I hoped there wasn't also a side of mortification along with it.

I could deal with a lot of things, but my best friend openly rejecting me was almost too much to bear. Asking anyone to kiss me and risking them saying no was a lot, but this...

"But... you're my best friend."

"I know. That's why it's perfect. It's *you*, and I feel safe with you."

"I thought..." He bit his lip, not finishing the statement.

Thought what? I wanted to ask, but I didn't.

He said nothing, and I moved to get off his bed, tugging my sweater down. "Never mind, forget about it. It was a bad idea. I don't know what I was thinking." I tried to ignore the embarrassment of the whole situation. Why had I even brought it up?

"Charlotte," he said, not a statement. A command. Ordering me to stay put. Not to disappear on him. I turned my head back to look at him. "Come here."

He tugged me in close to his side.

"O—okay."

Pulling me onto his lap, he brushed a strand of loose hair behind my ear.

"What are you doing?" I whispered.

"Close your eyes."

The smooth, confident tone in his voice had me instantly complying, my eyes fluttering shut.

I could feel him running his finger over my cheekbone before his hand cupped my face. He'd never touched me like this before. We'd done everything together, but never this.

We'd never touched each other like this.

He was my best friend, and I wasn't even interested in him like that, and yet...

"I'm going to kiss you now," he whispered.

Nodding my head, I hoped he didn't notice how my heart rate had sped up.

Then his lips pressed against mine and he was kissing me.

Daniel Bradford, my best friend—was kissing *me*. Charlotte Reynolds. *Was this a dream?*

I wrapped my arms around the back of his neck, intertwining my fingers in the hair at the base of his skull.

Sighing into it, he deepened the kiss, longer this time, but he didn't go any further, and I couldn't resist running my tongue against the entrance of his lips. Needing more. It might have meant nothing to him, just another kiss, just another girl, but I wouldn't regret one moment of it.

Daniel pulled away as our tongues connected, and it saved me from the moan I'd been so close to letting out, but I couldn't help but feel... disappointed?

"What, did you not like it?" I felt so small. Did he not want this? Maybe I'd coerced him into something he didn't want to do, and I'd ruined everything between us.

That was the last thing I wanted.

"No, it's not that..." He squeezed his eyes shut, like he couldn't stand to look at me. "I don't want to mess things up between us. You're the best friend I've ever had."

"I understand." I nodded, finding it too awkward to stay in this position sitting on top of him, and went back to sitting on his bed. "It won't happen again."

Because I could lose a lot of things, but not him. Never him.

And later, in the darkness of my room, I'd run my fingers over my lips, wondering... What if it hadn't?

What if he wanted me?

JUNIOR YEAR

"Marry me."

What? I wasn't sure I heard him right. There was no way. We were sitting on my couch, watching our favorite Netflix show on my laptop. I looked up at him, confusion written all over my face.

Noelle, Angelina and I had moved out of our dorm at the beginning of this academic year, and now it was spring semester. Which meant Daniel was graduating in just a few months. None of that explained what he just said, though.

I paused the show and moved to sit in front of him. "What? I'm sure I heard you wrong." There was no way he was saying we should get married. Not after the epic disaster of our kiss last year. We hadn't brought it up again.

Maybe he wanted to pretend it hadn't happened.

"I was just thinking. If we're both still single when we turn thirty, we should get married."

Yep, he definitely just said that. I bit my lip, watching as he plopped another piece of popcorn in his mouth. As if he hadn't just dropped a giant bomb on me.

"But you're my best friend." That was the only thought that I could come up with. The only reason us having a marriage pact was a terrible idea. If we couldn't even kiss and not have it awkward between us, how could we get married?

He nodded. "That's why it would work. Come on, Char, it's a good option. If neither of us finds someone, we should marry each other. I know I can put up with you, and I can take care of you."

"You're proposing we get married just because we get along?" I didn't know how to feel, or what I wanted in life, but I knew it was more than *that*. I didn't want to be someone's obligation or backup plan. Marriage, to me, was loving someone so much that you didn't want to be without them.

That was what I wanted.

"Think about it. If neither one of us finds anyone in the next eight years, we can just do it together. *Life*. We both want a family. It makes sense."

I agreed, perhaps because he was graduating soon and would have less time for me, or maybe something inside of me just wanted him to be happy.

"Okay."

"Okay, you'll think about it?"

I shook my head. "Okay, if I haven't met anyone by the time you turn thirty... we'll get married. A marriage pact." If we waited until *I* was thirty, he'd be nearing thirty-two. I really hoped neither one of us would still be single at thirty-two.

He cracked a grin, running his fingers through his dark hair. "Good."

"Now, can we get back to the show? I like this part."

Maybe it was because I didn't want to linger on the thought of us *together*. *Married*. I just wanted our routine, our comfort. To sit far enough on the couch that we weren't touching, just like always.

We didn't cuddle. We didn't hold hands. We were best friends, and that was enough.

Best friends who agreed to marry each other if they didn't meet anyone else, but... who was counting?

I hit play.

Daniel

SOPHOMORE YEAR

"ANGELINA," I called, huffing down the hallway with her box in my arms. "Did you *really* have to pack so much stuff? It's not like we can't go home on the weekends." I couldn't help but tease her.

My younger sister had decided to go to the same college as me —not that I minded, because we'd always been close growing up, but I was serious. She had packed almost her entire freaking wardrobe—and we only lived about twenty-five minutes from campus.

"Shush," Angelina said, brushing her long black hair behind her back. It was a trait we both had in common—hair so dark, it almost looked black. It was our Italian heritage on our mom's side that we got it from, as well as our olive-skinned complexion, but she had gotten our dad's blue eyes versus my brown ones.

I playfully rolled my eyes at her as I set my armful down in her dorm room.

"How much more is there?" She asked. It was still pretty sparse, but her new roommate had already started unpacking her stuff.

"Car's almost empty." I gave her roommate—Gabrielle, I tried to remind myself—a slight nod as she continued emptying a box, before we both headed back down for another load.

After we had finished emptying the car, I stood outside with the last load in my arms, staring up at Juniper Hall—the dorm my sister would live in for the year. I couldn't believe how normal it felt that we'd be going to the same school together again. That anytime I wanted to hang out, I at least had my sister.

All over the quad were families, parents dropping their kids off at school, but Angelina only had me. Not that our parents were gone, or anything—but after their divorce, neither one of them could stand being in the same place, and now it was just us here.

I locked my car and adjusted the last box of stuff in my arms and headed back into the dorm to take the elevator up to the third floor. Of course, Angelina hadn't waited for me, so I'd had to shuffle the box to press the up button, but I made it work.

When the elevator doors finally opened, I saw *her*.

Everything was hazy, and then she whirled around, retreating into a room in a blur of blonde and pink.

I blinked, and Angelina popped her head out of her door. "You coming with that?"

"Oh. Uh. Yes." I followed her into her room and plopped the box on the floor, looking for a glimpse of the blonde girl again.

Why did I have such a desire to get another look at her? I'd barely even seen her face, so it was crazy that I was feeling this way. My freshman year girlfriend and I had broken up before summer started, but it wasn't like I was longing for another relationship. I was fine with just having my few buddies, running track, and focusing on my engineering classes.

"I'll get going now," I said to Angelina, nodding briefly at Gabrielle, whose parents had left to get food. They'd brought their daughter all the way out here from Boston, and I was glad that at least someone seemed to have parents who cared about their whereabouts.

"Okay. See you later!" Angelina smiled at me before turning back to her mess of clothes she was attempting to fit in the tiny dorm closet.

"Have fun at Orientation, sis. Don't get into any trouble."

She made a little pouty face, like she always did when I called her that. That was the thing with spending all of your time with your sibling—you knew them inside and out. Even when she pretended to hate me around her friends in high school, we'd always been close. We'd go home, and after finishing our homework, we'd watch TV or play video games together.

I hated how she always beat me at Mario Kart.

"Daniel, I'm not twelve anymore. I can take care of myself, promise."

Sure, I knew she could, but ever since our parents had divorced, I'd felt like I needed to look after her more. It was weird thinking she was an adult now, living on her own. That she wouldn't *need* me.

I closed the door behind me, rubbing my shoulders. I'd carried a large amount of clothing up the stairs, and I was still trying to figure out why Angelina needed that many *shoes*.

As I turned, my body collided with someone else.

"Oh!" the voice—female—said, startled as I turned around to face her.

I opened my mouth to apologize, but there she was, standing in front of me. The girl from earlier. Long, blonde hair braided into two pigtails, bright gray eyes that almost sparkled, wearing a white t-shirt with a short pink overall dress.

"Shit. Sorry." I groaned. "I should have been looking where I was going." Wincing, I rolled my shoulder back once more.

"Are you okay?" She looked concerned as I tried to rub the muscles. "I was just... staring at my door." She pointed to the one directly opposite Angelina's. "It's all sort of surreal still."

I nodded. "I get it." I'd been there last year.

"Are you helping your girlfriend move in?" She asked, her head tilting to the door I'd just come from.

I blinked. "What?" *Oh.* I looked at Angelina's name on the door. "No. Just my sister."

"Oh." The blonde nodded. "That... makes sense."

I looked back at her door at the little door decoration that their RAs made with their names. They were cute as shit. The RAs on the floor of my dorm couldn't care less about making the decorations this fun.

"So are you Charlotte?" I guessed, reading off the names. "Or Noelle?"

"Charlotte. But my friends call me Char." A pretty pink shade spread across her cheeks. "Noelle's my roommate."

"Well, it's very nice to meet you, Charlotte." I couldn't help my grin. "I'm Daniel."

"It's nice to meet you, too, Daniel. I guess we'll probably be seeing a lot of each other?"

I raised an eyebrow, as if to ask why, and then I remembered. "Right. Because you live right across from my sister."

"Yep." She offered me a small smile. "I promise I'm not normally this much of a klutz."

"Hey, I go running every morning, and I still trip over my own two feet sometimes."

"Oh, you like to run?" Charlotte looked at me shyly. "I have to figure out a route myself around here... I moved up from California, so I'm not too familiar with the area, honestly."

"I ran track in high school. So I can probably show you a few routes. You know. Give you some pointers."

She grinned. "I'd like that. I'm a dancer. Running helps me stay in shape."

That day was the beginning of many morning runs, study sessions, and evenings spent together. We shared our favorite foods, music, movies, and eventually, what felt like most of our lives.

It was the first year where I felt like I really had someone who knew me.

All of me.

∼

JUNIOR YEAR

"What do you mean, you've *never* kissed anyone?" I stared at her, still in shock. Maybe I didn't have any right to speak, considering I'd barely kissed anyone, but still—I'd had a few girlfriends. None since meeting her, though.

Shrugging, Charlotte just shook her head as she continued to sit on my bed, plopping marshmallows into her mouth.

We'd been friends for a year, *best friends*, but somehow I still felt like there was so much I didn't know about her. And I spent more time with her than anyone else—even my roommate and my sister.

"Really?" I asked again.

She slumped back against my pillows, her blonde hair spilling across the dark gray pillowcase. "You know I haven't had a boyfriend. Why is *this* so surprising? Of course I haven't kissed anyone. Besides, I spend all my time with you, dummy." She threw a marshmallow at me.

I stammered. I didn't really have a reason that I couldn't believe it, but also... I knew I didn't *want* her to kiss anyone else. Was that crazy? She was my best friend. But... I couldn't help but stare at her glossy pink lips, covered in her favorite lip gloss she always wore.

What would it taste like? What would she taste like?

"I always wanted it to be with someone special," she whispered, looking shyer than I'd ever seen her. "And I didn't want to waste it on someone who wasn't."

And maybe I hadn't, but I understood that.

"How many girls have *you* kissed, anyway?" Charlotte asked, looking up at me as her blonde hair fanned out across my comforter.

"Um." I blinked. "A few, I guess."

Freshman year, in my newfound freedom, there had been more than a few. But now? I couldn't imagine kissing anyone else. She wasn't mine, and I wasn't hers, but it still felt like a betrayal to even think about having my lips against someone else's.

"What's it like?"

"What?" I blinked away my distraction, catching Charlotte staring at me.

"*Kissing*. What's it like?"

"Well..." *Was I sweating?* The room suddenly felt like it was a million degrees inside. I tugged at my collar. "I guess it's nice, with the right person."

"And have you found the right person?" Charlotte asked, dancing her fingers across my bed like she danced across the stage.

I shook my head. "No. That's why I'm not kissing them right now."

She sat up and pushed at me playfully.

We fell back into silence as Charlotte popped another marshmallow back into her mouth. Both sat there, looking at the opposite wall.

"Daniel?" she asked.

"Hmm?"

"What if..." Charlotte's cheeks turned pink, and she turned to face me. "What if *you* kiss me?"

"*What*?" I asked, astonished. She was asking me to kiss her?

"But... you're my best friend."

"I know. That's why it's perfect. It's *you*, and I feel safe with you."

She feels safe with me. I wanted to wrap my arms around her and bury my face in her hair, inhaling the strawberry smell of her shampoo.

She wanted it to be with someone special. Me? *I* was someone special? Her dorky best friend who spent all his time studying in the library? The shy engineer who was quiet and barely even went to parties? Who she probably never would have looked twice at if it wasn't for my sister living across the hall from her?

"I thought..." I bit my lip.

She blinked, moving to get off my bed. "Never mind, forget about it. It was a bad idea. I don't know what I was thinking."

"Charlotte," I said, not a question, but a statement, my voice thick with command.

She turned her head back to look at me.

"Come here."

I tugged her in closer to me.

"O-okay."

Her breath caught as I pulled her onto my lap, smoothed out a strand of hair and pushed it behind her ear. She had it styled in two little buns on top of her head today, with pieces hanging out the front. It was adorable, and so different from the ballerina buns she normally wore.

"What are you doing?" she whispered.

"Close your eyes," I instructed.

She did, her eyelids fluttering shut, and I rubbed my thumb over her cheekbone as I cupped her face.

I had never held Charlotte like this—had never imagined I would actually touch her like this—and I wanted to savor it.

But I also wanted to kiss her more than anything else.

"I'm going to kiss you now," I whispered, and she gave a tiny nod of permission as I pulled her mouth towards mine and connected our lips.

Just a press, the lightest of touch against her mouth. Simple, sweet. Like it should be. Charlotte kept her eyes shut, but her hands moved from her side and found their way behind my neck, intertwining, before she sighed against my mouth.

I kissed her again, longer this time. Wondering how far we would both go before we called this thing off. Knowing I needed to hold myself back as much as I needed her—this.

But when she swept her tongue into my mouth, I almost lost it. I pulled away.

Charlotte looked disappointed, like all she wanted was to sit here, in my lap, and make out with me.

"What, did you not like it?" She sounded hurt.

"No, it's not that..." I squeezed my eyes shut, trying to find the right words. "I don't want to mess things up between us. You're the best friend I've ever had."

"I understand." She nodded, but moved off of my lap, back to our original position.

You're more important than anything else, I wanted to tell her.

I care about you so much; I don't know what I'd do if I lost you.

If you let me love you, I'd never do anything else for the rest of my life. It was on the tip of my tongue.

But I didn't say that. I didn't say any of that. I just kept being her best friend.

～

SENIOR YEAR

"Marry me." I looked over at Charlotte as she sat next to me, eyes focused on the laptop screen in front of us.

I think her jaw dropped open as she paused the show and sat in front of me. "What? I'm sure I heard you wrong."

Fuck, that came out all wrong. "I was just thinking. If we're both still single when we turn thirty, we should get married."

Char bit her lip, and I popped another piece of popcorn into my mouth.

"But you're my best friend."

I nodded. "That's why it would work. Come on, Char, it's a good option. If neither of us finds someone, we should marry each other. I know I can put up with you, and I can take care of you."

"You're proposing we get married just because we get along?"

"Think about it." I hoped she didn't think I was insane. I just needed her to agree to this—to something, because I'd be graduating in a few months, and it felt like everything was going to change. But I didn't want it to. "If neither one of us finds anyone in the next eight years, we can just do it together. *Life*. We both want a family. It makes sense."

"Okay," she said.

"Okay, you'll think about it?"

She shook her head. "Okay, if I haven't met anyone by the time you turn thirty... we'll get married. A marriage pact."

She did always like to remind me I was older than her by a year and a half.

I cracked a grin. "Good."

"Now, can we get back to the show?" She rolled her eyes. "I like this part."

I couldn't stop thinking about what it had been like to kiss her the year before. How much I wanted to kiss her again, how easy it was to just be with her. I liked her presence in my life, from the pink to the ballet shoes tossed on my floor after she finished practice and came over to hang out. Even the smell of her champagne-and-berries perfume she always wore, and the glitter that seemed to follow her even when she wasn't wearing it. My life felt a little brighter because of her.

If I could spend the rest of my life basking in her happiness, I would be content.

And I wanted to make her happy. I wanted to make her happier than she could ever dream of being.

But she was my best friend—and I couldn't risk that right now.

I just couldn't.

CHAPTER 1

MANY YEARS LATER...

My pink dress fluttered to the floor as a pair of muscular arms wrapped around me from behind, cupping my breasts as he pulled down the tops of the lacy cups.

"Charlotte," he groaned in my ear as his fingers brushed over my hardened nipples.

I'd never felt anything like this before. Had never been so desperately turned on. Maybe it was the few glasses of wine I'd had during the reception. My friends infamously acknowledged me as a lightweight—or maybe it was simply the fact that it was *him*, but I was soaking wet.

And then there was the fact that no one had ever touched me like *that* before.

He pressed his erection into me—oh *God*, I practically whimpered—as he nuzzled into my neck.

"Daniel," I gasped when he kissed across my shoulder.

Daniel—my best friend for the last nine years—the man whose lips were currently searing into my skin, like a brand I never wanted to get rid of.

What was I doing? What were we doing? And why did it feel so good that I didn't want to stop?

"Are you sure?"

I nodded. I'd never been more sure of anything. I was sure that of everyone, Daniel was the person I wanted to take my virginity. Twenty-six years old, and I'd never slept with anyone. Truthfully, no one had gotten past second base. I hadn't known what I was saving myself for—not until tonight.

Not until Daniel pressed his cock into my back.

But I wanted him. Wanted him to take me—to teach me. Wanted to get it over with, because I was tired of waiting.

He unclasped my bra, pushing the straps off my arms as he let the fabric join my dress on the floor, and then he spun me around, and I hoped he couldn't see the blush on my cheeks in the dim lighting of our hotel room.

I tried to use my hands to cover my breasts, but he shook his head, pulling my hands away.

"You're so fucking beautiful," he said, reverently, his eyes mapping every inch of my bare skin, the only garment left my panties, covering the place where only my fingers had explored. "You don't ever have to hide from me, okay?"

I let his gaze hold mine instead of looking away this time, letting me drink in those beautiful brown eyes of his. "I know," I whispered, giving him the truth I'd known for a long time.

It was the reason it was so easy to give myself to him like this. I knew I was safe with him. Nine years of friendship made me comfortable telling him almost everything, and even then, this was new.

I hadn't kissed him since my sophomore year of college, and somehow that felt impossibly long ago, and also like yesterday.

But I couldn't get lost in memories of the past. Not right now, when all that separated us was a layer of clothes. His, to be more specific.

"It seems really unfair to me that I'm practically naked and you're still in all of *that*," I chuckled, gesturing to his suit.

God, Daniel in a suit was like fine wine; he was my personal brand of catnip. It was unfair how lethal it was to me, and I was sure that if I saw him like this daily, I would have lost my resolve a long time ago. Luckily, as an engineer, he wore slacks or nice jeans and a simple button-up to work most days.

Not the deadly suit, vest, and tie combo that currently had my mouth salivating.

"Take it off of me then," he said, his lips tilting up into a smirk as he let the suit jacket fall from his body.

Who were these people currently dancing around each other in this hotel room? Certainly not the Charlotte and Daniel who had flown here for his sister's wedding. I didn't know who they were, but something had irrevocably changed since this morning.

Maybe it was the lack of two beds. Maybe it was the alcohol. Maybe it was the fact that all our friends were in relationships, and we were the only ones still alone. Or, perhaps it was because I simply just wanted to *feel*.

And forget. I wanted to forget all the reasons this was a bad idea. I didn't want to think about what happened in the morning when we regretted this decision. Right now, I just wanted him.

I stepped closer, grabbing the end of his tie, and using it to tug his face down towards me—bringing his lips to my level. It had been far too long since I'd had them on mine.

"Kiss me," I whispered, and I wondered if he was thinking of the moment too. When I'd asked him to take my first kiss. Not much had changed since then.

His hand cupped the back of my head, his fingers weaving through the strands of my hair to massage the back of my skull. When his lips met mine, everything else melted away. It was just him and I, alone in this room. Nothing else mattered. No one else mattered.

We broke apart long enough for me to loosen the tie from his neck, and then I fumbled with the buttons as Daniel kissed me again, the way his tongue swept through my mouth making my knees go weak.

Truly, I thought it was unfair that he'd kissed enough girls to be this good at it. Why was I jealous of them, anyway? It wasn't like this was a thing.

This was just one night. Mutual pleasure, and nothing more.

Freeing the last button, he helped me ease the white fabric off his shoulders, before pulling off his undershirt and leaving his chest deliciously bare for me.

God. I'd seen him shirtless so many times before, but I'd never taken the time to appreciate it, had I? He worked every day to maintain his body, leaving the house before the sun even rose most mornings for his daily run, plus whatever time he spent at the gym.

I traced his abs with my fingers, wishing I could do the same with my tongue. Maybe I was inexperienced, but I definitely wasn't clueless.

"Easy, darling," he chuckled as I wrestled with his belt, trying to push his pants off his built frame.

"Need you," I practically panted as he pulled the belt from the loops, finally, *finally*, his pants hitting the floor.

Allowing him to guide me backwards onto the bed, I landed with an *oof*, before he pulled me to the edge of the bed, fingers hooking into my panties as he dragged them down my skin.

When his eyes met mine, the reverent look on his face almost broke me. He lifted my hips, that slow pull of lace driving me crazy with want.

"Please," I begged, "*Touch me.*"

Daniel kissed down my breasts, my abdomen, until he spread my thighs with his hands, his breath ghosting over my core. "Patience," he said against my skin, before licking a line up my slit. "I want to taste you first."

I moaned when his tongue made contact with my entrance again, and my eyes fluttered shut as he devoured me, brushing his tongue against my core. He was a man starved, treating me like the best feast he'd ever tasted.

And then he changed his focus, flicking that wicked tongue

against my clit, and *oh god*, I never imagined it would be this good, the pressure, the scrape of his teeth against me, and then he slipped a finger inside me.

"*Oh my god,*" I practically screamed.

"You're so wet," he practically hummed as he pushed his finger in and out, like he was getting me ready for later. "Is this all for me, Charlotte?"

I nodded, words failing me as he inserted another finger, plunging them in and out before he crooked them inside of me, hitting a spot I didn't even know existed inside of me, but one that made me grip his hair and push his face further against me, his lips descending on my clit again.

And I was greedy, because I just wanted more, more, *more*.

"Don't stop," I chanted, so close, so *very* close to coming apart just from whatever he was doing to me.

Ruining me, clearly, because how could I ever make myself feel this way after having his fingers inside of me? After he sucked my clit till I saw stars?

"You're so tight," he groaned. "I gotta loosen you up before you can take me, my pretty girl."

"Daniel, I—"

All thoughts eased from my brain when he flicked his tongue against me again, those fingers providing the perfect amount of pressure, and a shockwave of pleasure cascaded through my body.

He kept working me through it, only pulling his fingers out when I'd stilled, leaving me with a few last licks against me, and oh god, who was I?

Was I really about to do this?

With my best friend?

Before I could descend into a spiral, Daniel cupped my cheeks, pulling my face up to meet his, and he kissed me. Tasting myself on his tongue, I moaned into his mouth as he coaxed his tongue inside of mine, and my body loosened up instantly.

"Good?" He asked, his voice soft, reverent.

I nodded, because I wasn't sure I was capable of words right now. Not after what he'd just done. *God*. I'd read hundreds of romance novels, but I never thought someone could actually do that with their tongue.

"Stay here," he murmured, giving me one last soft kiss against my lips before he got off the bed, leaving me still panting from the force of my orgasm.

Hearing him rustling through his bag, I rolled over, watching as he pulled a condom out of his bag, which was probably smart. I hadn't even thought about protection myself, and I certainly hadn't brought any. Why would I?

Daniel pushed down his boxers, and I watched as his cock sprang free, the evidence of how much he wanted me painfully apparent. I liked how I affected him as much as he did me. The fabric fell to the floor, letting me appraise his fully naked body for the first time. The muscles on his thighs from his daily runs, the abs on his stomach that I still wanted to lick. And, lower, where...

My eyes widened. "Ohmygod. You're... huge. There's no way you're going to fit." I'd always been aware of how much taller he was than me, but I'd never thought about how much *bigger* he would be because of it.

"We'll go slow," he promised, climbing back on the bed with the packet in his hands. "I'll make it good for you, I promise." He kissed me again, once on the lips, and then on my nose, before he turned his attention back to the condom, tearing the package before rolling it on. I watched as he sheathed himself fully before returning to my side.

"Wait," I breathed, sitting up to look at him. There were so many thoughts fluttering through my brain that I didn't even know where to start.

"Do you not want to..." He swallowed roughly. "We don't have to, you know... I can just take care of myself."

"No, it's not *that*. It's just..." I was a virgin. I'd never been with anyone before. And even then, admitting that was... embarrassing. "Is this going to ruin everything?" I asked instead, wishing I could bury my face in his hands.

"No. It won't." He brushed his fingers across my jaw. "Are you sure, though?"

I kissed his jaw once, twice. "I want this. I want you." I pressed a kiss to his lips.

"Thank fuck," he said, dropping his head against mine as he eased me back against the pillows, positioning his body over mine.

I reached down to run a hand up his length, and he shuddered. "If you touch me... Baby... I'm not going to last long." Daniel groaned from on top of me, holding himself still. "I just want to make it good for you."

"You will," I said, cupping his face with both of my hands. "Please, I need you."

"Tell me if it hurts, okay? I don't want to hurt you."

"You won't."

I held onto his shoulders as he positioned himself at my entrance, rubbing the head back and forth over my wetness.

"*Oh!*" I gasped when he pushed the tip inside of me, head rolling back from the fit of him inside of me.

"Relax," he murmured, bringing our lips together and kissing me until I couldn't think about anything else but the press of his tongue against mine. My body sank into the mattress, and he eased inside of me, inch by inch, as his tongue kept up the relentless exploration of my mouth.

"You good?" He asked. "I didn't hurt you, right? Do you need me to wait?" He stilled inside of me, letting me adjust to his size. It was nothing like his fingers, or how I'd felt using a toy. This was completely different. "Fuck. You're so tight."

I shook my head, letting out a little moan from the fullness, how he was stretching me. He was fully inside of me, but I could tell how he was holding himself back, making sure he didn't hurt me, and something about that made my heart want to burst.

But as much as I loved his patience and care, I needed more. And even through the slight sting of pain, I wanted his relentless pounding, for us to find our climax together.

"Move," I begged. "Please. I need more."

With my command, he started moving inside of me, shallow thrusts as if he was working me up towards the harder, deeper motions I knew would come.

There was no holding in the moans that were escaping me, or the breathy noises I hadn't even known I could make.

"Look how well you're taking me, Charlotte," he encouraged. "Such a good girl for me."

I moaned. "*Yes.*" I was pretty sure I was babbling incoherently, chanting words like *more, yes, and please—*

Daniel pulled all the way out before thrusting back in, a punishing motion that had me pushing closer and closer towards the edge.

"Yes, darling, let me have it. Come for me," he murmured against my ear, and I never thought that would do it for me, but on his command, I exploded, shattering into a million pieces.

I didn't think anyone would be able to put me back together.

I wasn't sure I wanted anyone to.

Daniel followed closely behind me, giving me a few more thrusts as my orgasm pulsed around him, before the tension left his face and he came, filling the condom.

Even after coming down from our climaxes, Daniel just held me, and when he finally pulled out of me, I felt the loss of him immediately.

I knew I would be sore tomorrow, but I didn't regret the ache.

"You were perfect," he murmured against my hair before he got up to get rid of the condom.

My eyes fluttered shut before I could offer him anything back. But it didn't matter, anyway, right? They were just flowery words offered in the throes of sex. They didn't *mean* anything.

Right?

CHAPTER 2
Daniel

The spot next to me in the bed was cold.

"Oh." Charlotte came out of the bathroom, a towel wrapped around her body as she attempted to towel-dry her blonde hair. "You're awake."

"Mhm," I said, rubbing my hand over my face.

Last night, those strands had been curled, flowing down her back in ringlets of gold. She was the most beautiful thing I'd ever seen. I should have been focusing on my sister's rehearsal dinner, but all I could think about was how beautiful my best friend looked in her pink dress.

My head was pounding, a combination of the alcohol I'd drank last night and dehydration, I was sure.

"God, we really..." I looked at our clothes scattered across the floor. Sitting up in bed, the sheet fell into my lap, exposing my bare chest. We'd fallen asleep after, sweaty bodies tangled together, and I hadn't moved to put clothes back on.

Fuck. *Not a dream.*

She nodded.

"Charlotte, I—" I started, but she cut me off.

"I don't..." Charlotte tucked a strand of hair behind her ear as she avoided my gaze. "We shouldn't do that again. You're my best friend."

Another reminder that was all I was ever going to be. Even after last night, what we'd shared... Did she regret it?

"I get it." I said the words, but they felt hollow. Because I couldn't make myself regret it. I'd never regretted a single thing with her—except for one.

"Listen, I... I have to go get ready for the wedding." Charlotte looked towards the door as she dug through her bag, pulling on a soft t-shirt, forgoing a bra all-together. "The girls are meeting up soon to get ready, so I'm just going to go grab Gabbi and... go."

"Don't do this."

"What?" She blinked up at me.

"Run away. Avoid me, because you want to avoid what happened last night." I crossed my arms over my bare chest. "We need to talk about it."

"That's not..." She frowned. "That's not what I'm doing."

"Isn't it?" I cocked my head at her.

"No."

"Then explain to me why you're trying to run out of here like a one-night-stand would."

Her expression turned into a scowl as she speared her gray eyes at me. "Don't make assumptions just because we fucked last night."

Charlotte's words shot through me like a well-aimed bullet. *Fucked.* The word sounded so crude coming from her mouth, those lovely lips that had been all over my body.

Was that all it was for her? I didn't know why the idea of me being a quick fuck or some hook-up was so hurtful to me, but... No. I'd seen her face when I'd pushed inside of her. I'd felt her pleasure racing against my own. Last night had been anything but casual for me.

"Charlotte." My eyes caught hers, and she looked like a deer that was caught in the headlights. "Please." I hoped she could hear how serious I was, how desperate I was to make this right. We'd slept together, sure, but she was still my best friend. "You're too important to me to lose."

I climbed out of the bed, not caring about my nakedness. She'd seen it all last night.

She continued to ignore me, pulling on a pair of panties and then running shorts. If I hadn't been so irritated by her current behavior, maybe I would have been more focused on that tiny spandex garment.

Fuck. I needed to get my head on straight.

She's your best friend! I screamed at my head—and my dick, who didn't seem to get the memo last night. *Off-limits.* I shouldn't have touched her. But I had anyway.

She hefted her dress bag into one arm and her shoes in another. I knew her well enough from all these years to know that she would tuck everything she needed inside her bag.

"Char—"

"I have to go. I'm sorry."

"I'm sorry too," I said, and I meant it.

When Charlotte pulled the door shut behind her, leaving me alone in our hotel room, I couldn't hold it back anymore.

"Fuck!" I threw the pillow against the wall.

What had I done?

Had I ruined everything?

∼

"How's it going?" Matthew asked, plopping down in the seat next to me. I'd been sitting at our table at the reception, nursing a glass of wine and wondering how I'd messed everything up so quickly.

My eyes trailed over to Charlotte, laughing on the dance floor with Angelina. I hadn't been able to talk to her for most of the day with the ceremony and pictures, and it felt like everywhere I was, she wasn't.

She was avoiding me.

"I think I fucked up."

He raised an eyebrow. "How's that?"

I shook my head as I took another sip, thinking about how I'd run my fingers through her hair last night. What if I never got that chance again? "I don't even know where to start." How could I, with so much history?

"Tell her how you feel might be a good start." He ran a hand through his dark blonde hair.

"What if it's not that easy?"

"What if it is?" Matthew shook his head. "If you'd told me two years ago how happy I would be now, I would have never believed you."

"But..."

"But she's the best thing that ever happened to me." He looked over at his redheaded girlfriend. "And I think you feel the same away about her."

"She's my best friend," I said honestly.

Matthew slapped his hand on my back. "Then do what you have to do, man." He got up, heading over to Noelle.

Was he right? Was it that simple?

I took one last sip of my wine before standing up and heading over to her. I couldn't take this silence any longer.

She glared at me as I pulled her over into a corner by her wrist.

Taking her hand back, Charlotte crossed her arms over the top of her champagne colored-bridesmaid dress. It had a low neckline, and she must have worn some sort of contraption that pushed her tits up to the top, giving her the illusion of cleavage.

But more than that—she looked beautiful. They'd done some sort of pretty braid on the top half of her hair, and the rest was curled into loose blonde ringlets that draped against her pale skin.

"What?" she spoke in a hushed whisper as she whirled around on me.

"You know what."

"Enlighten me."

I leaned in close, enjoying the way her cheeks pinked from my proximity. I let my lips brush her ear as I whispered, "You look beautiful."

She pushed me away. "Don't do that. I told you... We can't."

Why not? My body wanted to scream. But I didn't. "Charlotte. You can't avoid me for the rest of the trip."

She quirked an eyebrow. "Sure I can." Her gaze was on anything but me, and I hated it.

"We slept together. It's not like it was the end of the world."

She looked around us, and mumbled something under her breath, what sounded a lot like, "*Maybe not to you.*"

"What?"

"Nothing." She waved me off. "Look, we both agreed it meant nothing, okay? So I don't know why we have to talk about it. I don't want to hear about how you regret it, I don't want to talk about how it ruined everything—"

"I don't. And it *didn't.*" I didn't regret it. And it hadn't ruined everything. Because I wouldn't let it.

She blinked. "What?"

I massaged my forehead, trying to figure out how. "You have no idea, do you?"

"No idea about what?" She asked, tilting her head as she watched me.

"Never mind. Forget it." I sighed, loosening my grip on her. "I just... I don't want to lose you."

"You won't lose me," she said, voice quiet.

"Then why does it feel like you're slipping away from me? Why does it feel like last night changed everything?"

Some voice in my head shouted, *because it did.*

"What if it did?" she whispered, echoing my thoughts. "What if we can't go back to what it was like before?"

"Then we move forward," I said, slipping a hand into her hair. "Together."

She shook her head. "I can't. I just... need some space, okay?"

Nodding, I wished I could give her the words to reassure her, but I didn't know what was in her head. And I didn't know how to get her to let me in.

So I just let her go.

Watched her walk away, link arms with Gabbi, dance with her best friends on the dance floor, and wished I could be out there with her.

Wished that I could fix it.

Charlotte

I'D BEEN AVOIDING him all night—all day, really. Was it fair of me?

No. It wasn't, and I knew it. I'd been the one to decide that it was *time*. That I was sick of the label, of feeling like I was stuck, waiting for the *right* person. And Daniel... I was safe with him. I'd trusted him.

But that wasn't fair for him either. Neither was how I was treating him.

Getting it *over with* seemed so easy whenwhen alcohol had seemed to light up every fuse in my body. I'd lost any rational thought the moment his lips connected with mine.

Still, I didn't regret it. Not one bit. I'd always thought my first time would be awkward, nervous fumbling. But with Daniel... it hadn't been. He'd been so focused on *me*, my pleasure, that it never felt like all of those awful loss of virginity stories.

But then we'd woken up, and the spell was... broken.

I'd slept with my best friend, given him my virginity—and what had I risked in the process?

Everything.

I was scared. Terrified, even. It felt like my skin was itching from the inside out, like everything was *wrong*. What was my usual course of action when I got scared? When I started thinking maybe things could be good?

I slammed the brakes. I walked away. I ghosted.

How could I do that to my best friend? The man who knew me almost as well as I knew myself?

Somehow, despite my ignoring him, no one had seemed to notice the weird tension between us. How even after I'd practically rejected him, I still kept catching him staring at me.

Distracting myself from his eyes, I helped Angelina to the bathroom—since she was a *little* tipsy. After we got her delivered back into the arms of her groom, Gabbi and I went to get her a glass of water.

You know, typical Maid of Honor and Bridesmaid duties. I certainly wasn't still ignoring the man who I was sharing a room with.

Not at all.

But Gabbi was quiet, too—not quite herself.

And I couldn't help but notice how her eyes kept seeking Hunter's out, too. I kept prying, sensing she was holding something back, but finally I just went for it.

"Is this about Hunter?" I asked, watching him across the room as he talked to his sister.

"No." She winced. "Sort of. Maybe." Gabbi looked down at the glass of water for Angelina, and then back at me. "I just..."

"You're seeing him?"

She gnawed on her bottom lip. "You could say that."

And, well... maybe I wasn't the only one who'd done something I shouldn't have last night. But Hunter... he looked at her like she hung the moon in the sky. It was so obvious, any of us could see it. Except Gabbi. She seemed clueless to how he really felt.

My eyes widened. "*Oh my god.* Did you sleep with him?"

"Charlotte! Shh!" Gabbi looked around, like she was terrified someone would have heard us. "I don't want anyone to know yet. It just happened."

And there was my opening. My chance to tell her what happened. Except... Something held me back. What was it? I couldn't quite describe the *reason* I said what I did. Why I lied.

But I pasted on my best pout, hoping she wouldn't see right through me, or the way I couldn't bring my eyes to meet Daniel's.

"Everyone's got a man except me. I'm still holding on to my v-card, for goodness sakes, and Angelina's married, Noelle's practically engaged, and now you're dating, too?" Even if I'd lost my virginity last night, the rest of it was true. And she didn't need to know that part.

Gabbi frowned. "Well... We're not exactly dating *yet*." She mussed with her hair, the curls that seemed to hold so much better in her hair than my long, straight blonde locks. "It's... complicated."

"Well... *un*-complicate it."

Take your own advice, Charlotte. My brain barked at me.

"I can't. Benjamin doesn't want us together, and Hunter doesn't want to ruin the relationship with his brother. Especially not during the wedding."

"But what do you think Angelina would think?" I squeezed her wrist. "I think she'd be happy for you. Better than that, she'd probably be ecstatic if you ended up as sisters-in-law. Think about it! Married to brothers."

The best friend's brother trope had always been one of my favorites, even if I tried not to analyze that too deeply. I had three best friends, but only one of them had a brother.

And we weren't going *there*.

Gabbi waved off my comment. "Don't get ahead of yourself there, Char. No one said anything about marriage." Looping my arm through hers, she looked around the dance floor. "Where's that man of yours, anyway?"

Oh god. I blushed. "He's not my man. He's just..." As if it was fate, my eyes connected with Daniel's. "He's my best friend."

The best friend you let kiss you last night. Who practically memorized your skin with his mouth. I tried not to let my skin flush. Even outside in the idyllic French countryside setting, I was warm recalling what exactly we'd done.

"*And?*" Gabbi was staring at me like I'd just grown two heads.

Maybe I had. That would certainly help explain why I'd made such reckless choices this weekend.

"And that's that. A fairytale is just that, Gabbi. A fairytale. It's never going to happen between us."

Even if we'd tumbled into bed together last night. That was all it would ever be. One night.

Anything more would jeopardize our friendship. Because I knew myself, and I knew I'd get attached, and if I fell in love, and he didn't feel the same... All our years of friendship would be gone, just like that. *Poof.*

"Sure, whatever you need to tell yourself."

Maybe we were all just experts at lying to ourselves. I frowned. That seemed to be a common theme here.

"If you're convincing yourself that this thing with you and Hunter is casual, maybe that's what *you're* telling yourself, too."

Gabbi looked down, still holding the glass of water for Angelina. "Shit. Where'd she go?"

I was happy about the topic change, so I looked around the room. "Maybe Benjamin kidnapped her and took her to the gardens? They're really beautiful, aren't they?"

Gabbi's cheeks flushed, the rosy color seeping through her tan skin. "Yeah. Yeah, they are."

I could only hope that one day I'd have my fairytale ending, the perfect wedding with the perfect man. But Daniel... he didn't feel that way about me, so there would be no happy ending to our story. Just two best friends who hooked up and wouldn't talk about it again.

That was just the way it was going to have to be.

CHAPTER 3
Charlotte

ONE MONTH LATER...

Smiling, I watched the tiny ballerinas spin in circles around the room. Sure, they weren't as graceful as my group of teenagers I taught, but they were still at the age when they were just here to have fun. Some of them might stay, committing to dance for the long haul.

That was how I'd been when I was a little six-year-old in a similar dance studio in California. But I'd fallen in love with it, and here I was, all these years later, teaching the next generation.

"Gwen, keep your chin up, sweetie," I instructed the tiny brunette, going through and giving them all tips on their form.

After we'd finished our hour long class, I dismissed the kids. The class was mostly girls, but we had a few boys who'd enrolled as well, and they seemed to enjoy ballet just as much as the girls. We always said we didn't pick favorites, but I had a few. Faith, with her big blue eyes, and Arzum, whose family had moved here from Turkey last year, and Gwen, who never failed to give me a big hug when she arrived.

"You all did really well today!" I smiled, giving high-fives to the kids as they moved to the sides of the room, to their parents who were waiting to take them home. "Remember, next week we're learning our new dance for the winter recital."

I'd been planning for it for weeks—the cute little costumes and the perfect dance to go along with it. It was one of my favorite parts of being a dance teacher, aside from taking them to competitions where they really got to shine.

Watching them pack up all their stuff, I felt a surge of pride.

"See you all next Monday!" I called out to the kids and parents rushing out the door, grateful for the silence. Exhaling deeply, I closed my eyes for a few moments to center myself before turning back to my friend.

"Excellent class today," my friend and the studio's owner, Juily, said with a smile on her face, brushing her dark brown hair off one brown shoulder. She'd told me a few months back that she and her wife were trying to start a family, so I'd been taking over more responsibilities to help while she was pregnant.

"Thanks." I bent down to take off my slippers. Normally, when I taught contemporary dance, I'd go barefoot or with half-soles, but for ballet I wore a leotard and tights.

Ever since I'd gotten back from Angelina's wedding last month, I'd felt like I was off balance. Like something was missing, and I didn't quite know what it was.

I loved my life—teaching dance and creating new choreography for our dancers while fulfilling one of my passions on the side—sewing. But was it *enough*?

Lately, I wasn't sure anymore.

"How've you been feeling lately?" I turned to Juily, who had her hand resting over her little bump.

"Good. I appreciate you picking up the slack since I've been working less, though. I know Naomi does too."

"It's no problem, really. Besides, I can use the extra money."

"Isabelle's been talking about picking up another class after this term is over, too, so that might help take some of the burden off of you."

"I really don't mind. I love these kids."

She placed a hand on my shoulder, squeezing briefly. "I know you do. And they absolutely adore you. I know a lot of the parents are already talking about re-enrolling for next year."

"Really?" I smiled. "That's good." I hadn't taught the younger kids in a while, since I'd mostly been focusing on my teens, especially the ones who were gearing up for competitions. But I'd missed this, even though there was a part of it that made my heart ache.

Teaching them reminded me of the one thing I wanted, and I didn't have. A dream that was in sight, and yet... so far away.

I had always planned on being married by twenty-five. Kids by 28. And somehow, that dream was floating further and further away from me. The last time I'd talked to my mom, I could practically feel her eyes roll over the phone.

You're not that old, she'd insisted. *You'll find someone, Lottie, I promise.*

But where? I'd tried the whole online dating thing, and it had never panned out. Had even gone out with a single dad from the dance studio once, but there was never that *spark*.

Maybe I'd have to accept that I was going to be single forever. I didn't want to spend the next two years frantically searching for the right guy. I just wanted to have what my friends did.

And I hated when my mom called me Lottie. It made me feel like I was still a kid. I'd stopped being Lottie when I moved away to college, choosing to go to Portland instead of staying in Sacramento. I missed California sometimes, but I enjoyed being my *own* person up here. No older sister to overshadow me, no parents who wanted me to stay living with them because they wanted to keep babying me.

"You know, Naomi's brother is single. I could see if she could set the two of you up." It felt like Juily read my mind sometimes, but as much as I wanted that, I was tired of first dates. Tired of dolling myself up just to feel like something was missing. The *spark*.

I shook my head, all but waving her off. "It's okay. I'm taking a break from all that."

She raised an eyebrow. "*That?*"

"You know..." I winced. "Dating." Ever since the wedding, the idea of it just sounded unappealing.

"I'm pretty sure for the last five years since I've met you, all you've talked about is how you want to find the right person. What happened?"

"Maybe it's just not going to happen for me. The fairytale. Finding *the one*. And that's okay."

That was the truth, after all. Nothing had happened. I just couldn't keep going on all of those first dates anymore, trying to ignore the nauseous feeling in my gut.

Maybe I wanted it too badly, and that was why it hadn't happened to me. So I'd sworn off dating for a while. I figured maybe if I stopped looking for the right guy, he'd show up. It was all I'd wanted for the longest time—someone to love me.

"I think someone's here to see you," Juily murmured, and when I looked up, through the little glass window in the wooden door, there he was.

The man I'd been avoiding for the last month. My best friend of nine years. Daniel Bradford.

A lot of things had changed in the last five years since graduating college, but there was one constant in all of it—*him*. He'd been my best friend since my freshman year. I had Noelle and the girls, too, but it was different between us.

But despite how perfect our meet-cute was, it wasn't the beginning of my happily ever after. It wasn't the romance story of the ages. In nine years, we'd only ever been best friends. Except for that one small moment where I thought everything might have changed, the one time where I asked him to kiss me—my first kiss—nothing had ever gone further. Until this summer, that was...

A mistake I was still trying to forget.

He knocked on the door, swinging it wide open.

"What are you doing here?" I said, unable to stop my surprise. When was the last time he visited me at the studio like this?

"It's your birthday," he said as a way of greeting. Like that explained everything. Like it explained the suit he was wearing or the flowers in his arms.

"I thought we weren't celebrating until tomorrow?" I frowned. "Your sister made a reservation at some fancy Italian place."

Daniel nodded. "We are celebrating tomorrow. With all our friends. But I thought maybe you'd like to get dinner tonight." He tugged at the collar of his shirt. "With me. Um. Just the two of us."

"Oh." I looked down at my leotard and tights. "I didn't bring anything to change into..."

I had planned on going home, sitting on the couch with a tub of cookie dough ice cream, and pretending like I wasn't turning twenty-seven years old.

Was spending the evening with him a better option? In some ways, it felt like it was more dangerous.

"We can swing by your place on the way."

I grabbed my bag and water bottle off the floor next to me, moving to stand next to Daniel.

"These are for you. You know." He looked shy, which was something I hadn't seen from him in years. "I know they're your favorite."

"Okay." I gave one last look to Juily, who gave me a small smirk before flipping out the studio lights behind us. I hadn't told her what happened last month, but I suspected she had an inkling. She always had some weird sense about that kind of thing. "Lead the way, then."

I followed him out to the parking lot, to his gray Tesla, and slid inside the car. It always smelled like him, with a faint air of apples and spicy musk. Relaxing into the seat, I inhaled deeply, and then let out a sigh of relief.

"You okay?" He looked over at me, and I knew he'd caught me smelling his car—him.

I bobbed my head. "Of course. Why wouldn't I be?"

He pinned me with a look that said *you know exactly what I'm talking about.* The reason we'd gone from hanging out multiple times a week to me almost going radio-silent. We'd seen each other a few times, and when Angelina and Gabbi had been in the hospital last week, he'd picked me up so we could visit, but everything was... different.

He nudged me with his elbow. "You know why."

"Oh." I picked at the seam on my leggings. "It's fine." It was, wasn't it? "We're gonna be fine, right?"

He gave me a nod, and then thankfully, he dropped it, and even though I didn't live too far away from the studio, I spent the rest of the drive deep in thought.

I went on dates, and so did he. And over time, it got easier to ignore the sinking feeling in my gut when I saw him smile at another girl. If I pretended like I didn't see it, it was easier to bear. And if I could just get over the nausea brought on by going out on dates, maybe something would come from it. But they were never *right*.

How many first dates had I been on? Dozens over the years. And yet, there'd been very few second dates. Less than a handful who ever made it to a third. Three who I'd even let kiss me. And it wasn't *right*.

But that night with Daniel, it had felt so *right*. And when he made me see stars, the first man to touch me like that, when he slid inside of me, everything felt changed.

I wasn't the same person that I was before.

But if I just kept searching for my Prince Charming, would I find him someday? Or had I been a fool all along?

Maybe I'd believed in the fairytale for too long. Maybe it was time to give up...

To find a new dream.

~

WE PULLED into my apartment complex, and I sat, staring up at my apartment and then back at my best friend. "Want to just wait here? I'll be quick." Having him upstairs felt like an intimacy I couldn't afford.

He shook his head. "Nah. It's fine. I'll come up with you. I can hang out on the couch while you change."

"Okay," I agreed, staring at him as he opened my door. I gave him a few hesitant glances as I headed to the sidewalk.

"What?"

"What do you mean, *what?* Why are you being weird?"

Daniel frowned. "I'm not. Can't I just make sure that my best friend gets into her apartment safely?"

"Sure..."

"It's your birthday, Charlotte. I'm not being weird. I'm just being nice."

Was that what it was?

My lips pressed into a straight line as I headed up the stairs to my shabby apartment, knowing he was right behind me.

There was a reason when we hung out that it was normally at his place, or out doing things. I certainly didn't invite anyone over to my tiny, one-bedroom apartment unless I had to.

Unlocking the front door, I tossed my keys on the kitchen countertop.

"Make yourself at home!"

I carried my dance bag into my room, hurrying into my closet to find something suitable to wear to dinner tonight with just the two of us. I'd stopped worrying a long time ago that I needed to dress up for him. He'd seen me in everything, from my sweatpants in college to running gear and everything in between. Sure, I enjoyed getting dolled up, but I did it for *myself*.

My eyes ran over the contents of my closet—color coded, the entire back row a layer of pastel dresses. Mostly pink, even though people liked to tease me for the love of the color. I'd made half of the dresses myself, a labor of time and love that made me smile every time I slipped one of my creations on.

Especially since I'd put pockets in almost all of them.

It was getting cold in Portland in late September, so I wore a pink dress with a tiered skirt and a white denim jacket. I slipped on a pair of heeled booties—I always felt like I needed the height when it was just him and I. All I needed now was to touch up my hair and makeup.

"Charlotte?" Daniel called out, and I heard rustling from the other room.

"Just a second!" I responded, swiping through my blonde locks with a hairbrush and pinning it back into a half-up, half-down style that would keep my hair out of my eyes. I ran another coat of mascara over my eyelashes, a thin layer of strawberry-flavored sparkly pink lip gloss over my lips, and then called it good.

It wasn't like this was a *date*, so I didn't bother to refresh the rest of my makeup that I'd put on this morning.

"I'm all ready—" I started, walking out of my bedroom, but stopped abruptly when I saw the look on Daniel's face.

"Char?" He said, standing in my kitchen, looking at—*Oh*, shit. "Charlotte, what is this?" Daniel held up a piece of paper. A paper that I clearly hadn't hidden well enough. I'd forgotten that I'd left it on the counter in the first place.

But I knew what it said without having to even look at it.

"Don't be mad." I winced.

Why hadn't I put it away?

"*Mad?*" He froze, looking at me in shock. "Charlotte, I'm not mad. I'd never be mad at you. I'm just... Why didn't you tell me?"

Despite being super close with all of my best friends, there was one teeny-tiny secret I'd been keeping from all of them.

A big, sort-of *terrifying* secret.

"Tell you that my apartment rent was going up so much that I can't afford it? That I've barely been scraping by as it is? That I'm close to being evicted?" I looked down at the floor, embarrassed, and my voice grew quiet. "I didn't want anyone's pity. Especially not yours. Not after everything."

I'd barely had anything left over lately, between my apartment, car payment, and the student loans I was still paying off. I was making ends meet, sure, but I wasn't *thriving*.

Not like the rest of my friends were. The worst part was, I knew they would have jumped in a second to help me. But I needed to do this myself. Still, I didn't want to confront that reality head-on just yet. Despite all of that, I was clearly going to, with Daniel standing in my kitchen. He had such a presence there, like he belonged, and I didn't know why the realization came to me so suddenly. I'd never thought that before, had I?

He set the paper down on the counter, striding over to me in what felt like two steps thanks to his long legs. Then he was staring down at me, his six foot one to my five foot four, and I suddenly felt so small.

I tried not to let the tears prick my eyes, to stand strong in front of him, but it felt like everything was falling apart. "I feel like a failure. Like... nothing is working for me."

He cupped my jaw with his hands, softly steering my head up to meet his gaze. "You are not a failure, Charlotte. I don't want you to think you are for even a moment, okay?"

I nodded my head, wrapping my jacket around my body, wishing I could retreat into myself.

My rent was going up at the end of the month and I couldn't afford it with my current income unless I got a roommate or moved. Even with my side business of making dresses and dance costumes, I wasn't making enough. And I didn't have enough time in the day to take on more clients unless I quit the dance studio, and I loved those kids more than anything. And even with the extra classes I was teaching at the studio, I was running on overtime for sewing.

So I was *stuck*.

My brain was working overtime, trying to think of ways I

could make up the difference any time I stared at my credit card bill on my laptop. I'd already cut my spending down, and what was left? I could sell my books. But that was the last thing I wanted to do.

My books were like my most prized possessions.

"We'll figure it out, okay? You've got me. You know that."

My shoulders dropped. "I know, I just... I wanted to take care of this myself. I've been taking extra orders, working longer at the dance studio, but it's just... not enough."

I'm not enough.

And maybe the thought rang so true that I finally let a tear drip from my eyes.

CHAPTER 4
Daniel

Shit. She was crying.

This was not how I wanted to start her birthday dinner. Of all the ways I had planned on tonight going, this was not it.

"I'm sorry," I whispered, wiping the tears from under her eyes. I really needed to step away—to put some space between our bodies. Mine liked this close proximity a little *too much*. And if I was going to ask her what I needed to ask her later tonight, well—I needed my wits about me.

Not to fuck up and cause a repeat of what happened at the wedding.

I wouldn't be able to take it if she pushed me away for another month.

"I came in here looking for a vase for the flowers—" I nodded at the glass that I'd filled with water and her pink lilies. Her favorite flower, and the way her face lit up when she saw them, made me want to buy them for her every week, just to see that smile. "And it was just laying on the counter. I didn't mean to pry."

"No, I—" Charlotte shook her head. She was my best friend, and it hurt that she'd kept something like this from me, but I knew it was her pride that kept her from speaking about it. "It's good that you know. I just..." She looked around her apartment. "I didn't want to admit it to anyone. I'm sorry for not telling you before."

Honestly, I hated her place. It was small and dark, and not in the best area of town. I'd told her as much when she moved in, but she'd just given me a big smile and told me it would be all right. That it was *her* place, and she loved it because of that. But I'd noticed how she'd let me come over less and less after we'd moved her in. Nowadays when we spent time together, it was with her friends, at my house, or around town.

"Why didn't you ask your family for help?"

She winced. "You know I can't do that. Mom, she..." Charlotte shook her head. "I don't want their money. I like my independence." She'd confessed that to me before. It was why she'd moved to Portland for college in the first place—and why she had stayed.

"Will you let me help? You know I have a guest room at my house." I'd bought a small starter home near my job a few years back, and I had to admit living there alone got lonely sometimes. I'd been thinking about getting a dog, but I hadn't bitten the bullet yet and started looking for one.

"I can't mooch off of my best friend, Daniel," she groaned.

"Okay." I pulled her into my arms, giving her a tight hug. I wouldn't accept that answer, but I'd give her time before she came around. For now, we had plans. "We'll figure it out later. We should get to dinner."

She wrapped her arms around my back, squeezing tightly, before letting go. "Okay. Yeah. Dinner." Charlotte pulled away and straightened her outfit, wiping her eyes before looking back up at me.

I gave her a small smile, hoping she didn't know how much it hurt my heart to see her cry. I liked to think I'd learned how to control my expressions over the years, but fuck if I knew what to do with her.

"Great. Only the best for my best friend's birthday."

That got a chuckle out of her, and the sound soothed me a little. I'd missed her so much, even if we'd still seen each other a few times.

"It's not like it's some big birthday. I'm only turning twenty-seven." She bit at her lip. "And we're celebrating with everyone else tomorrow."

Everyone else included my sister Angelina and her husband Benjamin, Noelle and her boyfriend Matthew, and Gabbi, who was now dating Benjamin's brother Hunter. The girls were all best friends, and I knew how much she looked forward to celebrating with them every year.

I couldn't help but be selfish and want a night to myself with my best friend as well.

"Where are we going?" She mumbled as I led her down the stairs, going first this time, so I didn't think about how much I wanted to pull her back into my arms.

Shit. I really needed to get myself back under control. Especially before dessert.

"It's a surprise." I extended out my hand to her when I got to the base of the stairs. "You'll like it, I promise."

And when she placed her hand in mine, nothing had ever felt so right.

I needed to stop thinking like that.

∼

HANDING the valet the key card to my car, I watched Charlotte stare up at the building with wonder in her eyes. I'd gotten us reservations at a restaurant in downtown Portland, thirty floors up, where you could see the view of practically the entire city.

Guiding her into the building and up the elevator, I could see the way her face changed as we stepped into the restaurant. "Oh my god. This place is amazing," she leaned over to whisper to me.

After checking in, they led us to our table, which was right next to one of the giant windows. I pulled out her chair for her and then settled into mine across from her, giving her a big smile. "Happy Birthday."

I had to get this back on track. Especially after I'd practically made her cry earlier by bringing up her apartment.

Her eyes roved around the restaurant. "This is really nice. Like, *way* nicer than where we usually go. Are you sure this is okay?"

Chuckling, I opened my menu. "It's fine. It's your birthday. Get whatever you want."

I could still remember the first day I'd seen her in Angelina's freshman dorm, with that blonde hair, her bright gray eyes. For a moment, I'd thought my heart stopped in my chest. She was wearing a cute white tee and a little pink corduroy dress, and yep —I was a goner. I laid in bed that night, preparing for my sophomore year, thinking about only one thing.

I'm going to marry that girl someday.

Had I known anything about her? No. Not yet, but I would.

I would, I promised myself. I wanted to know everything about her; how she took her coffee, how it would look when she was smiling at me, her favorite color and all the parts of her life. And damn if that hadn't made me feel weak inside—being this interested in a girl I had just met. Who literally only knew my first name, but there I was.

I'd never believed in love at first sight, and I wouldn't call it that, exactly, but there was something about her I wanted to get to know. That underneath her shy, quiet personality was someone who needed me—just as much as I needed her. Never in my wildest dreams would I have guessed that she'd grow to be one of my closest friends on campus. I had other friends over those four years, sure. Engineering students I talked to in class, my roommate, my sister who I'd always been close with, but Charlotte was always the one I wanted to spend time with. I still couldn't believe how much I relied upon our friendship.

But now, sitting in front of her tonight?

I wondered how I had gone from being so sure of what I wanted to being so terrified of losing her. Choosing friendship was better than the possibility of never speaking to her again. So I'd said nothing. I'd spent the last few years working so hard that I blinked and I was almost thirty, still single, and when was the last time I had even been on a date?

When was the last time I had wanted to? A voice nagged at my brain.

None of them had ever compared to Charlotte, anyway.

I decided it was better to remain just friends than risk losing her.

But I'd done just that and almost fucked everything up at the wedding, hadn't I?

The waiter came over with a bread basket and took our orders. Steak for me, and Charlotte ordered the pork loin, plus a side of mac and cheese for us to share.

"Okay, so... tell me about your week. Anything new happening at work?"

I thought about all the projects I was working on. As a structural engineer, I did a lot of calculations and design, but I didn't like to bore Charlotte by talking about specs too much. Sometimes, I'd show her some designs I created for the buildings my firm ended up building, as well as driving her by the finished project. I'd been doing this for over six years now, and I still loved my job. It was a good thing.

"Nothing much this week, but we got a new interior designer at the firm. Stella. She seems great."

"Oh, that's nice. What happened to your previous one?" She grabbed a roll out of the basket, tore off a piece, and plopped it in her mouth.

"He retired last month." I frowned. "Didn't I tell you that?"

"No."

"Yeah, they were..." Charlotte's phone buzzed on the table, interrupting my thought. She looked at it, her expression blank, and turned the screen over so it was face down.

I raised an eyebrow. "What was that?"

"Nothing."

"Seriously. Char. What's really going on with you? You keep avoiding me, dodging my questions, and I'm just... worried about you." Lately, she'd just seemed down, and nothing I could do felt like it raised her spirits for long. I just wanted to see her smile.

She took a deep breath. "Has there ever been something you really wanted, like *really* wanted, but you couldn't have it?"

"Sure." I cleared my throat. *You.* "What is it?"

"You're going to think it's silly," Charlotte mumbled.

I shook my head. "Not possible." I liked to think I knew her inside and out, enough that she could tell me anything.

She gave me a small smile. "Lavender's pregnant again." Her older sister. I nodded. "And I think I'm..." Her cheeks pinked, but she didn't finish the sentence. "I just thought I would already be with someone at this point in my life, you know? I didn't think I'd be twenty-seven and still be single. I want to have a family. I want all those things she has." Charlotte screwed up her face. "It just makes me sound jealous and ungrateful, and..."

"I get it."

"You do?"

"My *little* sister just got married. I'm fourteen months older than her, and she tied the knot first. How do you think I feel?"

"Oh. I didn't think about that."

"You can be happy for her and still want all the things she has. You're allowed to want things in life too, you know. And you should have whatever you want."

Her wet eyes shined into mine, and I cursed myself internally, because if she cried again tonight because of something I said, I would absolutely lose it. My need to comfort her was too great.

Our food came, interrupting our conversation as we dove in. We barely spoke two words the whole meal except for a few moans of *this is so good*, and *can I have more of yours?* Even her gluten-free pasta was incredible.

By the time we were down to our last few bites, I steeled

myself into finally bringing it up. Was it insane? Completely. Maybe she wouldn't even remember our conversation from college, and then I'd just look like a fool.

Instead, what she said next blindsided me completely.

"I want to have a baby."

What? My eyes shot up, meeting hers. A baby? "You..." I blinked. "*Now?*"

She nodded. "I've been thinking about it for a while, and I'm not getting any younger. I've always wanted to be a mom." Charlotte forked another green bean, not meeting my eyes as she brought it to her mouth. "What do you think? Should we get dessert?"

She was going to just brush over that like it was nothing?

"But..."

Who did she want to have a baby with? We'd slept together, but I didn't think that gave me any right to ask to be a part of this. But the thought of her having a baby with someone else... It hit me like a sucker punch.

Because I wanted her. And I wanted her to have *my* baby.

The realization hit me like a ton of bricks.

I couldn't wait anymore. Couldn't accept just being best friends. Because I was risking losing her by saying nothing, too.

Tilting her head, she just looked at me. "You're not too full, are you?"

She might have looked small, but between dance classes, and her workouts to stay in shape, it didn't phase me anymore how much she could eat.

"Listen, Char, I want to talk to you about something, and I know it might seem crazy, but hear me out, okay?" I took a deep breath. And then I said the single most important statement I'd ever said in my entire life.

"We should get married."

CHAPTER 5
Charlotte

"We should get married."

"What?" My eyes widened, food completely forgotten in front of me.

"We should—"

"That's what I thought you said." I frowned. "But—" My brain was running a thousand miles an hour. *What?*

Okay, *sure*, I'd just brought up having a baby, but I meant doing on my own. I wasn't asking him to do it with me. Even before we'd slept together at the wedding, I'd been thinking about it. And the last month, I'd been researching it.

I was an independent woman. I could have a baby on my own if I wanted to. Sperm banks were a thing, after all.

Still, his spur-of-the-moment proposal, if you could even call it that, was a surprise. I hadn't expected that.

"We said we'd get married if neither one of us had met anyone by thirty, right? We're almost there, anyway. I turn twenty-nine in a few months. Why don't we just get married now?" Daniel shrugged, like it was the most casual statement in the world."

"Just like that?" I stared at him. "You're cashing in on our marriage pact *now*?"

Damn, we should have ordered dessert. I could really use the distraction right now.

This man—my best friend, the one who stuck by my side for all my years of college, one I'd never really looked at like *that*, because his friendship was always too important to me—he just stared back.

"Yeah, just like that. Charlotte... you're my best friend. I care about you. Besides, we're both still single. Now that Hunter and Gabbi are together, we're the only single ones left, and god knows they've all teased us enough about it over the years." He said it with such certainty and clarity. Meanwhile, my brain was still trying to process what exactly was happening here. "And we already know we're good together."

"Hold on. What exactly are you saying right now?"

"What if, you know... we let them think we were *actually* together?"

He... *What?*

I gaped at him. "Like... A fake marriage?" I stared out the window at the view of downtown Portland, needing some time for my brain to process. The way he was talking about the rest of our lives, about being married to each other like some sort of transactional agreement made me take a pause.

After all this time, I thought that the stupid marriage pact we had made in college was nothing more than a *joke*. Brought on by senioritis, or maybe desperation he'd had with his impending graduation. I hadn't thought it was real.

Sure, no part of me wanted to admit to him that the idea of spending my last year in college without him had made me feel a little empty inside. Sure, I had my friends, and they were the best friends a girl could ask for, but something between him and I was... different. Maybe that was why I'd even agreed to it.

"I never thought..." It wasn't like it was something we'd brought up in the ensuing years. I'd dated, and he'd dated, and we'd never spoken of it again. Until today.

He raised an eyebrow and his face grew determined. "I just want you to be happy. Plus, I can give you what you want."

I wasn't sure that was possible, because if he knew *exactly* what I wanted, there was no way he'd be making this outlandish proposal.

"What is that, exactly?"

"You want to have a baby, right? I'll give you one."

I spit out my water. A baby? With... Daniel? "How exactly would that work?"

He raised an eyebrow, leaning one arm on the table. "The normal way, I'd suppose."

I swallowed another sip of water carefully, trying to prevent myself from spitting again. Or hyperventilating. Possibly both. "You... I... We can't do that again."

I should have assumed that would come with marriage, but that knowledge sent a whole other set of thoughts racing down my spine.

Delicious thoughts that I shouldn't be thinking about at dinner with my best friend. Thoughts that I never let myself entertain, for this reason alone. The reason I'd pushed him away after Angelina's wedding to begin with. It got too real, and it would never happen. He didn't see me like that. This was just... convenience. Maybe if I told myself that enough, it would sink in.

"We already know we work well together. Hell, we spend most of our free time together, anyway. This wouldn't be much different." It had been that way since college. Even with his guy friends, he had hardly ever chosen to spend as much time with them as he did with me.

"Except... We'd be married. So it would be a *lot* different."

He shot me a look, like he was telling me to be quiet. "We both want to have a family... It just makes sense." His hand covered mine. "We can be each other's family and start our own."

Looking away, I swore my eyes could have bored holes into my dessert menu. That was how determinately I was staring at it.

Was it wrong to want cheesecake at a time like this?

"Charlotte," he said, softly, barely more than a coaxing noise. "It makes sense. *We* make sense."

"But we don't... *love* each other." The words caught in my throat.

He just looked at me. "Don't we?"

"Not like *that*." Yeah, I loved him. Like you loved a best friend. The kind you'd shout "*love you!*" to from the car window as you pulled away. But I didn't love him in that big, crazy way. Even if I'd lost myself in his body for one night, giving him the piece of me I'd always kept for someone special.

But that wasn't love.

I'd always figured when I got married, it would be for love. I had always been waiting for that, hadn't I? That love-you-so-much-it-hurts kind of love. All the passion and fire that came along with finding your soulmate. The crazy, blinding-love that burned through your veins. But maybe I was kidding myself to believe I'd ever find it. I was too quiet, too scared, and too terrified to put myself out there.

And maybe turning twenty-seven came with my expiration date for finding the love I wanted. We'd still love each other, yeah —like best friends did, because we *loved* each other, but he wasn't *in love* with me. I knew that much. He had never looked at me like I was the only woman he had ever seen in his entire life, and I knew what that looked like—I had seen it with my best friends.

For the past two years, I'd watched them all fall in love, one by one. I was so happy for them. They'd truly found the loves of their lives, the perfect book boyfriends, like all the ones I'd read about for years. I yearned for it so badly. Because I didn't want to be alone. I wanted a husband, a white picket fence. A life together. But despite that, I was still always the one sitting at the end of the table—alone.

"Say yes," he whispered, "I know this wouldn't be a traditional marriage, that we're doing things all wrong... but I don't care. We can get married. You can have a baby." He squeezed my hand.

"Can I... think about it?" Even the question made me wince. It was a lot to take in all at once.

"Of course you can." Daniel's firm squeeze to my hand, and the warm smile on his face, somehow both made me feel better instantly.

I wanted to say something else, but stopped myself. No point in getting ahead of myself if I did actually say yes to him. "I think I'm going to get the cheesecake," I mumbled, still looking at the menu

He chuckled. "Char, I really meant it. You can have whatever you want."

For some reason, I didn't think he just meant dessert.

∼

FOR THE SECOND night in a row, I was celebrating my birthday with my best friends. Only tonight, there was no panoramic view of the city of Portland, or a distraction from Daniel's words.

We should get married.
I'll give you a baby.
We can be each other's family.

I finished my second glass of wine and deliberated ordering another one.

"I made a cake for you, back at the house." Noelle said, beaming at me as I picked at my dinner. She loved to bake, one of her biggest past-times besides writing steamy novels. "Gluten-free funfetti with vanilla frosting, your favorite. Pink, of course."

"Thanks." I gave her my best smile.

This year, I didn't have to think about what my wish would be when I blew out the candles on top of my birthday cake. There was no point, really. And honestly, I'd been making the same wish since I was sixteen years old. To fall in love. To meet the love of my life.

I'd been wishing on stars and dandelions and eyelashes as long as I could remember. But it didn't matter, because my life was definitely not the plot of a romance novel, no matter how many of them I read. Lately, it felt less and less like that was going to happen for me. Especially when all of my best friends were in serious relationships or married, and I was alone. But I didn't have to be. I couldn't stop thinking about Daniel's proposal last night.

Because this year... My best friend had offered me everything I had ever wanted. Except for the one thing I'd always wanted. True love. Could I marry him, accepting that we would never have that?

"You okay?" Daniel nudged my side, bringing me out of my thoughts. I'd been chewing on my thumbnail for the last few minutes, despite my bubblegum pink manicure.

Shrugging, I mumbled, "Fine." I tried to avoid his stare, because I knew he'd be able to see right through me. That was the thing about us—you didn't have almost a decade long friendship without knowing all of each other's tells.

And Daniel Bradford—he knew mine.

"Are you still thinking about what I said last night?" he asked in that low, smooth voice, which always distracted me from my thoughts.

"No. Maybe. I don't know." Meeting his eyes—those rich, brown eyes freckled with gold—I couldn't hold back my sigh.

He placed his hand on top of mine and squeezed lightly. "I'm here for you. When you make your decision." Then he flashed me a small smile—one I'd long since felt like was mine.

My stomach did a little flop as we continued holding each other's eye contact, and I looked away, trying to hide my blush.

That stare. So many women had been on the other end of it, I was sure, but never me. Not before. *So why now...?*

Noelle's eyes caught mine, and she gave me a little eyebrow raise, but she said nothing.

"So, everyone excited for Halloween this year?" Noelle's tall blond boyfriend—Matthew—asked all of us, looping an arm around his girlfriend's chair. "We've already started planning everything out."

Noelle grinned. "I'm glad we made this an annual thing. My cousin is even coming this year, and everyone's welcome to bring their friends again. The more the merrier. Only requirement is costumes."

At last year's Halloween party, they'd been the only official couple. They'd met her final year of Grad School, while she was working as a Hall Director on campus where he worked as a Professor. He'd already told us he was planning on proposing next month, and he had recruited us to help with the proposal. I thought it was cute that he wanted to include her best friends in it.

"It's my turn to pick this year," Angelina looked at him. Last year, she'd brought Benjamin, now her husband, to the event, though they were still denying their love for each other despite his obvious adoration. They'd dressed as Batman and Catwoman.

"Whatever you choose will be perfect," Benjamin agreed, kissing her cheek. She gave him a little eye-roll but didn't stop smiling. She was practically glowing with her post-European vacation tan, since they'd just got back from their honeymoon.

Hunter's lips tilted up into a smile of his own. "Ahh, the Halloween party. Wonderful memories."

He looked at Gabbi, who was struggling to eat on account of her arm cast after her and Angelina had been in a car accident last week. Luckily, everyone was okay, just a few bruises, and a broken bone, but it still made my heart flutter to see Hunter scoop up little bites on the fork to help her eat.

They'd met at the party last year, since Benjamin had dragged his brother there after he got off a shift at the hospital, where he worked in pediatrics. After being stuck together as Angelia and Benjamin's Maid of Honor and Best Man, they'd fallen in love, becoming the newest couple of our friend group. And then there was *us*. Best friends, but not together.

And then there were two, they'd said last week, glancing over at us. I fidgeted with my feet under the table, thinking about all of their teasing over the years. The girls had always told me that

Daniel and I should go out. What would they say if I said yes to him? If we actually got married? Over the last few months, they'd finally laid off me a little about him. The teasing had gone on for so long, and now that they'd stopped... I'd finally started wondering again.

"Can you believe how much has changed since then?" Gabbi leaned on her boyfriend, looking around the table. "Now look at all of us."

The dreamy sighs all around were almost too much for my mood.

Seeing all of my best friends happy made me happy, even if I also wanted what they had. It was like Daniel said—I could be happy for them and still want it for myself.

The four of us had all met freshman year of college, since Noelle and I had shared a room, and Angelina and Gabbi had been directly across the hall from us. We spent the next four years of college inseparable, and now here we were. The three of them were my best friends in the entire world. The girls who'd stuck with me through thick and thin, even when I'd thought everything would fall apart. I'd spent every birthday from the last nine years with them. We'd even skipped classes one year in college to spend a long weekend in Disneyland together. There was no way I was about to stop that tradition now.

It had gone from the four of us and Daniel to the eight of us, and I was so happy to spend time with the people I loved. I also couldn't help but think about what Daniel said last night. About how we made *sense*. I could see us with these three couples, growing old together. Raising families together. If I didn't do it with Daniel, who *would* I do it with?

Fuck, was I really thinking about saying yes to him?

After Angelina's wedding, it was a dangerous path to walk down. Especially now that he'd asked me to marry him. Even if it was just because of the marriage pact. Despite all of that, I was pretty sure I knew what my answer was going to be.

"So, what do you think?" Hunter's voice distracted me from my train of thought.

"Sorry, about what?" I asked sheepishly, looking around. Clearly, I'd spaced out longer than I thought.

Daniel frowned at me. "We're talking about going on a ski trip once the mountains have snow this winter. What do you think?"

"Oh." I looked around the table. "Sure. Sounds like fun."

I'd grown up in California, and while I'd seen snow as a kid, my parents had never taken us skiing. The most I'd ever done was when the girls and I had gone cosmic tubing during college. They'd take us up to the mountain at night and they would cover the course in black-lights and strobe lights. We'd race down it over and over until we were breathless from laughing so much.

I loved the snow, and all things about winter. My color palette might have been spring, but there was something magical about a city covered in a blanket of white.

"I think there are some cabins we could rent where we can all stay together," Benjamin commented, throwing his arm around Angelina.

"Like Angelina and Benjamin's joint bachelor party?" I raised an eyebrow, trying not to look at Daniel.

Matthew wrapped his arm around Noelle's chair, pulling it closer. "Something like that, but maybe a bit more privacy."

"Ah." My cheeks felt warm, and I hoped no one could see the way they flushed with the dim lighting in the restaurant.

If I agreed to Daniel's proposal, if we got married... They'd know by then. Which would mean all the couples would probably end up in our own rooms *together*.

Something told me that if I spent the night with him in the same bed again, it would change everything. I fought the urge to blush, thinking about what it had been like with him bracing himself on top of me. When he'd been inside me.

Best friend, best friend, best friend, I chanted to myself.

"Come on, what do you say, Char?" Angelina gave me a sly

grin. "We can sit in the lodge and read while the guys take the slopes."

"Oh, I definitely like the sound of that," Noelle agreed. "Maybe I'll have my next book done by then and you can all read it." She'd started writing her first one during her last semester of grad school, and with our encouragement, had decided to self publish. Angelina did her covers, and Gabbi helped with the social media promotions, but I mostly just helped by beta-reading and telling her my thoughts.

Either way, it was a mutually beneficial agreement.

"Okay," I agreed. But when I answered, I was looking directly at Daniel. "Let's do it."

CHAPTER 6
Daniel

The next day, I opened the door to find Charlotte standing on my doorstep, wearing a slouchy black sweater and denim leggings instead of her usual dance attire.

"Okay." Her response tumbled out, and I raised an eyebrow. "Okay?"

"You mean it?" She asked me. "You really want to marry me?"

"Absolutely."

Charlotte nodded. "Then... I think we should do it."

"Is that a yes?" My heart was practically in my throat.

She took a deep breath and nodded. *"Yes."*

It was my turn to say it. "Okay."

I looked at her, cheeks faintly pink on my porch, and opened the door wider. "Want to come in?"

She followed me inside without response, heading into my kitchen and opening several cupboards before I realized she was making herself a cup of tea.

I stood, mesmerized, as I watched her make herself at home in my house. Sure, she'd done it before, but now it felt like it meant something. Because maybe this would be her home, too.

I leaned against the wall that went into the kitchen, just watching her.

She hopped up on the counter as she waited for her water to heat, and finally turned her attention back to me. "We need this to look real. For starters, we need some sort of proposal story. Our friends are absolutely going to kill me if we just say *'hey, we're getting married!'* Even if it is a fake marriage."

Fake marriage? I tried to hide my frown. "Okay. I mean, can't we just tell them I proposed at dinner?" I'd had a ring in my pocket. I could have given it to her. But for whatever reason, I didn't. Maybe I was afraid that even if I was down on one knee ring in hand, she'd still say no.

Charlotte frowned. "Daniel. Benjamin flew Angelina to *Paris* to propose. You know Matthew has this giant scavenger hunt planned for Noelle. We need... something. Some cute story. They're going to think it's suspicious if we just suddenly say we're getting married out of the blue, aren't they?" She continued on. "So we should tell them we've been dating in secret or something. Or maybe we can tell them after we've officially gotten engaged? I mean, Hunter and Gabbi did that. Dated without telling all of us."

"Charlotte. Hey. Breathe." I stepped closer, standing in front of her in the kitchen and squeezing her thigh. "Don't worry about all of that. We'll just tell them the truth."

"Which is?"

That I'm in love with you.

"That you're madly in love with me, and when I realized, I immediately got down on one knee and asked you to marry me?"

She snorted. "Like that's believable."

"First of all, ouch. Second—do you have a better idea?" If she wanted a proposal story, I'd give her one. I'd do whatever she asked, because she was my best friend, and I wanted her to be happy. "We have to pretend to be in love, you know." I smirked.

She just shook her head at me.

"We'll come up with something."

"Okay." She looked up at me, like the realization had finally sunk in. "Oh my god. We're going to get *married*."

"That's kind of the idea, Char." I smirked, liking the idea of it just a little too much. Her being my wife.

"There's probably a million things we have to figure out." Leaning her head against the cabinet doors, she looked down at me.

"Like what?"

"Like... What happens if we meet someone else? If you fall in love, I... I wouldn't want to keep you from that, and..."

I squeezed her thigh again. "You don't have to worry about that."

I wouldn't fall for someone else. For the last nine years, I hadn't. I was an idiot. For not telling her how I felt years ago. For cashing in on our marriage pact instead of just telling her how I felt now. For somehow agreeing to something that wasn't even *real*.

My beautiful best friend Charlotte, who didn't know that I felt even an inkling of desire towards her. None, because I had made sure of it. Which was stupid.

Safe to say, not one bit of that explained why I had asked her to marry me. Or the pain it sent to my heart when she referred to what I had just proposed to her as a fake marriage. But I'd take what I could get with her, wouldn't I? I always had.

So I'd give her the wedding of her dreams, let her have the family she had always wanted, and if she never loved me as anything other than a friend... well, that'd be okay, too.

She giggled, and I raised an eyebrow. "What?"

"I just never thought I'd be living the plot of a marriage of convenience novel, or be agreeing to a fake marriage." She laughed again, wiping her eyes before looking at me.

It doesn't have to be fake. What was I thinking? I was out of my mind. I just couldn't help it when she started talking about wanting a family at dinner the other night. What was she going to do, have someone *else's* kid?

She wasn't mine, and I knew it. She'd never *been* mine, because I'd been a coward for too long. Too scared to lose her and too terrified to make a move. I couldn't sit around and wait any longer, though.

For her, I could be that person. We both wanted the life that I could give her: a marriage, a house, *kids*. A life with laughter and joy always surrounding us.

But calling it a *fake* marriage? I groaned to myself. Sure, I'd play along for now, but I was going to make her see that it was the truth, that my feelings for her were real. And hopefully, in time, she'd return those feelings back to me.

"Okay. Any other concerns you need me to ease? Or things we need to figure out right now?"

"Um..." Charlotte bit her lip. "Just that... I want to do all that typical couple stuff, I guess. Even if we're only faking it. After watching Angelina and Benjamin's wedding this summer... I want that. I want to have a wedding. It doesn't have to be a huge one, but one with all our friends, where we get all dressed up."

My sister was blissfully happy with her new husband, who she'd met at a work retreat despite insisting that she hated him. They loved to argue, but they loved each other even more. I was just glad she found someone deserving of her, because Benjamin was a really great guy. I enjoyed spending time with him when we all hung out together.

She tilted her head at me, like she was contemplating something. "If I'm only doing this once, I want to do it right."

Something made my heart beat faster at that admission. I liked that—that she would be *mine,* and no one else's. It fulfilled a strange, growly possessive part of me I wasn't sure what to do with.

"Of course. But... Are you sure you don't want to have a big wedding? I don't mind, you know. Whatever you want."

She shook her head. "My mom would probably insist, but... No. I want the dress, and the photos, and the memories, but I think who's *there* is more important. And that's just all the people who we love, who are actually important in our lives. And... us, I guess."

"I think that's perfect."

"You do?"

I nodded. "And I think you should move in with me."

"What?" Her mouth dropped open, like she hadn't even considered us living together, even though we'd just agreed to get married.

"Charlotte." I sighed. "Please let me help you with your apartment. I know you've stressed about it, and I want to help. I want to take care of you." I tilted her chin up, bringing our gazes together. "If I'm going to be your husband, let me help you."

She sighed as I wove my arms around her back. "Move in with me," I said against her hair, keeping her squished against my chest as I repeated it.

"I heard you the first time," she mumbled. "But..."

"Come on. We're going to live together eventually if we're married, right? You can just move in now instead."

"I don't know..." She looked around the room. "I have a lot of stuff. I don't want to... take over your space."

"Our space."

She looked at me with a befuddled expression on her face. "Our?"

"Yes. *Ours*. Besides, my house is enormous enough for the two of us. You can use the extra bedroom for a sewing room for your dresses and orders. And you're always over here, anyway. It just makes sense."

I hoped that appealing to her with logic would make her ignore how illogical all of this was. Getting married, living together, faking the relationship... All of it.

"Okay. You're right... We *would* live together if we were in an actual relationship. I just... have to give notice to my complex."

I nodded, relieved to get her out of there. "Do you want me to come with you? I can take care of it." Even if she could do it herself, I still wanted to be there for her. I was okay with her depending on me whenever she needed it. She *was* going to be my *wife*, after all.

"No."

Another thought occurred to me. I'd listened to our friends call their girlfriends sickeningly sweet nicknames for months, and I'd always just called her Char. No one ever really called me anything else, but I didn't think I would mind if it was her doing it.

"Okay. Now that's settled... What should we call each other? Like... pet names?"

She raised an eyebrow. "What about them?"

"Well... Are we going to keep calling each other our first names if we're in a relationship? If we don't want our friends to ask questions..."

"I don't know. We could... you know, play it by ear."

I smirked. "Okay, darling." I could think of a hundred different things to call her, but there was only one that would really matter. *Wife.* I couldn't exactly pull that one out yet, though.

"Daniel..." Her cheeks pinked slightly. "I don't know what I should call you, though. *Babe*?" She wrinkled her nose.

"We'll figure it out." I grinned. "And speaking of the wedding... What are you thinking?" I wanted to give her the wedding she'd always dreamed about.

Her eyes twinkled. "Well, we could always do a winter wedding..." She fiddled with her sweater. "I've always loved the idea of a wedding with snow. But is that too soon?"

"I don't see any reason to wait."

Because I'd marry you tomorrow, if you wanted it. I cleared the thought away. That was too much.

"Whenever is fine with me? We don't have to plan all the specifics out yet, though." Because I was dangerously close to blurting out my feelings, and that was the one thing I couldn't do. Not yet.

She nodded. "Great. Now... do you want to watch a movie?

The new Spider-Man is out. And my butt is going numb from sitting on this counter for so long."

"Yes. Want popcorn?"

"Is the answer to that *ever* going to be no?"

I laughed, going to pop a bag into the microwave before I let her lead the way to the couch.

We sat with a bowl of popcorn between us.

Even if we didn't sit thigh to thigh, I couldn't wait for the day I could bridge that gap between us, holding her in my arms and taking every bit of her she would give me.

"You know..." she paused the movie, looking between the screen and I. "Matthew and Noelle's Halloween party is coming up."

"Oh, yeah?"

She hummed in response. "Yes. And... I think I know the perfect costumes for us to do."

"As long as I don't have to wear shark teeth again, I'm game."

Last year we went as Sharkboy and Lavagirl. Even though Charlotte had looked absolutely adorable with her pink hair and the pink spandex suit, I'd felt like an idiot in my costume. But it made her smile, and that was worth it.

Everything with her was worth it.

∼

"Dad?"

We'd agreed not to tell our friends yet, but we hadn't said anything about our parents, and I needed someone to confide in who wasn't my sister. So I'd called my dad to tell him Charlotte and I's news.

"Daniel?" He answered, like it surprised him I was calling.

Maybe it did. I didn't call enough, and between my parents' divorce and eventual remarriages, sometimes it was hard to be in between their fighting. Angelina and I had always had each other, and we'd leaned on our parents less and less the older we got.

"Yeah, it's me. I have some news for you. I'm getting married."

"To who?"

I cleared my throat. "You know Charlotte, right? Charlotte Reynolds?"

"Angelina's friend?"

"She's my friend too," I grumbled. *Best friend.* And soon to be my wife.

He grunted. "About time, son. Have you set a date yet?"

I shook my head, even though he couldn't see the motion over the phone. "Char wants to have a winter wedding though, and we don't want to wait until next year, so..."

"Oh. Well, son... Why don't you use the ranch?"

"Are you sure, Dad?" I loved his place. Sure, he'd bought it after his divorce from mom, and both Angelina and I's relationships were strained with both of them, but this offer... "I know that's a lot to ask. I wouldn't want to impose."

"Of course. Tea has a friend who's a wedding planner. She'll be all over this. Just pick a date, and we'll see what we can do."

"That sounds perfect. And, if you can hold off mentioning it to Angelina? We haven't told our friends about the engagement yet, but I want to tell her myself."

He made a humming noise. "Sure. Have you thought about your honeymoon yet, son?"

I froze. "Um, I'm... not sure yet." I'd had a hard enough time keeping my hands off of Charlotte when we had shared a room over the summer. We'd clarified some things about our relationship, but the one thing we hadn't touched on in this arrangement was the physical aspect. Sure, we'd already slept together once, but... Would she even want a traditional honeymoon? "We might wait until summer."

That way, it would be warm. Knowing her, she'd be happy with us flying to Orlando and going to Disney World.

"Well, you'll want to do something nice to surprise your girl. I took Tea to Hawaii, you know. It was beautiful."

My girl. God. I liked how that sounded.

"I'll think about it. Listen, Dad, I have to go, but thanks for offering us the ranch. I'll talk to Charlotte and let you know."

"No problem, son. Talk to you soon."

I hung up with my dad, wondering if I'd regret it for the rest of my life if I didn't take her somewhere.

DANIEL
> Dad said we could use his house out in Damascus for the wedding. He and Teresa said they'd be happy to host us.

CHARLOTTE
> Really? When can we go see it?
>
> What did your dad say when you told him?

> Whenever you want. I just have to talk to him.
>
> And, nothing much...

It wasn't nothing. But I wasn't going to bring up the honeymoon, either.

> He's excited for us.

> Great.
>
> I got our costumes for the Halloween party today.

> Let's hope they fit.

> Ha. Ha. Did you forget who you're marrying? I'm a whiz with a sewing machine. I could fix it if they didn't.

> How could I forget? You made last year's costumes, after all.

It had surprised me how well she could sew on spandex, but I guess it shouldn't have surprised me. I'd seen her whip up dozens of dance costumes for her girls, and it was crazy how fast she could pull together a project anymore.

> See you tonight? We can plan more over dinner.

Sounds good. Have fun at work!

I leaned back in my office chair, settling in to work on my current project, but a new idea was forming in my mind. Charlotte was going to move into my house, but what if...

Pulling out a blank sheet of paper, I got to work.

CHAPTER 7
Charlotte

OCTOBER

Two weeks. That was how long it had been since I'd agreed to become Daniel Bradford's *wife*. Which meant that I also only had a month left in my crappy apartment, since I'd given notice that I'd be moving out at the end of my lease a few days ago.

Was I completely in over my head here? Maybe.

Juily was waiting for me after class, pinning me with her knowing stare. "Seems like everything is back to normal with that man of yours." She said, and I turned my head to hide my blush.

"He's not *my* man." I waved her off.

"Sure sounds like denial to me. No one shows up to whisk their best friend away on a romantic birthday dinner with flowers if they don't want to be with them."

"I... It's not like that. We're just friends."

Friends who agreed to get married because they made a marriage pact in college, but... Friends.

"Sure." She hooked an arm through mine. "How are the designs coming along for the winter formal costumes? I haven't seen them yet, and I'm just dying to know what you came up with."

"Let me grab my sketchpad from my bag, and I can show you. I went and got swatches this weekend for fabrics, as well."

It was safe to say I was obsessed. There was something about sewing the tiny dance costumes for our little students that filled my heart.

Would I make clothes for our kids someday? It was a topic Daniel and I hadn't brought back up, but I couldn't stop thinking about it. A fake marriage, but... I'd have my best friend by my side. And we'd raise our kids together. It was strange how fast I'd gone from thinking about having kids on my own, to knowing that I would have him.

I quickly shuffled through my dance bag for the aforementioned items to show to her, and she ran her fingers over the fabric. "Oh, Charlotte. This is going to be beautiful."

"Thank you." I practically beamed. I loved to teach dance, but dress design and sewing really was my passion. "They're like little snowflakes, see?" I picked up the white lace overlay fabric, running my fingers over the sparkles sewn in. They would glitter on stage, just like freshly fallen snow.

It would be a lot of work, but it would be worth it versus the cheaply mass-made costumes.

"I'm going to have to have you make something for our little one," she smiled. "We just found out it's a girl."

"Juily!" I exclaimed, pulling her into a hug. "That's incredible news!"

She patted her stomach. "We'll see if she takes after me, or her *infinitely* cooler programmer Mom."

I smiled, picturing a little dark-haired girl in a pink Leo and a black leather jacket, riding on a skateboard home from dance class. The perfect mix of girly and edgy. "She'll be perfect, either way," I decided.

"Yeah." She agreed, looping an arm through mine. "Now,

come on, let's go home. I'm sure your man wants to see you as much as my wife wants to see me."

"He's not my man," I mumbled again, but I wondered how much longer I'd even be able to deny the fact—before I felt like he really was.

I couldn't let myself get lost in that fantasy.

∽

CHARLOTTE
Hi.

DANIEL
Hey, darling.

I ROLLED my eyes at the text message.

You know you don't have to do that when it's just us.

Sure, but it's more fun this way.

Daniel...

What's up?

I've been so busy I've barely seen you all week. And...

We have things we should talk about.

Good things? Or bad things?

Why don't you come over here and find out?

Is that an invitation?

No.

I finished folding the top of another box when my doorbell rang, alerting me to Daniel's presence.

"Hi." I'd worn a purple t-shirt from our college, and a pair of running shorts as I ran around, packing up my apartment.

"You're packing."

"Great observation skills there, *babe*." I snorted at the nickname.

He smirked at the nickname. "What's up?"

I gestured to the boxes. "I'm packing."

"Is this your way of telling me you're moving in with me?"

"You already knew that."

Daniel laughed. "Maybe, but it's nice to see the actual confirmation. Need help?"

I pointed at the stack of boxes. "Want to tape those up? I'm trying to get all the non-essentials ready to go."

"Sure."

He started taping boxes, and we fell into a rhythm: him putting them together and me filling them with the things I didn't need around my apartment.

I decided it was finally time to talk about the topics we'd been avoiding.

"Well... we need to talk about ground rules. And... um..." My face flushed. "What happened at the wedding."

He set the tape down, turning to look at me. "When we had sex?"

"Yeah... that. We were both drunk, and I think we can both agree it's not a good idea. So maybe we should... not."

Bending to put another blanket in my box—I was always cold, so my blanket collection was quite expansive—I didn't notice him approaching behind me. Not before his arms wrapped around my middle. "And why, exactly, is it a bad idea, *darling?*"

I flushed. "You know why."

He pressed his body into mine, and I could feel him against my backside, already half-hard. I almost moaned as he rubbed against me. "I don't. Why don't you enlighten me?"

"Because we almost ruined e-everything," I said as he bent me over the couch.

"Did we?" He chuckled, the sound going straight through me as he nipped at my ear. "I think everything is turning out just the way it's supposed to. You're going to be my wife."

"We *can't*," I croaked out. I couldn't explain my hesitation, not without giving up all the cards I held to protect my heart. "And I don't... No kissing. No PDA."

"I'm going to kiss you, Charlotte. Married couples do kiss, you know." He kept me pressed against the couch, my hands gripping the top of my pillows.

I swallowed roughly as he crowded in next to me. "But we don't need to, um... in private." That seemed too *real*. Too intimate. And marrying my best friend because I couldn't find anyone else seemed like the exact opposite of that.

"Besides, we've kissed before, haven't we?" He brushed a hair back from my cheek.

"That was different." I diverted my eyes away.

"Was it?"

Was it? Maybe. Maybe it wasn't at all. Why had I asked him to kiss me in college? I was nineteen, and I still hadn't kissed a guy.

But then... Why had I kissed him in August?

"Charlotte." His voice was lower, softer, as he squeezed my thigh. "I want to kiss you. Okay?"

"Okay." I breathed out, closing my eyes.

But he didn't kiss me.

Not then.

He released his hold on me, letting me escape from between him and the couch, and it took a long time for my breathing to go back to normal.

Even longer for me to admit to myself that I'd wanted him to pin me down right there and claim me. That his breath against my ear had made me wetter than I'd ever been in my life.

That I was definitely not going to survive this fake marriage, if that was any sign.

"Happy Halloween!" Noelle smiled, her ginger locks held back with a purple headband and a green scarf tied around her neck over a purple dress. When I spotted Matthew in the living room, suddenly their costumes made perfect sense. Daphne and Fred from *Scooby-Doo*. Their hair colors already matched the characters, so it was perfect.

"Nice costume," I smiled, passing by the dessert table as I followed Noelle back into the kitchen area of her and Matthew's house. She was wearing her brand new sparkling engagement ring, which made me think of the one sitting on my bathroom counter.

"You should see Snowball. Matthew got her a Scooby collar and everything."

I laughed, wondering if that was the type of thing Daniel and I would do with our dog one day. The thought was shocking, considering we hadn't even told our friends our plan yet. And even though I knew we needed to—*soon*, I couldn't help but stress over all of their reactions.

"I'm surprised you and Daniel didn't come together."

"Why?" I asked, suddenly defensive. "There's no reason we would come together. It's not like there's anything going on between us. We're just—"

Noelle raised an eyebrow. "Char. I just meant that I know you don't like to drive. You almost always come with Daniel." The worst thing about having friends who've known you since your first year of college is that they *know* you. Maybe too well.

"Right." I tried to brush it off, to pretend I didn't just overreact to a harmless statement. "Because he's my best friend." I tugged my costume dress down, trying to feel less awkward.

"Uh-huh." She gave me another look, like she was trying to puzzle out my thoughts. Did she know I was hiding something?

Not that there's that much to hide. Just the ring sitting on my dresser, and the minor matter of me getting married to my best friend in a few months, and... I hadn't told any of them.

"He's just running late at work," I finally added. "I do have a car, so, you know..." And I *should* drive it more. I really should. But my apartment was walking distance to the dance studio, so it felt like a waste when I could get the fresh air, especially during the summer months when it wasn't constantly raining.

"Almost everyone is already here," she said as we entered the kitchen, and my eyes met my friends. "We're just waiting on Zofia and Nicolas, and Daniel, of course."

"Oh, good."

I stifled a laugh at Angelina and Benjamin, who'd dressed as Rey and Ben Solo from Star Wars. Ang had bubble buns in her hair, and Benjamin was currently crowding her against the counter, a lightsaber hooked on his waist.

"What do you think, Princess?" He murmured, low against Angelina's ear, and I felt like I was intruding on a private moment.

Turning around, I came face to face with Gabbi, who'd braided her hair and was wearing a gingham dress. Dorothy from *The Wizard of Oz*, with Hunter dressed as the Scarecrow, complete with a heart pinned to his front.

"Cute." I smiled at them.

Hunter rolled his eyes as a piece of straw fell out of his hat. "Next year we're getting the dragon onesies."

"Where's your other half?" Gabbi asked, referencing my costume.

"Oh." I blushed, wishing I could hide my face in the hood of my suit. "We're not really—"

Before I could deny it, a powerful pair of arms wrapped around me from the back, pulling our bodies together.

"Here I am," Daniel said, his voice deep against my hair, practically resting his head on top of mine. The position made my heart beat a million miles an hour, and I really hoped he couldn't feel how fast it was thundering in my chest.

"Sorry I was late, *Gwen*," he said, giving me a little wink as he pulled away from me, giving me a full view of his suit.

Oh, god. Why had I agreed to match costumes with him for the second year in a row? It was going to be so obvious something was going on between us when we were both wearing Spider suits.

I glanced down at the blue ballet slippers that were tied around my ankles. Ever since I'd watched *Spider-Man: Into the Spider-Verse* for the first time with Daniel, Gwen Stacy (AKA Spider-Gwen or Ghost-Spider) had been one of my favorite Marvel characters. Partially, it was just because there were so many similarities between us.

And even though the Peter Parker from her universe wasn't Spider-Man, well...

Turning, I took him in fully, the Spider-Man suit he pulled off better than I could imagine, and I hoped he didn't notice the way my breath caught in my throat when our eyes connected.

"Hi," I whispered, everyone else forgotten. For a moment, it was just Daniel and I standing in the middle of the crowded kitchen, the rest of our friends fading away into the background.

When had this thing started between us? When he'd asked me to marry him, or the wedding this summer? Or had it been long before, and I'd just been ignoring the spark I felt now in my blood?

"Sorry I couldn't pick you up," he said, and I just shook my head.

"It's fine. My car works just fine."

He gave me a little smirk, like he could see right through me. Like the passenger seat of his car was my throne, and all it needed was a *passenger princess* sign and we could call it good.

"Alright!" Noelle's voice commanded all of us to attention. "Now that everyone's here, we wanted to thank you all for coming to our first Halloween party as an engaged couple." She leaned onto Matthew's arm. "Hopefully, we'll make this an annual thing. We love seeing all our friends here, especially the ones we don't get to see as often." Noelle gave a warm smile as she looked around the room. "Don't forget to grab a drink from the kitchen, and snacks are in the dining room, but other than that, we're all just here to have fun!"

Matthew's best friend and his wife had brought their son, Theo, and he teetered around the floor, cute as ever, in his little Pikachu costume.

I wondered if in a few years, this party would be full of kids. My heart ached because I wanted that more than anything: a family of my own. Daniel had promised to give me that, and I could almost picture it: a little dark-haired girl, taking after him. A blonde one who took after me.

The vision was so jarring that when I came back to reality, I was startled for a second.

A cup being pressed into my hands. A pair of brown eyes looking down at me. A spandex suit that felt tight, hot. I tugged at the neck.

"You okay?" Daniel mumbled.

"Of course." I quirked an eyebrow. "Why wouldn't I be?"

He shrugged his shoulders, which caused the fabric to stretch. It should be illegal for someone to look good in a spandex Spider-Man suit, but there he stood. "You just seemed distracted."

"Just thinking." I hummed in response, taking a sip of the drink. It was some sort of punch, thanks to Noelle's excellent party planning skills, and it was delicious.

He nudged me as I took another drink. "About?"

I looked away. This wasn't the time for that conversation. A group had huddled around the couch in the living room, another gathered on the patio outside, happily chatting away. The rest of our friends had gathered in the dining room, surrounded by a heaping pile of goodies on the table.

"We need to tell them," I muttered, feeling guilty for keeping this from them. Feeling even guiltier knowing we were going to lie.

"When?" Daniel asked, squeezing my hand.

I shrugged. "Soon."

"Dad said we can come by this week, after you're done with dance one night. Teresa said she'd make us dinner, too."

Eyes wide, I nodded. We were really going to do this. *Oh, boy.*

"Oh, Charlotte," Noelle said, pulling me away. "I made you gluten-free cookies. And cupcakes. And..." She scratched the back of her head. "Well, there's a bunch of stuff for you."

"You're the best." I leaned against her arm. "As always."

"I know." She laughed. "That's why I'm your best friend."

Daniel gave a small noise of protest, but I ignored him.

"Forever and always, babe," I said, as I followed Noelle into the dining room. I wouldn't trade her for the world. She was more like my sister than my *actual sister.*

The engagement ring on her finger sparkled, catching my eye, and I couldn't stop myself from staring at it. She and Matthew were so happy, planning their wedding for the next year, and I looked over at Daniel.

Would we look like that when I had a ring on my finger? When he and I were planning our *fake* wedding?

Would we be as happy as our friends were, even if it was nothing but a marriage pact between the two of us?

I hoped so.

CHAPTER 8
Daniel

The week flew by, and despite work being slammed, Charlotte and I had been carving out little portions of each day to plan everything out with each other.

"So, we should tell them, huh?" I asked Charlotte, who'd been quiet ever since I picked her up from the dance studio after she'd finished her last class of the day.

She had changed into a long-sleeved t-shirt dress with a raincoat pulled over the top since it was currently gray and drizzly out, like any typical fall day in Portland.

"Hm?" She looked up at me, the question clear in her eyes. "Oh. Yeah. I feel guilty keeping it a secret." She fidgeted with the zipper on her jacket, clearly avoiding my gaze. "We need to tell them."

"I know we haven't really started planning the wedding yet, but..." I couldn't help but think about the ring that was currently hiding in my nightstand drawer.

"That'll change tonight." Since we were currently driving out to my dad's house.

"We're going over to Angelina and Benjamin's new house at the end of the week. Should we tell them then?"

"That works." She looked at her lap. "Do you think they're going to be mad?"

I snorted. "They've probably all been taking bets on how long it would take for us to hook up."

"Haha, very funny." Charlotte rolled her eyes.

She might have thought I was kidding, but I wouldn't have put it past them. Especially not after the conversation I'd shared with Benjamin last year. I'd practically confided in him I was stuck in the friend zone. This girl made me stupid, because I'd barely known him then, and I'd practically spilled out all of my feelings for my best friend.

"I don't want them to be mad that we didn't tell them," she said, quietly. "But I'm glad we have this time to just... figure it out. Before we have to play a part."

"Right. Because it's all fake." I didn't think she could detect the bitterness in my tone. Why had I implied that in the first place? Stupid. I was stupid.

She exhaled a sigh of relief. "Exactly."

I made a humming sound as we pulled into the driveway of my dad's ranch. It was a giant piece of property, with a horse barn and the little garden they'd planted two years ago, complete with a smattering of blueberry bushes. You couldn't beat the ones plucked right off the plant.

Turning off the car, I turned to look at her.

"Do you think we should have a code word?" She said, words spilling from her lips as if she'd been looking for something to say.

"Do you think we *need* a code word?" I asked back.

"Well, if something makes one of us uncomfortable, then we could say it and use it to change the conversation."

I shook my head. "I have a better idea." Charlotte raised an eyebrow as I leaned in closer to her. "We should practice."

She made a confused face. "Practice...?"

"Kissing."

"*What*?" Charlotte just stared at me.

"We need to practice being a *real* couple." Something I'd wanted us to be all along. "We're going to have to kiss in public. And at the wedding."

"I don't think we need to *practice* anything, Daniel."

She was right. We didn't. I already knew how good we were together—I just wanted an excuse to kiss her again. I'd almost kissed her the other night, when I'd had her pinned against the couch, those soft pink lips practically begging me, but I'd held myself back.

"But we're... best friends." She gave a small noise of protest.

"Friends don't kiss you the way I do, Charlotte."

I might have been a selfish bastard, taking what I could get from her, but I needed this. And that was why, after leaning across the center console and brushing a hair that had come loose from her giant clip back behind her ear, I cupped her jaw.

"Tell me I can kiss you, Charlotte." The words flew out before I could stop them, and I ran my thumb across her cheekbone as my hands held her face.

Her eyes fluttered shut as I traced her face, and I could hear her breathing grow deeper. "You can kiss me, Daniel."

She kept her eyes shut as I kissed her cheek, her jaw, the corner of her lip—just featherlight touches, but I could feel her tension gradually fading with each one. Feeling the way she opened herself up to me. A part of me had wanted to kiss her again since August, since I'd been so stupid at the wedding, and I wouldn't squander this opportunity now. Part of me didn't understand why I hadn't spent the last nine *years* kissing her.

Her tongue ran against the seam of my lips, and when I opened them, she flooded all of my senses.

Strawberries. She tasted like strawberries, and I practically groaned into her mouth. I wanted to lose myself in her, in her taste, because nothing had ever been so good. Nothing had ever felt so right. I hated that I'd ever kissed anyone else, because no one else would ever compare to her.

Letting our tongues dance, kissing her with all that I had.

When we pulled away, her cheeks were flushed, and she touched her lips.

"Damn. Quite a kiss, darling. Still going to insist we're *just* best friends?"

"I—We should probably go inside," she mumbled, but she didn't move to get out of her seat.

"Mmm. Yeah. I bet my dad is waiting for us for dinner."

Hopefully, he'd remembered my request to make Charlotte something gluten-free. I hated it when she could only eat meat and vegetables, because Charlotte loved all things bread and pasta. She would normally sneak sourdough, because it didn't make her sick, but most other things she tried to be good.

I got out of the car, and when I moved around to open up her door, she was still sitting there, staring at my dad's house.

"You don't think he saw us kissing, do you?" She whispered the question, and I held back my chuckle. She was so serious, her brow furrowed in worry, even though I knew it wasn't something that would phase my dad in the slightest.

I shrugged. "What does it matter? We *are* getting married, Charlotte."

And my dad had been married twice. I was sure two adults making out in a car wasn't anything new to him.

But I also sensed Charlotte's uneasiness with the situation, and I knew there was more going through her head. Reassuring her was my priority, but the second was her comfort. She'd met my dad before, but this time would be different. Because we were faking this entire relationship, and we were going to get married.

"Right." She looked away, still flushed. "Besides, that was just practice. It didn't... mean anything."

"Mm."

I didn't know quite what to say. She thought that was fake, and all I wanted to do was fix that. So... Whatever she needed to tell herself, because I was going to prove to her that this was real.

Holding her hand, we walked up to the door, side by side.

"If you need to make an escape, just squeeze my hand. I've got you, darling."

∼

"It's good to see you again, Mr. Bradford," Charlotte said, tucking her hair behind her ear as she gave a small wave to my father.

I tucked her in close to me as we sat on the couch in the living room.

"Dinner's almost ready!" My step-mom hollered from the kitchen as I looked around the room.

This house was nothing like the one I'd grown up in. My parents had both worked full-time jobs, but I couldn't imagine us living somewhere like this compared to our four-bedroom house. I hadn't come here much because of that. Because part of me wished I'd had this growing up. Two happy parents who never fought, where the family vacations hadn't stopped because of the grueling divorce.

A photo of Dad, Angelina and I from Disneyland sat on the mantle of their fireplace, and there was something about its placement that made me feel like an asshole for ever feeling that way.

Dad had tried his best, and no matter what, I knew he loved us in the best way that he could. For Angelina, maybe it wasn't enough. But for me...

All it did was solidify my need to give that to my future child. *Our future child.* I pressed my thigh against Char's, as if I needed the reminder that she was there. Maybe she was nervous, but I needed her too.

We were doing this together. We were doing *life* together.

Not because we'd had no other options, but because we'd both made the choice together. Hadn't we? Our marriage pact said nothing about *love,* but it certainly was a declaration to stand by each other through thick and thin.

I might not have known everything, but I was pretty sure that was the exact foundation you'd need for a successful marriage.

I just hoped that ours would be one of those.

"After dinner, Tea and I will show you around outside. We have a few ideas for the ceremony location, and we've got a contact who can do heated tents if you want to have the reception outside, too."

"Thank you, Mr. Bradford." Charlotte's eyes sparkled.

"You don't have to thank me, sweetheart."

"No, I do." She looked over at me. "We do. If it wasn't for you, we might have gone to the courthouse." Charlotte gave a rough laugh, and I didn't know why I hated that thought.

She'd even said she was only doing this once. That she wanted to do it right because she wanted the memories. The idea of her standing in anything less than her dream gown under a canopy of sparkling lights didn't sit right with me. Especially in something as cold and impersonal as a courthouse.

I frowned. "Well, maybe not a courthouse—"

"Of course, we can't all be your sister and get married in France," Theresa said with a laugh.

Wrapping my arm around Charlotte's side, I wished I could nuzzle my face against her soft hair. I wanted so many things I'd never wanted before, things I had never let myself think of before. Things I couldn't have. "We just want to keep it small. Personal, meaningful. But beautiful, too." Charlotte blushed at the last part. "Something you deserve," I murmured, placing a kiss against her temple.

She squeezed my hand, her eyes wide as she looked at me, and I shook my head with a laugh.

She had no idea, did she?

∞

"This place is perfect. It's absolutely... magical." Her breath caught as she looked over the grounds of the ranch, her eyes taking in every inch of the property. "And there are horses, Daniel! *Horses!*"

I chuckled. "Yes, darling. There's horses."

Angelina's dream when we were growing up was to have a horse, and now that she had grown up, well... My dad had horses.

Theresa pulled her dark hair away from her neck, pulling it up into a ponytail. "You know, we could get a sleigh for the horses to pull you away on after the ceremony. Assuming there's snow. Or maybe a carriage, if we don't get any."

"*Shut up,*" Charlotte said, her jaw dropping open. "Sorry. That's just... Wow."

"We were thinking about maybe a wedding around Christmas. I know there's not always a white Christmas in Portland, but, hopefully, this year..." I nudged Charlotte's shoulder.

She was clearly still focused on the whole *horse-drawn sleigh* aspect. I could see the excitement in her eyes as she thought about it.

The first year we'd been friends, I'd caught her in her dorm one night, crying over a Hallmark movie, a blanket wrapped around her entire body. Charlotte got cold easily, and she cried over sappy Christmas movies like there was no tomorrow. And what would you know? I'd crawled in next to her, and we'd watched another one.

Now it was our December tradition to watch the new ones together. Charlotte might have been all things pink and floral, but at her core, she was a lover of all things Christmas: the magic, the snow, and the romance.

Teresa smiled. "I know what you mean. And to think, your dad and I eloped in Vegas." She rolled her eyes. "The pinnacle of romance. I have to admit, the honeymoon made up for it, though."

Charlotte looked up at me, her big gray eyes looking into mine with worry. Sometimes I wondered if she could see into my soul the way it felt like I could see into hers. Maybe she could. Maybe I wanted her to. Maybe then she'd know my truth.

Right now, though, I didn't want her panicking about a honeymoon. Not when we'd barely even talked about *that* aspect of our relationship. Even if I wanted everything with her, there was no way I was going to book an elaborate honeymoon to some tropical destination if she didn't want that. If she still thought what happened at the wedding was a drunken mistake.

"I told Dad we were thinking about having our honeymoon next summer, since our wedding will be right before Christmas." I looked at Charlotte, who gave a brief nod of confirmation, like that was alright with her. *Phew.*

"Besides, we're going on that ski trip after the holidays with our friends." She patted my arm. "That will be like our honeymoon." Charlotte added.

Except in my mind, our honeymoon involved a lot less clothes.

And a lot more sweaty nights with her under the sheets.

I shook the thought from my mind. Thinking about Charlotte bare underneath me while I was touring my dad's property for our wedding was a mistake.

When Theresa and Dad wandered away, leaving us alone to wander, Charlotte looked up at me. Her big gray eyes reflected the stormy sky, her furrowed brow exposing her emotions. I watched as she gnawed on her lip, deep in thought.

"What's going through that beautiful head of yours, darling?" I asked her, my voice an inaudible murmur.

"I just..." She shook her head. "I hadn't even thought about..."

Chuckling, I ran a finger over the line of her jaw. "A honeymoon?"

She blushed, ducking her head away, clearly embarrassed. "Well... Yeah. I mean. We haven't talked about all of that. What's going to happen when we move in and live together and... *everything*?"

"Everything?" I raised an eyebrow. "You mean... *sex*?"

Chuckling, I lead her behind the barn. "I thought we discussed this last night." I pinned her between my arms against the siding.

Shit, had I taken the kiss in the car the wrong way earlier? I should have reassured her it wasn't fake. That I'd *wanted* to kiss her. Not that I was playing pretend.

"I mean..." Charlotte blushed. "I know you probably have... needs. We don't have to, you know... sleep together. Again. It's... not that kind of marriage, after all." She peeked up at me, practically hiding behind her curtain of blonde hair. "Right?"

What kind of marriage was it? Was it really just one of *convenience?*

"Charlotte, do you..." I swallowed roughly. What was I about to ask? *Do you want to?* God no. Just the thought of asking her after she'd all but ran out of our hotel room in August, how she was clearly pushing me away...

I needed to step away. Let her go. Put some distance between us, because maybe she was right. Maybe jeopardizing our friendship for sex would just ruin everything. And I didn't know what I would do without her in my life.

She wasn't just some hookup, not that I was prone to doing those, anyway. But it wasn't like we hadn't both seen other people over the last few years. Even some part of me burned with the thought of someone else touching her like I had.

But if I opened my mouth, I was bound to admit things she wasn't ready for. How I couldn't stop thinking about her, ever since the wedding. How sometimes I would dream of her underneath me, her blonde hair spilling over my sheets as I moved inside of her. How waking up from those dreams was the worst, because it meant coming back to a reality where I didn't have her in my arms.

No, it was better to stay on neutral ground here.

We were getting married, and we'd agreed on having kids together, but that didn't mean we had to do it the typical way. No matter what I wanted. All that mattered was that I had her in my life.

That she was going to be my wife.

That she was happy.

"We don't have to do anything you don't want to do, okay? I don't expect that."

She looked away, practically burying her cheeks in the neck of her coat. "Okay." She looked like a turtle when she finally popped her head back out, and I saw her face grow determined, like she'd decided on something.

"Okay." I nodded. "Now, should we go look at the rest of the property? Dad already said we can use the inside of the house to get ready on the day of the wedding, as well."

"Do you think..." Charlotte's eyes tracked towards the door to the barn. "We could go meet the horses?" Her eyes lit up.

I resisted a laugh.

"Whatever you want, Charlotte."

I always meant it when it came to her.

CHAPTER 9
Charlotte

"You're sure about this, right?" Daniel asked, looking over at me briefly as he drove us to Benjamin and Angelina's new house.

I nodded. "We need to tell them." I wanted my best friends involved in planning my wedding. Wanted to tell them it was happening. It felt weird that we were planning our wedding without our friends even knowing.

His hand squeezed mine before he gripped the steering wheel again. It was like he always knew that his little gesture reassured me, because every time he squeezed my hand, everything felt like it was going to be okay again.

I couldn't deny the truth to myself for much longer. I'd been dancing around my attraction to him, trying to pretend I didn't want to feel his body against mine again. Because I was *scared*. But last week, at his dad's house... I'd seen that flicker of desire once again.

And when he'd kissed me, I'd almost begged him to take me right there.

But we were already getting *fake* married. It was just a marriage pact. I had to remind myself about that, because I wasn't a hook-up kind of girl. I couldn't do no-strings attached sex. I'd given him my virginity, a decision driven by alcohol and pure *need*, and there was no part of me that regretted that, but if I slept with him again...

When he parked in front of their new house, he looked over at me again. "Before we go in there, I... uh... I have something for you."

"You do?" I raised an eyebrow.

He pulled something out of his pocket, leaning over to drop it into my hand.

"What..." I stared at my hand as he pulled his away. "It's beautiful, but I..." The ring sat in the middle of my palm, the stone set into a band of white gold, individual tiny diamonds set around it. "I didn't get anything for you."

"I don't need one." Daniel chuckled. "You can give it to me at the wedding. It's alright. I'll wait until we're married." He winked.

Married. Oh, god. I thought I was fine, and then he went and said stuff like that.

"You ready?"

"As I'll ever be," I said, giving him a weak smile.

Daniel leaned over and kissed me on the cheek. "We got this, darling."

"Yeah." I looked over at their house, trying to will myself to believe the words, and slipped my engagement ring into my pocket. We just needed to fool our friends into thinking we were in a real relationship, not that we were getting married because of a marriage pact we'd made when we were practically kids.

Daniel got out of the car, opening my door for me, and then we were walking up the paved sidewalk that led to the two massive front doors.

Before I could even ring the doorbell, it swung open, and Angelina was there. Her hair twisted up into a clip with her signature shade of red lipstick on, even though she was wearing a black turtleneck sweater and jeans.

"Hi," I said, smiling at the rest of our friends as Daniel and I walked into the living room. Handing Angelina the little plant I'd picked up for her as a housewarming gift, everyone crowded in to say hello, and then we all got swept up into a tour of the house.

Angelina showed us her new walk-in closet, and Noelle was jealous, because she wanted a room for her shoes, too. Afterwards, we went back to the kitchen to keep talking.

When Hunter and Benjamin came back inside from looking at the patio, Hunter tried to nestle Gabbi into himself when she practically yelped from the cold. I couldn't hear their exchange, but she was glaring at him, brushing the droplets of water from his coat. From his grin, I could tell just how much he loved my friend. Hunter leaned in and kissed Gabbi's cheek. I was glad they were happy.

But I couldn't help but wonder if Daniel would ever look at me that way.

"Anything cool out there?" she asked him.

Hunter nodded. "Benjamin was just showing me the place he wants to build a pool."

Gabbi raised an eyebrow, looking over at Ben. "A pool, Benjamin?"

"It'll be perfect for the kids." Benjamin grinned.

We all turned to Angelina, who waved her hands. "No, I'm not pregnant. I promise." She glared at her husband. "We're not even going to try until I'm thirty. At least." Ang pointed a finger at him before turning back to the rest of us. "*But*, one day, it might be nice if we can have all our families out there. And if we build a structure over it, we can keep it heated in the winter, so it'll be usable all year round."

"I like it." Gabbi grinned.

I felt lost in my thoughts all night. It was strange to see my friends move on to the next part of their lives: engaged, married, thinking about having kids.

I supposed that would be *us* soon, too. Maybe that *was* why I'd said yes. I didn't want to be alone anymore. And he... was my best friend.

Daniel handed me a glass of lemonade, and I gave Gabbi a small smile. Taking a sip, I made eye contact with him. He gave me a slight nod, as if to say, *go for it*. I set the glass down and took a breath before turning back to the rest of our friends.

"Hey, guys? Um..." I knew I was fidgeting, rubbing my ring finger almost absentmindedly, thinking about the ring that sat inside my pocket. The one he'd surprised me with tonight.

Daniel gave me another nod, as if he was encouraging me—and somehow, his eyes locked onto mine gave me the strength to keep going. "I have something to tell you all."

They all looked at me expectantly, not saying *anything*, just standing there staring.

I scooted closer to Daniel, who picked up my hand and wove our fingers together.

"*We* have something to tell you all," Daniel confirmed, squeezing my hand. "We're... together," Daniel finally said.

I expected gasps, some surprised expressions, but they all looked so excited for us.

"You *are?!*" Angelina shrieked.

"That's not all though." My lips curled up into a hint of a smile, and I pulled my hand free from Daniel's, grabbing the ring in my pocket. Sliding it on my finger, felt right. Like this was the correct decision. "We're getting married."

If it was possible, I was pretty sure the other six of our friends all collectively gasped at once. "You—*what?*"

There it was.

Daniel wrapped his arm around me, pulling me deeper into his side. "You heard her," he nodded. "We're engaged."

"Are you pregnant?" Angelina narrowed her eyes. "Daniel, you didn't accidentally get her pregnant, did you?" She looked at me. "I'll kill my brother if he did."

I flushed, my cheeks surely already pink from how warm they felt. "No. I'm not pregnant. We just... realized we both had feelings for each other at the wedding, and we've been trying to figure out the best time to tell all of you."

Gabbi blinked. "Since the *wedding*? But... it's been months?"

"Sorry." I winced. "I feel like I did this all wrong. We wanted to ask all of you if you'd be our bridesmaids and groomsmen."

"Of course!" Noelle squealed, throwing her arms around me. And then all four of us girls were in the middle of a group hug.

When I pulled away, the guys were all patting Daniel on the back, and I was so glad they'd all become friends. I liked that all our guys—now that Daniel was really *mine*, even if we weren't really in *love*—were a group too.

"Oh my god, you know what this means?" Noelle's smile radiated off her face, her freckled cheeks glowing as she looked over at Gabbi. "You'll be the last two to get engaged."

She raised an eyebrow at Hunter, and he gave her a dopey grin. "I think we're good for now." Gabbi laughed.

"I can't believe we'll get to plan our weddings together," Noelle said, squeezing my hand excitedly. "Matthew and I are planning on getting married next fall."

"When are you guys tying the knot?" Angelina asked, sipping on her glass of wine, practically staring us down through the glass.

"We're still deciding an exact date, but..." My cheeks heated. "It'll be in December sometime."

I didn't really see any reason to wait. Especially if we were going to get married at his dad's house, and we didn't have to rent a venue... Plus, I was making my dress. I'd already started on the sketches for it. All we had to do was book the caterers, and his step-mom was helping take care of most of it. She was a godsend I hadn't expected when we'd started all of this craziness.

"December!" Gabbi's eyes went wide. "Are you crazy?"

"Maybe a little," I laughed.

"Crazy in *love*," Daniel added with a little smirk, and I resisted the urge to elbow him in the stomach.

We certainly weren't Angelina and Benjamin who enjoyed a good verbal sparring, and I thought injuring my *fiancé* in front of all our friends might give off the wrong idea.

Still, my face flushed as they all launched into a million questions.

"How'd he propose?" Noelle asked.

"Yeah, Charlotte, how *did* he propose?" Angelina looked between the two of us, still standing next to each other.

Daniel gave me a little smile, like it was our own inside joke. "Why don't you tell them, darling?"

I fiddled with the ring on my finger. What had we agreed on? Something as close to the truth as possible? "It was my birthday," I started, looking over at him. "We went to this restaurant in downtown with this amazing view, and he surprised me over dessert." Close enough, at least. I'd spent most of that night thinking about how I wanted cheesecake.

"And the ring?" Gabbi asked Daniel. "It's beautiful."

"Thank you." He pulled me to his side.

"This is just... crazy." Angelina crossed her arms. "After all these years, I can't believe you two are actually together. And none of us even knew it."

"Yeah, well, we are." Daniel gave his younger sister a nod. "So you'll have to get used to it."

I was glad he was acting more confident than I felt, because her comment had only succeeded in me feeling bashful.

Why had we waited so long to tell them, anyway?

Because it was fake?

∼

Today was officially the day. I couldn't delay this any longer.

I looked over at my empty apartment, now devoid of all of my things. I'd sold some of my unnecessary furniture, the shitty stuff I'd gotten straight out of college: my bed, my kitchen table, and my living room set. I didn't need it anymore.

I'd kept my pink chair, though, and I packed all of my sewing supplies in boxes. The bulk of it, the guys would come and get later, but right now, Daniel and I were loading up the rest of my belongings. I was trying to pick up several bags of my dresses, but couldn't quite manage.

"I'll get those," he grunted, scooping them all up like they weighed nothing, even though I'd been struggling from all the weight.

"I can take one," I protested, but he just ignored me, heading down the stairs towards his car.

By the time we finished shoving my dress collection in, the car was full to the brim. Matthew was bringing his truck over later, and that was when they'd also get all of my boxes of books. I'd tried to rent a U-Haul, but the guys had insisted that they could take care of it.

Which left the two of us driving over to his house in silence. We'd already parked my car at his house when we brought the first load over this morning.

Our house, he liked to remind me. It was now *ours*, even though I still felt like I was intruding on his space. Sure, it had been the best option, and yes, we were about to get *married*, but was it my home?

He'd bought it a few years ago, a self-dubbed starter home. Even after having it remodeled, he'd been dreaming of building his own house for years. Another feat I was sure he'd accomplish.

It occurred to me with a start that he would probably do that while we were *married*, and I froze. Would that be *our* house? Or would it still feel like I was just living in his?

"What?" He stopped to stare at me.

"What happens if this doesn't work out?"

He frowned. "Living together?"

I shook my head, my mouth feeling dry. "That and, well... Being married."

"Charlotte." He dropped my bags onto the living room floor, coming over to stand in front of me. "We've been friends for nine years. I know you better than anyone else? What exactly are you worried about?"

I looked away, unable to meet his eyes when he looked at me like *that*.

What was I worried about? Everything. That he'd meet someone else, and realize he made a mistake marrying me. That the love of his life was out there somewhere, and it *wasn't* me. That I wanted this to work more badly than I could properly express. That the resolve I'd built up over the last few months was slowly chipping away, and if I wasn't careful, I was going to end up with a broken heart.

"What if we have kids, and then decide this doesn't work?" I couldn't help the worry that was festering in my gut. His parents' divorce had been hard on both him and Angelina, and no matter what happened, marriage pact or not, I didn't want to subject any of our potential kids to that. No matter how much I wanted a baby, I didn't want to risk them growing up unhappy. "Maybe this is a terrible idea. Oh god." I moved my hand to rub my forehead, but Daniel took it instead, squeezing it tight, before dropping our hands in between us. He just kept holding on tight.

Daniel smoothed a hair behind my ear. "If this doesn't work out, we'll be okay. You won't lose me, ever, alright?"

Part of me wasn't sure if that was true, but I nodded. Maybe that was what I'd been the most worried about all along. I had my friends, but losing Daniel—that was something I wasn't sure I'd ever recover from.

Not when he was the first person I texted every morning and the last person I thought about every night. When I saw something cute, he was the first person I wanted to tell about it. When I saw funny videos on the internet, he was the one I wanted to send them to.

Daniel was just my person, and I'd long since accepted that. He was my best friend.

Even when he pulled into the house, we both sat in the car in silence for a while. It was like neither one of us wanted to move, because we were about to change everything between us.

Daniel kissed my knuckles before letting go of my hand to get out of the car.

I focused my eyes on the numbers on his house, and I didn't even notice that he'd come around to my side and opened up the door for me. Extending out a hand, he helped me out of the car.

"Come on, I'll show you your room."

I blinked. "My... room?"

He gave me a weird look and then nodded.

Was I... *disappointed* that we weren't sharing his bedroom? I wasn't going to admit that to myself. It would be better this way, especially without sex to complicate things. I'd implied that much, hadn't I? He was just listening to me. Especially after we'd almost ruined everything with sex before.

"What about the stuff in the car?"

"We can just grab it afterwards. Come on."

"Right. My room. Perfect. Lead the way." I pasted on a fake smile, adjusting my slouchy pink sweater.

Daniel led me through the house, up the stairs and to the bedroom across the hall from his. When we walked in, my eyes tracked over the pink velvet tufted bed frame, nightstands and dresser all sitting there, just waiting for me to fill them.

"I thought this might be more comfortable for you. So you'd have your own space." He leaned against the door frame as I sat on the mattress. I couldn't decide if I loved how thoughtful he was or if I hated it.

After all, wasn't I going to be his wife? Wasn't he the one who had come up with this inane idea in the first place?

"Wasn't this your guest room?"

He scratched the top of his head, the tips of his ears a little red. "Yeah. But it's yours now. You can fill it with all of your pink."

I'd been over to his house so many times, for movie dates on the couch or eating pizza after a long day, but everything felt different now. Maybe it was because I knew this wasn't a temporary thing. I was going to live here—together, with him.

"I have one more thing I want to show you." He tugged my hand towards the front of the house, into the empty bonus room. But it wasn't empty at all—multiple bookcases sat there, just waiting to be filled up.

"You did this for me?" I was feeling a little choked up. Building me bookcases for my books shouldn't have made me feel like this, but I couldn't help the flutters in my stomach from the action.

Daniel squeezed my hand. "Yeah. I wanted you to have somewhere that you could make into your space. I cleaned out the closet, so you should be able to store your dress projects in there, and then I was thinking we could put your sewing desk against the wall." He looked at his watch. "Shoot. I only have an hour till the guys are meeting me at your apartment to get everything else. Are you okay here while I go?"

I nodded my head. "I'll just start unpacking, I guess."

"Let me go get the rest of the bags out of the car." He kissed the top of my head before heading outside, leaving me standing in my space. It was bigger than I'd ever had at my apartment, and I could already see it now.

Maybe everything wasn't perfect, but things were going to turn out just fine.

I needed to protect my heart. So I didn't get confused about what this was and what it *wasn't*. We weren't two people marrying for love. Sure, we loved each other, but not the way I needed. The way I craved.

And I was just going to have to accept that.

∼

THE GUYS HAD COME and gone, Matthew's truck carting over my sewing desk and the rest of my stuff, leaving the two of us alone once again.

Which meant that I needed to make the call that I'd been avoiding.

"Hello?"

"Hey, Mom."

"Charlotte!" I could hear my mom's surprise over the phone. "How's everything been?"

I looked at Daniel, who sat in the other room, fiddling with his guitar as he played with a few strings. "It's good. But listen, Mom, I have something I need to tell you."

My sketchbook was in my lap, the page opened to something I was working on for a dance commission, but I knew if I flipped a few pages back that my dress was in there. That I could run my fingers over the lines I'd drawn, and redrawn, over and over, until it had been perfect.

I shut my eyes as I prepared to drop this giant bomb on her.

"You're moving home?"

I scoffed. *As if.* I loved California, and I'd always be a California girl at heart, but this place was my home now. With these people, especially the guy sitting in the next room, over. "I've been in Oregon for almost ten years, and that's what you jump to? No. I'm..." I took a deep breath, trying to get over my initial hesitation. Why hadn't I done this sooner? "I'm getting married. Next month."

"What?!" she exclaimed. "To who? When did this happen? We're invited, right? Do you need my help? I can call my friends, and we can—"

I sighed. There it was. That was why I hadn't called. "Mom—"

"What do you *mean*, you're getting married?" She interrupted me, asking again. "I didn't even know you were dating someone."

That's because I wasn't, I thought bitterly, but I didn't say it. Of course I didn't.

There were a lot of things I'd do before ever admitting this ruse to my mother. She would have a heart attack and die.

"Mom." I took a deep breath. "The wedding's already planned. I just wanted to tell you." Pinching my nose, I figured I'd go question by question. "Daniel and I are getting married."

"The dark-haired boy?"

I flushed. "Mom. I've known him since college. He's not—" Oh, whatever.

Daniel's fingers stroked over the string of the guitar, and all I could think about was when he'd had those fingers inside of *me*.

Oh, god. Living in this close of proximity with him was going to be the death of me.

I needed to get off the phone before I continued this line of thoughts while talking to my *mother*.

"December twenty-third. If you want to be there. Invitations will be out in the mail this week."

Thank god for Daniel's step-mom. She was a godsend, and not having to ask my mom for help made me feel all the better about it. Sure, I could plan this wedding all on my own, but I liked how I didn't have to.

"Are you sure this isn't a little rash?"

Daniel's eyes met mine, and even though I didn't think he could hear her end of the conversation, I still held my head up high as I told her the truth. "He's my best friend. I've known him for almost ten years. There's nothing rash about this. If you can't support me in this, don't come. Okay?" I didn't give her a chance to respond before I continued. "I have to go now. My fiancé is home. I'll talk to you later."

I hung up without another word, and then put my phone on silent before I tossed it off to the side. She would probably call back and give me stern words for hanging up on her, but right now, I just needed my best friend.

"Hey."

His smooth voice had me looking up. He'd left his guitar on the floor and extended a hand out to me.

"Hi." I breathed it back as I took his hand, and he practically pulled me into his arms.

No matter what happened, at least I had him.

Fake or real, he was by my side.

CHAPTER 10
Daniel

He's my best friend. I've known him for almost ten years. There's nothing rash about this. If you can't support me in this, don't come.

The words filled me with a swell of pride. She was incredible in all aspects of her life, but hearing her stand up to her mother... Damn. I was proud of her. And a little turned on. I liked her boldness. I wasn't sure there was a single thing I disliked about her, in all honesty. There never had been.

I adjusted myself casually, hoping she wouldn't notice.

When we'd finished moving all of her stuff into the house, she'd brought all of her sketching supplies out into the living room. Her notebook was open to whatever she'd started designing before she'd called her Mom.

I leaned against the door frame as I observed her drawing; the pencil creating the folds and fullness of the skirt. She hummed softly as she worked. And even though I shouldn't have been spying, watching her work without a clue I was there, I couldn't stop myself.

I wondered if the design for her wedding dress was in there too. If she'd even started making it yet. Charlotte liked to be on top of her creations, and since our wedding was a little over a month and a half out...

Fuck. It would be here before we knew it, and there was still so much to do.

Charlotte had pulled her blonde hair up into a messy bun on top of her head, wearing a purple alumni crewneck from our college and a pair of black leggings with little criss-cross designs on the bottoms. It was... cute. Though there was a part of me who knew I shouldn't find loungewear adorable, I couldn't help it with her. Everything I saw her in took my breath away. Even barefaced and in sweats, I thought she was the most beautiful girl I'd ever seen.

And her mom had upset her.

But damn, if there hadn't been a little thrill that ran through me when she called me her fiancé for what was probably the first time.

"Do you want dinner?" I asked her, hoping she wouldn't retreat into her room now that I was practically holding her in my arms.

"You made something?" She asked, looking surprised.

"Mhm. I prepped something earlier. I figured you'd be hungry after moving all day."

She was still holding onto my hand, but Charlotte surprised me by wrapping her other arm around my back, squeezing tight.

"Thank you," she finally said when we broke apart. "I think I needed that." Charlotte exhaled deeply before turning towards the kitchen. "What's for dinner?" She made a face, looking skeptical.

Did she think I didn't know all of her food preferences? Going out anywhere new always proved a challenge with her gluten free diet, so most of the time, we went to places she knew and loved.

I grinned. "Take a seat. You'll like it, I promise."

Pulling out a bottle of wine—white, because that was what she preferred—and two glasses, I raised it up in question. Thankfully, she knew what I was asking, the sort of wordless communication we'd developed over the last almost decade of friendship.

Part of me wished that wordless ease extended to other aspects of our lives.

She nodded, and after I filled the glass and handed it to her, I caught her playing with the stem of the glass, deep in thought. "Listen, I think... maybe we should set some ground rules."

I raised an eyebrow. "Rules?" Taking a sip of the wine, I let the sweet flavors of it sit on my tongue. We'd started this conversation before, but had never finished it.

"Yeah. For living together. For this fake marriage." She gestured wildly around us.

God, there's that term again. *Fake marriage.* I hated it so much. Why did it grate on my nerves when I was the one who proposed this agreement in the first place?

Trying not to let myself react, I gave her a brief nod as I pulled the lasagna out of the oven. Angelina and I had come from an Italian-American family, so they had passed a lot of the recipes I loved to make down to me from our relatives.

"What are you thinking?"

"Well," she wrinkled up her nose, deep in thought. "What do people in marriage of convenience books normally agree on?"

I crossed my arms over my chest as she appeared deep in thought.

"Um... knock before entering the other's room?"

"How old are we?"

"Daniel. I'm serious." Her brows furrowed. "And no sex."

She really liked to drive that point home, didn't she? Had it been that bad?

"So am I, Char. We're adults.

"I just don't want to ruin our friendship."

But what if I didn't want to be just friends with her anymore?

"I have some rules, too."

She raised an eyebrow. "You do?"

Nodding, I continued on. "We eat dinner together every

night. Go out on a date at least once a week. Tell each other what we're thinking. Feeling."

"Right." Charlotte mumbled. "Honesty."

I could feel that she was holding something back from me, even as we sat at the table, eating lasagna and the garlic bread I'd made.

"Okay, if this is what I have to look forward to every night, I have no complaints about dinner." She moaned as she brought another forkful of the layered pasta to her mouth. "This is *so* good."

"Good." I said it with a smile, even though I didn't press for more. I couldn't ask her what was bothering her, what seemed to be on her mind. Not tonight.

Tonight, I was just enjoying sitting side by side with my best friend—and soon to be wife.

∼

A WEEK LATER, I was trying to figure out how the circus had come to town—or, rather, to my house.

Somehow, I'd always avoided having everyone over here. Not that it was too small to host, but simply that I'd never had a *reason* to. It was always either Matthew and Noelle, since they'd been dating the longest, or Benjamin and Angelina, with all the wedding activities.

But now, it was our turn, and everyone crowded on the couches in my—our—living room. Gabbi and Angelina were cooing over pictures of my sister and Benjamin's new kittens on her phone.

"What are their names again?" Gabbi asked, even though I wasn't sure how she'd forgotten.

"Bruce and Selina." My sister's smile filled my heart. She'd been so serious for so long, so unwilling to let love into her life, that seeing her filled with this much joy was everything I could have wished for her.

I wanted Charlotte to have that kind of happiness, too.

The guys were in the kitchen, talking about god knows what, while I sat on the couch with Charlotte's legs draped over me. The only thing that would make us be touching more was with her on my lap.

Gabbi looked at Benjamin. "How'd she talk you into that?"

Angelina rolled her eyes as Benjamin wrapped his arms around his wife. "She can be *very* convincing."

"I like that we both have black cats," Gabbi added. Her little black cat was named Toothless, after the Dragon from *How To Train Your Dragon*. Her love for dragons probably also explained the dragon-and-book tattoo on her wrist. Hunter had even gotten a dragon tattoo to match.

"And who could forget the big white fluff ball," Noelle added, looking at their dog.

"When are you two getting a pet, Char?" Angelina asked. "I know you mentioned it a few months back."

"Oh, uh..." She stiffened, turning her head to look at me as her cheeks pinked. "I don't know."

Huh. I didn't know she wanted an animal. I'd told her I wanted a dog before, but I doubted she remembered that.

"There's no rush," I told her. "We have time."

For now, I was content with just the two of us. The rest would come eventually.

She nodded, but I could still feel her discomfort, and I wondered what was going through her head.

"I'm just gonna... run to the bathroom," she mumbled, practically stumbling off the couch as fast as she could.

"Hey, babe, will you get me a refill?" Angelina gave her husband a sweet smile, and he kissed her cheek as he took her glass, Matthew and Hunter following her to do the same.

And then the three remaining girls looked at me.

"Why do I feel like I've done something wrong and I'm at the principal's office?"

Angelina rolled her eyes.

"Listen. We know that you've been friends with Charlotte for a long time," Noelle started, fiercely protective of her best friend. *Our* best friend. "But if you hurt her, I swear, you will regret it."

Gabbi crossed her arms over her chest, nodding in agreement. "Don't make us kick you in the ass, Bradford."

The three of them were like a pack of guard dogs—a little terrifying, because I knew they were serious. Not that they'd kick my ass, because I had the height over all of them at six one, but that they'd always have Charlotte's best interests at heart. They'd all been with each other through thick and thin. Breakups, graduation, navigating the years together—of course, they'd want to make sure I was going to treat her right.

And I would.

"Aren't you going to say anything?" I asked my sister.

Angelina raised an eyebrow. "What's left to say?"

"Thanks for the support," I muttered under my breath. Apparently, twenty-seven years of being siblings meant nothing for loyalty.

"She's one of my best friends," Angelina quirked an eyebrow.

"I thought I was too," I grunted. She gave me a small smirk, patting me on the shoulder as I turned back to the other two girls.

"Look, I... I'm not going to hurt her," I said, raising my arms in the air, as if attempting not to look threatening. It was clear that I needed to make a peace offering. Or maybe just the truth. "I care about her." More than I could say.

"But do you *love* her?"

I didn't know if I could answer that. If I could say those three words, knowing what they truly meant. "I—" They didn't know we were marrying because of the marriage pact, that somehow I'd convinced Charlotte to marry me for no other reason than I'd wanted her to. We'd agree we would fake it, that we were pretending to be together, so of course. "Of course I do." I loved her—I'd always loved her. As a friend, as the person I felt most comfortable around.

The guys came in from the kitchen, saving me from any further interrogation. Charlotte still hadn't come back from the bathroom, and I was worried about her after the way she'd left so suddenly.

"I'm gonna go check on her," I said, nodding to the three girls, who all gave me looks of approval.

Glad I was at least doing that right. I rolled my eyes after I was out of eyesight, thinking about them trying to protect Charlotte from me. I'd promised myself a long time ago that I would never hurt her.

"Charlotte?" I knocked on the bathroom door. "Are you okay?"

"Are you alone?" She sniffled.

Fuck. Was she crying in there?

"Yes, darling," I murmured through the door. "Want to let me in so we can talk?"

"N-no." Her voice was weak, shaky. "I'm fine. Promise."

"Charlotte." This time, my voice was low. "Let me in, please."

She opened the door just a crack, enough for me to slip inside and lock it behind me. Her eyes were red and puffy, rimmed with tears, and her chest was moving rapidly, like she couldn't get enough air.

Wrapping her up in my arms, I rested my head on top of hers, practically burying my nose in her hair. "Breathe," I murmured against her scalp as I rubbed her back.

"What's wrong?" I asked her once her breathing had returned to normal, but she still said nothing, choosing instead to shake her head against my plaid shirt. She would never call them anxiety attacks, but I knew she had them every now and again, when the panic would fill her eyes. I'd seen it once when she was driving, and she'd gripped the steering wheel so hard her knuckles had gone white.

Even if I didn't know what caused it, I always knew what I could do. Be there for her. Hold her hand and help her through it.

I lifted her onto the bathroom sink, wiping the tears from her eyes. "Talk to me, baby. Please."

"I'm scared." It was hardly more than a whisper.

"Of what?"

"That we're making a mistake. That—" She squeezed her eyes shut, not finishing her sentence.

I stepped inside her legs, trying to ignore how right it felt as Charlotte's arms came around the back of my neck, holding me tighter to her.

"We're not making a mistake. You're my best friend, and we're going to do it all together." I waited for her eyes to meet mine. "Okay?"

Another nod, and then she was intertwining her fingers with my hair, tugging my mouth down to hers. I was hopeless to do anything but obey.

"Kiss me," she whispered. "Make me forget all the reasons this is a bad idea."

"Fuck." I couldn't deny her anything. Our lips crashed together, and I murmured it against her lips before I was determined to consume her whole. "Your wish is my command."

By the time we opened the bathroom door, Charlotte's cheeks were pink and her lips puffy and swollen,

"Oh my god. They're gonna know what we were doing in there," she mumbled as I pulled her out into the hallway, back towards our living room. "Don't make me go back out there."

"Charlotte." I brushed a finger across her ear. "You talk about dirty books with your girls. But you're embarrassed about this?"

She was so bold and brazen the night in France, when she'd pushed her tongue into my mouth and then had let me go down on her. But this? Confronting her friends after I'd kissed her?

I kissed the top of her forehead, pulling her close. "It'll be fine, darling. I've got you, okay?"

And I did.

I intended to prove that to her for the rest of our lives.

"Daniel?"

The door to my bedroom opened and closed, jolting me awake. I'd always been a light sleeper, and I felt like it was even more so now that I knew only a wall separated me from her.

"Charlotte?" I mumbled as the bed creaked, her sliding underneath the covers. "Are you okay?"

I couldn't see her face in the darkness, but the sliver of moonlight that shone in from the blinds allowed me to see her faint outline.

"I just... Can I stay with you tonight?" She sounded unsure of herself, and I hated that.

"Of course."

She laid her head on the pillow next to mine, and I could feel her curling herself into a ball. I didn't know where her mind was, but she felt a million miles away.

"Do you want to talk about it?" I asked, my voice a low whisper.

"No." She shut her eyes tight. "I just don't want to be alone."

I should have kept my hands to myself, but I couldn't resist the urge to pull her closer to me, to hold her in my arms and reassure her that everything was going to be okay. Even if I didn't even know what was wrong, I knew I didn't want to see her hurting, didn't want her to be unhappy.

After a few minutes of silence, she whispered another confession. "I think I've been taking care of myself for so long... I think I've forgotten what it was like to let someone else take care of me."

I tugged on a strand of her hair, wrapping it around my finger. It might have been a more caring gesture than was normal for best friends, and there was no one around to pretend to, but I just needed to do it. Needed to have some connection to her as I murmured out my own words. "When my parents first divorced, it was just Angelina and I. We had to learn how to take care of each other. Both of our parents fighting... it took a toll on us. It was hard to watch. But she was my best friend. I'm glad we got to go to college together." I tilted up her chin to look at me. "But you're not alone anymore, Charlotte. Okay? I'm here for you. I'm never going anywhere, baby."

We fell asleep like that, her head against my chest and my arms around her, and something settled into my chest.

CHAPTER 11
Charlotte

"Charlotte?" The voice dragged me from my thoughts. Of how I'd woken up in bed next to Daniel and snuck out before he was awake. *Again.* The sun hadn't even risen when I'd tiptoed from his bedroom back to mine, pulled on a pair of leggings and a sports bra, and went for a run, an audiobook playing in my ear as I ran through his neighborhood.

I hadn't said anything. I'd just run away.

"What do you think?" Gabbi asked me, clicking through webpages on her computer as we waited for the other two in our favorite coffee shop.

I looked at her computer screen, seeing the lodging options for our group ski trip pulled up on her laptop. It was a little last minute, but we were looking at going in just a few weeks. The guys had already made sure we'd gotten our ski passes, so we just needed somewhere to stay.

And then once we got back, the wedding would be right around the corner.

"Oh, yeah. Sure."

Gabbi frowned, as if realizing I hadn't actually paid attention to anything she'd just said. "There are a few different options we can do, either renting a big house and we'd all have our own room, or there's a cute little lodge with individual cabins." She wiggled her eyebrows. "Then we'd all have privacy."

"Gabs!" I almost choked on my hot chocolate. Of course, she thought we were in an actual relationship, which meant all the intimate, physical aspects as well. Which, I supposed, we *had* done, even if everything else was a lie. *Was I the worst friend?* I hadn't even admitted that I'd slept with him during Angelina's wedding. It felt too personal to share that moment with anyone. Even just the thought of that kiss last week sent butterflies through my stomach, my body craving his touch.

"We haven't, um..."

Gabbi raised an eyebrow. "But you... live together?"

My cheeks pinked. "Yeah." It wasn't like I could deny it when they'd all just been over yesterday. They didn't know I was occupying the guest room. I'd slept in his arms last night, and for all they knew, that was my reality.

Luckily, Noelle and Angelina came in and saved me from the situation.

"What are we looking at?" Angelina asked, sitting down next to Gabbi and staring at the computer.

"Options for the ski weekend to Bend," Gabbi answered as Ang took the laptop and started going through the different tabs.

"Ooh, this one has a big hot tub on the deck outside that we could probably all fit in, and the kitchen is *enormous*." She flipped through the rest of the details before handing the computer over to Noelle. "That one's my vote. And it has four bedrooms with queen-sized beds, so we'll all have our own room."

Gabbi looked at me, knowing our conversation from earlier had gotten cut off. I just gave her a nod of confirmation. What else could I say?

I can't sleep with my future husband—again—*because I'm terrified that sex is going to ruin everything?*

Why had I said yes? In the first place? Ugh. I hated I felt desperate enough to marry my best friend. Sure, he was handsome, and charming, and I'd never found another person who I felt comfortable enough in their presence to want to spend the rest of my life with, but...

"Char?"

"What?" I looked up.

"Is that good with you?" Noelle asked. "I think we should book this place. It doesn't have the privacy of individual cabins, but the living spaces are nice, and the balcony has a fantastic view of the mountains."

"Plus the hot tub." Angelina added.

Noelle smirked. "Yes. And there's that."

"Yeah. Sure. Sounds good," I agreed, absentmindedly. I needed to get out of my funk.

Everything was going to be fine. I needed to stop second-guessing myself the way I had for years. Sometimes it felt like I'd been so terrified of failure that I hadn't ever reached my full potential. Sure, I loved making dresses, but it was still a side hustle. I loved teaching dance, but was it *enough*?

What was the dream that would make me feel like my soul was *alive*? Because when I closed my eyes, the only thing I desired wasn't a job or a pair of ballet slippers.

Giving them the best smile I could muster, I tried to ignore the feeling in my stomach that everything was about to change.

I just hoped it wouldn't be for the worst.

~

GLITTER COVERED the floor of my sewing room, as well as yards and yards of satin and lace, but I was determined to finish in time. To wear *my* dress on my wedding day—my dream dress, exactly how I'd pictured it.

Well, mostly, considering how much I had left to do, and how the wedding was getting closer by the day.

Two weeks had passed since I'd finally moved in with Daniel. Which meant we had around a month until the wedding, and there was so much left to do. Sure, we'd sent out invitations, and I'd booked a photographer and found a florist, but my to-do list felt like it was a mile long.

We were supposed to go cake tasting at my favorite local bakery tonight, even though I was pretty sure I already knew what I wanted. A part of me just wanted to make sure it was what *he* wanted, too. Daniel had been letting me making almost all the decisions, giving me a reassuring smile and telling me it was "*whatever I wanted.*"

Which was great, but... what I really wanted was for us to plan our dream wedding together. Not just my dream wedding. Because this was about us, wasn't it?

I sighed, pinning another layer of fabric together, when a knock sounded on the door.

Shit. Was it still bad luck to see the dress before the wedding when it wasn't a genuine marriage? I had a split second to decide that *yes;* it was. I was treating this like a real wedding, after all. We were pulling out all the stops.

So there was no way I was letting him see the half-made dress strewn all over the room.

"Don't come in!" I shouted, hurrying to drape a sheet over the mannequin currently holding the bodice of my dress as I was working on the skirt. "You can't see it!"

Daniel chuckled through the wood. "You know, for all your talk about a fake marriage, you sure seem determined to do this right."

He'd said he was going for a run, and I could only hope that he wasn't shirtless again. I'd already had to amend our rules yesterday to include being *fully clothed* in all common areas. Daniel shirtless was a reminder I did *not* need.

I opened the door, crossing my arms as I eyed him, kicking a spool away from me. "We're only doing this once."

"Mhm." His hair was damp, likely from a shower he'd taken post run. Why did I want to brush my fingers through it? Why did I want to see if he still smelled like apples?

I'd used his body wash this summer. We wouldn't evaluate why I enjoyed smelling like him.

Clearing my head of thoughts of Daniel in the shower, I refocused my energy on him. "That means it has to be perfect."

"Does that perfection involve me feeding you dinner?" He quirked an eyebrow.

As if in answer, my stomach growled. But... "What about the cake tasting?"

He frowned. "You're telling me you aren't hungry? *You?*"

Well... He had a point. Between dancing and working out to stay in shape, I had to consume more calories since I burned so many off. "Okay. Yeah. I could eat."

"Great. Follow me."

I never knew how special it would feel to have a man make dinner for me every night. I'd figured I would be the one taking care of him, but watching him cook so effortlessly was... *sexy*.

How on earth was I going to survive it if that was my view every night?

And how was I going to survive sharing a room with him during the ski trip next week?

∼

"There they are! Our fellow engaged couple!" Noelle grinned, waving at us wildly from their driveway.

"Oh, goodness," I muttered under my breath, tugging my jacket tighter around me as I fiddled with the engagement ring on my finger.

The ski trip I'd been dreading had finally arrived, and I was trying to remember why I'd agreed on this trip. It was a terrible idea. For starters, because I was in a fake relationship with my best friend, and none of them had any idea that it was real. That wasn't even touching on how I was always freezing cold. I'd bundled up in a sweater and a thick jacket just for the drive to meet our friends.

Putting on my best fake smile, I attempted to grab my bag out of the trunk of Daniel's car, but he swooped in and grabbed it out from under me.

"Oh. Thanks."

"Of course," he murmured, carrying it over to Matthew's truck. "I got you."

Noelle flung her arms around me, pulling me into a tight hug. "Hi, Char."

"Hey." I grinned at her, thankful that I had my best friend by my side.

"I've missed you," she pouted. "This last month has been way too busy."

"I know," I agreed with a groan. Between my winter recitals, and her finishing the end of the school year at her job, plus wedding planning, we'd barely seen each other. The last time I'd seen all the girls had been that day at the coffee shop. "But at least you're on winter break now!" We'd waited until there was enough snow on the mountain for the trip, and since classes had ended for the semester, it worked out perfectly. To everyone's excitement but mine. Never mind the fact that it was right before Daniel and I's wedding, so the trip was one big celebration for *us*.

I looped my arm through Noelle's as we watched the guys load Matthew's truck.

"Everyone excited?" Matthew stretched out his arms, carrying out an ice chest from their house.

"Oh, yeah," I said, feigning excitement. "Excited to read in the lodge," I said with a laugh.

My plans included consuming copious amounts of hot chocolate and digging into a new sports romance series. I might not have been a sports girl, but I couldn't get enough of hockey romances, especially during the winter.

Anything to distract myself from thoughts of my husband-to-be.

Noelle laughed. "I'm planning to brainstorm my next book when this one isn't trying to get me down the mountain."

Matthew ruffled her red hair. "You know you're going to love it. Plus, I'll be by your side the whole time, sweetheart."

"Babe," she groaned. "You're messing up my hair."

He smirked and kissed her cheek before leaving the two of us standing in the driveway.

"What are you guys doing with Snowball while we're gone for the weekend?" I asked her, thinking of their large samoyed that was always excited when we came over.

"Oh, Matthew's sister Tessa is in town for the holidays, and she's staying at the house while we're in Bend."

"That worked out well, huh?" I had met Matthew's little sister before, and like him, she had tall stature, striking blue eyes, and perfect Hollywood blonde waves. It was no wonder that she'd gone into acting, spending most of her year working out of Los Angeles.

Noelle nodded. "Really well. And I think he misses having her close."

"Good thing she's home for Christmas then, huh?"

"Yeah." She grinned. "What about you? First Christmas living with D, huh?" Noelle nudged me, and I couldn't help my blush as I watched Matthew and Daniel talking near the truck. "Any fun plans?"

"Oh. It's just a few days after the wedding, so... I'm not sure yet." I bit my lip.

Noelle raised an eyebrow. "When are you guys going on your honeymoon?"

How do you tell your best friend *I'm not, because this marriage is totally a sham to hide the fact that I don't want to be alone anymore and we're just faking being in love?* Oh, right—*you don't.*

Instead, I lied. "Oh, we're thinking about waiting until summer." I shrugged. "It makes more sense."

"Sure..."

"Ready to go, you two?" Daniel called out, distracting Noelle from asking me any further questions. Thank goodness.

"What time are we meeting the others?" He asked Matthew, the two guys promptly shutting the back of the truck bed now that everything was inside.

"Around thirty minutes, I believe." We were meeting them and then all caravanning down to the house we rented together. Hunter, Gabbi, Angelina and Benjamin were all riding in Hunter's jeep, since we figured carpooling would be easier than taking four cars.

"Shotgun," Noelle announced with a wink, like she was doing me a favor so I could sit next to my fiancé. At least, she thought she was. I should thank her, but I couldn't help but panic about our current situation. Faking it in this close proximity would be... interesting.

Daniel slung his arm around my shoulders, tugging me closer into his body, my head practically resting against his chest. "Let's do this."

Let's hope our acting skills were up to the test for the weekend.

Otherwise, our friends were going to see right through us.

CHAPTER 12
Daniel

"Are you good?" I murmured to Charlotte, squeezing her knee as we drove through the mountains, riding in the backseat.

Hunter, Gabbi, Benjamin and Angelina were riding in the jeep behind us, and I was grateful the weather on the pass wasn't so bad that neither of our cars required chains, and the snow tires we swapped to every winter were enough.

She gave me a tight nod, and I knew something was on her mind, and I had a feeling I knew exactly what was causing her to retreat into her mind.

"Hey." I wished I could reassure her further, but Matthew and Noelle were sitting in the front seat, and for all they knew, we were happily engaged. "It's gonna be fine."

We'd chosen to carpool for a good reason, but now I was wishing we'd chosen differently. We might have picked the best cars for going over the pass in the winter, but we could have been alone so we could talk. And now, that would have to wait until we got to our destination.

"Mhm," she responded, looking out the window at the snow falling outside.

A few moments later, my phone buzzed in my pocket, and I pulled it out to see a text message from Charlotte.

CHARLOTTE
Do you think we're going to pull it off?

DANIEL
No one suspects anything. What's got you worried?

It's just… I feel like we have to be super coupley. Like they won't believe it if we don't act like we're in love. We're about to get married, so we should be all over each other, right?

She had no idea how hard of a time I had keeping my hands off of her during the day. Her moving in with me had only made the desire that had flared up in August even worse. But I knew it wasn't what she wanted to hear, what would help her to not spiral into anxiety.

She thought sex would only complicate this, after all. And maybe she was right.

But these feelings weren't going away, no matter how hard I tried.

Breathe. We got this.

I just…

Is this wrong? That we're duping our friends? Should we come clean and just tell them the truth?

The truth? Charlotte, we are getting married.

Everything is going to be fine. Because you're my best friend. And we're a team. Fake marriage or not.

I could only hope it was the truth.

THREE HOURS LATER, we'd reached our destination, piling out of the cars in front of the rental for the weekend.

I helped Charlotte out of the car before we all went around to the back of the truck to grab our bags.

"Here," I said, lifting Charlotte's bag over my shoulder before she could grab it. "I'll take that."

She gave me a nod, following me inside our bedroom. The girls had picked a fairly large house to rent, complete with a hot-tub sitting on the back porch that was surrounded by trees—and lots of snow.

The house was a four bedroom, with a large kitchen and living room area, and thankfully, we each had our own room. Or not so thankfully, considering how hard it was going to be for me to sleep next to her and not think about our night in August.

I was so fucked.

"What's in here, anyway?" I asked, setting her bag down on a chair. She'd brought a suitcase and a duffel bag, and the bag I had carried was much heavier than I thought it would be.

Char looked away sheepishly. "Books."

I raised an eyebrow. "Why? Aren't you going to go skiing?"

"I've never actually, uh... skied before? I don't know how." She turned her head away, looking self-conscious, maybe even a little nervous?

"I'll teach you." The first time I'd gone skiing was when I was a kid, something my dad and I had always loved doing together.

"Are you sure?"

I blinked. "Of course. Why wouldn't I be?"

Charlotte shrugged and then looked over our room. They'd decorated it in a woodsy theme, complete with a little table and chairs, but there was only one bed.

"How do you want to do this?"

I raised an eyebrow. "What do you mean?"

"Well, I can take the couch, or..."

"Char." I walked the short distance across the room to her, wrapping my arms around her midriff. "We can share the bed. It's not like we haven't done it before. Plus, we're getting married. Want to tell me what this is really about?" She slumped in on herself, giving a small sigh, and I spun her around in my arms to look at me.

"I just... I don't know if I'm ready for *that*." She glanced towards the bed.

"Sharing a bed?" I asked. "Sleeping together?"

She shook her head. "At home we're... it's just us. We don't have to play pretend."

And she'd escape to her bedroom every night. Something I planned to remedy once we got home, after we said *I do*. Because if it was up to me, we'd have an actual marriage. She'd never have to pretend around me.

But she needed time to get there, and I'd give that to her. I'd just have to hope she'd fall in love with me.

"We don't have to play pretend here, either. It's still just us. Okay?" At least, inside this room.

She bit her lip, exhaling deeply. "Okay."

"Now, come here."

Charlotte raised a perfect blonde eyebrow. "Why?"

"Char." I extended a hand to her. "Please."

"Alright," she mumbled, taking my hand and letting me pull her into my arms.

I held her tightly, wrapping one arm around her back and smoothing the other over the back of her head. "We got this, alright?"

Pulling back from her embrace, I waited until she nodded, then kissed her forehead and pulled away.

"Now, let's go see what the plan is with the gang, huh?"

She stood, frozen, her fingers brushing where I'd kissed her head, even after I'd moved away.

"Don't look at me like that."

"Like what?" She breathed out, her brilliant gray eyes locked onto mine.

"Like you want me to kiss you for real."

"Oh." She blushed. "And what if we need... more practice?"

I smirked. "Do you think we need practice, baby?"

She stepped back closer to my body, her fingers trailing up my chest, even though I was wearing my North Face jacket.

"Couldn't hurt."

I hummed in response, cupping Charlotte's cheek with one hand as the other brushed through her hair. "Do you want me to kiss you, Charlotte? All you have to do is say the words."

"Kiss me, Daniel," she said, and I couldn't help but comply, crushing my lips to hers.

The moment our lips touched, a surge of rightness settled through my body. Kissing her had always felt so *right*, and I couldn't believe we hadn't been doing this for the last decade.

I knew more than ever that I needed to do whatever I could to keep her, to get her to fall in love with me, because I didn't want to kiss anyone else ever again.

The thought of Charlotte moving on, finding it with someone else... I didn't like it. Couldn't imagine it.

So I was going to get my fake fiancée to be my real one.

∽

WE WANTED to make the most of the daylight, so we headed to the mountain after settling into the house. Charlotte and I were the only ones left after the other couples had all gone their separate ways, as she was the only one who hadn't skied before.

"How do they feel?" I asked, checking Charlotte's ski boots, making sure I hadn't clasped them too tight. She made a face, clearly moving her foot inside the boot, and then swayed a little, so I caught her arm to keep her upright.

We'd rented our gear for the long weekend, but somehow she'd still ended up with a pink set. I liked that. Her snow pants were black, but even the ski coat she'd brought along was a bright shade of bubblegum pink, lighting up her face.

"Good. I think." Her cheeks were pink, but I wasn't sure if it was from the frosty weather or a blush. Either way, I liked it.

I grabbed her skis from where I'd propped them up, setting them onto the packed snow so she could snap her boots in.

"Shall we?" I asked, and she gave a slight nod.

I guided Charlotte's boots into the skis, showed her how to fasten them, checked that they were secure, and then put on my own skis.

"We're just going to start small, and I'll teach you the basics, alright?"

I started going through all the motions, and Charlotte was a quick learner. Maybe it was because of dance, but she had no problem picking up on what to do with her feet, and she was quickly mastering the little learner's hill.

"What do you think?" I asked as her face lit up with an exhilarating smile as she came down the hill another time. We'd been at it for a few hours, and she wasn't wobbly on her feet. "Time for the bunny hill?"

"Are you sure?" Her eyes grew wide.

"Yeah." I grinned. "I think you're ready."

She balanced on her ski poles, looking at me. "You'll catch me if I fall, right?"

"Of course, darling. I'll always be there to catch you." And I meant it.

She swatted at my chest. "I'm serious."

"I am too."

"You don't have to play pretend right now, Daniel. It's just us."

"Maybe I'm not playing pretend."

She looked away, her eyes connecting with the chairlift.

I resisted the temptation to pull her close and reveal my true feelings about our act, and watched Charlotte, who was still gazing into the distance.

"Why'd you never ski when you were younger?" I wanted to distract her by changing the subject. California had plenty of ski resorts as well, so it surprised me she'd never gone on vacation to one. "Or when we were in college?" We'd been within two hours of Mount Hood from Portland, so it wouldn't have been hard.

"I don't know." Charlotte shook her head, the motion freeing some of her blonde hair that was tucked inside her puffy jacket. "I was always so focused on dance, and we just... never went. And during college, well... you were there." She turned to look at me. "We went tubing almost every year. That was good enough for me."

Huh. It was funny to think that my girl, the one who wanted to have a winter wedding, had barely spent any time in the snow. Though this weekend would change all of that, I supposed.

"Still." I frowned. "I could have taught you before. If I'd... realized."

God, how much did I not know about my best friend? Maybe I knew the big stuff, but there was still so much I didn't know about her. And I wanted to know everything.

"It's okay." She gives me a small smile. "I like this." Her voice drops, even though none of our friends are around. "And I'm glad it's just the two of us. No pretending." The rest of our friends had already gone up, the girls each promising to go on a few runs before they retreated to the lodge for their inevitable book discussion.

"Me too," I agreed. "Now, want to head up the lift?"

She nodded, and the words flickered through my head.

No pretending. If only.

CHAPTER 13
Charlotte

After four times down the bunny hill, I was more than happy to sink into a chair in the lodge.

Gabbi was sitting there with her camera, looking at some photos she'd snapped. I admired her tenacity, because there was no way I could hold anything while also learning to ski. Absolutely not.

Dance helped me stay fit and strong, so I had no trouble with balancing on the skis or catching my breath. Still, I definitely underestimated just how much energy it would be, even with Daniel by my side to pick me up when I fell. Which, thankfully, had only happened twice so far, and neither was my fault. The first time, someone nearly run into me, and I'd had to hold Daniel back, so he didn't go off on them for mowing me down. The second, well—I blamed that one on the tree.

So, I was perfectly content to get a hot chocolate and curl up with a new book.

"How was it?" Noelle asked, cheeks rosy as she plopped right next to the fireplace in the main lodge, her ski clothes abandoned in a pile on the neighboring chair.

I busied myself by unwrapping my scarf from my neck, dropping it, my wet coat, and gloves onto a chair. "Good." I looked at my fake fiancé.

"You sure you don't want to go down one more time?" Daniel asked me, shaking out his dark hair that was stuck to his forehead from the helmet. I didn't know why I had the urge to reach out and touch it, and then I realized I *could*. Because everyone else thought I was his fiancé, right? So it didn't matter if I played with his hair, pushing it out of his eyes.

So I did.

"I think I'm just going to hang out in the lodge for a little while." I mumbled, enjoying how soft his hair was. What conditioner did he use to get his hair like that? I was so focused on combing it back that I barely noticed when Daniel cleared his throat.

"Darling." My eyes connected with his. "I think it's good now."

"Oh." I looked away awkwardly. "Right."

He grabbed my hand and kissed it before I let it drop into my lap, awkwardly fumbling with the zipper of my long-sleeved thermal shirt.

"Have fun," I said, wondering if I should give him a kiss on the cheek. Or the lips. What was the proper protocol here, anyway? Would my friends think it was weird if I didn't kiss him?

Thankfully, Daniel didn't leave me questioning for too long, leaning over to kiss my forehead before heading back out into the snow.

"So?" Noelle asked, raising an eyebrow. "Did you like it?"

"It was... fun," I finally admitted, sinking into the big lounger next to her, glad to be inside and out of the freezing cold. It felt like my nose was going to be permanently pink if I spent any more time out there on the slopes. "I'm getting the hang of it, that's for sure."

"Anyone see Ang?" Gabbi asked, popping her head up from her camera before tucking it into her bag.

"I think her and Benjamin were doing one more before she

was going to come in and join us, too. Something about him talking her into it…"

"I can only imagine," I said with a snort. Those two were constantly bickering, but it was obvious how much they cared for each other. Daniel might have teased me occasionally, but there was nothing like that between us. I wondered if it would ever be like that for us, the non-stop flirting and inability to stop touching each other that our friends all seemed to have.

Even if it wasn't, I thought it would be okay.

I had only read twenty pages when Angelina arrived at the lodge, looking stylish in her ski outfit. While I felt like an oversized toddler in all pink, Angelina looked like a bad-ass. We were practically opposites—the tallest and the smallest, the boldest and the *shyest*, but I'd always been grateful for her friendship.

And that she didn't think it was weird that I was friends with —and now marrying—her brother. Even if she didn't know it was all fake.

"I'm here!" She announced with a flourish, happily pulling off her own damp outer layer and piling it onto a chair next to me. "How's everyone faring?"

I nodded. "Good." The other girls echoed my sentiments.

"I still can't believe you'd never been skiing before, Char," Angelina added.

"Honestly, I'm kind of glad I got to do it this way. With all of my favorite people at my side." I smiled at the rest of the girls, and Noelle reached over, squeezing my leg.

"Is everyone excited about tonight?" Gabbi asked, and I couldn't help my surprise.

"What's tonight?"

Three dumbfounded stares looked back at me. "Charlotte, you're getting married in like two weeks. We're celebrating, of course!"

"No, no, no. I didn't want a bachelorette party for a reason," I groaned. I'd practically refused when Noelle had offered after I'd asked her to be my maid of honor.

Unfortunately, my Bridal Shower was another story, one I couldn't get out of, but that was a problem I'd deal with later—when I got home.

I could only imagine how embarrassing it would be for me. The parties I'd seen with dick-shaped cakes and strippers? That wasn't my scene. I didn't need any of that.

"It will not be like that, we promise," Angelina said.

"Plus, you saw what a great bach party I planned last summer!" Gabbi chimed in. I had to relent—she had me there. It had been nice. Classy. A few nights together in a rented house in Napa, California, and mostly, we'd all just drunk a lot of wine. I'd shared a room with Gabbi, except for the night she'd never come back to our room. I later found out she had been in Hunter's bed. "Nothing to worry about, I swear."

I tried to ease the pout from my face. "*Fine.* But I'm not wearing a sash."

Something passed between their faces, but they all agreed. "No sash. What about a crown?"

I groaned again. This was going to be one long weekend.

～

"Bottoms up!" They cheered, watching me throw back another shot.

Here's the thing: I knew my body. I knew exactly how much alcohol I could have before I got a little *too* drunk. And too-drunk-Charlotte liked to dance on top of tables and was absolutely way too giggly. Luckily, I wasn't the kind to make out with random guys, but also, my weakness was *here*.

Because the girls had planned a bar night to celebrate Daniel and I's impending nuptials, and we were all crowded into a booth at a bar in Downtown Bend.

"Anyone want food?"

"Pizza," I groaned, my head practically hitting the table. "I need pizza." Anything to soak up all the alcohol I'd drank. "And maybe a pretzel. With cheese dip, please."

Something that would stop me from looking at my best friend at my side through a completely new lens.

"You okay?" Daniel whispered in my ear when they'd all left to order food.

I nodded. "Don't let me drink anything else." I rubbed at my temples. "I don't want you to have to deal with me all drunk tonight."

He brushed a hair back behind my ear. "I don't mind taking care of you, you know."

"Skiing plus a hangover seems like a terrible combination," I said, instead, trying to avoid his stare. At how he was looking at me with so much emotion in those brown eyes that I loved so much. The ones that had captivated me from the very first day I met him. There was so much sadness clouded in those eyes, and I wondered if anyone had ever taken care of him?

I wanted to. I wanted to be that person for him.

"And I haven't been sick in ages, so I don't want to start now." I scrunched up my nose.

He chuckled. "Yeah. Maybe you're right." Daniel's arm came around me, tugging me closer. "But that doesn't mean you can't celebrate with your friends. If you want."

Kissing the side of his cheek, I mumbled a quick, "Thank you." If only he knew how much I appreciated it. How much I appreciated him. Ever since college, he'd always taken care of me. He provided me with food, walked me back to my dorm late at night, and was always there to study with me in the library.

Our friendship had just naturally fallen into place, and I guess this fake relationship had too. It wasn't weird when he touched me like this, when I leaned on his body for support.

"I'm gonna go dance," I said, my eyes tracking over the rest of the girls on the floor. "Want to come?"

He shook his head. "I'll be here. Come find me if you need anything."

"I will." I nodded. "Thanks, babe."

Every time I said it, it got a little easier. Felt a little less fake.

Maybe it was just the alcohol, but it didn't feel strange at all. It felt like maybe, for once, all the puzzle pieces were falling into place.

Like there might be something more buried underneath all of this.

~

"Put me down," I groaned, riding on Daniel's back as we walked back to the house. "I'm heavy."

After a few more hours of drinks, a scenery change to a new bar, and more dancing, we'd finally both called it quits. And the fresh air seemed like the best choice, so here we were.

"Char." Even though I couldn't see his face, his tone was rough. Commanding. "You're light as a feather. I can carry you." As if reassuring me, his fingers tightened on my thighs, and I sighed, wishing I could bury my face in his hair in embarrassment.

Not because his hair smelled like his shampoo, which was, frankly, delicious.

"Why did I drink that last cocktail?" I said, groaning. Clearly, I wouldn't stop beating myself up about the fact that I was swaying on my feet and my best-friend-slash-fake-fiancé had to carry me back.

I certainly would *not* think about how I was all pressed up against his muscles while riding piggyback on him.

"You were having fun with your friends," he chuckled. "That's a good thing. I feel like I haven't seen you let loose in a while."

It was true—I'd been so stressed with everything. Planning a wedding, maintaining a fake relationship, on top of my two jobs. "Maybe you're right," I said, settling my head onto his shoulder. The warmth of his body was close to lulling me to sleep, but I was fighting to keep my eyes open. "It's been a weird few months."

Thankfully, I wasn't completely drunk, but I had consumed enough alcohol to decrease my inhibitions. And I had a habit of confessing things I shouldn't.

Or doing things I knew would change everything, like I'd done in August.

Sometimes I thought it was a mistake, but I didn't regret it. I'd been worried it would ruin our friendship, but we were doing just fine now, right?

So why was I avoiding the tension between us? I'd seen how he looked at me. I knew what he looked like without a shirt on. Why didn't I let myself indulge in it again?

"Charlotte," he murmured, bringing me out of my trance-like state. "We're back."

I opened my eyes. When did I close them? His shoulder was comfortable, especially considering how fit he was.

"Oh." I mumbled, sliding down off his back, every inch of me rubbing against him. Why did that send a rush through my body? It must have been the alcohol. That's what I was choosing to blame it on, anyway.

Forgoing digging through my bag to find my pajamas, I flopped onto the bed, letting the mattress cup my body like a cloud.

Daniel sat down beside me, and it was his weight that reminded me of the last time we'd truly shared a bed.

"Daniel..." I started. "We should talk." Sitting up, I spun the ring around my finger a few times, staring at the diamond. Reminding myself what we'd promised each other. Honesty.

"What's wrong?" He looked concerned, even with his soft-spoken voice, looking at me like he thought I might break. Like what I was about to say mattered to him. Like, just maybe, he needed me to be okay.

Shit. Maybe I'd chosen the wrong words. When did *we should talk* mean anything other than *we should break up?* And I didn't want to break off our fake engagement. Even if it wasn't real, at least I had him like this. At least I had my best friend.

"We promised we'd be truthful with each other and..." I shrugged my shoulders up, turning back to the window, not making eye contact as I watched the snow fall outside. Central Oregon really was a magical place in the winter. "There's something you should know."

"Yeah?"

"That night in Paris... that was my first time." I bit my lip, wrapping my arms around myself.

Guess we were going with complete honesty now. I hadn't even known I was going to say it till it came out, but I didn't regret it. If we were doing this marriage pact right, it was the time for the truth. One at a time

"Your first?" He froze, like the puzzle pieces were connecting in his head. "You'd never..." He winced. "Fuck, baby. Did I hurt you?"

I shook my head; the concern coming off of him was almost palpable. "It wasn't like I was waiting for marriage, or anything, I just... I'd never slept with anyone. I'm sorry I didn't tell you, but..." An awkward, strained laugh slipped out from my lips. "I was twenty-six years old and a virgin, and it all just *happened,* and then I was worried you might regret it..." And I'd wanted to get it over with. Though that wasn't quite true either. I'd wanted it to be him.

"I'd never regret you, Char."

"I know that now," I whispered, because I *did.* Because he'd asked, hadn't he? I didn't even really know his motivations for doing it—not like he knew mine, but he'd still been the one to propose the idea.

"Hey. It's okay." He squeezed my hip.

"I was scared. I avoided you because it terrified me. We'd never..." I cleared my throat. It had never been like that between us. I'd never thought he looked at me like he *wanted* me until that rehearsal dinner. But those brown, gold-flecked eyes had been full of desire, *need*. It had made me unsteady, and everything had changed. "It wasn't like we had feelings for each other, but I just... I know this is all fake, that we're not a *normal* couple, but..." I buried my head in his neck.

"Charlotte." He reached out, one hand resting under my jaw as he tilted my chin up to bring our gazes together. The other reached down to grab my hand, squeezing it. "Look at me, baby." I always appreciated the way he would reassure me with his gentle squeezes. The way he held my hand had become like a lifeline, and I didn't want him to stop touching me. "You've been my best friend since I was nineteen years old and I walked into your dorm and ran into you. The only person who knows me, inside and out. I don't need any of that. I just need you in my life. By my side."

"I know," I murmured, exhaling a breath as he brushed a strand of hair back behind my ear. "But I'm not a one-night-stand kind of girl. That's just... not me." Something was stuck in my throat, and I wasn't sure I had the words to continue. There was more, but it wasn't the right time to admit it. I hadn't been waiting because I'd wanted to stay pure for marriage, and there had been opportunities, sure. I'd had other friends suggest to me I should just find someone to *get it over with*. But that didn't feel right. So, I'd waited.

Until Angelina's wedding this summer. Until... Daniel.

"So why me?"

"I knew I was safe with you. And I... wanted to." Lose my virginity, have sex. Experience what it felt like to be wanted by *him*. "But it was stupid, Daniel, if it meant losing you, because I wouldn't trade you, even for the best sex in the world. Or a million dollars."

"What if the best sex in the world was with me?" He asked, not hiding the bit of humor in his voice. "We can try again and see... If you want." Daniel brushed his lips against my ear.

I hit him in the chest playfully as I kept my eyes on the window. Better to not look at him. Because I was pretty sure I'd let myself have what I shouldn't want all over again. Not after that kiss earlier today. I wanted it, too, but... Why did I keep screwing everything up? "Don't say that. Your friendship is more important to me. Sex just... complicates things."

"Even when we're going to be married?"

My cheeks pinked, even as I stopped myself from saying anything else.

"Shit, Char. I knew... in college, when you asked me to be your first kiss, I figured then that you'd never..." He shook his head. "But to think, all these years... How come you never slept with any of those guys you dated? You never wanted to?"

"A guy I went out with once or twice, Daniel? I wouldn't give my virginity to someone who didn't care about me. Maybe that sounds dumb, but..." I sighed. I hated that I ever had dated any of those losers. None of them had ever meant anything. Maybe for a long time, I'd been trying to convince myself I didn't have feelings for my best friend, but... "It was never right." I added on as a mumble.

Even if I'd liked them well enough, I'd never had that spark with any of them. And I'd tried.

So I'd survived on self-love, hoping I'd meet the right guy one day. Maybe I'd met the right guy the day I'd moved into college. I'd just been too blind to realize it.

I shook my head, focusing on the way his arms felt as I drew circles around his muscles, not quite wanting to look him in the eyes. "No. I think..." I took a deep breath, and his fingers brushed my chin. Daniel's hand tilted my head up to look him in the eyes, and I was sure that my face was flushed. I cleared my throat. "I think some part of me always knew I was waiting for the right guy. Someone I trusted and was comfortable enough with."

"And I was that guy?" He asked, his voice low as he studied my face.

"I feel safe with you. I always have."

Daniel brushed a strand of my hair off my forehead. "Charlotte, I..."

"You don't have to say anything," I insisted. "I just wanted you to know."

"Thank you for telling me," he said, cupping my cheek. "For trusting me."

I trusted him with so much of me, and if I wasn't careful, I'd be giving him my heart, too.

CHAPTER 14
Daniel

Thankfully, after our eventful night of drinking and confessions, Charlotte hadn't been hungover in the morning. She'd practically jumped out of bed at the first glimmer of sunlight in the morning, ready for the day. After she'd slept close enough for me to touch—but not where I really wanted her, in my arms—I was painfully hard, trying to ignore the fact that I was pining over my best friend who clearly didn't feel the same way.

She'd chosen me to take her virginity because she felt safe with me, not because she loved me. But did it even matter?

She'd chosen me. She'd chosen to *marry* me. And she loved me, even if it was just as a friend. I knew that. I'd have to be okay with that.

So we'd gotten up with the sun, and after a quick shower, we'd been ready to hit the slopes again for the day. Charlotte and I did a few quiet runs together, enjoying the freshly fallen snow that seemed to glitter in the light as we rode up the chairlift. Eventually she went back to the lodge and find the girls, and I'd gone and done some of the other, more difficult slopes.

But when I got back to the lodge a few hours later, around lunchtime, she hadn't been there.

"Have you seen Char?" I asked the girls who were sitting around the table in the lodge, drinking hot chocolate as they read. Angelina's hair was still damp from the freshly falling snow outside, which meant she hadn't been back long.

Gabbi's head popped up. "I thought she went out to find you. She said she was going to go do another run with you. But… clearly, she didn't. Shit."

"The guys and I were all together, and…" I pinched my nose. "We went down one of the black diamond runs, and I thought I'd come back to check on her…"

We all turned our heads to look outside. Fuck, it was snowing harder now. And my girl had only just learned how to ski yesterday. So where was she?

"I'm going to go back out there and look for her. If she comes back here…" I shook my head. "Tell her not to go out again."

Gabbi pulled out her phone. "I'll send a text to everyone, just in case someone checks it."

"I'll send the rest of the guys out when they get back, too," Noelle added. "Don't worry. We'll find her."

Angelina gave me a reassuring nod, and I zipped up my coat, heading back outside into the rapidly falling snow.

Where could she have gone? We'd only gone down a few of the basic green runs together between yesterday and today, so I'd have to hope she went down one of those.

Pulling out my phone, I dialed her number, hoping she would answer. Chances were, she didn't even have reception, but I hoped that maybe if I could reach her…

When I found her, I was going to make her promise not to go up the mountain alone again, because I couldn't bear it if anything was to happen to her.

I went down a few of the runs before the guys caught up to me. Sliding my goggles onto my helmet, I slowed to a stop when I realized it was them.

"We heard your girl is missing?" Hunter said, eyes fraught with concern. "We've been looking too. We came as soon as we got back and the girls told us where you went." Benjamin and Matthew nodded in agreement, all of them bundled up in their snow gear.

It hadn't occurred to me just now how much these guys meant to me. They'd all become close friends, sure, but I realized now just how much they would do for me—for Charlotte. The lengths we would all go to for each other, for the girls we cared about so much.

Hanging my head, I just nodded. "I've checked the few runs we did before, but I didn't see her anywhere on them. I don't know—" I felt so helpless, not knowing where she was, or how I was going to find her. She'd come up here looking for me, and I'd failed her.

"Don't worry," Benjamin reassured me, resting his gloved hand on my shoulder. "We'll find her. Let's split the runs up and go again. You don't think she'd go on one outside her skill level?"

I didn't think so, but... "There's always a chance." I sighed.

"Let's all take one and meet at the bottom of the hill. If we don't find her, we'll run them again." Matthew, thankfully, was much more calm than me.

I was a mess, worrying about my girl.

She was, wasn't she? Mine. Mine to protect. Mine to care for, to take care *of*.

"Okay."

We were wasting precious time we didn't have if we didn't find her, but... what other option did I have?

The four of us split up, each taking a different run that we hadn't been down already. I really hoped she'd be on one of them. The mountain was too big, especially not knowing where she went. I was sure she wouldn't have gone on any of the Black Diamond courses alone, especially since I'd just taught her how to ski.

But the blue ones—shit. It was a lot of ground to cover.

I headed down another run, calling her name and trying to ski slowly, back and forth, inspecting the trees as I went.

"Charlotte!" I called, the worry and fear overrunning my body. What if something had happened to her? Or if she'd crashed into a bunch of trees and hit her head, and couldn't answer me? What if—*fuck*. I couldn't be thinking like this. I needed to stay focused so that I could find her. "Charlotte!"

"Hello?" The response was weak, but I heard it all the same.

"Char?" I said again, spinning around to look for her. "Keep talking!"

"D-Daniel?" There was her voice again. "I'm over h-here," she said, and following her voice, I finally found her.

There. There she was. She'd fallen into a snow ditch and had tried to shelter in between two pine trees. It did little in the way of protecting her from the snow that was falling faster and faster now, though.

Sending up a silent thank you, I popped my boots out of the skis, climbing into the small crevasse where she was sitting. She'd discarded the skis and poles beside her, and I was glad she'd gotten her boots out of them. It would have been worse if her body was stuck in an awkward position because she couldn't get them to unlatch.

"Are you okay? Is anything hurt?" I tried to inspect her for injuries, but I couldn't see much between the ski pants and her big puffy coat. Crouching in closer to her, I wiped snow off of her hat and cheeks, inspecting her face. The tip of her nose was bright red, and she was shivering. "Jesus, Charlotte. You're freezing."

She tried to give me a smile, but really it was more of a grimace. "I'll be f-fine once we get inside." She groaned as she tried to stand up on her feet. "I think I t-twisted my a-ankle when I was looking for you, and it hurt to put weight on, and I t-tried to stay out of the snow." Her teeth were chattering as she lifted her head to respond.

"Come on, let's get you out of there," I murmured, watching her eyes flutter shut as I pulled her into my arms. I'd have to come back for the skis and our poles, but I wasn't really worried about that right now.

After careful maneuvering, I got us both down the mountain and back to the lodge, aiming for the spot where I'd left the girls sitting. Her lack of tears made me believe her ankle wasn't terribly hurt, but she winced when I tried to set her down on her feet.

As fast as I could, I got my own skis off my feet and leaned them up against the post outside the lodge.

The rest of the guys weren't down yet, but I wasn't about to keep her outside any longer than normal. I'd have to hope that they'd check inside before they went back out again.

"Darling," I whispered in her ear. "I want Hunter to check your ankle and make sure it's not broken or sprained, alright?"

She nodded, wrapping her arms around my neck and burying her head in the crook of my neck.

Carefully carrying Charlotte into the lodge, I laid her on the couch near the fireplace. The girls ran over to check on her as I unzipped her coat and removed her outer layers.

"Are you okay?" Noelle asked, and Charlotte brushed her off.

"I'll be fine." The tip of her nose was still pink, but thankfully, now that she was in just her thermals and inside, she'd stopped shivering as much. Angelina came back over with a cup of hot chocolate, which was now firmly in Charlotte's hands, cupping it tightly.

"We were so worried when Daniel came back without you."

I spotted Hunter's curly brown hair walking into the lodge, and I breathed a sigh of relief. "Hunter."

"Hey." He kneeled down in front of Charlotte. "How ya feeling?"

"Fine," she said, grimacing only slightly when she tried to move her foot. "I fell, and I think I just twisted it... It hurts, but I don't think it's broken."

Hunter nodded, quickly looking over her and testing Charlotte's foot, as well as an all-around checkup to make sure nothing else was wrong. "You're right. It doesn't look broken to me, either. You probably just rolled it." He looked at me. "She just needs some rest, ice, compression, and elevation." Thank god.

"Is there anything else we should do? Do you think she needs x-rays?"

"The pain should go away on its own in a few days, but if it doesn't... I know some good ortho doctors back home, and we can get you all checked out."

"Thanks, doc," Charlotte gave him a fake smile when he finished up.

"And no more skiing this weekend, I'm afraid. Try to put as little weight on that foot as possible."

"What a bummer," she murmured, though I could see right through her fake pout. She wasn't disappointed at all.

"Let's get you back to the house," I said, hefting her into my arms. "We'll go warm you up, okay?"

She mumbled something incoherent into my chest, and I looked at the rest of the group. Hunter tossed me the keys to his jeep.

"We'll all get back in the truck," Hunter said. Matthew, now at Noelle's side, nodded in agreement.

Noelle frowned. "Do you want us to come back with you to keep you company?" She asked Charlotte, who shook her head.

"No, no. You guys have fun. We'll be okay." She looked back to me, and I could only nod.

"I'll take care of her," I agreed.

I always would.

∾

Unfortunately, the worst part of leaving the lodge to head back to the house had been getting her back in her wet jacket and boots. By the time we pulled up to the front door of the rental, she was shivering again.

Shivering wasn't a bad thing, though—it meant her body was trying to warm her up. We just needed to speed up the process.

"Baby, we need to get you out of those wet clothes and into the shower to get warm." I swallowed, thinking about how I was going to have to peel her clothes off of her. *Shit.* I shouldn't be thinking those thoughts right now.

I walked over to the bathroom and turned on the shower water, warming it up for her.

"Okay," she mumbled, fumbling with the zipper on her coat before I stepped in to help her the rest of the way.

Her coat came off, and then her ski pants and sweater, leaving her in just the thermal under layer that had clearly failed to keep her completely warm in the snow. The cold had seeped down to her bottom layer.

"Do you want me to..." I looked at the door, wondering if she wanted me to leave.

"It's okay," she whispered, leaning against me. "It's nothing you haven't seen before, right?" Charlotte gave a weak chuckle.

I let my fingers rest against the hem of her shirt, waiting for her slight nod before I pulled it off of her. After helping her out of her leggings, she stood there in just her panties and lacy bra, body still shaking from the aftereffects of the cold.

"Can you—" she asked, turning around, exposing her bare back to me besides her bra, which I quickly unclasped.

And then—creamy skin. Those little pink nipples, and—*fuck*—was I staring at her tits? I looked away, my cheeks burning.

"Is your ankle okay?" I asked, keeping my eyes diverted from hers as another tantalizing thought flickered through my head.

"Yeah," she said, voice low. "It's fine now. It doesn't really hurt as much anymore. Like Hunter said, I just need to rest."

I was still going to have her ice it once we got her warmed up and by the fire in the living room.

"I'll just leave you to it, then." My voice was rough, and I hurried towards the door, eyes practically squeezed shut as my hand gripped the doorknob.

What the hell was I thinking, trying to help like that? She still blushed when we talked about kissing, and I'd gone and seen her practically naked. *Fuck me.*

All I wanted to do was to take care of her. To make sure she was okay. I wasn't trying to take advantage of her. I never would. I just...

Shutting my eyes, I tried to shake off the image. Of her wide, gray eyes connecting with mine as she let her bra fall into the pile of soggy clothes on the floor. The way she didn't even try to cover herself as my gaze met hers. It was too much. All of it.

"Daniel," she called, her voice husky. "Aren't you going to warm me up?"

I turned around, finding her standing under the stream of water, her hands covering her nipples. The rest of her body—her slender curves, her pale skin—was all on display. For me.

I blinked. Surely, I was imagining it, right?

"Please," she whispered, and she didn't have to ask me twice.

Tearing my ski clothes, I stripped down to my underwear in a matter of seconds, stepping into the shower with her in only my boxers.

She bared her back to me as I moved in next to her, grateful that this shower was bigger than some. Not as big as the one in my bedroom at home, but still more than enough that we could both fit in it safely.

I brushed my fingers over a wet shoulder, brushing her hair off to the side before placing a kiss there. Charlotte moaned as I sucked on her skin as the warm water continued to rain down around us.

"*Yes,*" she practically hummed, as I replaced her hands with mine, running my thumbs over her hardened nipples.

I spun her around in my arms so I could kiss her, needing to taste her lips. It had been too long since yesterday. Too long since I'd tasted her strawberry lip gloss on my tongue.

Splaying my fingers across her back, I pulled her body flush against mine, and I knew she could probably feel my growing erection pressing against her stomach. Dipping my head down, I pressed my lips to hers, giving her a sweet, soft kiss for only a moment before I plunged my tongue past her lips, eagerly ravaging her mouth. I wanted to memorize every inch, to know every bit of her body. How she reacted. What made her squirm, moan, cry.

I wanted her to scream my name when I made her come, but it wasn't even a want anymore. I needed her.

Needed her with every fiber of my being. Needed her pink and her glitter, her never-ending smiles and the way she could be anything to anyone. The way she could talk for hours about *anything*, because even when she doubted herself, she was one of the smartest people I knew. I needed everything from her, because I couldn't accept anything less.

Charlotte moaned into my mouth as her tongue met mine. When we finally broke apart, almost panting from how hard I'd kissed her, there'd been no mistaking how hard I was.

"Do you need some help with that?" She giggled.

This girl. She'd been shivering from the cold five minutes ago, and now she was five seconds away from pouncing on me.

I chuckled, my voice rough. "What do you think, Charlotte?"

She pushed on the waistband of my boxers, freezing when I placed my hands on top of hers. "Are you sure?"

Her fingers danced up my bare chest. "Just because I was a virgin until a few months ago doesn't mean I'm innocent. Or that I don't know anything. You know?"

I smirked. "Char, you gonna teach me a thing or two from all of those smutty books you've read?"

"Mhm." She popped her tongue inside her mouth, giving me a wicked grin. "But first, I need you to take this off." My girl toyed with my boxers, and I was all too happy to comply.

"Darling, your wish is my command."

I sealed her lips with mine as I pushed the wet fabric off my legs, and let the fabric settle against the bottom of the shower basin.

"Thought we were supposed to be warming you up," I said with a chuckle as her soft, bare skin pressed against my chest and my cock jumped to attention. "Fuck." Her tiny hand wrapped around my length, her fingers not fully closing as she pumped me. "Charlotte." I groaned.

"I think about you all the time, you know." She whispered in my ear, my eyes fluttering shut as she kept up her motion, my hands bracing against the tile wall behind her.

"You do?"

She hummed in response. "How it felt to have you inside of me, your body weight pinned on top of mine... How sad I am that *I* didn't get to taste you."

My eyes flew open as I practically coughed out the next words. "You want to do that?" She'd been a virgin until August, and now she was offering to go down on me?

"I never thought it was particularly hot before, even when I read about it in books, but now I'm thinking that if it was you, I wouldn't mind so much." Her fingers explored my tip, running along the underside of the head, and I jerked just from her touch.

"Baby." Stepping forward, her back hit the shower wall as I found her lips, bringing them back to mine. There was no holding back, not now. She gasped as I nipped at her bottom lip, allowing me to plunge my tongue into her mouth. I kissed her until she was squirming against me, inhaling every one of her little moans as my hands explored her body. My fingers dipped inside of her, and I groaned as I felt how wet she was for me.

We hadn't gotten to do this in France. Just once hadn't been enough. I needed more.

But a thought broke through my haze of lust.

"Wait." I was gripping her hips as she looked up at me, completely still. "What are we doing?"

"Sex. Just sex." She moved my hands up to cup her tits. They were perfect, big enough that I could cup them with my hands with those rosy nipples that begged for my tongue. "Please. I need you. I'm so empty." She moaned as I squeezed her breasts, lightly kneading the skin.

"Are you sure?" I asked, receiving only a nod in response as I pinched a nipple, emitting another loud moan from her.

"Please."

"I don't have a condom, it's—"

Charlotte shook her head as I heaved her up into my arms, pinning her against the wall with my body. Her thighs spread apart around me, leaving her pussy exposed.

"Fill me up, Daniel," she begged.

"Fuck, baby. This might hurt." Before, I'd given her my fingers and my tongue until she'd come. This time, I would enter her bare. I just hoped she was wet enough to take all of me again.

I nudged the tip at her entrance, moaning from the feel as she welcomed me into her body. I eased myself in, one inch at a time, my sole focus on the way my dick was disappearing into her body.

Damn, that was hot. It was a sight I didn't think I'd ever tire of.

When I was almost fully seated inside of her, Charlotte wrapped her legs around me, pushing me the final inch.

"So good," she cried as I thrust inside of her, her back pressed against the tile wall as I held her in place with my hands. "Don't stop."

I didn't plan on it. I was going to worship this woman until the day I died, if I had any say in it.

The shower water continued running down around us as I pumped inside of her, my fingers digging into her thighs. Charlotte's head hit the shower wall as she emitted a long moan, and I could tell she was close. Knowing I'd found the spot inside of her that made her see stars, I kept up my almost brutal pace, driving us both towards our release.

"I'm close," she ground out, practically digging her nails into my shoulder blades as I fucked her within an inch of her life.

"Come for me, darling," I whispered against her ear, kissing a spot on her neck as I continued thrusting up inside of her in slow, punishing strokes.

I was barely hanging on, and when she clenched around me, her insides pulsing around me, I couldn't help myself from spilling inside of her, even as Charlotte interwove her fingers into my hair, tugging deeply.

Coming down from our high, I kept myself planted inside of her as I watched her chest rise and fall, both of our breathing returning to normal, before slowly pulling out.

She winced, and I watched as our combined releases dripped down her leg.

"Fuck," I muttered. "That was hot." I wrapped an arm around her waist to keep her from falling, steadying us both on our feet. "How are you feeling? Are you okay? I wasn't too rough, was I?"

She practically giggled, the blush on her cheeks from satisfaction instead of embarrassment. "You were perfect."

We quickly washed off, and after turning off the shower water, I grabbed a giant towel from the rack and wrapped it around her body. She turned around, smirking at me as she held the fluffy thing over her, keeping her beautiful body hidden from my view. "How was that for getting warm, huh?"

She scampered out into our bedroom in only her towel, leaving me to follow behind once I'd wrapped one around myself and collected our piles of wet ski clothes.

"You're going to kill me," I groaned as she disappeared to change.

Wordlessly, we both got dressed into our warm pajamas, and moved to the living room, where I spread a blanket in front of the fireplace. I pulled Charlotte down in between my legs as I started combing out her blonde tangles with a brush.

"How are you feeling?"

"Better," she said shyly, like she hadn't just started what might have been the most mind-blowing sex of my life. "Thank you."

"Of course." I kept brushing her damp hair, long after I'd gotten out all the knots, just because I liked how it felt to take care of her. How right it was with her in between me, relying on me.

I set the hairbrush down, and she leaned against my chest as we both watched the fire in the fireplace.

"We didn't use a condom..." I finally said, thinking about how we hadn't stopped while we were in the shower. How I'd watched the cum drip out of her. I'd liked it a little too much.

"I'm still on birth control," Charlotte mumbled. "So..."

"We haven't talked about after, what would happen when we were married—" I cleared my throat. "Do you still want to..."

"Have a baby?"

I nodded. "Yeah."

She looked away. "That's why we're getting married, right? So I could have a baby?"

Among other things. Namely, that I was in love with her.

"Maybe, after the wedding... We can start trying."

"Yeah?" I couldn't help but curl my lips up into a smile. If she wanted a baby, I'd throw her pills down the toilet now. We would have all too much fun trying to get her pregnant, that I knew for sure.

"Mhm," she hummed in response, settling further against my legs. "How long do you think we have until the others get back?"

"A few hours, I hope," I said, arching an eyebrow. "Why?"

She smirked, wrapping her arms around my neck and placing a kiss against my lips. "Might as well get some practice in now, right?"

I laughed. "I like where your thinking is at."

Laying her down on the blanket, I took my time this time, showing her just how much I liked that idea.

CHAPTER 15
Charlotte

It turned out that getting better acquainted with Daniel's body had definite perks. One of which was that when I wrapped myself around him in bed that night, there was no shame or embarrassment. We slept snuggled up next to each other, and I didn't think I'd gotten a better night of sleep in my life.

There was still another full day of the ski trip on our itinerary, but I took it easy as Hunter had suggested, staying at the house instead of going up to the lodge. My ankle wasn't bothering me anymore, but truthfully, I just needed a moment for my brain to catch up to my body, and figure out what was happening.

What had I told him? *Sex, just sex.* My brain was a blurry mess, but all I'd thought when he was walking away to let me warm up in the shower alone is that I didn't *want* to be alone. And I didn't want to ignore this feeling between us anymore, either.

Who was that girl? Certainly not me. I'd never been so bold or brazen in my life. Except for when it came to him.

"You're sure you're okay staying back?" Daniel asked, a little frown spread over his handsome face.

When had I started noticing how attractive he was? I couldn't keep my eyes off of him, off the little black curl that had separated from his hair and hung onto his forehead in the perfect Superman curl. I'd decided it was my weakness.

My pile of books was at my side, as well as a steamy cup of hot apple cider with a little something extra, courtesy of Noelle, who'd also taken up camp next to me. "Absolutely."

Apparently, we were operating in solidarity, and the girls had decided to send the guys up without us. The guys all loved to ski, and we loved to curl up with a new book boyfriend and dive into our fantasy worlds.

"What are you working on?" I asked Noelle, who was typing away on her laptop's keyboard.

"I had this idea for a single mom romance where she falls in love with her daughter's ski instructor, so I was just jotting down my notes."

Gabbi looked up from her book. "What if he's also her brother's best friend, and they've just reconnected at the ski resort?"

She was wearing one of Hunter's green henleys with a pair of leggings today, which was totally oversized and so cute. I, on the other hand, had pulled on one of the *Best Friends Book Club* sweatshirts Noelle had made all of us, and was enjoying how cozy and warm it was.

Noelle tugged the turtleneck of her cream colored sweater. "I like it." She leaned over to jot a few more notes down on her computer, before closing it and grabbing her Kindle. "What's everyone reading?"

Angelina plopped down on the loveseat across from us. "I just finished my book. I was trying to decide if I wanted to start something new or reread something from last year." We'd buddy read a lot of things, and the perk of all of us being readers was always having someone to talk about books with.

Gabbi held hers up in the air. "Want this one? It's got fated mates and a little *touch her and you die*. Plus, there's only one bed."

Angelina held up her hands. "Gimme." Gabbi tossed the

book to our dark-haired friend, before pulling out another one of her own.

Only one bed—I giggled. If only they knew the romance tropes I was living out right now.

"What about you, Char?"

I held up the cover of mine. "I've been reading this hockey series. Felt fitting for wintertime." And it had all of my favorite tropes. One book was a marriage of convenience, another accidental pregnancy—two of my favorites.

"One day, I'm going to drag you along to a game with me," Gabbi muttered. "You've read enough of it."

She'd grown up around it in Boston, and always talked about how they'd gone to see games. Meanwhile, I'd barely been to a handful of games during college, even though I ate up sports romance books like they were going out of style.

"Too bad there's no professional team in Oregon," I laughed.

"I'm just saying, next time I go home, you could come with me and we could go watch the Bruins…"

The thought about going with Gabbi to her home when I hadn't even been home to see my family in years settled weird in my gut. "Maybe," I said instead.

Thinking about my family also led me to the very real realization that when I got home from this trip, I'd have less than a week until they were in town for my wedding.

Maybe we should have just eloped, I groaned internally to myself.

But I'd always wanted that magical fairytale wedding. I only had a few final touches left on the dress I was making myself. It was everything I'd dreamed about since I was old enough to dream about my wedding.

"Are you ready for next week?" Angelina asked, looking at me, apparently able to read my train of thoughts. She didn't have the best relationship with her parents, either, and I knew it was rough after her mom had remarried. Daniel didn't talk too much about it, but the two of them had each other, and I was glad Daniel was closer with his dad. "I can't believe how soon the wedding is."

"Almost. I still have to finish my veil." I'd almost forgotten until I was picking up my shoes last week, and then I'd gone crazy, trying to make the perfect one. It was glittery, with little pearls spaced throughout, that matched the ones in the middle of the flowers on my dress and hem.

I was just glad we'd ordered the bridesmaid dresses.

Angelina huffed a small laugh. "I remember how jittery I was the week before Benjamin and I's wedding. I barely got any sleep until he started wearing me out." She winked.

I blushed. God, that certainly wasn't happening. I pushed those thoughts out of my head. After we'd slept together in front of the fireplace, we hadn't mentioned it again. Not that or our conversation about my birth control.

"Happy to say I fall asleep as soon as my head hits the pillow," I joked instead. "Besides, I've been sewing so much tulle when I shut my eyes, all I see is white sparkles. I think they might be embedded in the carpet forever." And in my skin, but I didn't really mind that.

Besides pink, glitter was my favorite color. Taylor Swift had said that once, and I wholeheartedly agreed.

"I'm glad we eloped," Angelina mused. "I can't imagine how stressed I would have been if we'd gotten married at home."

I was glad we were having a small wedding for the same reason. Our close friends and immediate family would be here, sure, but neither one of us had a bunch of cousins we were close with. So my friends from the dance studio would be there, Daniel's close engineer friends, and some other college friends we'd kept in touch with. I liked it that way.

"When Hunter and I get married, I just want to have it on the beach," Gabbi said, leaning her head against the top of the couch and looking up at the ceiling. "Small. Intimate. Beautiful."

"We'll be there." We all agreed with a smile, and I looked

around the room at my best friends, the girls I'd spent almost a decade of my life with, and my heart was filled with so much love.

"I love you three," I said, trying not to let my eyes fill with tears.

"Same," Gabbi agreed.

Noelle's smile lit up her face. "I love you too. You're like the three sisters I always wanted."

We all piled into a group hug until Angelina rolled her eyes with a smile. "Okay, okay, enough sappiness." Noelle, Gabbi and I laughed. "But I love you all too."

There was no place in life I'd rather be as long as they were at my side.

And when the guys came back from the mountain a few hours later, and they settled at our sides, I knew the same went for them, as well.

That we'd built something special here that went beyond just regular friendship.

And maybe... What Daniel and I had was enough.

∼

A WEEK LATER, I was wearing a knee length sparkly dress, surrounded by my friends in the fanciest hotel ballroom I could imagine for my bridal shower.

In hindsight, telling my mom that she could plan it since I wouldn't let her help with the wedding wasn't the best idea. Especially after Noelle had tried to insist that she could do it, but my mom had signed up for it, anyway.

I should have said *no*. We could have done it at one of our houses, a small, casual affair with just my closest friends.

If I'd had my way, I wouldn't have even had a shower. It wasn't like I really needed one. Daniel and I had both chosen not to have bachelor or bachelorette parties, besides the night at the bar during the ski trip. What was the point?

We were getting married because we didn't *want* to be single, so celebrating one last night of being single was, well... dumb. But I was just glad that no one had protested in the friend group. We'd gone all out for Angelina and Benjamin's wedding, so it was nice to go more low-key for ours. One big event per year was enough for me.

But, no. And since I'd given my mom such little notice (as she liked to remind me, five times a day), they'd planned it for the week before the wedding. Meaning they were up here in Portland for the entire week. It was the first time my mom and sister were visiting me in years. I'd had enough time to get used to it, to the fact that when I'd chosen to stay here with my best friends, with Daniel, they'd practically written me off.

But now that I was getting married... Somehow they wanted to be a part of my life again? It made me frustrated and upset, and I didn't like how I felt when I was angry. It twisted up my insides, and the person I became just wasn't me.

Yet I was here, playing the part of the dutiful bride, because that was how it always was in this family. I'd be the perfectly poised daughter my mom wanted, and when I got home, I'd take a long shower and try to figure out how I could never live up to their expectations.

"Oh my god! I can't believe my little sister is getting married!" Lavender smiled, giving me a brief nudge with her elbow as I sipped on the champagne from my flute.

I gave her a small smile. "Thanks, Lav."

It wasn't Lavender's fault that she was my mom's favorite, and I would never trade my older sister for the world. But sometimes it felt like whenever I was around her, I came in second place. Lavender was a model. She'd married a successful lawyer, and now she was pregnant with her second baby. I hated feeling like I could measure up.

Sure, it was part of the reason I'd stopped going home years ago. The way my mom made everything between us into some competition. Never mind that I loved teaching dance, had my own successful business selling dresses and dance costumes, and that I was marrying an engineer.

Sure, there were some things they didn't need to know. Namely, that my marriage was fake, and I'd moved out of my apartment because the rent was astronomically high.

"You okay?" Noelle slid in next to me, swapping out my empty glass for a full one.

I tried to force my face into a smile. This was *my* bridal shower, and sure, my marriage might not have been real, but it was the only one I was going to have. "Yeah." I tilted my fresh glass up, taking a sip. This occasion called for it. "Just thinking, I guess." I leaned my head against my best friend's shoulder.

"Promise me something," she murmured as I surveyed the crowd in attendance.

"Anything." I meant it.

"Let's do something a *little* more low-key for my bridal shower, please?"

I giggled. "You mean you don't want a champagne fountain?"

"Char," she groaned.

"I promise." I dropped my voice into a whisper. "I think she only did this because she's upset I wouldn't let her plan my wedding. The thought of a backyard wedding on Daniel's dad's property... It's a bit scandalous for my *high-society* mother." Never mind that I'd grown up in California, not New York. Or that we weren't heiresses to a giant fortune. She'd still carried those roots with her, even after marrying my Silicon Valley-based father.

"I think outdoor weddings are perfect." Noelle sighed. "We're touring some pumpkin patches nearby for our wedding next fall, and I can't imagine us doing anything else." Her eyes fluttered shut as she smiled, like she was imagining it.

"As long as we don't have to carry pumpkins with our bridesmaid dresses, you know I'm down for anything." I looped an arm through hers. "Now, do you think we can escape before the games begin?"

"With your mom?" She rolled her eyes. "Unlikely."

"We should probably go rescue them, huh?" Angelina and Gabbi were stuck in a conversation with some of my relatives. My fellow instructors from the dance studio, luckily, were all sitting around another table, just chatting.

"Yes. Definitely."

"When do you think Hunter and Gabbi are going to get engaged?" I murmured to Noelle, watching our brunette friend loop her arm through Angelina's and head towards the food table. Freeing themselves.

"I'll tell you one thing... If Hunter's anything like Matthew, he's going to make it special when he does. And they've only been dating for a few months. What's the rush?"

What's the rush, Charlotte?

I looked down into my drink as we headed over to reconvene with our friends.

The question echoed through my heart, bumping around a few times like a pinball machine before settling in my gut, a heavy weight I couldn't quite explain.

What was the rush? Why had I been so eager to say *yes*?

To rush into a fake marriage in the first place?

Was I that desperate for a family of my own?

But I knew, deep in my heart, that the answer was *yes*.

～

"You're home."

I looked up, darting my eyes away from Daniel's face, my eyes trailing down his tight white t-shirt and gray sweatpants as he stood at the top of the stairs.

Home. The word settled into my heart. I was home, wasn't I?

This, here, with him... It was home now.

Giving him a small smile, I set my purse on the side table in the entryway before reaching down to shuck my heels off. I should have taken them off after I left the venue, given that it was December and the walk to my car had been *freezing*, but I hadn't wanted to stop.

As soon as I got the all clear sign from my sister and the presents were open, I escaped the bridal shower.

When I looked up, heels discarded on the ground and brushing out my white satin dress, Daniel was in front of me.

"Hi." I swallowed roughly.

"Hey." He gave me a tight smile. "How was today? Was your mom on her best behavior?"

I shrugged. "It was fine. Nothing too crazy to report."

Surprisingly, for once, it had been a good day. Maybe because my girls had kept me supplied with champagne, and then we'd hidden away while my mom and her crew tore the building down. And the back of my car was full of gifts. Some that I'd decided my husband-to-be did not need to see—*ever*. I'd been scarred enough that I'd had to open them in front of my mom. The lingerie wasn't even the worst of it.

"I made dinner, if you want to join."

"Okay." I looked down at my dress. Knowing him, it was something that would stain my pretty white dress. "I'll just go shower and change, and then I'll be back down."

"Take your time," he said, shoving his hands in his pockets. "You know where to find me."

Once I removed my makeup and untangled my hair, I changed into a sports bra and my go-to black leggings, along with a roomy dance sweatshirt. Whipping my wet hair up into a loose bun, I made my way downstairs.

"Something smells amazing," I groaned. Sure, I'd eaten at the bridal shower, but most of it hadn't been gluten-free. The fact that my own mother didn't even remember my dietary needs, but Daniel always made sure I could eat, honestly flabbergasted me.

"What's for dinner?" I asked, following my nose to the kitchen, finding Daniel frying white corn tortillas on the stove.

"Tacos." He grinned. "Hopefully that's good with you?"

I could have cried with happiness. "Yum. Sounds perfect."

He finished cooking the tortillas, and after we'd both loaded up the shells and filled our plates, we sat down in the dining room, digging into our meals. I'd always liked them with just meat, cheese, and lettuce, but he'd also made a side of rice and beans.

"This is delicious," I moaned after the first bite of the taco, all the flavors exploding on my tongue. I quickly demolished the first one and started on my second.

He chuckled, watching me scarf down more tacos than I wanted to count. I was hungry, and he'd never once judged me for how much food I could shovel in.

"So..."

I gulped down a glass of juice as he finished his rice, settling his fork back down on his plate.

"So?" I raised an eyebrow.

"That's it? Nothing on your mind?"

"No."

"You sure?" He raised an eyebrow.

"Nope." I shoveled another bite into my mouth.

"Charlotte." He groaned. "You're killing me."

After finishing my food, I stood up to go rinse my plate off, standing in front of the sink, foot tapping to an indecipherable rhythm on the ground.

"What—" An arm snaked around my waist, spinning me around, pinning me in between the counter and his powerful body.

And then, wordlessly, Daniel kissed me.

His lips met mine, and I practically moaned into his mouth as I let my tongue brush against his, surrendering to the maddening inferno that was between us.

I broke away, reddened cheeks and swollen lips and all, and

instead of actually saying something, I just... escaped. Disappeared up the stairs to let my heart calm down.

    Because what was that?

    What were we doing here?

    And why did it feel like that kiss wasn't fake?

CHAPTER 16
Daniel

Gray eyes above me, rolling back into her head as she takes me in, inch by inch, taking her own pleasure, riding me—

My fist wrapped around my dick, stroking up and down my shaft as I pictured Charlotte's face in the throes of pleasure as she got herself off on top of me. I tried not to entertain this fantasy before, but the memory of her writhing beneath me was too alluring.

I couldn't bear being so close to her anymore, not without touching her. The scent of strawberries followed me everywhere, and then there was her parading around the house in those tiny spandex shorts. I was going crazy with need, but I was respecting her boundaries.

She'd escaped after I'd kissed her a few days ago, and I'd took that as a sign. This was fake, and even if our bodies responded to each other, that was all it was. I'd been giving her space ever since, knowing how stressed she was with the wedding only days away.

"Daniel?" Her voice came over the sound of the shower as I was getting closer, but this wasn't dream Charlotte, this was—

"Oh!" Her cheeks pinked as she entered my bathroom, clearly

catching me jacking off to thoughts of her. Obviously, I hadn't locked my door. *Fuck.*

I whipped around, wishing I had somewhere to hide, but the shower door of the master bathroom was completely clear, and even the fog did little to hide me from her.

"Charlotte," I groaned. "I thought we agreed not to come in without knocking." I braced myself against the shower wall, leaning my head against the cool tile. But I supposed we had broken a lot of our rules last weekend on the ski trip. But she was the one who had insisted on them in the first place, hadn't she?

"Well, I knocked, and you didn't answer, and your dad was on the phone, and I didn't realize you were in the shower, and—"

I wondered if I turned around right now, if her cheeks would be pink. If she was as embarrassed as I was of the position she'd caught me in.

"I'll call him back," I practically barked out. "Anything else?"

"Um..." Her voice was silken, barely a whisper. "No." I kept my eyes on the wall, knowing if I turned around, if I looked at her, that her cheeks would be bright red.

I grabbed my towel, wrapping it around my waist, sending a word of apology to my weeping cock.

Except for when I turned around, she didn't look embarrassed at all. She looked... annoyed? Was that the emotion that flared through her gray eyes?

"What?"

She shook her head, leaving the bathroom and me standing there, dripping wet. The water was dripping into my eyes, but I didn't care. I followed her, determined to figure out what had upset her.

Charlotte had retreated into her bedroom.

Because even though we'd had amazing, mind-blowing sex last weekend, nothing had changed for her. She'd come home and holed herself up in her sewing room. I knew she was finishing her dress, but she'd barely come downstairs for dinner every night before retreating into her bedroom.

"Charlotte," I practically barked, finding her standing in the guest bedroom. "What did I do?"

She shook her head. "Nothing. I just..." My girl wouldn't make eye contact with me. "It's stupid. Never mind."

"You have to tell me, or I won't know what's going through that mind of yours, darling."

"I thought that after last weekend..." She bit her lip, and I raised an eyebrow. "Besides kissing me the other night, you haven't tried anything." Her gaze dropped to her feet. "I thought you didn't want me anymore."

Did she think that was all I wanted from her? Just sex? I was trying to prove to her it was the opposite. That I wanted everything with her.

"Fuck. No. Charlotte. Why would you think that?" Stepping closer to her, I guided her chin up to look at me. "That would be impossible. I just didn't want to start it if that wasn't what you wanted. And you've been up here, practically avoiding me."

She frowned. "I have not."

I chuckled. "You have. But it's okay. We've both been busy. We're getting married in a few days." Like she needed the reminder. "And you've been making your dress."

Charlotte looked up at me through her lashes as she fidgeted with her fingers. "So... is sex back on the table?"

"Was it ever off the table?" I tried to hold back my throaty rasp. Fuck. Hearing her say those words, with the delicate lilt of her voice, was almost too much. Her angelic voice talking about sex made me hard, and I was still gripping my towel tightly.

"Just sex, right? That's what this is?"

I swallowed roughly. If that was what she wanted, that was all she could give me... I would take it. Even though I knew I'd want more.

I'd always wanted more from her.

"Just sex," I confirmed, dropping my towel, pulling her close to me.

And I proved that to her with my mouth, making her orgasm

twice before she fell asleep, and then I slipped out of the bed, retreating to my own to think about just how fucked I was.

∼

"So... Here we are." I said, dropping onto the guest bed and turning back to look at Charlotte, who was sitting at the vanity, not saying much.

We'd spent the last week with her family and mine, entertaining both and trying to keep the peace between everyone. Charlotte was distant, and even I knew it wasn't just our impending nuptials that had her withdrawn into herself.

We had been living together for a month and a half, and I'd thought the last week had been good—better than good. We'd coexisted in the way we'd always seemed to, spending our free time together. And falling in to bed together was *good*. But she wasn't her usual bubbly self.

Something *else* was bothering her.

I just needed to figure out what. After we got through this weekend, it would just be us, and hopefully she would talk to me then.

Since we'd opted out of a big wedding, we'd chosen to have the wedding practice and then dinner at my dad's house with our family and closest friends. The weather had been colder than normal this week, with a cold front coming from the north. We'd practiced walking down the aisle quickly while bundled up in our thick winter coats.

When we'd gotten back inside, the tip of Charlotte's nose had been pink.

I wanted to warm it up myself, but I held myself back.

"Are you ready for this?" I murmured, brushing her hair off her shoulder as she stared at me in the mirror.

Dinner wasn't for a little longer, and even though the rest of our friends were downstairs, we'd come up to change out of our clothes and into something nicer.

For Charlotte, that meant a white dress that cut off at her knees, complete with long puffy sleeves and covered in sparkles. It matched her sparkly hair clips that were pinned in the loose, curly up-do she had somehow done in the last hour.

She looked every bit the bride, even though she was still wearing her fleece lined tights.

"Honestly?" She tilted up her head to look at me, our eyes connecting in the reflection. "I don't know." She fiddled with the hem of her dress.

I slid onto the bench next to her, resisting the urge to swipe my fingers through her silky hair. "Want to talk about it?" I asked in a low voice.

Charlotte bit her lip. "Yes. No. I don't know." Her finger rubbed her finger over her ring absentmindedly, like she was still getting used to it sitting there. "Can we just pretend that this is actually real? Just for this weekend? That you're madly in love with me, and we're getting married because we can't imagine not being together?"

I am, I wanted to say. *We are*.

But it wasn't the truth. Because even if I loved her, she didn't love me. Not like that. She loved me like a friend, that was all. "Of course, darling," I said instead, leaning over to kiss her temple. "You're my best friend. I'd give you whatever you wanted, if you asked."

"Okay." She shut her eyes as she took a deep breath in before exhaling. When they reopened, those beautiful gray eyes shining into mine, she looked determined.

Whatever she'd decided, the worry had eased from her eyes, and I squeezed the hand that was resting in her lap. "You good?"

"Mhm." She inhaled another deep breath before turning to look at me. "Thank you. You always know exactly what to say."

This time, I kissed her on the cheek before extending out my hand to her. "Shall we?"

She slipped her hand in mine, and we headed down the stairs

together, bodies close and palms clinging tightly, and I could almost let myself believe what she'd asked.

Because all of this... it felt so *right*.

∽

Charlotte's hand had stayed wrapped around mine until we settled at the giant dining room table for dinner with our families and closest friends. Technically, it was our rehearsal dinner, but we'd kept it casual. Laid back. Food served family style, instead of plated. We'd planned no toasts, no speeches.

Just the way we wanted it.

"Last chance for me to be your Best Woman, you know," Angelina said with a wink as we all sat down in our seats.

"Hey!" Charlotte frowned. "You're not allowed to defect to the boy's side." She turned her head, looking at me, poking my chest with her dainty finger. "No stealing my bridesmaids." My wife-to-be gave me her best little pout, even though she looked like an adorable little kitten begging for food instead of someone you'd take seriously.

"Relax, darling," I said, grabbing her hand and kissing it. "I won't steal my sister from you." The irony didn't phase me, considering how I'd stolen Charlotte from her to be *my* friend in college.

"Besides, Angel, he has me," Benjamin smirked from beside his wife, and she rolled her eyes.

"Yes, but clearly, I am better than you."

Ben huffed before Angelina leaned over and whispered something in his ear before kissing his cheek.

"Ah, to be young and in love," my dad murmured from beside me, his wife smirking as they watched our friends.

Charlotte caught my eye, raising an eyebrow as if she was asking me a question. Instead of responding, I interlaced our fingers under the table.

"So, I heard you gang just got back from a ski trip to Bend, huh?"

It was Noelle who responded, her body language open and warm as she leaned against Matthew. "Yeah. We went down a long weekend after finals finished. It was fun. Even if Charlotte took a little tumble."

Charlotte's mom glared daggers at me, and I didn't want to know what she thought about the fact that I couldn't keep her daughter safe.

My dad looked at Matthew. "You said you're a Professor, right?"

My tall, blond friend nodded. "Yes. Noelle works at the University too. She's an advisor for the freshman and sophomores in the School of Business." Matthew couldn't help but boast about his girl regularly. In a lot of ways, I understood it. I wanted to sing Charlotte's praises every chance I got.

"It's nice that you're all still connected," Theresa said with a smile, putting her fork down. "I've hardly kept in contact with any of my friends from college."

I hadn't really either, except for Charlotte and the girls. My roommate and my closest guy friend during college had moved back home to Alaska, so now if I hung out with someone that wasn't in this room, it was probably one of the guys I worked with.

Charlotte laughed. "Even though we all missed our five-year reunion this summer because of Angelina's wedding?"

"Our wedding was better, anyway." Angelina played it off. "Plus, who else did you want to see? All the people I cared about from college are sitting around this table." She looked at me. "And my brother, too."

I rolled my eyes as she laughed. "Who would have guessed that my older brother would marry one of my best friends and college roommates?"

"Not me," I muttered as the rest of the table laughed. Maybe

I'd always hoped, but I certainly never would have guessed that she'd pick me. I was just lucky she had.

"Sometimes I wondered if those three were going to make bets on how long it would take for you two to realize you were in love with each other," Benjamin said. He pointed his fork between the two of us. "I was sure that a scheme would be required to push the two of you together, but then you figured it out all on your own."

"Yeah. You two were so oblivious," Angelina said with a smirk. "I just want to know what changed that led to this." She laughed off the last statement, like she didn't actually expect us to answer.

Charlotte and I locked eyes, and I wondered if she was thinking about the same moment I had. The one where we'd both said *fuck it,* and I'd pinned her against our hotel room door the second it was closed and kissed her.

Maybe Charlotte and I *had* been the only two who were so blind to what was between us. I'd always cared for her, but this summer had opened my eyes. I'd known then that I couldn't live with her being *just* my best friend. Couldn't watch her fall in love and get married to someone else.

"I just woke up one day and realized I couldn't live without her," I said, truthfully. "And the rest is history."

I squeezed her hand under the table.

Even if this whole charade was just a farce, at least I had her on my side.

Fake or not.

And tomorrow... Tomorrow would be real.

CHAPTER 17
Charlotte

I was getting ready for bed when I heard a rap against my door.

"Charlotte." His deep, husky voice seemed to almost drift through the wood, stopping me in my tracks.

God, did he even know what he did to me? How much he affected my body? I didn't think anyone else had ever flipped a switch in me like he did. Fortunately, it wasn't always like this. If I had to endure the last nine years of our friendship with an uncontrollable desire to touch and kiss him, I wouldn't have made it.

Certainly not with my heart intact. Because while Daniel wanted to marry me, I also knew that I was his backup plan. I was the last-case-scenario, and I had to remember that.

Pacing over to the door, I tightened my robe over myself, even though he'd already seen all of me. Twice. Something we'd both, apparently, decided not to talk about. How I'd watched him in the shower until I hadn't been able to take it anymore. How much I'd liked it when he'd treated me roughly, sparking things inside of me I hadn't even known existed.

Did I want a repeat? *Yes.* But also... this was different. We were at his dad's house.

"What are you doing here?" I whispered through the door.

"You know we're not supposed to spend the night together before our wedding day."

"Are you telling me you actually believe in that?" He murmured back as I cracked it open.

Daniel was wearing a pair of sweats, hung loose on his hips, and a sweatshirt pulled on top. At least he'd remembered my *no-walking-around-shirtless* rule. Sure, we'd already broken the other ones, but who was I to complain? Shirtless Daniel was my kryptonite, and at least if he'd covered up, I could make it through tonight without pouncing on him.

Maybe.

Daniel leaned against the doorway, practically resting against his arm and hip, just watching me. I had a hard time keeping the heat from rushing to my body just from his stare alone. He looked me up and down, taking in my appearance, even though I'd simply tossed my hair into a messy bun and wore my preferred pink, cozy robe. I'd worn the same thing dozens of times at his house. Somehow, it still didn't quite feel like home. Maybe it was because we were still sharing separate bedrooms, and he'd slip out each night after wringing every drop of pleasure from my body.

What had we been talking about again?

Oh, right. Our wedding. I cleared my throat, refocusing my attention on him.

"We talked about this. I don't want us to have bad luck. That's no way to start off a fake marriage." *Fake. Like I had to remind myself of the fact as well.* That if I didn't remember it, I'd let myself hope for things that wouldn't happen.

"Well, I wanted to show you something."

"And it couldn't have waited until tomorrow?" I raised an eyebrow.

"Nope." Grinning, he walked into the room, heading straight for the enormous windows that overlooked the yard.

"What are you doing?"

"Getting you to look out the window," he said with a smirk,

drawing back the curtains so I could see outside. "Seems like you got your wish, huh?"

It was snowing; the ground dusted in a white blanket, clear in the moonlight that streamed through my windows. Falling from the sky were those thick, fluffy flakes that promised to stick.

A white wedding, just like I'd dreamed about.

"Oh, Daniel..." I covered my mouth, taking in the view. "It's beautiful."

I never would have imagined that I'd actually get my wish. Since I was little, I'd always thought winter weddings, especially with snow on the ground, were beautiful. Never mind that I was always cold, or that I'd definitely need a blanket after the ceremony was over. It was everything I could have ever asked for.

"You're sure you want to do this, right?"

I loved that he asked, that he checked to make sure this was what I wanted and that I was okay. That he was so caring all the time. A part of me had always known this was how he was. It was part of the reason I'd loved being his friend so much. He really cared about the people he got close to, and he loved taking care of them.

Now I just had to let my brain—and heart—get the memo. That I could let him take care of me, without worrying about the consequences. About what happened when everything fell apart. But maybe, even if it was just for now, I needed to live in the moment. Enjoy the little things as they happened.

Not worry about what happened if my fake husband I was marrying for convenience didn't fall in love with me. This wasn't some plot of a romance novel where they were getting married because of a contract, and a dose of forced proximity would get her to fall in love with her.

Because we'd been best friends for too long for that.

I let him wrap his arms around my shoulders, swaying us back and forth as we watched the snow fall. He tucked me into his body, and it was an intimacy that almost came too easily to us, but I wouldn't complain. I enjoyed being in his arms. Honestly, ever since I'd crawled into his bed after having a nightmare, I wanted to be there all the time.

"Yeah," I said, my voice soft. If he wasn't holding me, I doubted he'd be able to hear it at all. "I want to be your wife. I want to marry you tomorrow." It was the truth, even if it was dangerous to feel that way.

I turned around and wrapped my arms around his neck, before raising up on my tiptoes to place a quick kiss to his lips.

"Yeah?" He asked, and I let our foreheads rest together.

I could feel his gaze on me, even as he lowered his lips to my ear and nipped at my earlobe.

"Y-yes," I said, trying to hold back my voice as he kissed my neck.

"Daniel, what are we doing?" I whispered into the darkness of the night as he sucked at my skin. *Sex, just sex,* flickered through my mind. Why had I ever said that, when it was the last thing I'd wanted?

"Forgetting the bad stuff," he murmured, and I almost let myself drown in him. "Making it real."

But as much as I wanted to... "We should go to bed," I whispered. "We're getting married tomorrow."

"Mm. You're right." He wrapped his arms back around me, pecking me on the forehead. "I'll be waiting at the end of the aisle, wife."

"Not your wife yet," I murmured, even though the word sent a rush through me.

And how he was looking at me.... like I was the most precious thing in the world to him?

Maybe none of my fears mattered, as long as I had him like this.

"Soon." He kissed me again, tenderly, on the lips, before disappearing back out the door, leaving me to watch the snow.

∼

"Charlotte, you look beautiful," Noelle said, squeezing my hand as if she was being careful not to touch my dress.

I'd added the finishing details three nights ago, and then it had finally been *done*. I overlaid the base of heavy white satin with a sparkly sheer fabric, and I decorated it with flowery lace details and sleeves. It was everything I'd ever dreamed of since I was a little girl, and I'd made it myself, down to the row of pearl buttons up my back and the long veil that trailed behind me tucked into my hair.

"The perfect bride," Gabbi agreed.

"*Shut up,* you're going to make me cry," I said, playfully swatting at my friends, who were taking turns making sure I looked perfect. "And I don't want my makeup to run yet."

I was sure it would later. I cried easily, and my wedding... Well, it was safe to say I'd almost cried a few times today.

Luckily, I had my girls by my side.

"You're officially going to be my sister," Angelina smiled. "*Finally.* Took you two long enough, huh?" She gave me a little wink to let me know she was kidding.

Each of my bridesmaids—Angelina, Gabbi, and Noelle, as my maid of honor—were wearing long, pink chiffon dresses with fur shawls around their shoulders. Luckily, we'd only be outside during the actual ceremony part and for photos. During happy hour and the reception, we'd be in the heated tent that Daniel's step-mom had rented. Honestly, she was a lifesaver, somehow throwing together our entire wedding in less than two months. But it felt right, *real* in a way that it hadn't before.

I was really going to marry my best friend. And after last night, well... Maybe we weren't in love yet, but I knew there was something more there. And I couldn't wait to find out *what* it was.

But first, I had to get through this ceremony—through the day. And then the rest of our lives and this fake marriage would be in front of us. No big deal.

"No cold feet?" Noelle asked me, and I shook my head.

"I mean, my feet will probably be cold when we get out there," I said, trying to be funny. "It is like 30 degrees out there, you know." I was wearing fleece-lined tights under my dress.

Why had I thought a winter wedding was a good idea again?

I looked out the window and smiled. Yeah, that was why. My little miracle that it had snowed for my wedding day. It wasn't super thick, but it coated the ground, like a white blanket dusting the outside world, so everything sparkled when the sun hit it.

"Yeah, yeah. At least you have sleeves." Angelina joked.

"Hey, I got the fur wraps!" I protested. "And they heated the reception tent. It should be nice and cozy."

Noelle laughed. "She's just messing with you, Char. We'll be fine."

"You should just be grateful it's not a long ceremony," I said, shooting daggers at my soon-to-be sister-in-law. "We could have gotten married on campus." A lot of my old college friends who had both attended had got married at the chapel at our university, but I'd wanted something different.

"Okay, okay, you win," Angelina groaned. "Short and cold. Tradeoffs."

"And an open-bar at the end." I wiggled my eyebrows.

"Hope no one forgets their birth control tonight," Angelina muttered.

"Right," I said, giving a strained laugh. I'd been planning on stopping mine—not that they knew about my plans. The real reason I'd said yes.

And then I pushed it all out of my mind, something I would worry about later.

Because I was getting married. Today.

Now.

∽

"Are you ready, sweetheart?" My dad asked me, studying me intently after the girls had walked away to get in place to walk down the aisle.

Dad and I were still inside the main house, so I could have my big reveal. The dress deserved nothing less.

"Yeah, Daddy." I hugged him tightly, careful not to press my face into his suit so I didn't get any of my makeup on it.

I'd spent an hour making sure every detail was perfect, down to the shimmer on my eyelids, and this was one day I wanted everything to be perfect.

"You're happy?" He asked, voice quiet as he stared out the glass doors.

I didn't even have to hesitate. "I am." The last month, living with Daniel, having dinner together every night, the ski trip... I'd never imagined things would be like this between us. Maybe I'd still worried about what we truly were for each other, but he was my best friend. No one else in the world knew me better. "He's everything I could have ever dreamed of."

My dad extended out an arm to me. "Shall we take you to your husband, then?"

"Yes," I murmured, my eyes tracking to where Daniel stood.

He was standing underneath an arch wrapped in greenery, little white and pink roses interwoven throughout. A layer of snow dusted everything, somehow heightening the look.

It was a fairytale. One I didn't know if I'd earned, but had gotten all the less.

His eyes came up towards the house, and even though I knew he couldn't see me, the butterflies rumbled through me.

So much for trying to deny my attraction to my best friend.

The man who was about to be my husband.

CHAPTER 18
Daniel

Four months ago, we'd been at a different wedding, one where everything had changed. And today—it was our turn.

Benjamin patted me on my shoulder, giving me one big smile before I turned towards the house, to where I knew Charlotte was waiting on the other side.

Her best friends were already standing on the other side of us, dressed in that blush pink shade Charlotte loved so much. They each carried bouquets of white and pink roses with baby's breath —I didn't even want to know how hard that had been to get in the middle of winter—in their hands.

I was sure that behind me, each of the guys had their eyes glued to them. They were all spectacular women, but I only had eyes for one girl.

The door opened, and there she was.

My bride. My wife-to-be.

Ever so gracefully, she practically floated towards me, the sun behind her making it look like she had a halo against her soft blonde curls. And she didn't take her eyes off of me for one breath.

There was no chance that I would ever look away.

I was misty-eyed before she'd even taken the first step, but the closer she got to me, the more choked up I was.

Charlotte. *My Charlotte.*

With a veil tucked into her hair and the brightest smile on her face.

She'd been working away on that dress in her sewing room for the last month, and I hadn't gotten a single peek, but I never would have imagined *this*. It clung to her skin, dainty lace sleeves down to her wrist, and a corseted bodice, the skirt flowing down to her feet before extending in a long train behind her.

And the dress—the entire damn dress—glittered like the snow that had coated the ground.

She pressed a kiss against her dad's cheek before he settled down in the row with her mother, sister, and her sister's family.

Charlotte passed her bouquet to Noelle as she stepped up to join us.

"Hi," I whispered as she stood beside me.

"Hi." A few loose curls framed her face, and I resisted the urge to touch them. To touch her.

God, had she always been this beautiful? Was I crying? *Fuck.* Charlotte's thumb came up to my face, wiping away one singular tear.

"Don't make me cry, Daniel," she whispered. "Or I will throw you to the dogs." She tilted her head to indicate her best friends.

"Sorry," I whispered. "It's just that..." I sucked in a breath. "You're so beautiful, Char."

"Thank you." She tilted her eyes down, as if she could hide her adorable blush. It was my favorite thing in the world.

Finally, we nodded at our officiant that we were ready to start the ceremony, and Charlotte's hands slipped into mine.

"Family and friends, thank you all for coming today to share in this wonderful occasion. Today, we are gathered together to unite Charlotte and Daniel in marriage."

I was sure if I had turned out into the crowd, I would have seen countless friends. We hadn't invited too many people—our closest family members, friends, and co-workers, but I knew they were all here to support us.

But I couldn't keep my eyes off of Charlotte.

The officiant gave a brief speech—he'd talked to us yesterday about what to prepare, so none of it was much of a surprise.

And then... it was time.

We'd agreed not to do our own vows. Partially, because Angelina had teased me, saying I would probably cry my way through them. Maybe she was right. I didn't cry often, but for my family, the ones I loved? I was a wreck. And trying to express to my best friend how much she meant to me? That was practically impossible. It was too soon, too, to lay all of my cards out on the table. Plus, it wasn't like she was in love with me. I didn't want our vows to be fake like this marriage was.

"Daniel, do you take Charlotte to be your wife? Do you promise to love, honor, cherish, and keep her, in sickness and in health, in good times and bad times, for richer or poorer, to have and to hold, from this day forward, as long as you both shall live?"

"I do." I squeezed her hands, staring into her beautiful face.

The one I'd happily see every day for the rest of my life. That I'd do anything just to earn a smile from.

"Charlotte, do you take Daniel to be your husband? Do you promise to love, honor, cherish, and keep her, in sickness and in health, in good times and bad times, for richer or poorer, to have and to hold, from this day forward, as long as you both shall live?"

"I do."

I brought one of our joined hands up to my lips and kissed her knuckles. There weren't enough words to communicate how I was feeling at that moment. How much I wanted this to be really real. For her to be truly mine.

Maybe she could see it in my eyes. How thankful I was for her, how grateful I was for her very presence in my life. Because I needed her smiles, her laughs, her love of Christmas movies and romance novels just as much as I needed the air we breathed.

And today, as the snow fell on us in large, fluffy flakes as we said our vows of commitment to each other, I knew that there would never be anyone in my life that would compare to my Charlotte.

The officiant cleared his throat once again, bringing our attention back to him.

"Charlotte and Daniel have chosen rings to exchange with each other as a symbol of their unending love. Daniel, please take the ring you have selected for Charlotte. As you place it on her finger, repeat after me: With this ring, I thee wed."

I repeated it back, sliding Charlotte's wedding band down on top of her engagement ring. We'd have to get it soldered together soon, but a part of me liked that she'd kept wearing her engagement ring, not wanting to give it up even for a few days.

Coming downstairs and seeing her on the couch, unconsciously twisting the ring back and forth as she watched something on TV or the way she rubbed her finger over the stone when she was thinking—it filled me with a sense of possession I didn't deserve.

Mine. She was mine.

And now I would be hers. And maybe that was the most important part of all of this. Being hers. I'd made a promise to her, to love and honor her, and she'd done the same.

It was all I could ask for—all I could hope for in this life.

To love her and be loved in return.

"You can finally give me mine," I whispered into her ear, reminding her of the promise she'd made when I'd unceremoniously given her the ring. The one I'd had for longer than I wanted to admit.

"Charlotte, please take the ring you have selected for Daniel. As you place it on his finger, repeat after me: With this ring, I thee wed."

She repeated the words as she pushed a black wedding band down my finger. I'd joked with her about it when I'd first given her the ring I'd picked out, but... I was happy to have it. To have her.

"By the power vested in me by the state of Oregon, I now pronounce you husband and wife. You may now kiss the bride."

And because we were pretending, because this was *real*, if only for the day, I did what I wanted to more than anything. I pulled her into my arms, dipped her down, and kissed her like my life depended on it.

She wrapped her arms around my neck, kissing me back, and if it wasn't for the cheering of our family and friends, I could have gotten lost in it. In her lips, the taste of her mouth. There was no joining of tongues, no deep desperation to join our bodies together, but maybe we were holding ourselves back. Because we knew what would happen if we gave in.

And it was good. *So good.*

When I was kissing Charlotte, it felt like everything was right in the world.

"Should we go, Mrs. Bradford?" I asked as I set her back on her feet, turning to go back down the aisle, still dusted in snow.

We hadn't had a flower girl to scatter petals, or a dog to come down the aisle with our rings tied to its collar. What we had was mother nature's beautiful display of winter, and two magnificent beasts waiting for us.

Her eyes opened wide as she took in the view of what we'd ride away in.

It might not be the perfect fairytale wedding, riding away in a carriage towards a castle, but this was our little slice of magic. And Charlotte deserved no less.

Theresa had come through, and a horse-drawn sleigh waited to carry us away.

"Daniel." Her eyes filled with tears. "I told you not to make me cry. Damn you."

Leaning down, I kissing the tip of her nose. "I can't help it, darling. I just want to make you happy."

Her hand slipped into mine, the other holding tight to her bouquet, and we practically ran down the aisle as our guests cheered for us.

Everything, at least for now, was perfect.

∽

We finished taking photos, and I'd lost count of how many times we'd kissed during them. The amount of times I'd have to hold myself back from swiping my tongue inside. All I knew was I wanted to keep kissing her, and there was still so much time left before I could reveal my last surprise of the night. Hopefully, she'd like that one as much as the horse who'd carried us away from the ceremony.

The photos of her petting the horse's muzzle and stroking its mane were bound to be some of the best from the whole day, if only because her entire face had lit up. It wasn't like one of Charlotte's fake smiles—this was real. She was beaming.

I wanted her to look at me like that.

Fake echoed through my head. Even if that was true, the show we were putting on certainly looked real. And my feelings—those were real, too.

Because I wanted this to be a proper marriage. I was going to prove it to her, too. She just needed time to see how good this would be—us, together. But this wasn't fake—not for me. Not anymore.

"Hi, wife," I said, dropping into the seat next to her, my hand finding hers in her lap.

"Hi, husband," she whispered back, nibbling on her gluten-free roll.

We ordered everything with Charlotte in mind, our favorite foods—all things she could eat. The worst part of going to parties for her had always been the lack of options. So even though our guests weren't eating gluten-free meals, it was all her favorites that now decorated her plate.

I set down the glass of champagne I'd grabbed for her before grabbing her plate and cutting her chicken up into bite-sized pieces.

"You didn't have to do that," she mumbled.

"Why not? I wanted to." I'd also hated watching her struggle to try not to get anything on her dress, and if I could do anything to ease that... I would.

"Oh." She looked up at me, and I kissed the side of her forehead. "Need anything else?"

"No." Charlotte shook her head. "Thank you."

"Of course. You're my wife."

My wife. I didn't think I would tire of saying that. Never.

We'd both changed so much over the last month, and the last two weeks since the ski trip had been different.

I couldn't stop thinking about what she'd told me that night after the bar.

I'd been a fool. If I had known that I was her first, that she hadn't been with anyone before me... I would have been more gentle. Had I made it good for her? I thought I had, but... It wasn't what she deserved.

Tonight, at least, I'd make it special.

I hadn't earned it, but I wanted her. I didn't want her regretting this—regretting me. If things didn't work out between us, Charlotte would be okay. I'd make sure of it.

But me... I'd never be the same. If I was being honest with myself, I hadn't been the same since that night in August when she'd walked out of the hotel bathroom before the rehearsal dinner.

I still couldn't explain what had happened, if she'd felt the way I did that night. When we'd locked eyes, something fundamental had changed between us. I'd wanted to kiss her as soon as I saw that shimmery pink lip gloss swiped over her lips.

And after two glasses of wine... *Fuck it.* My resolve had been gone.

But then she'd shut me out. And it had broken a piece of me when she'd tried to avoid me. What was she so afraid of?

I thought I knew every part of Charlotte, but I realized there were so many things she kept hidden, not wanting the world to see underneath her bright, smiling face.

All this time, I thought I'd loved her. But I hadn't known the first thing about that, not really. She'd always been important to me, but now... looking over at her with her cheeks warm from the outside temperature and a slightly pink nose, I thought maybe I had known nothing at all. She'd always been mine, yet I'd had no claim over her. I'd dated other women, too. When I realized friendship with Charlotte was more important to me than any attraction or desire I felt towards her, I tried to move on. Get her off of my mind.

But it never worked. Because they were never *her*.

And now... I extended out a hand towards her.

"Shall we dance, darling?"

CHAPTER 19
Charlotte

Daniel pulled me into his arms, twirling me around the dance floor.

I'd never known how fast my heart could beat just from a man's embrace. There certainly hadn't been any dances like this before. One arm was curled around my back, resting on the small of my back, but just that touch heated me through the fabric. The other was holding my hand, even as we swayed around the floor for our first dance.

We hadn't taken lessons, but Daniel knew I didn't need it. I'd taken ballroom lessons since I was little, and dance was in my blood. But he never once stepped on my toes. His steps were in perfect harmony as mine, every bit as graceful as I was.

My heart swooned. "When'd you get so good at this?" I murmured to him as I rested my head against his shoulder for a moment.

He cleared his throat. "I, uh... Took lessons."

I looked up at him, right into those brown eyes I'd spent almost a decade looking into. But this close, I could stare at the little flecks of gold in his iris. The deviations in color that made up the rich hue.

He'd taken dance classes? For *me*?

Was this my quiet best friend who preferred a night in to going out, the one who loved math, who I'd catch strumming along to his guitar or playing piano—who always watched me dance and hardly ever joined me?

But then, he'd come to every one of my recitals in college. He'd walked me to class when I was wearing my pink leotard. He'd picked me up when I got off late from teaching classes. And he'd surprised me by learning all on his own.

"Daniel..."

"It was no big deal, really." He raised his shoulders in a shrug.

"Maybe not to you," I muttered. But it was a big deal for me. Because this didn't feel fake.

It wasn't like the cake tasting where we'd pretended to be one happy couple, or holding hands as we walked around his Dad's property while deciding where we wanted to have the wedding. Doing it on his own meant no one was there to witness the gesture. He did it for *me*.

It was like our little secret, a kernel of knowledge that warmed me from the inside out.

"Who told you that you could be so perfect?" I murmured under my breath, but when I looked up at him, the way he was gazing at me took my breath away.

Would it ever stop?

"Only for you," he promised, resting our foreheads together.

The butterflies exploded in my chest, and I had a hard time reminding myself that this was all just pretend. That it was just a fairytale I wanted to believe in.

Daniel kissed my forehead as our dance ended, and I gave him my best smile as he pulled me to his side, letting the masses come over to congratulate us.

"I can't believe you're *married,*" Angelina nudged me as my three best friends surrounded me later, pulling me into one corner of the thankfully warm tent.

Looking down at my ring, I couldn't help but agree. Because

it didn't feel real. "I know," I giggled, sipping on my champagne. "It feels surreal."

Noelle sighed dreamily. "I can't believe I'll be next." She looked over at Matthew, who was standing at the edge of the bar with Hunter, while Benjamin and Daniel were talking next to the dessert table.

Angelina nudged Gabbi. "When are you two tying the knot, Gabs?"

"Hey, he hasn't even *proposed* yet." She elbowed Ang right back. "Give us some time to just be together first. What's there to rush?"

"Yeah, it's not like these two crazy kids who got engaged without even telling us they were dating." Angelina pinned a stare at me.

I blushed. "I'm sorry! We weren't trying to keep it a secret from you. It was just that it all happened so fast." And that we hadn't even been dating before we got *fake* engaged. But I wasn't telling them that.

What had been the rush? I'd had the same thought at the bridal shower. I'd wanted to be married. I wanted to start a family. And was it that crazy at twenty-seven? I didn't think so.

"Can you believe how fast time has gone by? It feels like we all just graduated from college, but next thing we know, one of us is going to have a baby." Noelle ran her fingers through her curly red hair.

"Well..." I blushed.

"*Are you?*"

"No!" I put my hands up. "Not yet, anyway. But..." I looked over at Daniel. The thought of a baby with his eyes brought a smile to my face. We might have started this marriage off for all the wrong reasons, but I couldn't deny that my best friend was going to make the best dad. "Maybe soon," I whispered, unable to stop the joy from spreading through my face.

"Charlotte!" Noelle exclaimed, squeezing my palms.

"Yeah." I ducked my head down to hide my blush, taking another ship of champagne as I let the bubbles flow through me.

"Who'd have thought?" Gabbi laughed.

"Me." Angelina raised a hand.

"Definitely me," Noelle agreed.

"Okay, so maybe we all did," Gabbi added.

"Thanks, just keep rubbing it in that you all saw it before I did."

"Come on, Charlotte, it's been so obvious that he has been in love with you since freshman year. You just never saw it," Gabbi snorted.

"Really?" I blinked, looking across the room at Daniel—my *husband*. Had he really been in love with me all this time? "But we were always just best friends..."

Noelle nodded. "You were so deep in the friend zone, I'm surprised you found a way out. How did that happen, anyway?"

"Um, well, actually..." I didn't know if it was the champagne that loosened my tongue, but the words just spilled out of me. "At Angelina's wedding, we both just realized that we'd rather be together than be apart. I'd gone on so many dates in the last few years, but none of them ever felt right. Maybe my heart knew I was waiting for the right person."

I didn't even have to lie. It was the truth.

And maybe I had, in a roundabout way, been waiting for Daniel Bradford.

"Well, Mrs. Bradford," Angelina said, looping her arm through mine, "I'd say that worked out for you."

I laughed. "It feels a bit like I've stolen your last name."

"Nah, just my brother." I watched as Angelina's eyes looked across the room at her own husband. "I'm happy with my new name." She winked at me.

"Well, that's good."

"But, I have to admit, I felt a little like my brother was stealing *you* from me when we all first became friends." Angelina fidgeted with her fingernails. "I love him—we've always been so close—but it felt like I finally had something that was mine, and then he swooped in and stole you from me." She laughed. "But I enjoyed seeing how he was with you. How he always made sure you got back to the dorm safely, walking with you around campus... I guess it was nice, in a way. Knowing he had someone like that in his life. Like you."

"Angelina..." My eyes filled with tears.

She cleared her throat. "Now enough sappiness for the evening." She flicked her eyes back to her husband. "I need more champagne."

"Yes, please," I agreed.

Because I couldn't stop thinking about what they'd said.

Did Daniel love me?

Maybe I hadn't asked him enough about *his* motivations for this fake marriage.

Or was it fake to him at all?

∽

"They're all gone," Daniel said, practically slumping against the door in exhaustion.

"Do you think they bought it? Did we look believably in love?" I said, taking another bite of our wedding cake. As the flavors exploded on my tongue, I practically moaned. It was delicious, especially for it being gluten-free. And it was *pink*. "I could eat this for the rest of my life and never tire of it, I think."

The cake was amazing—pink velvet with the best cream cheese buttercream. Our friends had given toasts, reminding us of all the times we'd adamantly refused there was anything between us. Of how we'd both thought we were in the friend zone. How wrong they were. Because we might not have been just friends anymore, but we weren't really lovers, either. Somewhere in the middle.

I'd given him my virginity, and he'd given me the best night of my life. And then I'd run away. Still, we didn't love each other.

And exploring his body during this fake relationship wasn't wrong, was it? We might not have done this for love, but I was damn well going to take advantage of the benefits.

The tension between us was too intense to ignore.

His dad's couch was so comfy, and I'd plopped myself on it when we came inside after everyone had finally started leaving the tented venue area. And the cake that was currently resting in my lap was just the icing on top of the whole day.

I let my eyes float shut as I relaxed further into the couch. Feeling the weight of the plate being lifted off my abdomen, I opened my eyes to Daniel staring at me.

"Charlotte." His arms came down around me, caging me in. "It's our wedding night, darling." His voice was a low rumbling in my ear, and there was something about it that set my body aflame.

We hadn't talked about the other day when I'd joined him in the shower, or the way he'd thrust in to me and we'd both lost our minds. I'd been sore afterwards, but there was also a part of me that had felt like I was floating on clouds for the rest of the day.

So... maybe now was the time to talk about it. "Um... about the other day..."

He positioned his forehead over mine, his lips close enough that I could have leaned up and touched ours together if I moved just a hair. "We said it was sex, right? Just sex?"

I closed my eyes as he intertwined his fingers in my hair. "Yeah."

"We don't need to talk about what it means," Daniel agreed. "Let's just make each other feel good."

That I was on board with. I hummed in agreement.

"I need the words, Charlotte."

"I want this," I whispered, tugging him down further on top of me. "I want you."

"Good girl," he murmured against my skin, lighting my body on fire.

I looked up at him, feeling all too exposed on the couch of his dad's house. "Should we..." I didn't know what the protocol was here.

Would we drive home? Stay at his dad's? The idea of doing anything in his dad's house didn't sit right with me, even if we were technically married now in everyone's eyes. No one else knew it was fake. "Go upstairs?" I finished, lamely.

Daniel shook his head. "We're not staying here tonight."

"We're not?"

"No." He scratched his head, looking away sheepishly. "I might have, uh, one more surprise up my sleeve..."

"You do?" I blinked. "What about my stuff?" I'd left it all in the guest room this morning.

"I got it."

"Oh." I thought about some of the stuff I'd packed in my bag. The lacy thing I'd gotten *just in case*. Oh god. We were doing this, weren't we? Did I want that?

Yes. Yes, I did.

He extended out his hand. "Come on. Let's go. Your carriage awaits, darling."

"Okay." Placing my hand in his, I couldn't help the surge of rightness that came in the moment. It might not have been real, but there was no one else I'd rather do this with than him.

Even if he was being secretive and sneaky by not telling me his plans beforehand, I trusted him enough that I'd go with him anywhere.

He placed a kiss on my lips before sweeping me off my feet and hefting me into his arms. I was grateful for my small stature and how tall he was with how effortlessly he picked me up, even in my wedding gown.

I nuzzled into his tux jacket as he carried me to the car, hoping my makeup had set enough that it wouldn't rub off on his jacket.

The snow was falling down around us as he gently placed me on the passenger seat of the car and helped me get buckled in my dress. "Wouldn't it have been a better idea for me to take this off before we left?" I mumbled, but he just shook his head, closing my door to go around to the other side of the car and slide into the driver's seat.

"Where to, babe?" I asked, suppressing a yawn. The buzz the champagne had given me of had long since worn off, and now I was just sleepy.

"I got us a hotel." He looked over at me mid-yawn and winced. "I hope that wasn't too pretentious, but—"

I silenced him by putting a finger over his lips. "It wasn't. And that's perfect."

He nodded, starting the car. "We talked about how we weren't going on a honeymoon before, and even if this is fake, I still wanted tonight to be special."

My heart lept in my chest at the gesture. How caring and thoughtful this man I'd married was. "It will be." Looking up at him as he intertwined our fingers, kissing my knuckles, I couldn't help the way my heart stuttered in my chest. "Take me away, Daniel."

I was certainly in for a night I'd never forget.

⁓

THE HOTEL WAS BEAUTIFUL, and he'd reserved the honeymoon suite for two nights. The *room was enormous*, complete with its own jacuzzi, something I wanted to take advantage of later.

But first, I wanted my husband.

I reached around his neck, pulling him down to my lips.

Ever since last night, I'd wanted *more*. The kiss had set me on fire, and every touch throughout the day, every little kiss, left me wanting more.

Which was dumb. Because it was fake. None of this was real.

Except why was my heart racing faster as he lifted me up, carrying me bridal style into the bedroom? Why, when I was firmly back on my feet, did we not break apart?

I wove my arms around his neck, curling my fingers into the nape of his hair. And brought my lips to his.

Fuck, I needed him. I wanted him, too. Desire was pooling low in my gut, and if I didn't kiss him now, I was going to lose it.

"Need you out of this tux," I muttered, pawing at his jacket to push it to the ground. A three-piece suit shouldn't be this attractive on anyone. Like he was a modern god, dressed specifically to make my stomach flop just from the sight of him.

He chuckled, letting the garment fall from his shoulders. "Easy there, darling." Daniel nipped at my earlobe as his fingers tried to undo the buttons on my back.

I couldn't help it—I laughed. "We should probably get this off of me before we rip it."

He looked me up and down. "It would be such a shame to rip something this pretty, huh, *wife*?"

Spinning me around, he undid the long row of pearl buttons, far faster than I'd gotten into them.

"What else can those fingers do?" I murmured to myself, thinking of the delicate way he could play the piano. Of the way he'd pushed them inside of me, making me come faster than I'd ever thought possible.

And now we were... *married.*

I practically shivered as he ran his fingers over the bare skin of my back. My dress fell down around my hips, leaving me only in the little lace panties I'd gotten specifically for the occasion. I'd built cups in my dress, leaving me with a beautiful open-backed design for my wedding dress—and no bra on.

Daniel picked up the dress reverently, carrying it over to the closet to hang it up inside. Maybe we weren't in love, but the way he was treating my dress—so reverently—made my heart thrum up in my chest. I'd spent weeks making it, dozens of hours as I sewed each individual detail, and it had all been so worth it.

"Your turn, *husband*," I said, giving him my best coy smile, reaching out to unbutton his vest. It was a crime that I was practically naked while he was fully clothed, only his jacket discarded.

I wanted to run my fingers over his abdomen, trace each rib of his abs with my tongue. Tonight, I wanted to do it all, because I'd never gotten the chance to before.

Once we'd stripped him down to his briefs, a flurry of hands and fabric, I ran my hands over his erection, finding him already hard and wanting. Why did that turn me on so much? Knowing how much he wanted me made my heart race even faster, the wetness pooling between my thighs. I went to push my hand inside his waistband and run my fingers up his shaft, but he pushed me away.

"Come here," he murmured, and before I could say anything, he'd guided me to the edge of the bed, plopping me down on the mattress so he could pull out the dozens of bobby pins holding my hair in place. "I'm going to take care of this first."

Oh. Because he knew my hair would be a giant mess if we didn't take it all down now.

I couldn't help but think about the other day on the ski trip, when he'd brushed out my damp hair just because he wanted to. Not because I'd asked him to. He ran his fingers through my curls, separating the strands.

When he'd finished, I plopped against the giant king-sized mattress, throwing my arms out as if I could make a snow-angel on the bed. "Mmm," I said, settling myself in. "That's better."

Daniel joined me on the bed, climbing over top of me and letting his body weight drape over mine.

"Darling... You're so beautiful, all spread out for me." He kissed my neck, my collarbone, down towards my breasts.

"Just for you," I agreed, trying to hold back a moan as he sucked at my skin.

"Fuck, I like that," he groaned. "I feel so possessive, but I liked thinking that I'm the only one who gets to touch you. Taste you. That no one else has explored every inch of your body except for me."

There was some part of me that liked how possessive he felt, too. Because I wanted to *just* be his. I liked when he called me darling, especially in private. It made me feel like, maybe it might have started off as something fake, but now it felt like *more*.

"More," I panted as his lips connected with my nipple, sucking lightly as his tongue ran over the hardened peak.

I wanted this to be real between us. Wanted the ring that was on my finger to mean more than just a pact we'd made back in college. Than us choosing to be together because we were the last two singles in our friend group.

I whined, practically writhing underneath him. I didn't know what I needed, but I knew I needed *more*.

He chuckled, transferring his attention to my other breast, those maddening circles he was drawing with his tongue, and when I whimpered, he pulled away. "What does my girl want? My fingers or my tongue?"

I moaned in response. How could I possibly choose? "Both," I pleaded. "Anything. *Everything*."

Daniel's eyes were dark as he inched down the bed, kissing down my stomach before reaching my little white lace panties. Every bit the bride. I wouldn't admit that they'd been an impulse purchase or that I'd felt insecure about my everyday underwear. Because I wasn't analyzing how I wanted to look good for him.

How I wanted him to see me like this: beautiful, sexy, desirable.

Reaching down, he hooked his finger around the fabric, dragging it down my legs intimately, his eyes only leaving mine as he kissed the inside of my thigh, my knee, my ankle. Leaving me so desperately writhing for him as I was bare underneath him.

"What do you want?"

"Touch me," I whispered.

"Words, Charlotte."

Oh, God. I groaned. Were we really doing this? I squeezed my eyes shut. "I want you to fuck me with your tongue. *Please*."

His breath ghosted over my slit, and I practically jumped out of my skin from the sensation when his tongue darted out to taste me.

But he didn't give me what he knew I wanted. *Bastard.* "Is this what you want, hmm? For me to taste your sweet cunt with my tongue? Tongue fuck you till you're screaming my name, because you're my wife?"

"*Yes,*" I cried out when he plunged inside of me. "*Yes. Please.*"

I'd never been the sort to beg for anything, but I thought that perhaps now, for this man... I'd do anything he asked of me.

He gave me a filthy smirk before ducking back down, spreading my legs apart with his hands and burying his head in between my thighs. Daniel's mouth... *Oh god.* I'd been missing out on this for too long.

Taking his sweet time feasting on me, he licked and sucked like a man *starved*. I couldn't hold in my moans when he switched his attention to my clit, thrusting two fingers inside of me and making me call out his name. Never one to go back on his word, he kept up his pace until I was panting, practically coming out of my skin as I dug my fingers into his hair, pulling him into me even deeper, every languid lick or circle of his tongue against me sending sparks through my body.

"I'm so close, Daniel, don't stop—" I cried, rocking my hips against his mouth. He crooked his fingers inside of me, brushing against that spot, and I lost it, the pressure between my clit and inside of me too much.

I came as he kept working me with his fingers, my back arching off the bed as I tugged on his hair. It was probably to the point of pain, but I was too blind to my orgasm to think properly.

"Fuck," he groaned, popping his fingers into his mouth, licking me off of him as he watched me. "You're the sweetest thing I've ever tasted."

"That was..." *Wow.*

I sat up, scrambling to push down his boxers and get my mouth on him in return. But he just shook his head.

"What? You don't want me to return the favor?"

"Fuck. No. But... tonight's about you. I want to worship you."

I couldn't exactly argue with that. As much as I wanted to taste him, I was also eager to get him inside of me.

"This," I said, pushing against the fabric even as he sat on the bed. "Off. Now."

He chuckled, complying with my request, letting his cock spring free.

I didn't care if this was still *just sex*, because I was going to enjoy every moment. Especially all the orgasms he was willing to give me.

Daniel's boxers joined our other discarded garments on the floor, and then he was over top of me, kissing me with a new fervor as we coiled our bodies and tongues together.

Finding his cock, I swiped a finger over the liquid that had oozed out, guiding him towards me.

He groaned as I notched the tip of him at my entrance. "Wait. Charlotte."

I stilled, my eyes growing wide. Did he—he wanted this just as badly as I did, didn't he? I hadn't read this all wrong when I attacked him earlier, had I?

"Are you still okay with no condoms?" Daniel's eyebrows furrowed, focusing intently on me. Making sure I was okay.

Oh.

Oh.

We'd talked about it before, and after the shower on the ski trip, but this... I shook my head.

"I don't... I don't want anything between us."

Not after I'd experienced him bare before. And I'd planned to go off birth control after the wedding, anyway.

My cheeks heated. Even though we'd been intimate before, there was something different about *this*. This wasn't our first time, but in some ways, it felt like it. It was the first time we were bearing ourselves to each other as husband and wife. Maybe it was because this time, I knew it was something more. That this wasn't just a one-night-stand, a quick fling.

It was Daniel.

"I'm clean," he said, curling a finger around my hair. "And I haven't been with anyone besides you in years. I meant to mention it before, but..." But time had gotten away from us, because I'd insisted we *practiced*. Something I wanted to get back to right now.

And *years?* I'd have to take the time to analyze that statement later, but right now, I just wanted him inside of me. I was so achingly empty, and I just needed him to fill me up.

To make love to me on our wedding night.

To make me forget that this marriage was fake.

"There's only ever been you," I murmured, kissing his jaw as I slid my hands down to his shoulders. "I want you inside of me. Please."

CHAPTER 20
Daniel

There was nothing as beautiful as the sight of my wife bare underneath me.

If what happened in Paris was a moment of weakness, both of us surrendering to our desires, this was different. And tonight, I planned to thoroughly take my time.

You're everything I've ever wanted, is what I wanted to say. But I didn't. I just sealed my feelings by placing another kiss on her lips, this one deeper, longer. I ran my tongue across her lips, seeking entrance, and when Charlotte moaned into my mouth, I couldn't control myself any longer. *Oh, if only you knew just how strong my feelings were,* I thought as I plunged inside of her, gritting my teeth at how good she felt, wrapped around my dick.

"Goddamn, you feel so good," I groaned, holding my hips still as I waited for her to adjust to my size. It was always a tight fit, given how much bigger I was than her, but I didn't want to hurt her. "Are you alright?"

She nodded, intertwining our fingers together. I leaned down, kissing her and running my tongue against her lips. Letting her body relax, opening up for me even more. "You can move," Charlotte whispered, cupping my jaw with her hand.

Lingering against her lips for a moment, I let myself savor before I complied, rocking my hips against hers.

"Oh, *Fuck*. You're so deep," Charlotte gasped when I pushed inside of her fully.

Her fingers spread over her abdomen as I rocked inside of her, short shallow thrusts that were eliciting those tiny mewls I was coming to love so much.

"That's it," I praised. "Look at you taking all of my cock like a good girl."

"*Daniel,*" my girl moaned.

I thrust into the hilt, but before I could pull out again, Charlotte wrapped her legs around my back, burying me even deeper inside of her wet heat. She surprised me when she flipped us over, leaving me flat on my back as she positioned herself on top of me, hands planted against my chest.

Who was this brazen girl and what had she done with my Charlotte? Because I was fucking *obsessed*. I was all too happy to let her ride me, to watch her take her own pleasure. If she hadn't told me, I never would have guessed she'd never done this before.

Her big gray eyes met mine, that captivating color that always seemed to reflect the world around her, and my heart pounded in my chest.

And, *fuck*—"I'm not going to last very long if you look at me like that, baby."

"Like what?" She fluttered her eyelashes as she rolled her hips, causing me to grunt. "Besides, we have forever for you to show me just how good you can make it for me, right?" She leaned down, kissing the side of my lips.

"We can go all night, and I still won't be able to get enough of you," I practically growled, slamming up into of her.

Charlotte groaned as we found our rhythm, her hips rolling against me, grinding her clit down against my shaft, and I thrust up into her.

She shut her eyes, letting out a moan as I picked her up before sliding her back down onto my cock. She was so light, goddamnit, and all I could do was watch her tits bounce as I fucked her. As she got herself off like this.

Head tilted back, I couldn't look away from the look on her face as she orgasmed, the gorgeous flush that she had from being well-fucked.

It was beautiful.

She was the most beautiful thing I'd ever seen. Had been, ever since I'd first walked into that dorm freshman year. Ever since she'd become my sister's friend. My best friend.

"Charlotte," I grunted, quivering as her body clenched around me, milking me. "I'm gonna—" My balls tightened, and I could feel myself getting close. Every motion brought me even closer to losing it.

"Inside me," she whispered. "Come inside of me, Daniel."

Fuck. There was something about this girl commanding me that made me want to obey her every whim. Spilling inside of her, I painted her insides with my cum, all too satisfied when our combined releases dripped out of her and down my length. There was no taking my eyes off of it, even as she remained seated with me inside of her.

"That was hot," I said, pulling my girl down on top of me so I could hold her, not pulling out even as I softened inside of her.

"Told you I wasn't some virgin prone to maidenly blushing," she muttered, and I laughed, tracing my fingers over her cheeks.

"No, but I love it when you blush for me." I tucked a blonde curl behind her hair, wanting to run my fingers through it once again. She'd had it up earlier, and yet she still looked so beautiful, even now, with slightly tousled sex hair.

"Oh." Her eyes looked up, meeting mine.

Running my fingers down her back, I was just enjoying the moment, holding her against my body.

"I didn't realize it would be so good," she murmured, almost quiet enough that if I hadn't been entangled with her, I wasn't sure I would have heard it. "Sex. Is it… always like that for you?"

I shook my head. "I don't know what your books say," I said, flicking her nose. "But it's not. This thing between us? It's never been like that for me before."

Not that I'd ever been prone to that many hook-ups, anyway. Perks of being a nerdy engineer. Sure, I'd lost my virginity in high school, and I hadn't exactly abstained from sex in college, but it was never like that for me. I'd never lost my mind wanting someone so much before. Had the desire to bury myself in their body, repeatedly, because I was lost without it.

"Good," she said, eliciting a laugh from me. "I don't like thinking about you with someone else."

I liked that my girl was possessive over me. Because I was over her too. I'd gotten almost all of her firsts, and I'd be taking all of her lasts, as well. Running my nose against her cheek, before burying it in her hair and smelling her flowery shampoo, I confessed the same. "I don't like thinking about you with anyone, either. Especially none of those guys who wouldn't have treated you right. Not like I wanted to. Not like I can."

I tilted her chin up so I could place a gentle kiss on her lips.

Charlotte yawned. "I should take my makeup off before we fall asleep." She'd done some pretty pink shimmer and glitter for her bridal look, and as pretty as it was, I knew she was right. I'd heard Angelina complain about what happened when she left hers on overnight. I didn't think my girl would like that, either.

But I was going to take care of her, and more than just helping her get her makeup off. Pulling out of her, I already felt the loss of her warmth, surprised at how much I liked that connection.

The fact that even after we'd both come, she hadn't been in any rush to separate from me. To move away. How far we'd come since August.

"Come on," I said, heaving her up into my arms, carrying my wife bridal style towards the bathroom.

"What are we doing?" she muttered sleepily, nuzzling her head into my chest.

I chuckled. "I'm cleaning you up."

"Oh." She hummed. "I like the sound of that."

So did I. We'd never had a night like this before. I'd never gotten to experience caring for her so intimately. Even after she'd hurt herself in the snow, it hadn't just been about us. That had been making sure she was okay, and then Even though I wouldn't admit it out loud, I liked it. A lot.

But I didn't want to scare her with my feelings. I knew how I felt about her, but I needed to give her time to feel the same way back.

My wife.

I put her down so she could use the bathroom as I filled up the giant tub, thankful that I'd had the foresight to make this reservation. Sure, we could have spent our first night as husband and wife at my house, or my dad's, but this was better. Less... cold. More real.

Settling her down in the tub, I stepped in behind her, nestling her much smaller body between my thighs, the two of us comfortably fitting, thankfully, in this giant tub. The warm water was soothing, almost lulling her to sleep, a fact I only knew because her head was resting against my pecs. Her eyes fluttered shut.

Letting her relax in the warm water, I tried not to let her little sighs of contemned

I shifted her so my already-hardening cock wouldn't dig into her back, but she blinked her eyes open.

"Daniel?"

"How are you feeling?" I asked, kissing her neck.

"Good," she confirmed, wiggling back further against me. I wanted to warn her to stop, what exactly what was going to happen if she continued down that train, but fuck me—I was so gone for her that I didn't. "I think I'm going to be sore tomorrow," she moaned. "So you're going to have to take care of me."

"*Fuck*, darling." This girl. She knew what she was doing.

"I'm not going to be gentle this time," I said, sliding my tongue against her lips as she twisted around to wrap her arms around my neck.

"Take me back to bed, husband," she whispered, and who was I not to comply?

"Your wish is my command, wife."

And then I carried her back to the bed, and after I gave her two more orgasms, first with my fingers, and then draped over the bed as I plowed into her from behind, we were finally cuddled up and on the verge of sleep. Her thigh between mine, a mess of tangled limbs as I fell asleep holding my dream girl.

And all I could think was there wasn't a single way I would have rather spent this night.

∽

WE'D WOKEN up two more times in the middle of the night, seeking out each other's bodies for pleasure, and by the time both of us roused from the bed in the morning, it was almost ten.

"Good morning," Charlotte said, rubbing her eyes as she stretched her arms, her pebbled nipples peeking through the sheet.

"Morning." And because I could, I bent down to kiss her. Just a simple kiss on the lips.

"What's on the agenda for the day, husband?"

God, I liked that.

"Well, wife, I was thinking we could hide away and see no one, and do absolutely nothing."

"Mmm. That sounds nice."

Besides, after we checked out of our room, we'd be home for Christmas, and since most of us didn't have family in town, we were celebrating with a gift exchange with all our friends. And then we'd go back to pretending.

It was weird that somehow this, just the two of us, felt more real than when we were pretending for our friends' sake.

"Want to order breakfast?" I held up the room service menu I'd thankfully requested the day before.

And I had already ordered champagne for tonight. Might as well celebrate getting married while we could, right?

"Pancakes?" Her eyes lit up as she looked at all the options. Luckily, I had splurged on an extravagant hotel, and their room service menu wasn't too shabby.

I chuckled. "Breakfast of champions. Let's do it."

She took the menu from my hands. "Better get me a ham and cheese omelet and some breakfast potatoes, too. Maybe a side of bacon."

"Work up an appetite there, baby?"

Charlotte looked bashful, as if I hadn't just been inside her yesterday, the blood rushing to her cheeks. "Maybe." Her posture straightened, and she turned to face me fully. "But it's okay, because you can help me work it off later." She winked.

I choked. Who was this girl, and where was my blushing bride? Except, I liked it.

"Oh, I fully intend to." I gave a playful wiggle of my eyebrows before heading to the phone to place our order. Knowing we'd eat all of it, I added fruit as well as some additional items for me.

I'd go for an extra run tomorrow to make up for all the cake from yesterday as well. Not that I minded. I enjoyed staying fit, but that second slice of cake wouldn't hurt. Neither had the third.

After making sure that Char's pancakes were gluten-free, I hopped in the shower, knowing full well that if we took one together, we'd spend too much time doing things that would just get us dirty all over again.

When I got out, I pulled on a pair of navy sweatpants, letting them hang loose on my hips, and with a towel slung around my shoulders, a knock sounded at the door.

"Oh, perfect," Charlotte groaned. "Food. I'm starving." She'd pulled on a satin robe, tied at the waist with a sash, and her blonde locks were tumbling out of the messy bun she'd pulled her hair into last night after we'd gotten out of the bath.

Carrying over the tray of food onto the bed, I sat beside her on top of the covers.

I popped a piece of bacon into my mouth before turning to look at her, finding her staring at my bare chest.

"Now feed me, husband," she said, batting her eyelashes as I swallowed roughly.

Picking up a strawberry, I brought it to her lips, mesmerized as I watched her bite into it, the juices spilling all over my fingers, but I didn't care.

But then my brain stuttered to a halt as she sucked my finger into her mouth, the strawberry forgotten as she licked up the juices. *Fuck me.* I was losing my mind. She wasn't even trying to affect me, and she was.

That was always the case with us, wasn't it?

I'd been losing my mind over her since she'd sat on my dorm bed, eating marshmallows by the bag.

"Charlotte." I muttered.

"Hm?" She looked up at me, my thumb perched precariously between her teeth, and finally let go with a pop. I swiped my thumb over her bottom lip before bending down to take her lips with mine. Sweeping my tongue in her mouth, I groaned at the lingering taste of the strawberry.

"You always taste so fucking sweet," I groaned.

She blushed, pulling away from me and moving back to the tray, digging into her pancakes without looking at me again.

But fuck, I couldn't take my eyes off of her.

What was I going to do to make this our everyday reality? I needed her by my side every night. Needed her to not pull away.

So I was going to do everything in my power to keep things like they were now.

It would have to be enough.

CHAPTER 21
Charlotte

Looking over at the hallway, I hesitated. After this weekend, should I go back to my room? I hated that I even had to, but this was still fake, wasn't it? We'd agreed on casual sex, but that didn't mean what we did this weekend came with any feelings. Sure, he exhausted my body until I fell asleep each night, but...

Was it okay for me to admit to myself that I liked sharing his bed?

As if noticing my dismay, Daniel stopped, pausing in his tracks, and came back over to where I stood at the top of the stairs.

"You're sleeping in here from now on." Daniel wrapped his hand around my wrist, tugging me along—making my decision for me. "With me."

I was okay with that. This marriage might have been all because of our pact, but I *liked* not sleeping alone. And I wanted a repeat of this weekend. I didn't want that to stop. Even if it wasn't real.

"Okay," I agreed.

"No more guest room?"

"No more guest room."

He dropped his forehead against mine. "Good."

I simply hummed in response, dropping my bags on the floor. Everything else was in the guest room—my room—but I had no desire to unpack right now. Instead, I flopped on his bed, burying my nose in the pillow to inhale his scent, before watching him flitter around the room, putting his stuff away.

"I can't believe tomorrow is Christmas," I said, stretching out my arms. "It feels like it was just summer."

"Mmm," he said, absentmindedly agreeing with me as he shoved his dirty clothes into the hamper.

Where had this year gone? He might not have been thinking about it, but I was. Angelina and Benjamin's wedding, my birthday, Noelle and Matthew's engagement... Our wedding. It had all gone by so fast.

It would be the new year soon, and once school was back in session, I'd be back at the dance studio teaching classes five days a week. Even if I missed the kids, I would miss all this time I got to spend just the two of us even more. And Daniel's birthday was right around the corner. Sure, I'd planned stuff for him in the past, but this year, we'd be celebrating as husband and wife. So that was something I needed time to work out in my head.

"You know, I didn't think we were going to make it this far with no one suspecting something," I muttered, still sprawled out on his dark gray comforter. I'd been in his room before, but I couldn't help but notice it was pretty devoid of a lot of personal touches. Something I supposed I'd fix after I moved all of my stuff in here.

"Guess we're pretty good at this relationship stuff, huh?" Daniel laughed.

"Yeah. Guess our friends wanted us to be together too much to question it." They hadn't even batted an eye when we'd said we were getting married so quickly. Maybe that should have scared me, but it... didn't.

"Makes you wonder why we didn't do this before," I said with a small laugh.

Why hadn't we? Why hadn't he made a move in college? Maybe I hadn't seen him like that until this past year, but...

Really, it was too bad it was fake. Even though I felt like I was forgetting it *was* fake half the time. Which I couldn't do. If I let myself forget that this wasn't real, that I was just a backup, the last resort... if this fell apart, if he fell in love with someone else? I didn't know who I would be without him anymore. Two months of us faking it, and it already felt like something different from when we started.

And I didn't want to have my heart broken.

Losing him would destroy me.

~

"CHARLOTTE."

"Mmm?" When had I closed my eyes? I popped them open to find Daniel leaning over me, his lips inches from my face. If I leaned up, we'd be kissing.

"I'm going to go for a run," he said, voice rough in a way I couldn't quite identify. "Do you want to join me?"

"Oh." I thought about the numerous calories I'd consumed over the last few days, even with the copious amounts of *physical activity* we'd engaged in. And then about the dance studio, the grueling hours I put into staying in shape for teaching dance. "Yeah. Let's do it." I rubbed my finger over my wedding ring, admiring the band on his finger that proved we were irrevocably tied. "Let me go get changed," I said, hopping off the bed.

Lacing up my pink tennis shoes, I met Daniel by the front door before pulling on my favorite raincoat and slipped my phone in one of the zippered pockets. It was damp and chilly outside, thanks to the Portland winter, but that was nothing a raincoat and a good run couldn't fix.

I couldn't remember the last time Daniel and I had gone for a run together, even after I moved in to his house. Maybe that was a mistake I should have fixed sooner. Back in college, that had been one of our very first things we'd bonded over. He'd shown me all the best routes, the best trails nearby, and we'd been able to talk for hours about everything. Life. TV shows. Books. Sometimes we'd gone in silence, just the sound of our feet hitting the pavement or splashing in puddles on a rainy day.

But we'd always been together. It was a friendship borne not of necessity, but because we genuinely enjoyed spending time together. And that had always been enough for me, hadn't it? He'd been my best friend, and even if I knew he'd never look at me like that... Well, things were different now.

Shoving my bluetooth earphones in my other pocket, we took off at a leisurely pace up the hill.

Normally when I ran alone, I listened to music, but it felt weird to do that when we were *together*.

Sure, I knew I liked to listen to workout playlists when they ran, but I normally either listened to Disney music—nothing got me pumped up like *Go the Distance* from Hercules—or my Taylor Swift playlist. No matter what anyone said about my girl, her music had got me through everything. Even if I hadn't gotten my heart broken, I could belt out one of her breakup songs like no one's business.

"So..." I said, finally breaking the silence a few minutes into our run. He was matching me, stride for stride, which I knew wasn't easy since I was way shorter than him. Even if I had fairly long legs for my height, he always towered over me, and his pace was much longer than mine.

Except he seemed content to stay just like this, right by my side. He always had, and maybe that was why we worked. Because no matter what happened, we always had each other. As best friends, now husband and wife, and maybe... something more. *Lovers?*

The thought had me wrinkling my nose at the word. Was that what we were? No. Even if we were going to try to have a baby now that we were married, even if we were sleeping together... We weren't in love.

"So." He raised an eyebrow. "What's going through that pretty little head of yours?"

"Why do you think there's anything?"

"Charlotte." He stopped moving, turning his body fully to look at me. "There always is."

"Everything's different," I said instead of an acknowledgment of his statement. My eyebrows furrowed. "Us. This. I'm just..."

Overwhelmed. Happy, but still... confused. What was this thing between us? Did I want there to be more?

"We're married." Daniel ran his finger over my ring. "Of course everything is going to be different," he chuckled. "Because now I have an excuse to kiss you any time I want."

"Oh." I busied myself by tugging my fingers into the sleeves of my fleece-lined jacket. "And that's... new? For you?"

It was for me. This inability to stay away from him. To not want to touch him. Wasn't it? I'd never felt this magnetic attraction to anyone before, not until him. Not until he taught me all the ways my body could want him. How it felt when he touched me. If he was like a drug, I wasn't sure I ever wanted him out of my system.

"Charlotte," he murmured. "I've always wanted to kiss you."

"You..." I blinked. *What?*

But this man, my stubborn, infuriatingly handsome husband, said nothing else. He leaned down to retie his shoe, even though I knew he'd double knotted them before we left. He always did.

"How about we take it one day at a time?"

I couldn't shake off what he said earlier. *Always*? He'd always wanted to kiss me?

When had always begun? Before or after I'd asked him to take my first kiss in college? Before or after he'd asked me to marry him in a marriage pact?

My brain was close to overloading, but he just took my hand in his. Squeezed it, the way he always did. Grounding me. Preventing me from getting lost in the labyrinth of thoughts I was about to enter.

So, one day at a time? I nodded. "Okay." I could do that.

When he stood up, I expected him to resume his pace, but he cupped my jaw. So heartbreakingly intimate for a fake relationship, wasn't it? And there was no one around. No, *just sex* to hide behind. No friends we were trying to fool.

"I promise, I'm going to make these the best days of your life," he said, and I tipped up my face, expecting him to kiss me.

My eyes fluttered shut, but he just kissed my forehead, leaving me speechless as he turned around and resumed our path. I settled back in behind him, wondering if this was too good to be true.

Would this last, or would it all just come crashing down around me?

Would I let him break my heart?

Because I was worrying he already had it, and I was pretty sure I'd give him anything he wanted, if only to make him happy.

∽

THE LIGHT STREAMED in through the windows, illuminating Daniel's bedroom. Our bedroom now, I supposed.

I hadn't shared a room since college with Noelle. While she was the best friend and roommate I ever could have asked for, somehow I knew that this experience would be a lot different.

Except... when I woke up that Christmas morning, the bed next to me was already cold.

My body protested as I forced myself to get out of bed. I trudged to the bathroom, where I quickly brushed my teeth and fixed my hair. After I pulled on my soft robe, I made my way down the stairs, finding Daniel sitting on the couch, staring out the fogged up windows into the backyard.

"Hi." I wrapped my arms tighter around myself as I sat on the cushion on the opposite end of him. *"Brrr.* It's cold." I was always freezing, a condition not made better by living in the Pacific Northwest, but I loved it up here. How it was always green and beautiful, even if the sky was gray from October to March.

"Good morning," he said, sipping on a cup of coffee. "You want some?" He tilted his head to the counter.

I shook my head. I wasn't a huge coffee girl, much preferring hot chocolate to the bitter taste of coffee, but a hot drink did sound nice... "Maybe I'll just go make a hot chocolate."

"Stay here. I'll make you one." He stood up and draped the blanket from the back of the couch over my lap before going to the kitchen.

While Daniel was making me a coffee, I couldn't help but notice how quiet the house was. How empty it felt. And then my heart raced, thinking about the present I had waiting for him. I was pretty sure he was going to be shocked, and I couldn't wait to surprise him.

I was lost in thought until Daniel appeared with my favorite mug—Taylor Swift's albums as book spines—the chocolate and coffee scent wafting out of it.

"What is this?" I raised an eyebrow. It certainly wasn't the black coffee with a splash of milk he was drinking.

"It's a mocha. Try it."

I sipped it, and *damn*. I couldn't hold back my soft moan. "That's good."

He smiled. "I know you don't really like coffee. Even when I leave a pot out in the mornings, you never drink it." Grimacing, I turned to him to apologize, but he shook his head. "But I thought you might like it like this."

"I do." Which surprised me, because I'd never grown to like the taste of coffee. The girls knew that, and normally when they got me something, it was extra sweet. But this was perfect. And he'd done it all without me even having to ask. "What'd you put in it?"

"Milk, caramel, and half a container of chocolate." The corner of Daniel's lips curled up into a smirk. "Not really, but it's better this way, right?"

I took another sip, enjoying the sweet combination of chocolate and caramel as it danced on my tongue. "Yes. It's so much better."

Daniel sat back down on the couch, closer to me this time, moving my legs on top of his lap before spreading the blanket back out over them.

"Merry Christmas," I whispered, staring at the tree we'd put up after Thanksgiving. There were a few boxes wrapped underneath, gifts for our friends, even though my actual surprise wasn't in the living room at all.

After the run yesterday, I showered quickly and went to do some errands, hiding Daniel's present somewhere where I hoped he wouldn't find it.

"Merry Christmas." His hand squeezed my ankle lightly. "After presents, I thought I'd make us French toast and we could watch a Christmas movie and sit on the couch."

"Hallmark?" There'd be an all-day marathon, and after the last two days, nothing sounded better than lazing on the couch and doing nothing.

"Of course." He kissed my forehead.

"Sounds like the perfect day, then." I stretched out my legs, settling onto him further, but it didn't phase him. Daniel just let his hand rest against my upper thigh, drawing circles on the fabric as we sat enjoying the quiet, sipping our drinks.

One day at a time.

Maybe I could get used to this.

CHAPTER 22
Daniel

There was something about this display of domesticity that filled all the gaps in my chest. When I was younger, Angelina and I used to have Christmas mornings just like this with our parents. We'd open presents on Christmas Eve from our family, and in the morning after opening whatever Santa brought us, we'd drink hot chocolate and eat breakfast—waffles, french toast, chocolate chip pancakes—whatever my mom made that year. And I'd always loved when we turned on *Rudolph* or *The Santa Clause*. I liked to tease Angelina that she looked like the little elf girl who made Santa hot chocolate when she was younger, too, because I'd been a little shit back then.

Thankfully, we were still best friends. If she hadn't gone to the same college as me, if we hadn't been so close all our lives... I never would have met Charlotte. And I definitely wouldn't be sitting here right now.

She smiled, and it took everything not to lean over and kiss her. But we were still working on that, weren't we? The small displays of affection. Outside the house, when we were playing pretend, that was when I could show my true feelings.

Suddenly, I couldn't think about anything else besides seeing *our* baby bundled in her arms, running my fingers across tiny little chubby cheeks that resembled my wife. Because fuck, I wanted it. I wanted to be a dad, wanted to raise a whole bunch of kids with her. It had always been a dream of mine, but it wasn't something I'd seriously thought about until Charlotte had brought it up on her birthday.

But as for now, things were different. Even if we'd decided that sex was on the table. Even if our conversation from before was playing on a non stop loop in my mind. Was it too early to bring it up? Or was that just my own selfish wish coming through?

"What?" I murmured, pacing over to the fridge to grab a glass of water, which I quickly guzzled down.

"Nothing." Charlotte rested her chin on the back of the couch as she tracked my movements. Her lips tilted up into a small, soft smile as she watched me, and my heart sped up in my chest from the casual moment.

I wasn't wearing something weird, right? I looked down at my clothes. I'd pulled on a long-sleeved t-shirt and sweats this morning, but nothing out of the usual. Was there something on my face? No use in trying to solve that mystery right now, though.

I had my girl to surprise.

"Mmm. Ready for your gift?"

Abandoning my glass on the island, I pulled out the card from where I'd stashed it behind our tree and walked back to her.

"What is this?" Charlotte asked, looking at the envelope I'd placed in her hands.

"Open it," I murmured, settling back down on the couch next to her. "I know we didn't discuss if we were doing presents, but..."

I hadn't been able to help myself. And we usually got something for each other, anyway. Even if those gifts had been small and inconsequential versus this. Before, even something as small as buying her the perfume she loved so much seemed like *too much*. This year, my ring was on her finger, and I didn't care if she thought the gesture was too big. All I wanted to do was see her smile. Make her happy.

What I'd bought was non-refundable, anyway.

Charlotte tore into the top of the card gently, like she was afraid to rip the envelope.

My graceful girl.

I watched as her eyes scanned the card, reading the inside before pulling out the contents. She blinked, her eyes filling with tears.

"You got me Taylor Swift tickets? How'd you even get these?"

"I have my ways," I said with a smirk.

She didn't need to know how long I'd sat there, in the queue, trying to get her VIP tickets and a chance to see her favorite artist perform live. I'd almost cursed out the damn website so many times.

Charlotte threw her arms around me, hugging me tight. "Thank you. Thank you. Oh my god, I'm so excited."

It had been worth it. For this.

I wrapped my arms around her, my hands cradling the small of her back. "Merry Christmas, baby." I didn't know why *baby* kept slipping out, but I couldn't help it. I kissed the top of her head as she held on to me.

Pulling away, she cleared her throat. "I actually have something for you, too."

I raised an eyebrow, looking around. "You do?"

Everything stashed under the tree we'd put there together. Gifts for our friends, things we'd wrapped together. I knew what every present was, and I was trying to figure out where she'd stashed an extra one when she stood up from the couch, letting her blanket fall behind.

Charlotte nodded. "Uh-huh. You stay here, though. I'll be back." She eyed me nervously, and then headed upstairs.

though that was something I planned to remedy soon, because I wanted all of her stuff in mine, her clothes hanging next to mine in the closet, her bathroom stuff on our bathroom counter... But what had she stashed in there?

"Close your eyes!" She shouted, and I obeyed her, if only because, well, I was curious what her surprise was. I liked that we'd both done something without discussing it beforehand. We might have been just settling into this fake marriage, but we were already in sync.

My wife. Every day the sound of that got better, and it had only been a few days since we'd tied the knot. A few very sweaty days of *just sex*. But even if the marriage was fake, even if we were only indulging in each other's bodies, that was real.

A weight dropped into my lap, and a cold, wet thing pressed into my hand.

"You can open your eyes," Charlotte whispered from in front of me, as a tongue licked up my face.

My hands reached out to grab the thing—the *puppy*—as I opened my eyes. It had been a nose that pressed into my palm.

"Surprise," she said, her eyes glowing with happiness.

"A dog?" I blinked. "You got us a dog?"

She scratched the top of the German Shepherd puppy's head as it nuzzled into my hand. "I got you a dog, but yeah. He's all yours." Charlotte beamed. "Merry Christmas, Daniel."

The puppy barked, demanding my attention on him instead of focusing on Charlotte's face.

"Did you name him?"

"No." She shook her head. "I left that for you." Settling onto the couch next to me, she sat on her knees as I ran my fingers over his still floppy ears.

"Oh." I studied his little brown face, the black wet nose that had pressed into my hand. His soft pink tongue that was all too happy to lick me.

"He's so cute, right?" Charlotte murmured next to me. "When I went to pick one out, he came right over to me and curled up in my lap." She ran her hand over the puppy's snout before resting it on my thigh. "It was love at first sight. I got to pick him up yesterday, and I really thought I was going to spoil the surprise last night."

Love at first sight?

"Yeah." I looked at her and smiled, thinking of the first time I saw her. "It was."

"What do you think, boy?" I asked our dog—because no matter what she insisted, he was *ours*—"What should we name you?"

"You know, I did have an idea, but it might be stupid..." Charlotte started, her eyes connecting with mine. "But if you have something better, you can go with that." A faint pink blush danced over her flawless cheeks. Even when she had no makeup on in the mornings, just like this, she was absolutely beautiful. Stunning beyond compare.

"Pretty sure that's impossible, darling." Because nothing she said was stupid. Most of it was just plain adorable.

"Brownie." She smiled shyly. "I've always thought food names for dogs were so cute. Marshmallow, Cookie, Oreo... At one point, I told my mom we should get a whole brood of dogs and name them all after desserts."

No surprise that it didn't happen, but... It fit. I looked at the puppy, and then back to her. "I like it, actually. What do you think, Brownie?" The puppy tilted his head at me before licking my hand again. And then he barked excitedly. "I think he likes it too. Then it's settled. Brownie."

Charlotte leaned her head on my shoulder as we watched our puppy curl up in my lap, his head resting on my leg.

"Thank you," I said, kissing the top of her head. "This was the best gift ever."

"I know you've always talked about getting a dog. And now that we're, you know..."

"Married?"

She nodded, like it was still weird for her to say. "It felt like the right time. To start our family."

My mouth went dry, thinking of other ways we planned to start a family.

Was this crazy? Having a fake marriage—one of convenience, because of a marriage pact in college—and still wanting to have it all? I didn't know, but I knew one thing: there was no way I was letting her go.

∼

"Oh," Charlotte said, sounding disappointed as we passed it. "It sold."

After a lazy day of Hallmark movies and cuddling with our new pup on the couch, we loaded Brownie and his crate up to drive to Benjamin and Angelina's house for Christmas dinner.

Of course, as we'd driven onto their street, the plot of land that always caught my eye popped up again.

Had she always looked at it too? I couldn't think of a better place to live than on the same street as my sister, especially once we had families of our own. I knew that most people would think it was crazy, but Benjamin had been trying to talk the rest of us guys into it ever since they'd moved here. It was a neighborhood full of enormous houses with big lots, which you rarely saw in new construction, let alone in the Portland area, but it was in a wealthy area.

One that luckily, all of us could afford. Sure, Benjamin might have been making the big bucks as a CFO, and Hunter was a Doctor, but as an engineer, I had a decently large salary as well, and I'd been squirreling away most of it for years.

"There's other lots," I said, reaching out and squeezing her thigh as I drove.

"I know. But that one was..."

I knew exactly what she meant. It called to me too. Which solidified the plan I had in mind. The plan she didn't even know I'd put into action yet.

"Perfect?" Letting my hand rest on her thigh, I guided my car into the driveway behind Matthew and Noelle's truck. "It's just an empty lot, darling."

"But it had so much room in the backyard for the..." Her voice grew quiet, trailing off.

"The kids?" I put the car in park and turned to look at her.

She avoided my gaze, playing with her fingers in her lap, picking at the nail polish that was still on there from the wedding. "Well... Eventually. You want more than one, right?"

I nodded. Charlotte had no idea how much I wanted all of it with her. "I've always liked the idea of having a big family. However many you want." Two, three, four—I couldn't help but smile, thinking about us raising them together. There was no one I'd rather start a family with than her. My best friend—my wife.

She dipped her head. "We can talk about it later, anyway."

Showtime. I collected Brownie's crate, thankful the pup had slept for most of the drive. It was probably a bit nuts to bring him over to meet this many people on our first day, but—this was our family. Even Matthew and Noelle, not related to us by blood or marriage, were the people we'd chosen. The family we'd chosen.

Snowball, the dog, was wearing a Santa hat with *Santa Paws* embroidered on the rim. I couldn't believe how well behaved Matthew's dog was that she was just sitting there, not even attempting to eat the pom-pom.

"And who's this cutie?" Noelle said, kneeling on the floor in front of our puppy as he barked in excitement. Something we'd work on, but for now, he was just an eight week-old puppy. And we wanted him to get socialized.

"Everyone," Charlotte said with a smile, as the entire gang looked over at us, Charlotte's wedding ring catching the light. "This is Brownie."

I pulled her to my side as Noelle scratched in between his ears. "Charlotte got him for us for Christmas."

"For *you*," she whispered.

"Same difference." I flicked her nose.

"Aww, look at him," Angelina said, crouching down next to

Noelle. Brownie tried to jump on her to lick her face, and she sternly told him *no*. "Anywhere but the face," she playfully scolded before peppering his sweet little face with kisses.

I was smitten. I'd always wanted a dog, and the idea of a protector dog that Charlotte would have by her side while she was home alone was just the icing on top of the cake. We'd spent all afternoon after I'd made us french toast cuddled up with Brownie on the couch, or playing with him on the floor. As soon as I'd gotten him leash trained, I'd train him to run by my side every morning too.

Gabbi was scratching the top of Selina's head as Brownie eagerly sniffed the house. "I wish we could have brought Toothless, too."

Bruce and Selina, the kittens Angelina had practically begged Benjamin to get (though he'd caved easily in the end), were happily perched up high on their cat tree, wearing matching pink and blue collars, eating up all the attention.

Hunter chuckled. "I think she's perfectly happy staying at home with her brand new toy and taking a nice long catnap." He ran his hand over his girlfriend's back.

"I know, I know." Gabbi bit her lip. "I just like this. Everyone bringing their pets along."

Matthew strolled in from the kitchen. "Everything's all prepped and ready to go. Ham is cooking in the oven."

"Another fantastic Matthew Harper meal," I said with a smile, clapping my friend on the shoulder.

"You know it."

"Need any help?"

"Nah." He looked at our girls—my wife and his fiancée, still fawning over our puppy—and smiled. "I got it. You just enjoy."

I followed him back into the kitchen, anyway.

"Thanks, man."

"I'm happy for you two. You know, we weren't sure sometimes if you two were going to figure it out, but I'm glad you did."

"Me too." We were *still* figuring it out, in fact, but that wasn't important. "It's nice to not feel like I'm stuck in the friend zone anymore," I said, speaking truthfully. I'd spent too long being content being her best friend, while being in love with her from a distance: always by her side, but never the way I wanted.

And now, everything was different.

Hunter plopped on a barstool, beer bottle in hand. "Ah, friendship. What a beautiful thing." He chuckled. "I still remember when Gabbi tried to insist we were *just* friends. As if she couldn't see that I was fucking crazy for her."

I resisted a snort, because I wasn't sure Charlotte could see that I had feelings for her either. Somehow, I didn't know how she didn't see how much I loved her. How none of this was fake for me. How playing pretend came as second nature to me.

Tonight, Charlotte had pulled a pink velvet dress out of her closet—because what other color would she wear—paring it with a pair of snowflake earrings and white heeled booties. I'd watched her tie her hair back into a curled ponytail with a ribbon before she swiped on some makeup. She looked beautiful with and without it, but I liked the way she'd always brighten up with some sparkles on her face.

Plus, I would never complain, because I'd wordlessly leaned against the doorframe the entire time she'd been getting ready. It had only taken me a minute to run a comb through my hair, pushing back the hair that I'd let grow a little longer on top, and putting on a dark gray button up and slacks had taken even less time.

Now, it was as apparent as ever that she fucking sparkled, lighting up every room that she was in. Her cheeks were pink—a combination of blush and the buzz from the alcohol she was drinking—as her face lit up with happiness. I'd happily orbit around her, forever living in her shadow, just so I could watch her shine.

"Daniel?" Hunter called, pulling me from my trance.

I'd been staring at her across the room, zoned out, for far too long. "Hm?"

But he just shook his head, laughing.

My brother-in-law strolled into the room, straightening the sleeves of his dark blue button-up shirt. Arguably, I thought we'd all have preferred wearing pajamas today, but the girls insisted we dress up a little. Even in the depths of winter, we'd all pulled it off nicely.

"Hey, Benjamin," I said as we clasped hands, the closest thing to a hug any of us normally shared.

"Can't believe you two agreed to come right after you got married," he said, shaking his head. "I was all too happy to spend a few weeks doing nothing with Angelina."

Nothing? I quirked an eyebrow, holding back a smirk. But that thought sobered up pretty quickly at the girls gathered around the fireplace. "You know we wouldn't miss spending Christmas with our family."

"Yeah." Matthew looked around. "I'd say they built a pretty good one."

I couldn't agree more. The girls had brought us together, and there was no way I'd trade any of these moments with all eight of us for anything. "We got lucky."

We all clinked our bottles together in agreement, before Benjamin chimed back in. "What was that about the friend zone that you guys were talking about, anyway?"

Matthew muttered a few words under his breath, and Hunter just rolled his eyes. "Unlike our boy Daniel over here, you wouldn't know what it's like to be in the friend zone."

Benjamin looked over at his wife with a grin. "Only because she wouldn't admit that we were friends, or that she liked me." Angelina raised an eyebrow as she looked over at us, and he gave her a cocky smile. "Turns out neither one of us was very good at lying to ourselves about that."

I laughed.

If only he knew.

CHAPTER 23
Charlotte

Wrapping paper littered the floor as a Christmas playlist pumping through the speakers, switching from Ariana Grande's *Santa Tell Me* to the ever popular Michael Bublé Christmas album. We'd let the boys have some input, and their taste wasn't the worst. With some things.

Although dinner was still cooking in the oven, we had gathered in the living room with hot steaming mugs filled with more liquor than intended, alongside a plate of cookies.

Because of that, I'd laughed harder than I had in weeks.

Taking another sip of my drink, I let the warm liquid settle against my belly, savoring the feeling. "I can't drink another cup of this, or I'm going to be *drunk*," I sang the last word for emphasis. Ah, to be a lightweight.

"Just one more!" Noelle protested, poking at my side. "Besides, you haven't even let us know how the wedding night went."

"Oh, god. We're not talking about this." I said, cheeks pink with embarrassment.

"Come on, you gotta give us *something*," Gabbi elbowed me, wiggling her eyebrows.

"Who was it I recall asking everyone else to stay out of her business?" I said, crossing my arms as I glared at my brunette best friend. We all seemed to share that exact trait: not wanting to talk about our own sex lives, but absolutely loving to get the dirty details about someone else's.

"I second that. I don't want to hear about my *brother*." Angelina wrinkled her nose. "Especially not how he is in the bedroom."

The guys were still in the other room, now playing fetch with Brownie. Or... trying, because our brand-new, eight-week-old puppy wasn't exactly good at bringing the toy back once they'd thrown it.

But our guys were stubborn, so they kept trying anyway.

"Thanks," I said, giving a small smile of appreciation to Angelina. At least she had my back.

"But how was it? Was it everything you thought it would be?" Noelle whispered, and I couldn't help but recall the last few nights in Daniel's arms.

I leaned my head back against the headrest of the couch, staring up at the ceiling. Honestly, I'd always imagined that when I lost my virginity, I'd have told my friends that it happened, *when* it happened. They'd even joked about getting me a cake to celebrate the occasion.

It was never something I was ashamed of, or felt like I needed to remedy. It just was. And because I'd kept it from them, well... Now I just felt guilty. It felt like an eternity had passed since Angelina's wedding. Since I'd said *fuck it* and experienced a night of pure passion with my best friend. A night that had turned into... this. A ring on my finger, a marriage pact fulfilled.

And maybe it was because of all the *just sex* we'd been having, toeing the line between something physical and casual and... whatever was happening between us.

That somehow, this fake marriage agreement was feeling less fake by the day, especially when I was living in his house and spending every second in his presence. I couldn't admit that to any of them. Not while they thought this rouse of ours was *real*, instead of a marriage pact agreed upon out of desperation.

Because I was too chicken to admit that I might have been feeling things for my best friend. Better to stay in this territory of fake marriage and sweaty nights than to admit anything else.

Right?

"It was..." I blushed furiously. I'd always been like this, but it didn't stop me from reading *filthy* smutty romance novels or straddling my best friend slash fake husband the other night. But talking about it... "Honestly, I didn't really know what to expect the first time. Everyone always said their first time was bad. But..." It wasn't. And I'd been lying to myself for months trying to prevent it from happening again, because I knew what would happen if I admitted to myself how right it felt. How incredible we were together. "It was perfect."

The wedding night. Daniel. Every minute since we'd said I do. All of it had been utterly perfect, and completely devastating to my heart.

How was I going to survive without falling madly, hopelessly in love with him?

"That's what it's like when you're with the right guy," Noelle said, giving me a knowing wink. "Sure, romance novels romanticize it, but..." She sighed dreamily as she looked at Matthew. "It's better when you love them, too."

Did I? It was too soon for that, wasn't it? He was my best friend, so of course I *loved* him, but like that? Was I already *in love* with Daniel? I didn't think so.

I still got butterflies whenever he smiled at me, when he called me darling, and when he looked at me with that heated gaze, but... Love?

Honestly, if I wasn't already, it wasn't that far off. He'd been my best friend since 18. I'd loved him as my best friend since then, even if this feeling, this new pounding in my chest, was completely new.

Not that I could admit that. Because they all thought we were married for love. Not some fake marriage pact from college, or that I'd been lonely, and he'd agreed to start a family with me.

"So glad your man's an official member of the Book Boyfriends now," Gabbi said, referencing the guys' group chat they had without us. We'd gotten the idea to rename it one day, and after a grand heist (also known as Gabbi stealing Hunter's phone), it was set in stone. I think they all knew if they changed it, we'd just change it back.

"We're going to have to change it to Book Husbands soon," Angelina snorted, looking directly at our brunette haired friend.

Gabbi held up her hands. "Don't look at me! We're not even engaged yet."

"Key word being *yet*, Gabs. If he's anything like his brother, he'll ask. He's probably already thought about how."

"We've only been dating for four months officially. It's no rush."

I snorted. *What was the rush, Charlotte?*

"What?" Angelina turned to me.

"I was just thinking about how Daniel and I'd been..." *together?* That wasn't the right word. We weren't completely together, anyway. Just married and having sex. "Seeing each other for even less time than that when he asked me."

Yes, because we were two totally sane people who hooked up once, proposed a marriage pact relationship, and then got married within three months. Totally normal.

"You said something happened at my wedding, didn't you?"

Did I? I didn't remember at this point. I'd tried to say as true as possible, but...

Angelina grinned, a devilish smile that told me she was all too proud of herself. "Look at Benjamin and I, bringing everyone together. He'll be way too pleased with himself if we say anything, though. It's bad enough at work with Zo and Nic."

"Are they dating now?" Gabbi asked.

Ang shook her head. "No. I mean, I don't *think* so. It's fun watching them try to play frogger to avoid each other, though. Especially when he's his personal assistant."

I wasn't envious of that situation. The only reason I'd been holding my heart back from my husband was because I was afraid of losing him as my best friend, anyway. But to have to worry about her job, her livelihood? I didn't envy Zofia at that moment.

Noelle sat up with a jolt, pulling out her phone and typing viciously.

"Everything good?" Gabbi raised an eyebrow.

A twinkle shined in our red-headed best friend's eyes. "Book idea. I will one hundred percent forget it if I don't make a note."

We all laughed. "You write it, and we'll read it, Charlotte."

"And draw it," chimed Angelina.

"I love you girls so much."

And honestly, there wasn't a single thing I would have changed about that night. Surrounded by my best friends, and all our guys... Everything felt right. Like this was where we were meant to be. Like we'd been put in those dorm rooms across the hall from each other for a reason, and every single decision we'd made had brought us here, together.

Noelle moving home to Portland and going to grad school, where she met Matthew. Angelina's email feud with the man who would break down all of her walls and show her what it meant to fall in love. Gabbi's perfect man, coming in the shape of Benjamin's brother.

And me, with Daniel... It fit. It made sense.

So why was I holding back? Why wasn't I embracing this fully?

Why wasn't I letting myself love my husband?

Maybe it was time that I stopped running from the things that scared me.

And start running towards the things that truly made me happy.

Towards my home.

I COLLAPSED ON THE COUCH, Brownie bundled up in my arms, and let my eyes flutter shut. We'd stayed until the late hours of the night, till all four of us girls could barely keep our eyes open. Laughter echoed through the room, and love filled every corner.

We'd finally agreed to go home after I'd practically fallen asleep in Daniel's lap watching another Christmas movie. I was so intently focused on his fingers caressing the skin on the inside of my thighs that I couldn't even remember what we watched. My panties were absolutely soaked, and I was so turned on I could barely see straight.

Sighing, I nuzzled my face against the puppy's. Desperate to have the ache between my legs filled.

"Darling."

"Mmm?" A set of brown eyes were staring into mine when I opened them. My husband leaned over, practically pinning me in place between his arms.

"Did you have a good day?"

I could still feel the flush of my cheeks from the wine I'd consumed, but even sleepy and drowsy, that smile hadn't left my face. "The best." Brownie had also apparently had a good day, because he was fast asleep in my arms, letting me cradle him like a baby.

Daniel traced my cheekbones, tucking a lock of blonde hair behind my ear.

"W-what?"

He smiled. "What? Can't I touch my wife?"

I blushed. Damn, I needed to stop doing that. Get my face under control. "Well..." I looked at the sleeping bundle in my arms. "You'll wake the baby."

"Let's make one."

"Now?" I blinked. We hadn't talked about it lately, not since the wedding.

Cupping the back of my neck with his palm, Daniel rested his forehead against mine. "Yes. Unless you think it's too soon?"

"No." I shook my head, fully awake now. "I don't want to wait."

"Mmm. Good." Turning my head to look at his expression, the focus in his face was single-handedly on me. I wasn't sure if I'd remembered to breathe.

I burrowed my head into his chest so he couldn't see my expression. The longing on my face. How much I wanted this. Wanted him. "I've always wanted to have kids before I turned thirty. And I'm not getting any younger," I laughed.

"True." Daniel wrapped his arms around me, pulling me into his lap, Brownie still cuddled between us.

"And you *want* to do it the normal way? With me?" He looked so vulnerable that I wanted to cry. This man constantly exceeded every expectation of mine.

A laugh escaped from my lips as I moved to straddle his legs, my hands moving up his chest. "It's not like we haven't had sex before."

"But this is different."

"Is it?"

"This is where we have to admit it's not *just sex* anymore, Charlotte."

I stifled a laugh. Had it ever really been just about sex? Ever since Angelina's wedding, it felt like I lit up from just a single glimpse from him. And now, the heat in his eyes, the way he ran his tongue over his lips as he bored his eyes into mine…

I drew circles on top of his shirt with my fingers. "I'm not on birth control anymore, you know."

I'd never really needed it, but it helped to regulate my periods, and it helped with hormone control and keeping me acne free. Honestly, I hadn't even worried about it even when we started sleeping together. Even if we'd had an *oops* baby, it would have been the best blessing of my life just to do this with him. It always would be.

"So…" I sucked my bottom lip into my mouth.

"So, I think it's time that this little one goes in his crate," Daniel said, rubbing a finger over Brownie's snout.

I giggled. "You're not letting him sleep on the bed with us?"

My husband shook his head. "Not tonight. Tonight is about me and you. Showing you how much I want this. Want *you*."

In one swift motion, he gathered both Brownie and me into his arms and carried us up the stairs, my head cradled against his chest. He carefully placed me on the bed, treating me as if I were the most valuable thing he had ever carried. Daniel carried Brownie to his cozy crate filled with blankets and toys before standing in front of me.

I was still wearing my pink velvet dress, even though I'd ditched my shoes the moment we'd walked through the door.

Sliding his hand into my hair, he held the side of my face before bringing our lips together. But it wasn't a sweet kiss, no. It was a promise of what was to come. The filthy way he was promising to touch me communicated only by our lips and his tongue. The saliva intermingling in our mouths, the way I wanted his body closer, closer, closer. Needed it.

Needed his body on top of mine more than I needed air, and not once did my head try to convince me that this was anything besides what it was. Us, needing each other. Drowning in lust.

Breaking the kiss, Daniel kneeled in front of me, pulling me to the edge of the bed. "I need these off, now," he said, tugging at the toes of my tights. "I need to taste you. Have that sweet cunt on my tongue."

"*Daniel—*" I moaned, and he made a tsk sound with his tongue, as if urging me to be quiet.

"Are you going to be a good girl for me and do what I say?"

I nodded. "Yes, *please.*"

There wasn't a chance as hell he wouldn't see how turned on I was just from my panties alone.

"Good. Now." He ran his fingers up my thighs. "Let me lick your pussy, wife."

I complied, and when his fingers skimmed the skin at my bare stomach, before he started rolling the waistband down, I almost moaned from the sensation alone. Squirming, I did my best to lift my hips so he could drag them down, leaving my dress pushed up above my hips.

"That's better."

He dipped his head down, his nose running over my panties, and I felt a rush of heat when he pulled them to the side to run his tongue up my slit, his nose bumping against my clit and giving me just the slightest bit of pressure.

"*Oh,*" I practically squeaked, the sensation driving me crazy.

"You're soaking wet, aren't you?" He murmured. "And it's all for me. Just for me."

Yes, I agreed, though the only sounds that emitted from my mouth were a series of gasps and moans as he put his tongue to work, doing just what he promised, his tongue buried inside of me, tasting me like I was the sweetest thing he'd ever had. Burying my hands in his thick, dark hair, I held on to him with every fiber of my being as he feasted on me.

Oh my god. He didn't stop his ministrations, just continuing to lap me with that glorious, talented tongue of his, and I was already so, so close, and—*Oh my god. Oh my god.*

My orgasm hit me like the weight of a freight train, and it was all I could do to just let him coax me through it, the sensation from his tongue and his nose driving me *mad*. God.

Daniel laughed as he stepped back in between my legs. "It's just me and you in this room, baby." I hadn't even realized I'd been chanting it out loud. "But I'm happy to be your God if you want me to be."

The only thing that stopped me from slapping him was the way he kissed me, letting me taste myself on his tongue as he explored every inch of my mouth the way he'd just stirred up my insides.

And all I knew was I needed every scrap of clothing off of our bodies. Now. I didn't want to wait any longer for him. Not when he was looking at me like *that,* lips slightly puffy from all the rough kissing, and not when his hair was all mused from my fingertips. From how I'd held him closer to me as he licked me to climax.

Wordlessly, I started unbuttoning his shirt, and then we were a whirlwind of clothes and hands—dress, bra, panties all discarded on the floor next to my tights. His slacks, button up, and boxers in another pile.

Pushing him down on the bed, I couldn't quite resist myself.

"You know," I said, straddling his lap, letting my soaked core brush against his arousal. "What you did to me earlier was very mean, *husband."*

"Hmm?" He asked, cupping my tits. "You'll have to remind me which part." Then he licked my nipple, and I almost forgot everything I was going to say.

Almost.

"You were teasing me," I muttered, barely keeping my cool as he sucked the tip of my breast into his mouth, brushing his teeth against me, "in front of all our friends. Driving me crazy. And I couldn't do anything about it."

He gave a knowing grin, but I didn't give him what I knew he wanted. What we both wanted. I wanted to torment him back first.

Instead, I just rocked against him, a feather-light touch of my lips against his shoulder. He repeated his actions on my other nipple, a few sensual licks that had me squirming against him.

"You liked it," he whispered, revealing the truth I already knew.

"Yes."

"And if I'd slipped a finger inside you, I would have found you dripping wet for me, wouldn't I? Even in front of all our friends?"

"Yes," I groaned as I rocked against his length again, needing him inside of me but enjoying this too much.

"You wanted all of them to know you're mine, didn't you? That I treat you right? Whose pussy this is?"

"Daniel," I pleaded, because the answer was *yes, yes, yes*. I needed all of that, and more.

"Mine," he practically growled. "Only mine. Because I'm the only one who will touch you. Fuck you. Make love to you."

Words left unspoken, but even through all the filth he was spilling, I could hear it, couldn't I?

Love you.

"The only one," I agreed. My first, and my forever. "No one else will ever have me."

"And why is that?"

"Because you're my husband," I said, my eyes fluttering shut with the words. "And I'm your wife."

"That's my good girl," he praised, tracing a finger over my spread outer-thighs, currently poised above his hips. "Now, tell me what you want, darling."

"I want you. Inside of me."

"Words, Charlotte."

My cheeks heated. "Please, *husband*. Fuck me. I need your c-cock." I moaned the last word as he helped me rub against him, and before I could beg any further, he shifted us, allowing him to plunge up inside, barely giving me time to adjust to his size.

"Fuck. It's like you were made for me."

Maybe I was.

Daniel kissed me, his tongue ravishing my mouth as he held himself still. By the time he pulled away, I was a panting, writhing pool of *need*.

"More," I begged, needing him to move.

He shook his head, giving me a devilish smile. "Take your pleasure, baby. Fuck yourself on my dick."

Daniel's hands wrapped around my waist, and I was suddenly reminded how much bigger he was than me just at the sight of his enormous hands on my skin.

And I began to move, rocking against him, back and forth, my arms around his neck as he helped guide my body, rolling my waist as I ground down on him, my clit sending sparking sensations from each movement.

It was good. Too good. And I was so close to coming again, just from his hands on my body and the way we were both chasing my pleasure together, that I could feel myself tightening around his length.

"Daniel, I'm—"

"Shh," he said, coaxing me through it as he held my body tighter to his, my hardened nipples rubbing against his firm chest. "Let go."

And so I did, letting myself tumble over the edge for the second time that night. Throwing my head back, I surrendered myself to my orgasm, letting the sensations overtake my entire body as I gave him everything. All of me.

When I finally came back to myself, I didn't miss the fact that he hadn't come himself—like he was still holding back.

"You didn't—"

He shook his head. "Needed you to come twice first." And then he grinned widely, his beautiful and brilliant face lighting up, and I leaned over to kiss him. Our lips locked together tightly, just like our bodies were intertwined.

Daniel moved down, kissing my neck as I remained in his lap, his cock still snug inside of me.

But he touched me languidly, like he was in no rush to end this.

"Inside me," I begged, as he marked my neck. "I want you to let go, *husband.*"

"Charlotte..." He all but groaned. "Are you saying what I think you're saying?"

I nodded, splaying my hand across my stomach, practically feeling him inside of me. "Please. Come inside of me. Fill me up, Daniel."

"*Fuck.*" His voice was guttural, deep as he moved inside of me. "You want me to get you pregnant? Put a baby in you?"

"Yes," I practically moaned as I ground myself down on him. "*Yes*. Please."

Pulling out, he flipped me over, my knees planting into the mattress as he pulled my hips up to him. Not pausing for a moment, Daniel thrust into me from behind, causing me to gasp from the fullness as I clawed at the sheets, seeking stability as he gripped my ass, fingers digging into what I knew was creamy, perfect skin. Skin I wanted him to paint with his cum. The dirty thought occurred to me so fast, of him pulling out, spraying it all over my back, my ass. Having him clean every inch of my body in the bath. Taking me again in the shower. Moaning, I let the fantasies spur on the sensation of his punishing thrusts, each one practically bouncing my whole body.

But as much as I wanted all of that, I needed it—him to lose himself in me, even more.

I gasped, clutching the sheets. "Y-you're so deep." This position, the way he was filling me, how sensitive I was from my last orgasm—it was all too much. Every shallow thrust inside of me that pushed against my womb, every place his hands touched my body, all of it set every nerve ending on my body alight, and I was practically shaking as he rutted into me from behind. "I can't—"

He leaned down, his lips touching my neck, before I felt his breath against my ear. "You can. You can take it. You're such a good girl, Charlotte. Do you like this, hm? Me getting ready to fill you with my seed?"

"Yes," I whimpered, squeezing my eyes shut as if that could stave off my impending orgasm, trying to prolong the pleasure. "I want you to knock me up."

My orgasm exploded through me, and before I could utter another word, he slowed down, and I could feel him harden even more inside of me. Moaning into the pillow, I practically pushed my ass further against him, burying him further inside of me.

A groan slipped from his lips—I couldn't hold back my voice, and neither could he. "*Fuck*, baby. I'm gonna cum. You feel so good like this." as his fingers dug into my waist and his hips bucked, and I didn't even have the words to beg for it anymore, not when he'd made me come three times and I could still feel myself pulsing around him.

I could feel the warmth spilling inside of me as he shot rope after rope of cum inside of me,

Wrapping his arms around my chest, he pulled me into him as we collapsed onto the bed, exhausted and spent. Even with him softening inside of me, he didn't pull out yet, just buried his face in my neck and held me tight.

"That was... wow."

I only wished I could have seen his face when he came.

Combing through the sweaty strands stuck to Daniel's forehead, I pushed his hair back as I stayed in his arms, content like that.

When he finally pulled out of me, I winced at the feeling of emptiness. I could feel the cum trickling out, down my legs, which should have been embarrassing but the way he was looking at me, the heat in his gaze as he watched the liquid drip out of me... I'd never felt more desired.

Using two fingers, he pushed his release back into me, and then shoved a pillow under my hips, keeping me propped up.

I giggled. "Do you really think that's going to help?"

Daniel looked down at me, a reverent look on his face as he leaned down and placed a kiss on my forehead. "Can it possibly hurt?" He whispered, and I shook my head.

Placing another kiss on my lips, he got up and went to the bathroom to clean off, returning to the bed a moment later with a pair of boxers on.

"How long do I stay like this?" I murmured, letting my eyes close shut.

I could hear Daniel's deep chuckle. "I don't know. I saw it on a show."

Cracking an eye open, I peered at him. And then I pulled the pillow out from underneath me and playfully whacked him with it. "You're ridiculous."

He took the pillow from my hands, tucking it back under our heads.

"Come here, love," he said, opening his arms, and I happily complied, burying my face into his chest.

And when my eyes shut, it was with a smile on my face, warm and burrowed into the arms of the only man I'd ever truly loved.

CHAPTER 24
Daniel

Watching my cum drip out of her, spilling onto her thighs, might have been the sexiest thing I'd ever seen.

Even now, watching her pull her hair up into a high ponytail, I couldn't take my eyes off of her. Maybe it was the fact that something had changed between us last night, something I couldn't quite put into words.

"What?" Charlotte pulled her brush away, raising an eyebrow as I watched her from the doorframe.

"Nothing." My lips curled up into a smile.

"You're smiling."

"I didn't know that was a crime."

Stepping up behind her, I wrapped my arms around her stomach. "So, do you think we did it last night? Made a baby?"

Charlotte had flushed cheeks. "I doubt it. It doesn't normally happen the first time, you know?" Her eyes met mine in the mirror.

"That's okay." I brushed my nose against her cheek. "It just means we get more time to try, right?"

She wiggled out of my arms, turning around to face me. "Is this... are we getting too serious?"

I frowned. "What do you mean? We're married. You want to have kids. Is this not what we agreed upon?" I raised an eyebrow. "Because if this is too much, just tell me." I crossed my arms over my chest so I wouldn't reach out to her.

Charlotte worried her lower lip. "No, I mean, it's great, it's just..." She shook her head, pasting on a smile. "It's nothing." She brushed her fingers over my cheek before stepping up on her tiptoes to place a kiss to my jaw.

"Okay. If you're sure."

"Mmm. I am."

I sighed. "I wish I could spend another day at home, but..." I had to get back to work. We had what felt like a million projects going on, plus my special one I'd been working on. One I hadn't told Charlotte about.

"I know. It's okay. I have to get back to commissions, anyway." She'd stopped accepting orders for her dresses because of the wedding, but now that it was over, it made sense that she'd want to get back to it.

"I'll see you tonight?" I offered, running a hand down my shirt to smooth out any potential wrinkles. My engineering office didn't require formal attire, but I still dressed nicely for work and client meetings.

Bending down to give Charlotte a quick kiss, I straightened up, reflecting on how good the moment felt. Like we were a *real* husband and wife, saying goodbye to each other before work. I liked it.

"Yeah." She gave me a smile before turning back to the bathroom mirror, running the brush through her blonde hair.

Mentally, I started planning a surprise for tonight. I needed to show her how much she meant to me, what this meant to me.

All of it.

∽

I'D NEVER BEEN SO excited to get home from work before. But knowing that someone was waiting for me—who was waiting for me—made it all better.

Pulling into the driveway, I smiled as I saw her silhouette in the upstairs window, sitting in the little sewing room I'd built for her. It wasn't much—nothing like what I hoped she would have one day, but for now, she was here, in this house that finally felt like ours. Our bedroom, and tonight I'd make love to her in our bed.

How it should be, except I needed to ease whatever fears were running through her brain. I'd noticed it this morning, and it was what had spurred me into action for tonight.

Besides our fake engagement, we'd never even been on an actual date.

Well, that was changing right now.

Before interrupting her, I took a moment to lean against the doorframe and watch her work.

She was blaring Taylor Swift, singing along as she ran stitches down two pieces of fabric on her machine, and I watched her head bob along to both activities.

When she finished, I cleared my throat.

"Oh!" Her hand flattened over her chest. "Geez. You scared me. I didn't expect you home so..." Charlotte's eyes widened as she checked her phone. "*That's* the time? I guess I got a little caught up..." A brief look over her pile of work could easily explain why.

"Come on." I reached out a hand, outstretched towards her so I could pull her up from her desk.

"What?" Charlotte blinked at me as she stood, standing in front of me.

"Let's go."

"Go where? I didn't know we had any plans tonight."

"I know." Because I wanted to surprise her, so that was what I was doing. I just had to hope this didn't all backfire on me. "I'm taking my wife on a date."

"Oh." She looked down at her clothes, wrinkling her nose. "Can I change first? I'm all covered in fur and glitter."

Nodding, because I would never tell her no, I followed her into our bedroom. "That's quite the combo of supplies."

"I was making costumes," she said, a blush spreading across her pretty cheeks. "Nothing weird, I promise."

"You could tell me you were Tinkerbell all covered in pixie dust and I wouldn't bat an eyelash, darling."

With that, she laughed. "You know, I did actually dress up as Tink for Halloween one year. I had the big pom-poms on my shoes and everything."

"When was this?" I'd spent the last nine Halloweens with her, and I definitely don't remember seeing anything so cute. "Do you still have the wings?" I couldn't help but think about how it'd be a cute costume to do in the future.

"Senior year of High School, I think. And... maybe. They're probably still at my parents." She grimaced.

For good reason—it was a place she didn't talk about much. Honestly, she didn't talk about her family much at all. I knew her older sister had two daughters, but besides that, she'd avoided going home as much as possible since she'd moved to Portland.

"Would you ever..." I started, and then stopped. It wasn't my place to ask. And I didn't want us going into tonight with any negativity hanging over our heads.

"Hmm?" She pulled her long-sleeved t-shirt off her body, and then her leggings followed, leaving her standing in the middle of the closet in just a bra and her little lace panties.

Stepping close to her, I pulled her body in flush to mine and leaned down to whisper in her ear. "If you stay like that for too long, we won't go anywhere, darling." I ground my cock, half-hard already, against her ass, before pulling away. "Later, I promise."

The back of her neck was red as I stepped away, forcing myself out of her presence.

Dressed in a figure-hugging white sweater dress and tights

with heeled booties, she stepped out, and I was momentarily taken aback by how good she looked.

"Ready?"

"Mhm. Do I look okay, or should I change?"

"You look perfect. But you always do."

Grabbing her pea coat off the rack, she looked at me with a nod. "Okay. I'm ready."

"Great." I cracked a grin. "Let's go."

Guiding her out into the car, I made sure she got buckled in before going around to the other side and sliding into the driver's seat.

～

"So..." Charlotte fidgeted with her wedding ring. "Any hints where we're going?"

"Nope." I leaned in close to drop my lips against her ear. "It's a surprise."

Did she feel it too? This didn't feel fake between us. It never had. I wanted to tell her, so she'd know exactly how I felt about her.

I'd loved her for a long time, but this was different. Now I knew, with one hundred percent certainty, that I was *in* love with her. My wife, who'd agreed to marry me because of a stupid marriage pact. Because I'd been so scared about ruining something between us, I'd hidden behind that instead of just telling her I wanted us to be together.

She crossed her arms over her chest, giving me a small pout before turning back to the windshield and watching the freeway pass us by.

There'd been somewhere I'd been wanting to go for a long time, and tonight had been the perfect occasion. Thankfully, when I'd called, there had been a last-minute cancellation, so I could get us in at the last minute.

We parked by the dock, and as we got closer, the name painted on the boat became visible, a surprised expression on Charlotte's face as she looked over at me. *PORTLAND SPIRIT* it read, the three decks visible complete with a string of lights hung from one end to the other.

"We're getting on that?" She said, looking mystified.

"Mhm. I got us a table for the dinner cruise. Shall we?" I offered her my arm, feeling rightness surging through my body when she looped hers through mine.

"How'd you pull this off?" She whispered to me as our seater led us to the table.

"I guess I'm just lucky," I murmured back. Lucky to be here—lucky to have her.

Charlotte smiled back at me as we sat at our little table by the window, able to watch the city lights out the window as we sailed along the river.

Our dinner was exceptional, and we continued the evening on the upper deck, surrounded by the soft glow of the string lights. The chilly air only added to the romantic atmosphere.

As we leaned on the rail, the boat cruised down the Willamette. I intertwined our fingers together, kissing her knuckle.

"Listen, I was thinking earlier and…" I looked her in the eyes. "Do you ever think about going home?"

She blinked at me, a weird expression forming on her face. "What do you mean? This is my home."

I shook my head. "To California. To your parents."

"You mean to visit?"

"Yeah."

"Oh." She worried her lips through her teeth. "Like… Together?"

I nodded. "If you want me there. You know I'd go anywhere with you." Picking up one of our adjoined hands, I kissed the top of her palm.

Her face melted, the tension and worry instantly fading away. "Maybe. I should really bring all the rest of my stuff up here."

"We don't have to make plans now, I just thought…"

She cupped my jaw with her hand. "No, it was a good thought. Thank you."

I kissed her forehead. "You know I'll always be by your side."

Charlotte wrapped her arms around me.

"This is just beautiful," she said, her eyes alight as she looked out over the city.

"Yeah." I brushed a hair off her cheek. But I didn't take my eyes off of her, not for a single second. Because she was the most beautiful sight of the night. Of any night.

"Thank you," she whispered.

"You never have to thank me," I repeated. A sentiment that would never stop being true.

Because everything I did—I did it for her.

~

"Are we old?" I asked, curled up on the couch at Matthew and Noelle's house. With a contented sigh, Charlotte snuggled into my lap. The dogs were both running around outside in the yard, and Charlotte cracked an eye open.

She frowned. "No. Why?"

I raised an eyebrow, watching the other guys who were in the middle of a Mario Kart tournament with Angelina. She was determined to win and beat the rest of them. "You were saying?" I asked, referring to our quiet gathering for New Year's Eve.

Last year, we'd all gone out to one of the rooftop bars in Portland, which thankfully had a heater, but Charlotte was still cold. She always was, even tonight, which is why she was curled up next to me, happily absorbing my body heat.

No complaints here.

"Personally, I think there's no better start to the year than kicking all of their asses, but maybe that's just me," my sister said, a grin spread across her face.

"You're just lucky I'm not playing," I said with a snort. "I always won growing up."

She furrowed her brow. "Did not."

"Did too."

"What are you, children?" Charlotte scolded, flicking me on the head, as if I wasn't older than her—and she wasn't the youngest person in the room. "Besides, I kind of like this better than last year. It's gross outside, anyway. It's definitely too cold to get dressed up and go outside." She pretend-shivered as in example, snuggling even further into me.

I used that as an excuse to wrap an arm around her, holding her tighter against my chest. Not because I wanted to play pretend, but because it felt so fucking good just holding her like this. Pretending it was real. Like we were the perfect couple of newlyweds the rest of them thought we were.

I leaned in close and whispered in her ear. "I think I know a way that I can warm you up."

"Daniel!" she whispered, smacked my arm, blushing furiously, as if she hadn't been complaining when I did just that last night.

Angelina just raised the corner of her lip up as Charlotte buried her face in my chest. "Want in the next round, bro? Gonna let me prove you wrong?"

"Nah." I looked down at the top of Charlotte's head. "I'm good here."

I was perfectly content with her in my arms. There was no part of me that needed to prove to my sister that I could kick her ass in Mario Kart when I had the girl of my dreams in my lap.

With a gentle smile on her lips, Charlotte looked up at me, and I bent down to press a kiss to her forehead before pulling her close.

"How are you doing?" I murmured to her, my voice low.

A contented sigh slipped from her lips. "Good."

"I'm gonna get up and grab another drink. Want anything?"

"Nah. I'm fine here." She waved me off, and I adjusted our

position so I could stand before letting her settle back against the couch cushions.

Hunter joined me in the kitchen as I pulled another two beers out of the fridge, the two of us clinking them together before we took our first sips.

"You still been looking at that plot of land?" I asked him after setting my beer down on the counter.

"Yeah." He scratched behind his head. "I haven't told Gabbi about it yet, but it feels right."

I looked over at Matthew and Noelle. "Think we can convince them to join us, too?"

A grin spread over Hunter's face. "Yeah. I do."

"You two ready for the countdown?" Matthew asked, coming into the kitchen as he looked back towards the living room. "It's almost midnight."

Nodding, we both followed behind him, me settling back behind Charlotte, and Hunter pulling Gabbi into his lap.

"Happy New Year!" We all cheered as the clock struck twelve in Portland, officially bringing us into the next year.

And then I kissed her, thankful that I'd get to do this for the rest of our lives. That after so many years of wanting to, I could finally kiss her like this, in front of everyone.

"Happy new year, darling."

"Happy new year, Daniel."

Rubbing her nose against mine, I happily stayed just like that, with her cradled in between my legs, in my arms. And even after she'd fallen asleep, and I'd carried her to the car, all I could think was, is there anything more perfect than this?

Was there anything more I could want out of life?

CHAPTER 25
Charlotte

Our routine as fake-married newlyweds blurred the lines between us to the point where I couldn't distinguish them anymore. Between dance classes, dress commissions, and trying to conceive, the past month had been a blur since the wedding.

Certainly not my feelings for my best friend slash fake husband.

My eyes lingered over the empty dance studio. I'd stayed late, working out the kinks of a new routine I'd been working on. Some days, this felt like enough. Teaching the next generation of dancers, coming up with new choreography for performances, and some days I missed that *rush*.

Observing my movements in the mirror, I did another turn. A blonde bun sat tightly on top of my head, keeping my hair in place. Gracefully, like the moves were second nature to me now. In some ways, they were. I'd been in ballet since I was six, and I'd always felt at home in the studio.

But *was* it enough?

What was that *more* I'd been searching for?

I went to do another spin when my eyes caught on someone leaning on the door frame, arms crossed as he watched me.

Daniel.

His lips turned up into a smile when he realized I'd seen him.

"Hi," I breathed out, dropping my form and bending over to grab my water from my bag.

"Hi, beautiful."

"What are you doing here?"

"What, I can't come watch my best friend dance?"

"Daniel..." I whispered, as he came to stand in front of me. He pulled a bouquet of lilies and other mixed flowers out from behind his back. "You didn't have to."

"I know." He smiled. "I wanted to. Happy one month."

Thoughtful didn't begin to cover it. He was looking at me with so much conviction, so much care, and those butterflies erupted in my stomach again. Was it just because we were trying to have a baby that I felt like this?

"Why are you looking at me like that?" I whispered.

"Like what?"

Like this is real. I looked away, blushing. "Like I'm beautiful."

"Because you are."

"What?" I was a sweaty mess, my hair falling out of my bun, wearing a sports bra and leggings.

"You're beautiful, darling. And why can't I look at you like that? Because you're mine," he said. "Even if our marriage isn't real, Char, you're my *wife*, and you're the most stunning woman I've ever laid eyes on."

His wife. There were the butterflies again. Lately, they happened whenever he called me that. Not even darling sent the same rush running through me.

His eyes narrowed in on my ring finger—currently devoid of his ring. I gave him a sheepish grimace. "I didn't want to lose it during class. It's too pretty."

Truly, it was too much. And too expensive. As an engineer with a good salary, it wasn't surprising that he got me a nice ring for our fake marriage. However, I couldn't shake the feeling that something might happen to it.

I pulled it out of my dance bag, where I'd safely zipped it up into an inside compartment, and held it up to him. "See? It's safe."

Daniel plucked it out of my hand, slid it back onto my ring finger, and then kissed my knuckle. "That's better. Now, do you think I could take my wife home so we can eat dinner? Or does she plan on hanging out in an empty studio all night?" He gave me a little smirk.

"*Fake* wife," I corrected him. I needed the reminder, especially when he was acting this sweet. "And we can go. I'm ready." I'd been working off my nervous energy, but now that he was here, it was suddenly all gone. Nothing seemed to really matter when I was in his presence. In his arms.

He grumbled something under his breath that I couldn't quite catch before taking my dance bag from me after I'd tugged on a sweatshirt, and I followed him to the car.

Getting in to the passenger side, I connected my phone, turning on my Taylor Swift playlist, letting it play on shuffle.

Daniel's hand rested on my thigh the entire time, a warm and comforting presence. Like he was reminding himself that I was here, that I was his. Or maybe it was the opposite entirely—that he was mine.

To my surprise, he didn't drive home. We were—"What are we doing here?" I said, raising an eyebrow as Daniel parked in front of our local bookstore.

He smiled, those brown eyes sparkling with joy. "You can buy whatever you want."

My eyes lit up. "Really?" He knew me all too well. I enjoyed going and grabbing new releases each week, as well as whatever pretty indie books my store was carrying. When I found them, I always liked to buy them, hoping they'd stock more.

I practically jumped out of the car, rushing in through the rain into the store.

"Have fun," he murmured into my hair as he caught up with me at the front. "Go crazy. I'll carry the ones you pick out."

"Okay."

As I browsed the romance section, he trailed behind me, observing as I deliberated over which books to choose. Each time our eyes met, I couldn't discern the emotion behind his gaze. If I did, my heart might actually burst. Because he was so caring and thoughtful that he knew that *this* was the surprise that would make me happy. Books—and the flowers that were resting in the car's backseat. Not expensive jewelry or things I didn't need. Just things that would put a smile on my face.

"I'm gonna go look over there one more time," I whispered as Daniel moved into the fantasy section, giving me a brief nod as he looked over the options as well. He was carrying around my large stack of books—I might have overdone it, but he said to get whatever I wanted, didn't he?

"Do you need any help?" While I browsed the romance tables, a bookseller startled me by asking if I needed help, as Daniel was engrossed in a science-fiction book across the store.

"Oh, no, I'm okay." I gave her a small smile. "I come in here all the time."

"Oh, great! Were you looking for anything in particular?" She gestured at the table in front of us. "Romance is my favorite genre, so if you need any recommendations…"

I shook my head. Partially because, *no,* and secondly because there was already a pile of books I'd grabbed. "I've actually already picked out a bunch," I said, waving at Daniel. "He's got them."

She looked down at my ring finger, the wedding ring that sat on it, and then back up at me. "*That's* your husband?"

I blushed. "Yeah." *Fake husband.* Currently living out my favorite tropes. No big deal.

"Oh my god." The girl grinned, pushing her glasses back onto her nose. "Please don't let him go. I say this for us book girls everywhere."

"I don't plan on it. We're actually… He's my best friend. Since college." I blinked, looking back over at him, catching his eyes as the corner of his lips tilted up.

"That's so cute! How long have you been married?"

"Only a month, actually. It took us a long time to figure things out."

Maybe too long. I'd often wondered why he'd never asked me out in college. But then again, maybe I was asking all the wrong questions. Maybe I needed to ask myself why I never asked him out in college.

Because I was a shy, sheltered girl with no dating experience and no idea what it was like to fall in love. But I had, hadn't I? I'd loved my best friend since I was eighteen, and there was nothing that had changed that in all these years. Not when I'd tried to date other people, and not when I'd imagined him with someone else.

"Newlyweds!" She clapped her hands. "That's so cute. Let me know if you need anything else, okay? I'll be floating around."

When she'd left, I wandered back over to Daniel.

"Everything okay?"

"Mmm." I curled an arm around his waist. "Thank you."

"You don't have to thank me," he said, kissing my forehead. "You never do."

"Eh." I was going to do it, anyway. Every day, for the rest of our lives. Because he deserved it. My gaze flickered between the towering stack of books and his face. "Let's go home."

And so we did.

Home.

∼

LATER THAT NIGHT, we were back at home, curled up on the couch, feeling content after indulging in the *Happy One Month Anniversary* cake he had bought earlier.

Maybe it was the girl's words from our earlier conversation that had stuck with me and got me thinking. As I looked back on the last decade, I couldn't help but question why we'd stayed just friends when we were clearly meant for more. For this.

"Daniel." I sat up on my knees, turning to him. "I wanted to tell you something."

"Hm?" He raised an eyebrow, even though I was sure he had no idea what I was about to say. It was something I'd buried deep down inside of myself for the longest time.

"You know I used to have the biggest crush on you?"

That got him sitting up straight. "When?"

Always.

"Well... freshman year."

He moved a little closer to me, brushing a strand of hair off of my face. "Why didn't you say anything?"

"I didn't want to ruin our friendship. If we did this," I paused, looking at the man I got to call my husband, "and it ended badly, you wouldn't be in my life anymore. And I couldn't risk losing you."

"Oh, baby. You'd never lose me." He placed a gentle kiss on my forehead. "I promise."

"I know." There was no doubt in my mind about it now. We'd make it through this. Even if we didn't say the words... I'd fight like hell for him. And I was pretty sure he felt the same.

"Why didn't *you* make a move?" I asked, turning my body so I could look into his eyes better.

"Didn't I?" He grinned, leaning in to whisper into my ear, "I asked you to marry me, Char."

"Yeah," I groaned, "At twenty-seven, not eighteen. We could have had so many more years together, Daniel. I could have—" I sniffled. *Loved you* was on the tip of my tongue. With a shake of my head, I leaned back onto his chest.

"Maybe things were always supposed to be like this. We just had to find our way together." He kissed my lips softly. "No regrets, right?"

I shook my head. In so many ways, I'd needed those years. To find myself. To learn who I was on my own. I was stronger because of that.

And I was stronger with him by my side.

"Is it weird that I think I was waiting for you?" My whole life, I'd never felt like I had my place. Not until college, until Portland. Because being with him, with Angelina, Gabbi, and Noelle, that had been where I'd fit in. Where I'd felt home. *Peace.*

"Charlotte..." He took my hand, squeezing it tight. "I wish..." He shook his head, words left unspoken. "I wish I'd waited for you."

"But..." Oh. He thought I meant *that?* No. "I know your first time wasn't with me." I gave a half smile, even though I went a little red thinking about someone else knowing him that intimately.

"It didn't mean anything." He winced. "Freshman year of college and... fuck, Char. I hadn't even met you yet when it happened, but I wish you were my one and only, baby." His fingers brushed over my ring. "But you're the only one who will ever matter to me, I promise."

I knew it was true, even if I didn't want to admit the truth.

That I was falling in love with my best friend—was probably already in love with him, if I was being honest. I opened my mouth to tell him that, but those three little words didn't slip out. Instead, what did was, "You're the only one for me, Daniel Bradford."

Which was as much of a confession as my heart was ready to give.

∽

I'D NEVER HATED the sight of blood before. Not until now.

My heart dropped a little. It wasn't like I'd expected it to happen right away, but why did I feel so disappointed that it *didn't?*

"Charlotte?" Daniel's voice called from outside the bathroom. "You okay?"

I sniffled, wiping the tears that had dripped out of my eyes off my face.

Why was I crying? Shit, Charlotte. *Get it together.*

"Um... Yeah, I'm fine." I called out, even though I was feeling anything but.

"Are you sure? Want me to get you anything?"

Quickly finishing up in the bathroom, I pulled my leggings back on, opening up the door and crashing into a brick wall.

Right. Not a brick wall. My husband.

"Oh." I squeaked.

"Darling..." He frowned, looking at my eyes, which I figured were probably red. If they weren't, that meant he could read me too well, and I didn't want to consider that possibility. "What's wrong?"

"I just..." I played with the ties on my shorts, trying not to look at his face. "I got my period."

He slid his finger under my chin, tipping it up to look at me. I wanted to wipe the expression off of his face, too. Pity.

For me. I hated it. What would happen if I couldn't have kids? Would everything fall apart if my reason for being here wasn't working? I couldn't think that way. But I also couldn't help the doubts swirling through my mind.

I always cried easily, and the hormones didn't help.

"It's fine!" I said, trying to paste on a cheery expression. "I'm just going to go to bed. I'm pretty tired after everything today."

"Charlotte..."

I tried to slip away from him, but he caught my wrist.

"Talk to me, baby," he pleaded in a low voice.

That was what did me in. The way he injected so much care into his voice. How even though he was holding on to me, it didn't feel like a leash. It felt like a lifeline. Like Daniel was my lifeline, my life preserver. If I was drowning, he'd save me, wouldn't he?

"I'm not pregnant," I whispered, voice cracking with emotion.

His hands cupped my cheek, the warmth instantly making me feel a little better. "You're not pregnant."

I shook my head. "No."

"It's okay." He rubbed a thumb over my cheekbone. "We'll keep trying." He offered me a warm smile.

I nodded. "I know."

"Then why are you crying, love?"

"I just... I really want this, Daniel." *To be a mom.* "You know?" That was all I'd ever wanted—not to be a dancer. Not to be a dress designer. But to have a family to love. To have a family to give my one hundred percent to, knowing I'd get it all back.

And that was what love was, wasn't it? Giving everything you had to someone, and getting everything of them back.

In my life, I'd experienced that with very few people. Noelle. Gabbi. Angelina. Daniel.

It always came back to Daniel.

The man whose chest I desperately wanted to burrow my face into. Because I knew what it felt like to be comforted by him.

He'd been doing it for the last nine years.

"I do," he murmured, smoothing down my hair. "Besides, trying is fun, right?" He chuckled.

Maybe he could see the way I'd been retreating into my head, panicking. Maybe he meant it, and this was still just sex for him. Just good sex, and no romantic strings attached. It was easy to think about it like that if I didn't think too much about what we were doing.

Trying.

I let him wrap his arms around me, swaying me even as we stood on the tile floor.

"Everything's going to be okay," he murmured against my forehead, his soft lips moving against my skin.

I wanted to believe him.

Maybe it would.

Either way, I had him.

CHAPTER 26
Daniel

Charlotte roughly erased something from her sketchbook, pursing her lips, before retracing the line with her pencil. She couldn't seem to get it right and gave up in frustration, burying herself in her blankets.

I couldn't help the chuckle that escaped from my lips.

"Oh." It startled her when she looked up and saw me there, arms crossed over my chest as I continued watching her. "Hi."

"Hey." I smiled at her. I couldn't help that, either. "How are you feeling?"

"Better." She pulled the blanket tighter over her shoulders. "Thanks."

"I brought you something to cheer you up," I said, pulling the pack of marshmallows and her favorite chocolates out from behind my back. "I thought you might like this better than flowers."

She'd kept the last bouquet on the dining room table until the flowers had shriveled up, but I knew the way to her heart. And I'd watched her eat entire bags of marshmallows multiple times during college.

"Daniel..." Her eyes filled with tears, and I set the goods down on the coffee table.

"Don't cry," I said, kneeling in between her legs. "Please. It breaks my heart when you cry." It made me want to do anything I could just to make her stop. Because I couldn't stand seeing her hurting.

I knew she was disappointed and upset, but I'd do everything I could to make this happen for her. It was her reason for agreeing to all of this in the first place, wasn't it? Why we'd gotten married. What would happen if we couldn't have kids? Would all of this crumble around us? Would she leave me if I couldn't give her the thing she wanted most of all?

Just the thought made me wince.

"I don't know what's fake or real anymore," she whispered, looking so vulnerable that it squeezed my heart. "This thing between us, I... I don't even know. What are we doing? Are we still pretending? Because if we are, I can't—"

None of it is fake.

I needed her to know that. Needed her to know how real this was for me. How much it always had been.

"So let me show you." I rubbed my arms up her sides reassuringly before squeezing her palm the way I always had. And then I took a deep breath. "Let me love you. Let me prove I can love you. Because I don't want this to be fake anymore."

Her eyes were watery. "You don't?"

"No." I shook my head. "Maybe I never have. Shit, Charlotte, it's... It's you. It's always been you for me. Since the first moment I saw you, standing in the middle of that hallway. So let's do this. For real." I slid my hand back, cupping her neck.

"I... I don't know what to say," she said, frozen in place and unblinking.

"Say yes. Say you want this too."

"I do." She closed her eyes. "But what if..."

Running my thumb over her bottom lip effectively shut her up. "No what if's. No unhappy endings allowed. Because this is us, Char, and we were meant to be together."

And I believed that, with every fiber of my being.

"Come here," I whispered, holding out my arms for her. My wife.

Charlotte slid into my lap, letting me cradle her in my arms.

"I don't want to pretend anymore," I confessed. "I'm tired of pretending I don't want you, Charlotte. All of you. In whatever way I can have you."

Charlotte wrapped her arms around my neck. "I don't want to pretend either."

"Good." I kissed her softly,

"Okay. So we're doing this? For real?"

"We're doing this, baby."

She fluttered her eyes, looking down at me as I brought our lips together–happy to show her just how real all of this was.

⸻

"Happy Birthday," Charlotte whispered, brushing her lips against mine as I woke up.

A few weeks had passed since we'd decided that this was real, and I couldn't believe how great it was between us. No holding back. No hiding behind a fake label.

"Thank you," I murmured, gripping her waist to pull her on top of me. Her tits, even through a thin layer of cotton, were hard as she settled on top of my body.

"Twenty-nine. How's it feel?"

"Mm. The same as twenty-eight did." I placed a kiss on her nose. "But at least I have my beautiful bride by my side."

Charlotte blushed. "Can you believe you're only one year away from our original pact?" The one I'd proposed in college—that we'd get married at 30 if neither one of us had found someone.

"Yeah." I ran my fingers through my hair. "I was so fucking stupid, wasn't I?"

If she had found someone else, if I'd missed my chance—I

never would have had this. Wouldn't have had her in our bed, my ring on her finger.

She froze. "What do you mean?"

"Should have asked you to marry me a lot sooner," I said, kissing her collarbone. "Should have spent a lot more time doing this. Making it real." I kissed her shoulder.

"Oh." Her body relaxed, practically melting into mine. "Yeah."

I was seconds away from tugging down that tiny strap and tasting her taut nipples, dying to get my tongue on her. Inside of her.

I'd been absolutely ravenous for her lately. She'd been more diligent, tracking her menstrual cycle to determine her fertility window before we had sex again.

But I'd had plenty of experience with wanting her. I could wait a few more days.

"Do you want breakfast?" Her fingers trailed up my bare chest. "I could make pancakes."

"Or," I said, sliding my hands up her thighs, pushing up underneath that tiny little nightgown she wore. "I could have you for breakfast."

She swatted me away. "Not yet."

"Just a taste," I begged. The sweetness of her body was like a drug, and I found myself addicted to the taste of her while I was between her thighs. Going down on her was heaven.

"You're *incorrigible*."

"Only for you." I gave her a peck on the lips before slipping out of the bed, pulling on a pair of sweatpants, and heading downstairs to let Brownie outside.

When I came back, Charlotte was standing at the kitchen counter, staring at the bowl of pancake mix and the griddle she must have pulled out from somewhere.

"You good?" I raised an eyebrow.

"Oh! I, uh…" She blushed. "I've never made pancakes before."

"Mm. I got it." I wrapped my hands around Charlotte's narrow waist, hefting her up onto the counter. "You can just sit there and watch."

"But..." My girl frowned. "I was going to do this for you."

"And this is for me," I said, pulling a spatula out and pointing it at her. "Because feeding my wife is the hottest, sexiest thing I can think of."

"Still," she whined, still pouting. "It's your birthday."

"You can make it up to me later," I whispered in her ear before rubbing our noses together.

Her eyes lit up with a spark, and she nodded.

I planned on cashing in on that *later,* as soon as we got upstairs and into the shower.

Because no matter what she thought, I already had everything I wanted this birthday.

Because I had her.

∽

"Surprise," Charlotte smiled, her grin taking over her face as she tugged my hand, pulling me into a ritzy, upscale swing dancing club in Downtown Portland.

"You did all this?" I blinked, seeing all our friends gathered around a booth in the corner, complete with their own dorky smiles.

"Mhm." We kept our hands intertwined as we walked to our table, not wanting to lose the feeling of connection.

Char and I getting married seemed to have brought us all closer together, and I couldn't think of a way I'd rather spend my birthday.

"Happy Birthday, man," Benjamin said, shaking my hand and patting me on the shoulder. Angelina's sudden embrace surprised me, but I quickly returned the rare sibling hug. We had always been close, but I couldn't resist teasing her.

"Thank you," I whispered in her ear.

"For what?" Angelina pulled away. "I didn't do anything. This was all Charlotte."

But how did I explain I was thanking her for everything? Without her, I wouldn't have even had Charlotte by my side—as my best friend for all those years, or as my wife now. I owed it all to my sister, who hadn't batted an eye when I fell in love with her friend. Sure, she'd huffed about it when we were younger—how all her friends always were crushing on me, getting close to her to get to me, but she'd never complained when Char and I spent countless hours sitting and talking in the dining hall, or sitting on my bed in my dorm and watching movies.

That she'd gained three best friends and yet I was always the fifth wheel, tagging along simply because Charlotte was there. And until Matthew, Benjamin, and Hunter had come along, I hadn't truly felt my place at Charlotte's side. But as I watched all the girls fall in love, and it had been even more clear to me I could never just accept friendship.

So I just shook my head. "For everything. Thanks for being the best sister I could have asked for."

"Yeah, yeah." She rolled her eyes, even though there was a smile spread across her face. "You're a pretty great brother yourself." She playfully punched me in the shoulder.

"Should we order some drinks?" Hunter asked, and the table erupted into cheers.

"I'll take that as a yes," I said with a laugh, and we waved a waiter over, quickly ordering a round for the entire table.

After we'd all sat around for a while, polishing off a few appetizers, the girls got up to dance, leaving the four of us guys sitting at the table, talking about construction projects and other work-related things. We might have all worked in different sectors, but it was still interesting to compare jobs.

Even through all our conversations, I was only half paying attention, my focus solely on Charlotte. Her lavender dress swayed against her hips as she danced with the other girls, the four of them laughing and clearly having a good time. I was content just like this.

Hunter laughed to himself.

"What?" I turned, looking at him.

He shook his head. "I was just thinking about our conversation at Benjamin and Angelina's wedding. How we'd watched our girls' dance then, too. But now... We don't have to hide how much we love them." He raised his glass up in the air. "Six months later, and everything is different."

For the better. I took a sip of my whiskey.

Then I set my drink down. "You're right. And I'm going to go dance with my wife."

He chuckled. "Good plan."

"You coming?" I asked the other three, who waved me off.

"We'll get the next one," Matthew added, taking another sip of his gin & tonic.

Weaving in through the crowd, I quickly found the girls.

"Mind if I cut in?" I said to Noelle, who was twirling Charlotte around following the steps of the dance they'd just learned tonight. Char already looked so graceful, gliding across the floor with every step.

Noelle's freckled cheeks flushed with pink, and her dress hugged her curvy figure. Despite the surrounding beauty, I fixed my eyes on my wife as she stepped away.

Charlotte's blonde hair flowed around her like a halo, and her skin glowed as if she were lit from within. Her purple, sparkly dress shimmered with each step she took.

"Hi."

She smiled back at me. "Hi."

"This is great," I said, leaning my forehead against hers as I took her hand in mine, wrapping my other hand around her waist.

"I'm glad you like it. I wanted to do something special for your birthday."

"You did. It's been a perfect day." Ever since we'd gotten out of the shower, she'd spent the day pampering me, taking me to my favorite places.

The best part? When we'd bundled up and taken Brownie for a nice, long walk around lunchtime, she'd held my hand the entire time.

We danced a few songs before the other guys joined us on the floor.

"Mmm. You know, I took a test earlier." She had a mischievous look on her face, and it made me want to kiss her.

"Oh?" I pulled her in closer to me, and she stepped up on her tiptoes, her arms wrapping around my neck so she could tug my ear down to her lips.

"I'm ovulating."

"You're—" My dick practically jumped in my pants, which was a problem. Partially because a quickie in the bathroom on my birthday was definitely not how I wanted to spend the night, and because the rest of our friends were also here. "You're trying to kill me, aren't you?"

She laughed, winking at me, before twirling out of my arms.

Grabbing her by the waist, I spun her back into me.

"Oh, no, you don't," I said as she shrieked, laughing as I hauled her back into my arms.

"Everything okay here?" A man appeared out of nowhere, my demeanor instantly shifting.

Charlotte stepped back further into me, letting me wrap an arm around her waist, like she trusted me to protect her. Felt safe with me.

"She's my wife." I said, practically growling.

"We're fine," she added, playing with my fingers that rested on her abdomen. "Just playing around."

The guy nodded, disappearing back into the hordes of people on the dance floor.

We both burst out laughing.

"You're going to get us in trouble, darling."

"Daniel," she whispered, tugging me down until my ear was level with her lips again. "Can we go home?"

I frowned. "Don't you want to enjoy hanging out with your friends?"

"I know it's your birthday, but..." She blushed. "We can try again."

"Now?" I asked, and she nodded. I leaned down so I could place my lips against her ear. "What excuse are we giving our friends, darling?"

Charlotte shrugged. "We're still newlyweds. I think we can come up with something."

Smirking, I pulled her off, back towards our table, where Matthew and Noelle were sitting entangled in each other's laps.

"Hey. You having fun?" Matthew asked, brushing the red curls off Noelle's shoulder.

"I'm actually feeling a little tired. I think we're going to head out." As I wrapped my arm around Charlotte's waist, I felt her body relax into mine.

"Good call. It is getting late." He looked around for our other friends. "Let me go find everyone else, so we can all say goodnight."

Thirty minutes later, after we'd all exchanged hugs (mostly the girls) and another round of birthday wishes, Charlotte and I were finally back at the car.

She dangled her keys in front of my face. "You want to drive, or should I?"

"Hand 'em over, darling."

Because we had somewhere to be.

~

AND THAT SOMEWHERE WAS OUR bed, clothes quickly discarded on the floor.

"*Fuck.*" Charlotte shimmied out of her shorts, leaving herself bare to me. "You've been teasing me all night." I groaned, palming her ass as I massaged each cheek.

Tormenting me was more like it. Ever since she'd dropped that bomb, it felt like she'd done everything possible to rile me up. Sitting on my lap, brushing against me so innocently, fluttering her eyelashes and licking her lips—I was at wit's end.

"I have one more surprise for you," she said against my lips, before darting off into the closet, leaving me on the edge of the bed, painfully hard and waiting.

When she emerged, my eyes practically popped out of my skull.

Delicate, white lace covered her torso, barely covering the tips of her rosy nipples.

"Happy Birthday," she said, pushing me down to straddle my thighs. "You're always taking care of me, but now it's my turn to take care of you."

"Mmm." I ran my hands up her outer thighs, fingering the little straps on her hips. "I like this."

"Do you like your gift?" She asked, before bending down to press a kiss to my neck, her sweet strawberry scent filling my senses, intoxicating me.

"It's the best."

Charlotte's lips kissed a trail down my chest, before she circled my nipple with her tongue, lavishing it with her attention before she moved to the other one, repeating the motion. Then she traced the ridges of my abs with her tongue.

"I've always wanted to do that," she admitted, running her fingers across my naked torso.

"You're welcome to anytime." I went to put my hands on her, but she made a *tsk* sound with her tongue. "No touching. Not until I've had my fun."

By the time she'd reached my lower abdomen, a path of open-mouthed kisses left behind, her tiny hand wrapped around my dick before I'd realized her plan.

"Charlotte," I groaned. "You don't have to."

"But I want to," she whispered, licking her lips as she gave a slight squeeze with her fingers. Her hand didn't quite wrap around all the way, which really shouldn't have been a surprise, given how much bigger I was than her, but part of me liked it. That weird, growly, possessive part of me, who

"You'll have to teach me what you like," she breathed, sliding her hand up and down my shaft. "I want this to be good for you."

"*Fuck*. Baby. There's nothing you can do that would be wrong." I shut my eyes as she increased the pressure, trying not to blow my load right then.

There was only one place I wanted to lose myself tonight—buried in her tight, wet heat. Not down her throat.

And then she leaned down, swiping her tongue over the tip, licking up the pre-cum that had oozed out.

"I told you I wanted to taste you, too," she said, voice husky, before her mouth explored the full length of my dick. First, with her tongue, and then, when she opened her mouth and took me inside of it.

As she bent over me, those pretty little lips wrapped around my cock, her eyes connected with mine, the vulnerability in them clear.

"More," I groaned, trying my best not to push her down further as she traced her tongue around the rim. As much as I was loving this, I didn't want to hurt her. And there was no way she could take all of me down her throat—certainly not comfortably.

I wrapped my hand around hers, showing her just how I liked it, both of us stroking me together as she sucked on my length, her tongue still playing with the tip.

"Charlotte," I groaned.

When I felt my balls tighten, too close to blowing my load, I pulled her off with a pop.

She frowned, wiping a few dribbles of saliva off her face. "What? Was something wrong?"

"No." I laughed. "It was too good. If you kept going, I was

going to lose my mind. And if I'm coming anywhere, it's not going to be down your throat, baby."

"Mmm."

Sitting up fully, I pushed her thighs apart, exposing the thin strap of lace that covered her slit. Pushing it aside, I roughly pushed two fingers into her, surprised when I met little resistance.

"You're so wet, aren't you, darling? Just from sucking me off?"

She agreed with a moan as I scissored my fingers inside of her.

"Gotta get you nice and wet so you can take my cock. You'd like that, wouldn't you?"

"Yes," she gasped as I held her tightly, moving her hips to increase the intensity of our connection.

I pulled my fingers out, eliciting a whimper from Charlotte. After all of her teasing, it was my turn to make her crazy.

"Now, let me have a taste of you. I've been dying for it all day." Laying back down on the bed, I patted the area next to my head. "Come sit on my face."

"Daniel," she squeaked, planting her hands on my chest. "I…"

"Come on," I coaxed her. "Show me just how dirty those little books of yours are."

"Oh, that's how it is, is it?" She murmured, climbing up towards my mouth.

Spreading her thighs further apart, I guided her onto my face, my nose lined up with her clit as my tongue darted out to taste her.

The little breathy noises that slipped from her lips only spurred me on further, and I increased my pace, fucking her with my tongue.

"It's too much," she cried, her thighs tightening around my head.

I could already feel her clenching, and I knew she was close, so I kept up the motion, digging my fingers into her flesh as I licked her senseless.

When she came, a rush of wetness soaked my face, and I eagerly lapped it all up.

"That was—wow." Her face was flushed, and she had a slight sheen of sweat on her forehead.

I grinned. "Best. Birthday. Ever."

I flipped her over onto her back and kissed her deeply, savoring the taste of her on my tongue. Our unhurried kiss was filled with the sensation of my body pressing against hers as my length pushing against her stomach.

"Daniel," she moaned. "I need you inside me. Right now."

With one last lick of my tongue against hers, I lined myself up with her entrance, settling my body in between her hips. Charlotte's eyes rolled back into her head as I pushed all the way inside of her, squeezing my eyes shut as I adjusted to the feeling, the way her insides hugged my cock.

"So fucking tight," I praised, savoring the way it felt to be inside her body.

Interlacing our fingers, I let our hands rest on the mattress, and I maintained eye contact with each time I slowly thrust inside of her. This wasn't a race to the finish line—it was us, entwined in pleasure, passion, succumbing to our mutual desire for each other.

"Kiss me," she breathed, our lips barely inches apart.

And so I did, giving her every piece of my body, heart, and soul. I kissed her with every bit of love for her I had, hoping she could feel it, too.

Hoping she knew how much I loved her, cherished her.

And that thought had me barreling even closer to the edge, that telltale tightness building, and I sputtered a curse. Groaning her name, I buried myself even deeper in her body.

"Not yet," Charlotte moaned. "I'm s-so close."

"Come for me," I murmured, tightening my grip around her fingers as I focused on hitting that spot inside of her I knew would push her over the edge, every push in scraping against her insides. "Be my good girl."

"Yes," she cried out. "I am. I'm yours."

I could feel her muscles contracting around me, and the pleasure was so intense that I thought I might climax right then and there. But Charlotte came first, always.

"*Fuck.* Yes you are. All mine."

Her body trembled, and I inhaled her little gasps before her body tumbled into oblivion, screaming out my name as she came, her inner walls pulsing around me as I kept fucking her through it.

And then, muttering her name, over and over, I let go, spilling inside of her, buried to the hilt, never losing the eye contact between us.

Her gray eyes, rimmed with red, conveyed everything she was feeling. And I wanted a photo of it to remember it forever. Because the love and emotion in her eyes were just for me. All mine.

I'd do anything to keep her—us, just like this.

CHAPTER 27
Charlotte

"**A**nything?" He asked as I slid into the car, looking so hopeful I thought I might cry.

I shook my head. It had been a month since Daniel's birthday, and this morning, I woke up to the familiar discomfort of my period arriving. I'd tried not to get my hopes up again, but it was hard.

"These things take time," I said, offering him a fake smile. It was true, after all. I'd even considered lying with my legs against the wall if that was what it took. Even if it didn't really help, I'd still feel like I did *something*. "I'm okay."

He reached over and squeezed my hand, our fingers intertwining as we rested them against the gearshift.

"Are you sure you want to come?" I asked, changing the subject as I looked over at him.

My dance school had a competition this weekend, and he'd insisted on coming along for moral support. He'd been doing that a lot lately, and I couldn't bring myself to complain about it. Sure, I wasn't pregnant, but this is how a husband would be with his wife, wouldn't it?

And we were happy. So I was ignoring everything else. All the little doubts in my brain. The way we hadn't said *I love you* yet.

None of that mattered when he held me like that during sex, when he interlaced our fingers and kissed me so tenderly I couldn't imagine he *didn't* love me.

"Why wouldn't I?" He raised an eyebrow. "Besides, it's not like you really wanted to drive yourself, did you?"

Right. Why did it sting a little that he felt like he *had* to chauffeur me? What did I want from him, anyway?

I was glad he was here. Pasting on my best smile, I reassured myself that it would be an enjoyable weekend. We'd booked a suite for the competition, and I had no doubts that Daniel would do his best to cheer me up, even if I was on my period.

Turns out that orgasms were great relief for period cramps, and the man I married had absolutely no qualms about delivering them, even through the period blood.

Was it possible that I'd married some superhuman instead of a normal one? Especially when that little black curl rested against his forehead—my Superman. He'd swooped me off my feet and saved me. Maybe not literally, but in every way that mattered.

Of course, I was giving my heart to him. I'd never stood a chance, had I?

"Charlotte?"

"Hmm?" I looked up from where I was still staring at our hands.

"I was just asking if you wanted anything." He'd pulled into a drive through.

"Oh." I blinked, like I could comb through the rest of my brain fog.

After we'd gotten our drinks and snacks, we were back on the road, driving towards the competition.

"So. Give me the rundown. Who all will be there?" Daniel asked me.

"Well, Juily's home with the baby, so from the studio itself, just me and Isa, but a few of the parents will be there too." Our new dance teacher, Isabella, had been hired by Juily a few months back while she'd—*mostly*—been on maternity leave, just running things behind the scenes.

Daniel nodded. "Good. No strange men I have to worry about?"

"Worried about a single dad sweeping me off my feet and stealing me away from you?" I flirted, running my hand over his thigh.

His expression grew serious. "Yes. I'm worried you'll find someone better than me."

"There's no one better than you," I mumbled, looking straight out the window instead of at his face.

There never has been, I thought to myself.

He kissed my hand before turning back to the road. "Thanks for letting me come with you."

I gave him a small smile. "Thanks for being by my side."

"Always."

∼

THE NEXT MORNING, we all arrived bright and early to the school auditorium they'd rented out for the event, and I plunged into the fray to go check us all in.

Since this competition was out of town, everyone had driven up separately, but we'd all be meeting up in a bit to go over everything, touching base with all of them and letting them know what time their performers were going on over the weekend.

Isabella found me in our assigned classroom where our dancers could change and get ready.

"How's everything looking?" She asked me, tightening her long, straight black hair behind her in a ponytail. Dressed in our dance school's quarter zip and leggings, she looked like the dancer she was. At only twenty-two years old and fresh out of college, she eagerly picked up everything we did at the studio.

"Good. I just have to corral all the parents and get them in here to pass these out." I held up my stack of envelopes.

"Want me to look around?" Isa asked, looking out the door. "I can send a text, too."

"That'd be great. I'd like to run the group performance one more time tonight too, just to get any jitters out." Keep the muscle memory fresh.

"I think that sounds perfect," she agreed.

"Okay. I'm going to find Daniel—erm, my husband, now."

She clapped her hands together. "He's here? I haven't gotten to meet him yet."

Surprising, considering how Daniel insisted on picking me up most nights, because he knew I hated driving.

I nodded. "He just went to go pick up coffee."

We'd been running late this morning—partially because we'd chosen to shower together, and that never ended quickly. I flushed.

After our meeting with all the parents and guardians of the dancers, I was heading back to find Daniel when a familiar face made me stop in my tracks.

"Charlotte, is that you?" Her tight curls bounced as she ran over, wrapping her arms around me.

"Oh my god. Grace?" I hugged my old friend. "It's been forever." We'd been in the same ballet class growing up, attending the same studio until we were eighteen. Until I'd moved to Portland.

She grinned. "How's everything been with you? Still dancing?"

"A little. I mostly just teach my kids and choreograph on the side now, but every once in a while I do a routine just for me. What about you? How have you been?" It was crazy to run into her here. As far as I'd known, she'd stayed in California. Most of our competitions up here were regional, unless one of our dancers was good enough to go to a national competition.

"Oh my god, I've been amazing. I'm actually opening a summer intensive in California, and even the extended session is almost full."

"Wow." I blinked. "That's amazing."

Regular dance studios didn't operate in the summer—it was a chance for kids to just be kids. Normally, in the summers, I used that break to come up with new ideas. Choreograph new routines for competitions. Usually, some of the top dancers got invited to intensives all across the country. I'd even gone to them myself when I was younger.

She shrugged. "You know the type. Dance is their life. It was ours once too." She looked away. "Though it practically still is," Grace said with a wink. "Those were the good ol' days, huh?"

I laughed, but the statement didn't feel true anymore. Dance hadn't been my life in a long time.

"What do you say you come down to California and be one of my instructors this summer?"

"Oh, I..." I fidgeted with my ring. "I couldn't."

Her eyes tracked the motion. "Oh my god. You're married."

I grinned, sticking my hand out so she could inspect the ring. "Yeah. Almost three months."

"Shut up! Who's the guy?"

"My best friend from college. His name's Daniel. He's actually here with me this weekend."

"That's incredible. Wow! I'm so happy for you."

"Thank you."

She shook her head. "My news pales in comparison now. But listen, if you change your mind, and want to come down for the summer—even if he wants to come with you—let me know. I can send you the info letter with all the details."

"Yeah, I'll let you know if anything changes," I agreed, even though I didn't see myself going.

And there he was. My husband.

Holding a cup of coffee and a little bag that I was sure contained food for me, too. Because he was always taking care of me like that—making sure I was fed, that I'd been drinking water. My heart beat faster in my chest as he approached me.

"Hi," I whispered as he leaned down to kiss my cheek before handing me the coffee.

"Everything good?" Daniel asked.

"Yeah. I just ran into an old friend." I offered him a small smile.

"That's fun."

I took a sip of the coffee. "Oh, this is *good*. Not as good as yours, but," I took another sip, sighing happily. "Thank you."

And just like he always did, he said, "Anything for you," and I couldn't hide the blush on my cheeks even if I wanted to.

"How do you always do that?" I murmured.

"What?"

"Make me feel so..." I was at a loss for words.

He quirked a dark eyebrow. "So...?"

I shook my head. It wasn't one little thing. It was how he made me feel every day. Special, loved, worshipped. Everything from his gentle touches to the way he made love to me—because that was what it felt like even if we hadn't called it that.

I just kissed his cheek instead. "You're pretty great, Mr. Bradford."

"Pretty perfect yourself, Mrs. Bradford."

Smiling as I took another sip of my coffee, I let that settle into my bones. And it felt like nothing ever had before. Right.

Home.

༄

"You're going to do amazing, Lily," I promised, smoothing over my teenage student's red hair that was styled into a tight bun. "Just remember that you've got this. You know this routine by heart, backwards and forwards."

We'd already done the group performance earlier, and the littler kids were mostly tomorrow, leaving all our teens to go on during the evening.

She hugged me tightly. "Thank you, Miss Charlotte."

"I didn't do anything," I said with a smile. "It's all you. My little superstar. So go show them all how you shine."

Lily gave a quick nod as she broke the hug, wiping her tears away. "You always know just what to say to make me feel better."

I laughed. "Don't forget, I was in your shoes once. Now, no crying. You'll smudge your makeup."

"Yes, ma'am," she said, blotting at her face with a laugh.

"Go get 'em, tiger."

After a deep breath and she pasted a smile back on her face, Lily left the room looking way more confident than she had before. Knowing her, she got pre and post-performance anxiety, so I was sure I'd be offering her more words of encouragement later, but I didn't mind.

"You're good with her," Daniel murmured, stepping into the room with two drinks in hand.

"Yeah, well, she's a good kid. I'm lucky."

He kissed my cheek as I took the cup from his hand. "I'm proud of you."

"Me?" I looked up at him. "I'm not even doing anything. They're the ones performing."

Shaking his head, he took my hand as we headed towards the auditorium where the girls were doing their routines. "You're the one who inspires them. And they look up to you, you can tell. You're not just their dance instructor, you're their mentor. It's pretty cool."

"Oh." I blushed. "I love it, you know? Mom always wanted me to go be a ballerina, or join a dance company, but…"

"But this makes you happy."

I nodded. "This is a *life*, you know? Dancing professionally would fulfill me, but it's not my dream. It's just not the life I saw myself living. I love to dance, but I don't want to be surrounded by it all the time. I like that I have time to sew and make my own creations. To read and to see my friends whenever I want." I sighed into his arm. "That I can have a family without worrying about how my life is going to change."

"And you're happy?" He looked worried for a moment. "With this life? With *me?*"

"Yes." There was no hesitation, no ounce of doubt in my voice. "Sometimes I think it's impossible for me to be this happy. Like I'm just waiting for the other shoe to drop." I looked up at him. "But it's not going to, is it? This is… good. No matter how it started out."

"It's better than good." He kissed the top of my head. "And no, it's not going to change. Because I'm not going anywhere."

We slipped into the room and watched my girls perform, and I couldn't help my cheers for them as Daniel sat by my side, holding my hand. Even as the night went on, he supported me from the sidelines without complaint, like he was just happy to be there.

Happy to be here with me.

But was he right? Was I finally secure and safe with him? Did I not have to worry about something bad happening that would ruin everything?

I hoped so. Because losing him, now? That would crush me.

CHAPTER 28
Daniel

Wrapping my arms around her, I pulled her back into bed. "What are you fretting about?"

She just shook her head, a small smile covering her face as she looked up at me. "I used to get nervous for *me*, but now I feel it for all of them, too. Sometimes I just have to remind myself that I taught them the best I can, and I've watched them all nail it at the studio. But still... I just have all this extra energy I need to burn off."

I grinned. "I can think of a few ways."

She wrinkled her nose. "I'm still on my period."

"So?" I raised an eyebrow.

"I was thinking more like... a midnight doughnut run."

"You know I'll never say no to doughnuts." Once, in college, she'd texted me at 8pm that our favorite donut shop had *dog doughnuts*—and we'd had to race over there to get them. Did I have homework that needed to be done? Certainly. But I'd dropped everything to drive her.

Charlotte kissed my cheek, hopping back off of the bed to find a pair of her dance sweats to pull on. Grabbing my own, and a sweatshirt from our school, I grabbed my phone and wallet.

"Ready?"

"Hold on," she hummed, pulling her hair up in a high ponytail before leaning over and plucking my crewneck sweatshirt—the one that I'd gotten from my engineering firm—out of my bag. Once it was over her head, she turned back to me. "Ready."

"I don't think that will ever get old."

"What?"

"You in my clothes." I wrapped both of my arms around her middle. "It makes me feel like a caveman, like I take one look at you and all I think is *mine*."

She leaned up, leaving a kiss against my neck. "Good."

"You like that?"

Charlotte stared at me, unblinking. "Have you missed every word of what we say at book club?"

"I wasn't aware I was *supposed* to be eavesdropping when you talked to your friends."

"In this one instance, I'm willing to overlook it." She smirked, eyes focused on the spot she'd kissed. "But yes. I love it."

"What are you staring at?"

I moved to the mirror—to see a little pink kiss mark on my neck.

"What's this for?"

"So that they know that you're *mine*."

"Mmm. The wedding ring isn't enough?"

She cracked a grin, interlacing our fingers together. "Nope. I don't want anyone else getting any ideas."

Turned out that I liked it when she was a little bit possessive, too.

And I was all too happy to drive her to get doughnuts, even though all I wanted was to pin her against the bed and show her how wild she drove me.

How much I adored her.

∽

THE ROOM WAS FILLED with tiny dancers, each dressed in a sparkling costume and sporting a neat, tight bun.

"So you're Miss Charlotte's *husband?*" They were inspecting me as if I was fresh meat. Maybe I was.

Still, I'd agreed to come with Char to her dance thing this weekend, and now was being relentlessly questioned by a group of girls who could be no older than ten.

"Yeah. She's my wife." It still made me smile to say that. My *wife*. God, I liked it. "She's Mrs. Bradford now." Legally, too. All the paperwork had been done last month, and her brand new driver's license had my name on it.

"We're still gonna call her Miss Charlotte." One of the little girls gave me a toothy grin.

I laughed. "Sure, kiddo."

Charlotte came out into the hallway with one of her older dancers—a teenager who'd been having a meltdown over the days' events. I'd learned from her a long time ago how stressful this kind of thing could be. The pressure to be perfect, to perform your part just perfectly—and even if they nailed everything, sometimes they still didn't feel like they were enough. It was hard, but the way she was hugging the girl gave me hope.

Her eyes connected with mine, and she flashed a smile my way.

"Did she make your costumes, too?" I asked, looking at the rhinestone fabric.

The little girl—Gwen, I was pretty sure her name was—nodded. "Uh-huh. Miss Charlotte's the *best*."

I leaned down conspiratorially. "I think so too."

"Don't you think she looks pretty today, Miss Charlotte's husband?"

I laughed. I loved that my entire personality boiled down to my wife. "She looks beautiful." But she always did.

Everyone broke out into giggles, before one girl—the little dark-haired dancer—looked around, and then whispered to me, "Are you two going to have a baby? Because when my mom remarried my step-dad, she had a new baby." Charlotte eyed me, and all I could do was smile at my wife, who was walking this way, her gray eyes bright.

"And Miss Juily just had a baby, too!"

My heart clenched, thinking about a baby. The thing she wanted more than anything, that I only hoped I could give her. Sure, everything had started out with her thinking this was fake, but now—things were good. Better than good.

"We'll see," I said as she slid in beside me.

"Are you all interrogating my husband?" Charlotte asked, wrapping her arm around my waist.

"No!" they exclaimed quickly, dissolving into a fit of giggles.

"Autumn, your solo is coming up soon, so do you want to run it one more time with me? I'll meet you in there in a minute."

The little dirty-blonde girl nodded her head, heading back to their little changing room. The hallway suddenly felt a lot less crowded as the rest of the group departed, leaving just the two of us.

"I'll see you later?" she whispered softly, taking the girl's small hand into her own.

I nodded. "I'll be the one in the back row. Do you need anything? Another coffee? Lunch run?"

"I'm okay for now." She blew me a kiss. "Thank you."

You don't need to thank me, flashed through my mind once again. *I'd do anything for you.*

"You're welcome," I said, as I watched her go, my gaze lingering on her figure until she disappeared from sight.

~

WE LEFT THE FOLLOWING DAY, after loading up our bags, and drove back to Portland.

"It's so good to be home," Charlotte said, practically collapsing on our bed after dropping her bag on the floor.

I lugged the rest of the stuff in behind her, chuckling as she burrowed herself into our bed. Brownie jumped up beside her, our dog desperately trying to lick her face.

"We were only gone the weekend, you know."

She giggled as Brownie's nose pressed into her skin. It felt like our puppy already took up half of the bed, and she was definitely nowhere near close to full grown yet. But I'd always loved big dogs, and Charlotte getting her for me made it all that much better.

"Maybe, but... I like our bed."

"Oh, our bed, hm?" I grabbed her ankle, pulling her to the edge of the mattress.

She looked up at me from underneath her eyelashes as her golden locks fanned out around her.

This girl. *Fuck.* She looked like an angel, all rosy cheeks and supple skin, movements so graceful I thought my heart might skip a beat. And she was mine. My girl. My wife.

"Mhm. Ours."

She was my everything. I knew I couldn't let her go, so I was prepared to do everything in my power to keep her by my side—happy, sated, cared for. To make sure she wanted for nothing, because there was nothing more I wanted to do than to spoil her.

I leaned down, kissing her exposed skin, trailing my fingers up her stomach as I pushed her shirt up.

"Daniel..." she protested with her words, even though her body arched into my touch. "I'm still..."

She trailed off when my fingers skimmed over her hardened nipples through her lace bra.

"I don't care," I said, leaning down to kiss her breast through the lace. "I want you."

Pushing the cups down, I freed her tits, exposing her rosy pink buds to the air.

"Fuck. You're perfect."

Bending down, I sucked one into my mouth, giving it all my attention. Even if she didn't want sex, I could still make her feel good. Soothe her cramps and pains. Get her mind off of the other things, too.

Because I knew that having her dance students around had distracted her from what her period really meant. I thought of her tears last month, and *fuck*. I couldn't do it again.

I used my mouth to drive her wild, and when she begged for more, I added my fingers to intensify the sensation. Working her into an orgasm, I didn't stop until she came, and I felt her entire body relax into my hold.

"That's my girl," I whispered, righting her clothes. "Feel better now?"

"Mmm. Thank you." Her eyelids drooped shut, like she was boneless and a little drunk off her orgasm.

"Sleep," was all I said, kissing her forehead, before I slipped into the bathroom to take care of myself.

And when I was done, I slid back in next to her, marveling at her wearing one of my shirts as a giant sleep shirt, and held her close all night.

Wondering if this was enough. If I was enough for her.

And fuck, I hoped I was.

∽

OUR MONTH WAS EXACTLY what I had envisioned married life to be: returning home to my wife, spending time with our beloved dog Brownie, and enjoying the company of friends.

It was everything I'd ever wanted, and I was working even harder to make all her dreams come true.

CHARLOTTE

Dinner tonight?

DANIEL

Work's keeping me late. Not sure I'll make it. There's leftovers in the fridge if you're hungry.

> Oh, okay.

> I'm sorry. This project is just keeping me busy.

> You don't have to apologize. Work is important.

> So are you.

I hated that what was keeping me away from her was my biggest surprise of all. That I couldn't tell her why I was spending longer evenings in the office. That even though this was real, and good, and better than anything else I'd ever imagined, I was keeping a secret from her.

Sighing, I put my phone back down and went back to my project. I'd tell her soon.

∽

My wife was determined to torture me. That was all there was to it.

CHARLOTTE
> The girls and I are going shopping. Need anything?

DANIEL
> More of those lacy things you wore on my birthday.

> I meant from the bookstore, silly.

> But... noted.

> Can't wait to see.

> Guess you're just gonna have to keep waiting. ;)

> Darling, you're killing me.

> I'm at a work meeting with a client.
>
> They want us to design a building for them, and now all I can think about is you. In that.

Oops.

I guess I shouldn't send a picture of it on then?

> Lord help me, if you don't...

I'll be waiting at home.

In our bed.

Wearing only that.

> Fuck me.

That's the plan.

~

CHARLOTTE

Brownie and I are going on a walk.

I miss you. I feel like you've barely been home when I am lately.

DANIEL

> Sorry, baby. I promise, this weekend is all yours.

It's almost that time of my cycle, you know...

> Are you saying what I think you're saying?

Only that you better bring your A-game tonight, Mr. Bradford.

> Don't tell me you need a reminder of the way I tongue-fucked you til you screamed my name last night, Mrs. Bradford.

> You're the worst. Why did I say yes again?

Because you love me? I hoped. I wished.

CHAPTER 29
Charlotte

"Daniel?" I raised an eyebrow, dropping my arms before going to pause my music.

He flipped the lock on the dance studio door, even though I knew no one else would come here this time of night.

"Why are you here?" I asked, crossing my arms over my chest. "I was going to head home soon."

"You're ovulating."

"I'm—*what*?" I blinked. "Why do you know that?"

"I get the notifications from your tracker on my phone," he muttered sheepishly.

"Oh." I blushed. "You…" He'd synced my app? How had he even known to do that?

"Yeah."

"We can wait till I'm home, you know." I looked down at my dance attire. I'd pulled on a slouchy sweater over my leggings, but other than that, I wasn't feeling sexy. Plus, this sort of felt like desecrating hollowed grounds.

I looked around the studio. It was late enough that everyone had gone home, Juily and Isabella included, leaving just me here, working on choreographing a new routine.

He smirked. "But I'm here now... And we've both been so busy lately." Daniel stepped up behind me, leaning down to inhale my hair. I'd been using the same strawberry scented shampoo for a long time, but lately it felt like he went feral for it.

"Daniel... We can't," I whispered, looking at the mirrors that surrounded us, the ballet barre installed on one side of the wall.

But we *had* both been so busy lately.

With both of our busy schedules, we only seemed to cross paths when we climbed into bed at night. Thankfully, it was spring break this next week, and my load would be a little lighter.

He kissed the top of my shoulder. "Why not? No one's going to catch us, darling." Kissing up my neck, I couldn't keep in the little gasp that escaped from my lips. "We're—" another kiss, this one to the sensitive skin behind my ear. "—alone."

"We shouldn't..." I said again, but when he dipped his fingers under the band of my leggings, I knew exactly what he would find. How much I was craving this, too.

"You say that, but you're already so wet for me, aren't you, baby?" He murmured against my ear, his eyes connecting in mine through the mirror as he ran his fingers against my slit.

I gasped as he pressed one finger inside of me. "*Yes.*"

"What do you want, hmm, my good girl?"

"Fuck me," I moaned, "Please."

Grasping my chin, he turned my head back to interlock our lips before dipping a second finger inside of me, exploring me deeply. As always, I turned into a puddle around him, because he knew exactly how to play with my body to make me come.

Sex with Daniel was better than I ever could have imagined, and it just kept getting better.

"Take those leggings off for me, Charlotte," he whispered in my ear. "I want you to watch as I fill that sweet little pussy of yours with my cum."

Oh, God. Why were even his words spurring me on this much? This was wrong—so wrong, but I couldn't find it in me to care anymore. Not when his fingers pulled out of me as I moved to obey his command, leaving me feeling empty. But I knew I wouldn't be for long.

I stripped off my leggings and panties, dropping them to the floor. I stood there, wearing only my sports bra and a thin sweater.

"Hold on to the barre, wife."

With my hands on the wooden bar, I watched him in the mirror as he stretched me out with his fingers, preparing me for what was to come.

Daniel knocked my feet further apart as he guided my ass into the air, my back practically parallel to the ground.

"Such a good girl," he praised me, before thrusting inside, all in one go. His hands were gripping my hips so hard I was pretty sure they would bruise, but I couldn't find it in me to care.

"Oh, *fuck.*" I moaned from the sudden pressure, feeling him *everywhere.* "Daniel, I'm—" This angle, the way he was so deeply inside of me... It was *too much.* "I'm so full." No matter how many times it had been, he always filled me so *full.*

"I know, baby. Going to keep you all stuffed with my cock until my seed is seeping out of you."

My eyes fluttered closed as I kept a tight grip on the wooden bar, thankful for it for keeping me up as he started moving, rutting into me from behind.

One of his hands released my waist to tug on my ponytail. "Watch us," he instructed, thrusting into me.

Raising my head, I watched his face, the way he was so focused, the sweat dripping from his temple, the same way I knew it was down my legs, and the pure determination on his face was almost enough to make me lose it right there.

"I can't wait to see you all swollen with our child," he whispered against my ear, filthy, delicious words that shouldn't have been so sexy, but when our eyes connected in the mirror, everything else faded away. It was just him and I, and I didn't care about anything else.

"Harder," I pleaded, needing more. "I need—"

My knuckles were white as I gripped the wood even harder,

thankful the thing had used so much there was no chance of getting splinters.

"I know what you need," Daniel muttered, reaching around with his other hand to finger my clit, rubbing at the sensitive bundle of nerves.

"Yesss." I cried. "Right there, please, I'm so close."

"Come for me, darling. And then I'll fill you up, just like I promised."

His words—and his thumb, moving circles around my clit like he knew just how to make me see stars—set me over the edge, and I cried out. The noises echoed through the empty dance studio, and if I was in my right mind, maybe I would have found it in me to be embarrassed.

But I was floating up to the heavens, my whole body tingling with pleasure, even as Daniel kept up fucking me with those slow, shallow strokes inside of me, while tugging on my ponytail and paying equal attention to my clit.

"So good. So fucking good for me."

He was a god. That was the only explanation. No man should have been able to make me feel like this.

I could feel myself spasming around him, the force of my orgasm nearly knocking me off of my feet if it wasn't for Daniel's arms still wrapped around my body.

When I finally came back to myself, I turned my neck just enough so I could actually look at him—not just through the mirror, and I giggled at the way his black, slightly shaggy hair was just about in his eyes. No part of him resembled the shy, collected engineer I'd known for almost a decade. This was Daniel in his rawest state—uncontrolled, caring about one thing and one thing alone. My pleasure.

But now I wanted to make *him* come. Wanted to feel the warmth rushing through me as he poured his release into my womb. I wanted to get my hands in his hair, to mess it up even further, but then he was picking me up, settling us onto the ground while still inside of me.

Shallow breaths filled the room as we sat there, me speared on his dick, his face flushed from the exertion and face twisted as he held himself back.

But I didn't want that—I wanted him to come undone.

He guided my hand down to his cock, spreading my fingers so I could feel where he entered me as he thrust up with his hips just slightly, his shaft rubbing against my still-sensitive clit.

"Do you like that?" He asked. "Feeling how I fuck you?"

A moan was my only response.

"Daniel—" I cried as we both watched ourselves through the mirrors, him spreading my legs so I could see the way he was parting my folds, my fingers still feeling it every time he moved inside of me.

"Look how good you take all of me."

And I did, watching the way he would thrust up into me, doing practically all the work as he held me in place with only his upper body strength.

Clenching down my muscles, I started rocking against him, moving in tandem with his thrusts, feeling him growing even harder inside of me.

"*Fuck,* Charlotte. You've ruined me for everyone else, you know that? I don't know how I ever went without you."

My breath caught as our eyes connected, and all I knew was I wanted to see his face as he came inside of me, if this was the time it took, I didn't want to watch through the mirror. Sliding off of him, I stood up, wincing at the loss.

I whipped my sweater off, exposing my breasts to the nippy studio, though that wasn't what had hardened my nipples.

"Fuck. I can't wait to suck on those pretty little tits."

Daniel grabbed my hand, trying to tug me back into his lap, but I shook my head, embarrassed despite what we were doing.

"Can we..." I bit my lip, wishing I had something to hide behind as his eyes trailed over my naked body. My cheeks pinked. No, they were on fire.

"What is it?" He looked concerned. "Are you okay?"

I shook my head, and he started to stand up, but I stopped him.

His cock was standing at attention, red and swollen with pre-cum oozing from the tip, and all I wanted was

"I want to look at you when you come," I muttered, practically looking at the ground.

"Charlotte..." He gave a deep chuckle. "Come here."

Scrambling over to him, he pulled me into his body, kissing me roughly as his hand found my ponytail holder and pulled it out, letting my blonde locks tumble over my pale skin.

"You're so beautiful," he murmured as he lowered me onto the ground, kissing down my body, spending time to worship each of my nipples with his tongue and mouth, sucking and licking and biting, driving me wild. He dropped a kiss to my stomach, before moving down lower.

"I need you," I begged, when his teasing was driving me crazy. "Please." Another kiss to the inside of each thigh, and then he positioned himself back at my opening, sliding home.

And then we didn't need words. My fingers were digging into the skin of his back as he held himself up over me, his hips doing all the work as I wrapped my legs around his waist, holding him even deeper inside of me, if that was even possible.

I knew the moment he was close, and he tumbled over the edge with a string of muttered *oh fuck, and Charlotte*—and I lost myself a moment later, succumbing to the feeling of bliss and happiness as I kept him locked inside of me, as if that would keep a single drop from spilling out. Right where it was supposed to be.

"We should really go home," I whispered, even as he buried his head against my breasts and kept holding me.

"Just give me another moment," he muttered, even as I could feel him softening inside of me.

Was it weird that I liked that? When he'd stay inside of me, even after we'd both finished?

"Brownie's waiting for us," I said with a giggle as Daniel sighed, pulling out and looking sheepish.

I winced. "We made a bit of a mess."

"You stay there. I'll go get something to clean up." Finding his jeans, he pulled them on, tucking himself inside.

I wouldn't object to that, not when I was pretty sure my legs were jelly. But also... I wiggled over to the wall, moving the bottom half of my body vertically as I kept my head on the floor.

Shutting my eyes, I must have only dozed off for a minute, but when I woke up, Daniel was standing over me. "What are you doing?"

"Figured it couldn't hurt," I mumbled.

He laughed. "Let's go home, wife."

I stood back on shaky legs as his cum dripped onto my thighs, creating a sticky mess between my legs.

"Mmm. My caveman side is coming back out, because I like that far too much."

Finding my leggings on the floor, I quickly shuffled over to pick them up and pull them and my undies on. I winced as I pulled them up over my thighs.

"I wasn't too rough, was I? Did I hurt you?"

I shook my head. "No. I... liked it." My cheeks flushed. I was sure I'd have marks there tomorrow, but it surprised me how much I *liked* him marking me. Proving I was his. Because it felt even more real. "I was just surprised, that's all." I looked around the room.

"Well?" He smirked. "Better than your books?" Daniel came over and wrapped his arms around my abdomen. "I was originally just going to pick you up and take you home, but you looked so hot with that look of concentration on your face that I just couldn't help myself."

"We're *never* telling Juily that we fucked in her studio. Oh, *god.*" My cheeks pinked. "I'm mortified. I cannot believe we just did that."

But the truth of the matter was, I *really* liked it.

"Maybe we should get some mirrors for home," I pondered out loud when we got into his car, and his laugh was unmistakable as we drove home.

Everything was going great, but then what was this sinking feeling in my gut? Why did it feel like the closer we grew together, the more scared I became? Maybe that was why I couldn't sleep. Certainly, there was something wrong, wasn't there?

Maybe the thing that was wrong wasn't with *us* or with him at all. Maybe it was just me.

~

INHALING DEEPLY THROUGH MY NOSE, I took another sip of water and glanced at the oven clock; the numbers glowing in the dim light. *3:00 am.*

Brownie was curled up under my feet, ever the loyal dog. He'd abandoned his bed in our room when I'd gotten out of bed fifteen minutes before.

Drumming my nails against the counter, I listened to the silence. All I'd ever wanted was a house full of happiness—joy and laughter. The sound of kids cartoons and giggles over fingerprinting. Baking cookies together. Teaching them how to ride a bike.

It was everything I'd ever wanted, and it was so close, but... I rested a hand over my flat stomach.

"Why are you awake?" Daniel padded into the kitchen, looking at me with eyes still filled with sleep.

"Hm?" I set my water down, moving my attention off of the time and onto him. "I couldn't fall asleep. Just... stuff on my mind, I guess."

Even after he'd given me multiple orgasms tonight, my mind hadn't been able to settle down. I couldn't seem to shut off all of my worries, even if I knew most of them were just my anxiety bubbling through. Sometimes it was hard to ignore them, to listen to the rational part of my brain who knew how crazy things sounded.

Daniel, my best friend, my husband, wrapped his arms around me from behind and nuzzled into my neck. "Come back to bed, darling. I can't sleep without you next to me."

I sighed, leaning my head backwards on his shoulder before just staring up at his jaw. He was so handsome and loving, and somehow, he was mine. We'd been friends for years, nothing more, and yet I didn't regret a moment of that. Because I had him, and I was definitely, one hundred percent, in love with him.

So I tried to banish the thoughts in my head that said something could go wrong. How could it, when he was looking at me like that?

He spun my chair around, pulling me into his arms and onto my feet—or more accurately, his feet, since he was holding me so close that I was standing on his toes.

"Hi," I whispered as he dropped his forehead to mine.

"Hi."

Wrapping my arms around his neck, I let him sway us back and forth. And then we were slow dancing, at three am, in the quiet silence of our home, and I wondered if a moment had ever felt so wholly and wonderfully mine as this one did between us.

Resting my head on his shoulder, we kept going like that, dancing to non-existent music, until I yawned, remembering how tired I was.

He brushed the hair away from my eyes. "What do you think? Time for bed?"

"Mhm," I agreed, sighing sleepily against him as he scooped me up, one hand on the small of my back, and the other under my arms, like he was protectively cradling me.

I'd never felt more at home than I did in his arms.

Maybe this was what it meant to be married. That your spouse was the place where your heart lived. It didn't matter where you went, as long as you were together, because they were your home.

And maybe those sleepy thoughts were still pinging around my brain, even as he slid me under the covers and moved in next to me, holding me against him even in sleep. Daniel's breathing evened out, and I couldn't help but brush the small black curl that had fallen onto his forehead back before tracing his jawbone, admiring his face as he slept.

Maybe that was why I said what I said. Or maybe it was simply that the words were true, and yet I hadn't said them yet.

"I love you," I murmured as I fell asleep, cradled against his body. He was already asleep anyway, so I knew he wouldn't have heard it. Nevertheless, even as sleep pulled me under, I knew it was true. It had been true for a long time.

I was so in love with my best friend.

CHAPTER 30
Daniel

I love you. There had been no mistaking it when she'd whispered it last night. At first, I thought I'd hallucinated the words. Thought that there was no way I'd heard her properly. But I had. She'd said the words, incoherent and half asleep.

She loved me. The thought rocked my core. She didn't mean as just friends, did she? This wasn't a casual remark made among passing. And I'd been in love with her for a long, long time.

Now it was my turn to tell her. Make my own confession.

Because I was so in love with my wife. I always had been.

And yet... She was quiet. Withdrawn. Something about the way she had been staring at the oven last night with glassy eyes didn't sit right in my gut. Something was *wrong*.

I'd watched her for three months, putting on her best brave face every time her period had come that I knew it was killing her inside. But all I could do was wrap my arms around her while she cried. I couldn't fix it with a snap of my fingers the same way I could make something with my hands. Build a house. Strum the cords of my guitar. Play a quiet melody on the piano. Those were all making something from nothing, and yet...

"What?" Charlotte looked up at me from her coffee cup, having clearly caught me staring at her.

I shook my head. "It's nothing."

Was I just being paranoid? Maybe it *was* nothing. Maybe I was reading too into her moods, even though I knew Charlotte as well as I knew myself.

I knew what her favorite candy was. How she liked to eat marshmallows as a casual snack. The way I'd catch her crying at Hallmark movies I knew she'd already watched before. How her eyes would fill with lust when she was reading something dirty in one of her romance novels. Her closet was stuffed full with every shade of pink imaginable, pastels that never seemed to end but were so perfectly her. How glitter seemed to go wherever she did. Her little look of concentration when she was threading a needle, or putting a hem into her newest creation.

The way she would light up when someone complimented the dress she'd made, and her response was always, "Thank you! It has pockets!"

Not bragging that she'd made it. She'd stick her hands in and the other girl would be in awe, because fucking pockets, man.

The way she'd cuddled up on the couch with a blanket over her lap, drinking the sickly sweet coffee I'd made for her because she hated the taste normally. Brownie's head resting on her lap.

Fuck, I loved her.

"We should get out of the house."

She blinked, her eyes wide in surprise as she looked up at me. Brownie's head popped up too, his ears perked forward. "What?"

"It's the weekend. We're just sitting here like an old married couple. We should go do something fun. Get our minds off of..." Trying to get pregnant. "Everything."

"Yeah?" Charlotte set her cup down on the side table next to her and scratched the top of our German Shepard's head. "What are you thinking?"

"Trust me?" I held out my hand to her.

"I've always trusted you," she breathed back, placing her hand in mine.

The words sent a thrum of satisfaction down to my bones. Something about the way she was looking at me, the phrase she'd uttered when she thought I was asleep last night—it was everything. Everything I'd wanted. Everything I needed was right here by my side.

I squeezed her hand, the unspoken tradition that we'd had as long as I could remember.

It was almost April, meaning the temperatures were getting warmer outside. But still, it could be chilly out there. And I didn't want her catching a cold.

"Go put something cute on. And grab your coat."

"I'm always cute," she muttered under her breath as she walked away, giving me the perfect view of her tiny pink pajama shorts that hugged her curves.

I swatted her ass.

"Hey!" She turned around to glare at me.

Shrugging, I gave my best innocent face. "Your cute ass was begging for it."

"So are you joining me in the shower, or…"

I gave her a wicked grin. "Right behind you, wife."

∽

"Where are we going?"

"You're terrible to surprise, you know that?"

Charlotte batted her eyelashes. "Maybe."

After a long shower, we'd eventually gotten everything loaded into the car, Brownie included, who was sitting in the backseat.

While Char had been doing her makeup and got dressed, I'd snuck downstairs and packed a picnic basket and everything we needed for the afternoon inside. It was a beautiful weekend, sunny and no rain, and I wanted to take advantage of it.

Taking the back roads towards our old university, I pulled off at Cathedral Park. We used to come here a lot when we were in college, especially when the weather was good, at the beginning and end of the school year.

"Daniel," she gasped as I spread out the picnic blanket. "When did you have time to do all of this?"

"Do you like it?" I asked, a grin spreading over my face.

She playfully pushed my arm.

Sitting on top of the blanket, I patted the space next to me. "Come here, love."

"Mmm." Instead of settling next to me, she nudged herself between my legs.

That's my girl.

"Listen..." I wrapped my hands around her midsection. "I know things haven't been perfect lately. But I want to be there for you."

"Everything's fine," she murmured, picking at the grass underneath the blanket.

"Charlotte." I frowned. "I know you. I know everything's not fine."

She leaned her head against my shoulder, looking up at me, her hand brushing against my jaw. "I don't want to think about anything but us right now, babe."

Babe. I couldn't stop my lips from curling up into a smile. I'd started calling her darling when we'd started all of this, but she'd never actually called me anything before.

"Food?" I asked, pulling out a bottle of sparkling cider and two glasses.

"Guess marrying you had perks after all, huh?"

I laughed. "Sure, I suppose that's one thing." Kissing her cheek, I pulled out the rest of the spread. Strawberries, gluten-free sandwiches, a bag of her favorite chips, gluten-free cookies for dessert. "Now eat up, wife."

Charlotte grinned, popping a strawberry into her mouth.

After we'd finished our food and thrown the ball enough for Brownie to be passed out on the grass next to us, Charlotte pulled one last item out of the bag.

"Why did you pack one of my books?" Charlotte said, laughing. It had been on the coffee table, her bookmark marking the spot she'd left off.

"Read to me," I said, resting with my hands behind my head on our little picnic blanket—the one that somehow had started living in my car a few years ago.

You never know when it will come in handy, Charlotte had argued.

I'd raised my eyebrow. *Sure, but why does it need to live in my car?*

She'd shrugged. *You always drive.*

It had been with us through countless adventures, from trips to the beach to outings with friends, but now I could truly appreciate it.

When I cracked my eyes open, she was staring at me, dumbfounded, the book in her hand.

"What?" She looked around the mostly empty park. We'd picked a quiet corner, so no one was close enough to hear our conversations. "You're crazy. You know this is...." She lowered her voice, cheeks flushed. "*Spicy,* right?"

I quirked an eyebrow. "So?"

"So, we're in public, and I..." She flushed. "It's embarrassing."

"Charlotte." I sat up, facing her fully, taking her jaw in my hand, my thumb resting against her chin. "You rode my cock to no abandon in your *dance studio* the other day. Why is this too much?"

She bit her lip. "You'll make fun of me."

"No, I won't. I'm your husband."

My girl gave me a cute little pout.

"You don't even know what's in here, do you?" Her blush had creeped up her neck now, like she couldn't possibly fathom it.

I smirked. "Mmm. Maybe." I had some idea. The guys talked, too, and they had informed me long ago about the girls and their tabbing systems for their books. Maybe I hadn't read all of them, but I'd found her most-tabbed books and read some of the sex scenes in them.

Some of them made *my* eyes grow wide.

I'd resisted asking the rest of them if they reenacted them with their girls. Partially because I had no desire to know what kind of freaky shit my sister and her husband got up to, and partially because I was pretty sure the answer to that was *yes.*

Before I could blink, Charlotte was straddling my hips, her center brushing against me. Even through my jeans, I was already half-hard and if she put her hands on me, I was at serious risk.

She leaned down to whisper in my ear. "Maybe I don't want to read it out loud here because it's going to make it too hard to *stop.*" Biting my earlobe, she tugged on it before rocking her hips against me.

I growled. "You're going to be the death of me."

"Mmm. That's kind of the idea."

"Get in the car," I ordered, already scooping up all of our stuff and shoving in the bags.

She laughed, the sound chasing me through the park as Brownie ran alongside of her.

And when we got home—she read it to me. Her cheeks were pink, and she blushed every time she read the word *cock* out loud.

But once she had finished, I gave her the best prize in the world. I did everything she'd read to her. Orgasm after orgasm, until she cried out that it was too much.

It might have been the best afternoon of my life.

∼

"THAT LOOKS AMAZING. WOW." My eyes scanned the living area. I couldn't believe it.

"Everything turned out perfect." My co-worker, Stella, who'd been helping me with everything, had given me a walkthrough of the house. The structure was done, and now that the walls were up and painted, the cabinets and countertops were next.

She was right—it had turned out perfect. The entire project was going to be incredible. Every single touch was turning out just like we'd planned it.

And the fireplace in the middle of the living room was my favorite part. It might have been a little impractical to have an actual wood-burning fireplace, but this was Oregon, and I had a feeling I knew exactly what it would be used for.

A wicked grin spread across my face. "She's going to love it."

It was the best surprise. Better than Taylor Swift tickets or a puppy.

I looked at my watch. Shit. It was already much later than I thought it would be.

"I gotta get going. I'll see you at the office tomorrow?"

She nodded. "Tell your wife I say hello. Are you going to bring her by to meet all of us sometime soon?"

I'd been by the dance studio many times, but somehow I'd never brought Charlotte by my work. She'd never come with lunch to surprise me, and I was always the one who picked *her* up. Whenever possible, she avoided driving because she hated it. Sometimes I joked about selling her car, because we always just took mine. Not that we needed the money, really.

But that wasn't that shocking, was it? She had a job too—a life. And we'd been faking it for so long that I wouldn't have expected her to meet my coworkers.

"I will," I said, already thinking about the future. Of how I was going to surprise her.

Everything would be perfect.

I just needed the right moment to tell her.

I love you.

Three little words that I'd known since college. I'd said them before, but never like this. It meant so much more now.

I'm in love with you, Charlotte Alexandra Bradford.
So very in love with you.

I just had to tell her.

CHAPTER 31
Charlotte

> **CHARLOTTE**
> I'm making dinner tonight. Your favorite.
>
> See you when you get home, husband.

I sent off the text before finishing dinner—homemade lasagna and garlic bread, which smelled absolutely amazing. And it was his favorite, so I knew he'd like it.

I'd followed the recipe in his recipe book, thankful that I'd bothered to learn to cook when I was younger. Daniel might have made dinner most nights, but I knew my way around the kitchen, too, and I wanted to spoil him. Because he deserved it.

Because I loved him, and I had taken the coward's way out instead of telling him. Whispering it after he'd gone asleep because I couldn't keep it in my chest one moment longer, but maybe I should have told him a long time ago.

I was pretty sure he loved me too, but it wasn't like he'd said it either. We'd decided it wasn't fake, but...

Since spring break was this week, I didn't have any classes to teach, and I hadn't started taking dress commissions again this year yet. With trying to get pregnant and everything else, I had enough on my plate, so thankfully, I had time to just *breathe*. Or try to. I'd somehow gotten more and more exhausted the more the night went on.

With dinner in the slow cooker and garlic bread ready to pop in the oven on broil, I sat down on the couch with my kindle. I had a few highly anticipated books from my favorite authors I wanted to catch up on, since I'd been reading less lately. Rubbing my sore ankles, I opened the first book, diving in to the world, fully immersing myself in my favorite author's writing.

The next time I looked up, the slow cooker was beeping at me that the food was done, and the clock read 6:30. Daniel normally got home from work at six.

Where was he? I rubbed my eyes, feeling more tired than normal. I didn't think I'd been overdoing it this week, but what did I know?

Opening my phone, I saw a text had come through while I'd been reading, and I scrambled to open it.

DANIEL
Sorry, things ran behind. I'm on my way home now.

CHARLOTTE
It's fine. I was just reading. Food will be ready when you get home.

Yawning, I moved to put the bread in the oven on broil and clean up my mess in the kitchen. I needed a nap. Maybe I'd go to bed early tonight.

"Darling, I'm home!" Daniel shouted from the door, and I instantly perked up at the rightness of those words. Of how much this felt like home. Not this house—but here. With Daniel.

When he came into the living room, I opened my arms for a hug, but he picked me up by the waist instead, pulling me up off of the couch and into his arms.

I squealed, unable to stop myself from laughing as he threw me over his shoulder before we both settled on the couch, me nestled into his lap.

"Hi," I said, a little breathless from laughing.

"Hi, wife." Daniel grinned, before placing a kiss on my lips. "Did you have a good day?"

"The best. I'm working on this incredible project, and..." He practically sighed in contentment. "I can't wait for you to see it."

"Me?" I hadn't seen much of his work since college.

He nodded. "I think you'll like this one."

"So, when *do* I get to see it?" I curled my fingers into the short hair at the nape of his neck, rubbing through his hair.

"When it's done."

I pouted. "Shouldn't your wife get to see it early?"

Honestly, I had no idea what it even was, but I wanted to see what he'd been working on for the last few months. Wanted to be the kind of wife who showed up at his office with a basket of muffins and got to know all the people he worked with. So the fact that he'd even thought of me in that regard made me smile.

"So, what was that about dinner?"

"Oh." I could feel my cheeks turning pink. "I know you normally cook, but..." I'd wanted to surprise him. "I made lasagna. Just like your Mom's."

He grinned. "You didn't have to."

"I know. But I wanted to. You're always taking care of me, and I thought maybe... it was my turn to take care of you." For a long time, I'd always taken care of myself, and then he'd shown me what it was like to let someone else take care of me. I wanted to show him how much I loved that. How much it meant to me.

Daniel's face lit up, and he delicately brushed the hair away from my face. "I want to kiss you so badly right now."

Playfully, I smacked his chest. "You can't. The food will get cold."

This time, it was him who pouted, especially after I forced myself to climb off of his lap before I kissed him myself. He was too tempting, especially with that dopey expression on his face.

I winced as a prickling feeling went through my stomach.

"What?" Daniel rushed to my side. "Are you okay?"

"Yeah, just... a cramp, I think." I bit my lip. *Probably just my period.* I didn't mention that, though. It was due any day, and I didn't want to think about it. "I'm fine now."

He frowned. "If you're sure..."

I nodded. "Yup. Now... dinner?"

Daniel extended his hand. "Shall we?"

"Lead the way, husband," I said, wondering if this would ever stop feeling like we were just playing house. Wondering how to work up the courage to tell him how I really felt.

∽

MY PHONE RANG, a four-way FaceTime call with the girls. Gabbi had started it, and when I joined, three other smiling faces looked back at me.

"Hello?" I blinked at the tiny screen on my phone.

"Charlotte!" Gabbi beamed. "I have news!"

Is that why you're calling at this time of the morning? I grumbled as I rubbed my eyes. I'd been feeling extra tired this week, and I'd laid down for a mid-morning nap, which was now, unfortunately, over.

All of my complaints came screeching to a halt when Gabbi's hand lifted into the frame of the camera—her left hand, now sporting a gorgeous diamond ring. "We're engaged!"

We all squealed, practically screaming in excitement at our friend.

"Oh my gosh!" Noelle exclaimed. "I can't believe it!"

Hunter poked his head into the frame, wrapping his tall frame around Gabbi's much smaller one. "Hi, girls."

"Hi, Hunter," Angelina said, batting her eyelashes. "You better take good care of my best friend, you hear me?"

He gave her a wink through the phone. "I plan on it."

Gabbi pushed him away playfully. "And I have someone else I want you all to meet, too." She hefted up a little bundle of light brown fur into the frame. "This is Rowan. Guess it was time we joined the dog circle, too. Hunter surprised me with her this morning. The ring was on her collar."

"Oh, Gabs." My heart melted. "She's beautiful."

"Can't we get a dog?" I heard Benjamin mumbling in the background of Angelina's call, and she shushed him. I laughed. Those two already had their hands full with their two black cats, though I couldn't imagine either of them as anything other than cat parents.

"Guess the group chat name officially needs to change," Noelle said with a laugh.

"Best Friends Book Club? No way. That name's like your *baby*," Angelina added, a little gasp at the end for emphasis.

"No." Her cheeks pinked. "Theirs. Book Boyfriends no longer, huh?"

We'd had this conversation a few months ago, and back then, everything with Daniel and I had been fake, a show we'd put on for our friends, but now...

"We got really lucky, didn't we?" I murmured, watching Daniel who was sitting on the floor of his office, strumming chords on his guitar. Try as I might over the years to get him to share his musical talents even with our friends, he never sang in public—or for anyone.

Except for me.

And now... I *was* really lucky.

Even with everything going on—I had the best friends a girl could have ever asked for. Sure, we all liked to tease each other, but we also pushed each other when we knew we needed it. And I wouldn't have traded them for the world.

"We did," Gabbi agreed with a hum, burying her face in Rowan's fur. "Now, I know we'll celebrate soon, but I just wanted to share the news real quick. Hunter and I are going to go have a celebration of our own." She winked.

"Gross," came Benjamin's voice again. "That's my brother you're talking about."

"Ben, I swear to God—" Angelina chirped back, narrowing

her eyes at where he was out of frame. "Love you, Gabs. So happy for you."

"Thanks."

We all said our goodbyes and made plans to see each other soon, and I couldn't help but smile as I ended the call. With Daniel spending even less time at home, I was feeling unsteady and uncertain, as if the ground was shifting beneath me. But talking to my girls, the ones who had been with me through thick and thin—it always brightened my spirits.

Daniel walked into the kitchen, opening the fridge to pop a few pieces of cheese into his mouth.

"Was that your girls?" He asked, settling down on the couch next to me, adjusting my blanket so it rested over both of us.

"Yeah." I gave him a small smile. "Hunter proposed to Gabbi."

"Oh, did he?" Daniel's smirk lit up his face.

"You totally knew, didn't you?"

He popped another cheese cube in. "We don't have a group chat for nothing."

"I can't believe you didn't tell me! I'm your *wife!*"

Daniel quirked an eyebrow. "Hunter asked me not to."

"I see where your loyalties lie," I said, crossing my arms and huffing my breath.

He leaned over, kissing my cheek. "To you."

"Mhm."

"Charlotte."

"What?"

A deep laugh emitted from his lungs. "Are you actually mad that I didn't tell you?"

"No," I said, even though I didn't make eye contact with him as he pried my arms apart and pulled me into his lap.

"Good." He kissed my neck. "Because I am."

"Am what?"

"On your team. Always."

It felt like as much of a vow as our marriage had been.

Always.

"I'm on yours too, you know," I said, my words barely audible. A breath.

"I know."

And then he kissed me like it was true.

Like there was nothing that could ever pull us apart.

I could only hope that nothing would.

∼

DANIEL and I had found our rhythm, but the sinking feeling in my gut lingered. Our nightly ritual of eating and cuddling was comforting, but it couldn't bridge the gap between us. I didn't know what to do.

Maybe I was a coward. That was the best explanation for it.

"What's this?" He picked up the envelope, and I froze.

Shit. It was an accident that I left it out. I had a vague memory of tucking it away in a drawer, but it obviously hadn't been. I could only blame that on my sluggish nature over the past week, because my brain clearly was malfunctioning from a lack of sleep. Even my mid-day naps weren't helping.

"It's nothing." I waved him off, trying to grab it from his hands, but since he had nearly a foot on me, it was no use.

He held it above his head, and when I finally gave up, slinking against the counter, he opened the envelope and read the paper.

"You got offered a job in California?" He raised an eyebrow. "Charlotte... What is this?" He looked crushed. Absolutely devastated.

What was that expression everyone always used to say? The calm before the storm? Of course, now that everything was perfect, something would come up to derail everything.

Why'd I been ignoring that feeling in my gut for so long?

I shook my head. "It's not what you think. I didn't even apply."

"But you want to do it? You want to go home?" The way he

said home broke my heart. Didn't he know that this was my home?

That *he* was my home?

I winced. "It's a wonderful opportunity, sure, but—" But no, I didn't *want* to go. He was my husband, and I didn't want to leave him. I didn't want to be apart from him, or the life we were building together. Even though I wasn't sure what the future would bring, I knew that much.

"If we weren't married, would you go?"

"I..." I blinked. Would I? *Maybe.* "But we *are* married." And we'd been trying to have a baby. Even if it was early April and I'd been off my birth control for four months. I wasn't *that* naïve, I knew these things took time.

"You should go."

"What?" My mouth dropped open.

"If it's your dream, if it's what you want—you should go."

I blinked. "Daniel. You're... You can't be serious?" My mouth dropped open. "You want me to leave you? What about us? Our marriage?"

He looked up at me, his eyes wounded. Had I really hurt him this badly? I hadn't even asked for this. "I don't want you to give things up because of me."

"I'm not giving anything up. I'm just choosing *you*." My fingers traced the contours of his face as I cupped his cheeks. "Because I love you, okay? I love you, and I'm not going anywhere."

"Charlotte—" His eyes were glassy, and I searched them for answers.

His jawline was defined as I traced it with my fingers, feeling the slight roughness of his unshaved skin. I thought I liked it like that, even though he had always been clean-shaven before.

"You don't have to say it back," I murmured. "But I'm here. I'm in this for the long haul. Okay?"

Continuing to hold on to his face, I felt him nod in acknowledgement.

My phone rang, breaking the silence, ruining the moment. But I didn't move.

"Charlotte."

"Hm?"

"Your phone."

"Right."

I picked it up. *Mom*. Our eyes connected, and that sinking feeling told me something was *wrong*. When was the last time she'd called me? Before my wedding, that was sure.

"Hi, Mom," I said, sucking in a breath as I picked up the phone.

"Charlotte." That was it. No hello. No preamble. Just my *name*.

"What's going on?"

"Your sister needs you. I—she's not due for another two weeks, and her husband is busy with a case, but—"

"Mom." I frowned, interrupting her. "She can call me herself, you know."

My mother sighed. "Lavender doesn't want to bother you. She knows you just got married."

"Okay?" I raised an eyebrow, even though I knew she couldn't see me.

"She's in labor. They're worried that there will be complications, and—" My mother choked out a sob.

My eyes widened as I listened to her explain what was happening, and when I hung up the phone, I promised I'd be there soon.

"What's wrong?" He asked me, his face full of worry. For *me*.

It broke my heart a little, knowing what I had to say next.

"I have to go."

CHAPTER 32
Daniel

I have to go? She had just confessed her love for me when the phone rang, cutting off any chance of my reply.

Fuck, I had the worst timing on the planet. But she looked panicked, and I knew something had happened with her sister. Her mom might have been an overbearing helicopter parent who didn't know quite when to step out of her daughter's lives, but Charlotte still cared.

"Is everything okay?"

She shook her head *no*.

"What?"

"I have to go to California. Home." The word made me wince. "My sister's gone into labor. She..." Charlotte squeezed her eyes shut. "She needs me. There's complications, and..." she said, and I could sense the weight of responsibility in her words. She trailed off, her voice fading as she shrugged her arms.

"Do you want me to come with you?" I'd told her I would. That I'd be by her side. She'd said the same thing to me, too, only minutes before, hadn't she?

She shook her head. "This is something I need to do on my own. And besides, you have that big project. You can't leave right now." Her voice was quiet, withdrawn.

Only she didn't know what that project was.

That it was all for her.

And I knew that this wasn't forever, wasn't a goodbye, but it felt like something fundamental was broken if I just let her go without telling her how I felt. Without making sure she knew how much I loved her.

"But..." I frowned. I didn't like the way her family treated her. How they belittled her career, the things she'd chosen in this life. "I don't want you to be alone."

"No matter how I feel about my mom... That's my sister. And I love her. And my niece." Her eyes filled with tears. "If we lose her..."

Because deep down, no matter how badly they treated her, Charlotte would always want one thing. Her family's love and acceptance.

"I know," I murmured. As I held her close, I could feel her body trembling. I rubbed her back and ran my fingers through her hair, whispering soothing words into her ear until she finally relaxed. "When do you want to leave?"

She gave me a sad smile. "Can you drive me to the airport? I'm going to go pack a bag and try to get on a last-minute flight."

I nodded, kissing her forehead. "Yeah. Anything you need, just say the word." I meant it.

Even if the idea of her being there without me, dealing with this crisis all on her own, broke my heart.

I'd do whatever she needed me to do for her to realize just how much I meant it when I said I was on her team.

"So... I'll call you?" Charlotte said, her pink Duffel bag slung over one arm and a matching backpack on the other. I'd snuck in a few new books into her bag when she wasn't looking, hoping that the small surprise would provide some modicum of comfort. It wasn't enough, but it was all I had.

I nodded. "I'll be the one waiting by the phone." It was a bad joke, but I meant it.

She held the one-way ticket in her hand, clutching her phone like it was her lifeline.

"I should go." She turned to look at the security line.

I pulled her in tight, wrapping my arms around her in a big hug, kissing her forehead.

"Bye."

She turned around, but I couldn't let her leave like this. With just a short goodbye. Not for her.

"Charlotte, wait—" I said, and she turned around.

Flung herself into my arms.

Kissed me like there was no tomorrow. Like nothing else mattered. Like we weren't at the airport in public. Like this wasn't just a temporary separation.

"I'm sorry," she whispered against my lips as we pulled apart, my hands still wrapped around her tiny waist, hers around my neck.

"Come back. Come home to me." It was a hoarse whisper, but it was all I could say. All I could offer.

She nodded, giving me a sad smile as she ran her finger over my wedding band. The one I'd never taken off since we'd said our vows. Because they meant something to me.

Because she meant something to me.

I love you. It was right on the tip of my tongue. But here, like this? It wasn't enough. "Charlotte, I—"

She kissed me again, a soft press of our lips, before separating our bodies. Picking up the bags she'd dropped on the floor.

"I'll miss you," I whispered to her back. *I love you.*

And I stood there, watching my wife walk through security, away from the life we'd been building. Away from *me*.

∽

THE CONSTRUCTION on *the* project was going well. All the floors were in, and when I stood around, watching as the carpenters installed the kitchen cabinets, I could almost imagine the life that would be lived here.

A wife, dancing with her husband in the fridge's light. Baking cookies in the oven. A glimpse of blonde hair and a strawberry scent that had seemed to disappear from my sheets. Our sheets.

God, I wanted to show her every square foot. Every little detail I'd handpicked.

And I would.

I'd tell her I loved her, like I should have done in the kitchen weeks ago when I'd caught her staring off into the distance. Like I should have told her on our wedding night.

Like I should have told her in college, when I'd proposed our marriage pact.

Despite knowing every detail of how we got here, I'd do it all again a million times over if it meant she'd be waiting for me at the end of the aisle. Dressed in white, her cheeks pink and her golden hair cascading in curls down her back.

My bride.

She was everything.

My Charlotte.

My wife.

Graceful owner of my heart.

The can of pink paint stared back at me, and I got to work, rolling the wall myself. I'd make it perfect, because while I was here, and she was there, I had nothing else to do.

So I threw myself into making sure every single piece of the project was perfect.

Because someone special deserved it.

CHAPTER 33
Charlotte

I heaved Leila up onto my hip, walking over to the sink with my sister's two-year-old.

"How's everything been?" Daniel asked on speakerphone.

"Good. It sounds like they're going to release Lav and the baby soon from the hospital." I'd already been down here for almost a week, and my sister, her husband and their new baby girl —Lauren—had been at the hospital that entire time. Following a hard labor, they took Lavender to the operating room for a C-section, which resulted in a longer recovery time than she had expected.

And I was good, mostly. The line was quiet. "I miss you," I whispered.

"I almost bought a flight down for this weekend. The house is too quiet without you."

"You can't leave Brownie," I said, suddenly wishing to bury my face in his fur. "Besides, I'll be home before you know it. Maybe another week. I promised I'd help a bit while everyone settles in."

He sighed. "Okay, it's just..." Daniel trailed off, not finishing his sentence.

"Hmm?"

"Never mind. It's not important. I just can't wait to have you back here, in my arms."

"I know," I said, because I wanted that too. More than he knew. "I gotta go, okay?"

"Yeah." His voice was sullen, withdrawn. "Talk to you soon."

After I hung up, I cried.

Because all I wanted was for him to say *I'm coming anyway*, and he hadn't. Of course he hadn't.

For the same reason he wasn't here in the first place.

Because I hadn't asked.

~

MY SISTER ARRIVED home a day later, her arms wrapped tightly around a sleeping bundle that radiated warmth and love. Of course, I'd visited in the hospital after she'd been born, but those first days had made all the difference.

"Thank you for everything," my sister said, wrapping me up in a hug after settling her newborn into a crib.

"Of course. You're my sister." I picked little baby Luna up in my arms. "And I wouldn't have missed this for the world." I nuzzled my face against her, inhaling the sweet newborn baby smell. I lived for it. And for once, there was no ounce of jealousy thrumming through my veins. Just genuine happiness for my sister and her little family.

And maybe it was the warmth settled in my gut that someday I would experience it too. That I knew I'd get that chance. Because I had Daniel. Because it wasn't fake, and I loved him. Even if I'd run away before he could say it back.

She hesitated before speaking again. "Look, I... I know it wasn't easy growing up with Mom. All those pageants and modeling gigs growing up... She tried, but it wasn't enough, was it?"

"But... I thought you loved it?"

"Maybe I did. Maybe I loved the attention I got because of it. Either way, it wasn't my dream. And neither one of us ever really got to be kids." She kissed the top of Leila's head. "Not like they will. And I know mom always compared you to me, but—"

"Stop." I held up a hand. "It's not your fault. None of it is."

"But you moved away, and you got as far away from here as possible. In the past ten years, you've barely come home. And I know you love it up there, even if I think you're crazy because it's always raining, but I never got to tell you how I felt. How much I loved being your older sister and wished things were different. I did my best to reign Mom in at your wedding, because you saw how she was with mine."

"All that to say, I'm really proud of you. And I love you so much."

"Lav..." My eyes filled with tears. Maybe it was time I be honest with her, too. "I never wanted to compete with you over Mom's attention. You were my big sister. I looked up to you, admired you. I know I haven't been around much. But that's not because I resented you or anything. It was just... hard."

"Hard?" She raised an eyebrow as I cupped the back of her daughter's head.

"I wanted this, too." I looked around the house. "A husband, a home. A life. But I didn't have any of that."

"But..." She frowned. "I thought you loved living in Portland."

"I did." I sighed. "I do. It's not that. It was that I was chasing this fairytale, thinking that if I just found the right person, everything would click into place for me like it did for you. But that isn't how life works, is it?"

Lavender chuckled, taking Luna from me, rocking her in her arms. "No. It's not."

"Because love—genuine love—it takes work. But I've found that. The person who adores me. Who takes care of me, supports me. Has my back. And it's nothing like the fairytale I'd dreamed of."

"No?"

I shook my head, but a big smile spread over my face. "It's better. It's... *Everything.*"

"So, why are you still here? Go home and get your man, silly."

I opened my mouth to tell her just that, but then a wave of nausea hit me. *Not again.* Feeling dizzy, I clutched the side of the table.

"Charlotte, you look really pale. Are you sure you're okay?" Lavender asked me, the worry clear on her face.

I shook my head. No, I wasn't okay. It was getting harder to ignore the truth. I'd thrown up almost every day since I'd been here, and all I wanted was my husband. I could hardly keep up lying to myself.

"Why don't you call your husband?" She rubbed my back as I tried to push my sweaty hair off my face.

I'd almost done it every night, asking him to come get me. But I was trying to prove something to myself, wasn't I? Except I didn't know what that was.

"Yeah." I nodded, trying not to dry heave. I hadn't kept anything down all day, so there was nothing left to come up, anyway.

"Go home," she whispered. "To Mom's. I got everything here. I'll tell her you weren't feeling good and you can get in a good nap."

"Are you sure? I know you wanted some time to bond with your new baby..."

She waved me off. "We've got plenty of time for that. Besides, we're a family of four now, you know? I just want to savor all these moments while they're this little. Charlotte, it's... It's not just a bug, is it?" Lavender asked as I grabbed my bag, slinging it over my shoulder.

Tears pricked at my eyes as I shook my head. "No. We've been trying and I'm..." *I'm late.*

"Have you taken a test?"

I swallowed roughly. "Not yet. I can't..." Not without him. I needed him by my side. He wanted this just as much as I did. So I couldn't.

And I was being a coward and hiding in California. He'd told me to go, and I'd gone. But being here wasn't right. It was all wrong. Because he wasn't here. He'd said he'd come, and I'd told him no.

"Call your husband, Charlotte. Tell him, and he'll be here." She offered me a small smile. "You know he will. Because that man—he loves you. So much. I think he always has."

I looked up at her, cradling her baby against her chest, and I wondered if she was right.

"You think so?"

She nodded. "He's looked at you like you were his entire world since college, Charlotte. I was just surprised it took you this long to realize it. But I'm glad it worked out for the two of you. It's good to see you this happy. Now, go. Before I call Mom and make her drag you home yourself."

"Okay." I agreed. "I love you."

She wrapped an arm around me, hugging me tightly. "I love you too, Char. Now go. Call your man."

Getting back to Mom's house, I peeled off my sports bra and leggings as I hopped in the shower. Letting the water rush over me, I let the tears drip from my eyes, even though I didn't know why I was crying. Finally, when I got out and wrapped a fluffy towel around my clean body, I forced myself to do the thing I'd been avoiding.

I picked up my phone and hit his name.

It barely even rang before he picked up, and he hadn't even gotten a word out when I spoke.

"Daniel... I know I told you not to come, but... I need you." The tears were flowing down my face, and all I wanted to do was bury myself in his arms. Where I felt safe. "I don't want to be alone," I whispered.

"You're never alone," he murmured, something that felt a lot more like a promise than just a casual statement. "I'm on my way, baby, okay? I'll be there as soon as I can get on a flight."

I nodded into the phone, even though he couldn't hear me. "Okay," I whispered back.

∼

I'D SPENT most of the day curled up in my bed, only finally heading downstairs that night in search of food that might curb my appetite. I was sick all morning, but I'd barely eaten anything today, and now I was practically ravenous.

Standing in the kitchen, I closed my eyes, picturing Daniel's face. *He's coming,* I reminded myself. *He'll come get you, and then you can go home, and—*

"Charlotte?" my mom asked, but I couldn't quite focus on her face.

I blinked, the rush of dizziness hitting me again. But it was different this time. I tried to grip the top of a barstool as another round of nausea hit me.

Morning sickness my ass, I scowled, but the thought didn't last long. "I don't feel so good, mom," I got out, hoping I'd managed to put together a string of coherent words as I swayed on my feet.

She rushed over to me. "What do you need, honey?"

"Daniel. Call Daniel," I said, and then everything went black.

CHAPTER 34
Daniel

"Where's my wife?" I barked as the door opened, not caring who stood behind it.

The last eight hours had been chaos, trying to get on a flight and get down to her after she called me. But I didn't mind one bit. I'd missed her too much, hurt too much without having her by my side. I'd known it wasn't forever, but I still couldn't stand us being apart. Charlotte was the missing piece that made me feel complete, and I was taking her home.

Because we were supposed to be together.

Matthew and Noelle had agreed to keep Brownie until we got back, knowing that I needed to be with her.

Her dad pointed me up the stairs. "Second door on the right."

I nodded my thanks, not even stopping for a *hello*, or a *how are you, sir?* I had one goal in mind, a singular focus driving me.

Charlotte.

I eased open her childhood bedroom door, walking into the quiet room. It was funny, after all this time, seeing where she grew up. The light pink glittery walls, the dance trophies that sat on her shelf. A small collection of books that she must have read when she was younger. The fairy wings I assumed she'd used for her

Tinkerbell costume. All these little pieces of her life, coming together to make one complete picture. Every part of her made her who she was, the strong, resilient girl who jumped to help her family, even when they didn't deserve it.

Thank goodness her dad had let me in, showing me upstairs to her room.

"Charlotte?" I called out, not hearing any movement inside the room. "Love?"

"I'm in here," her voice called from the bathroom, sniffling. My backpack hit the floor with a thud, and I realized I had no idea what was inside. Without wasting any time, I packed my things and left as soon as I received the call.

Pulling open the bathroom door, I found her tear-stained face, her arms wrapped around her knees as she hugged herself tight.

"Baby," I whispered, and pulled her into my arms.

"You're here," she breathed, nuzzling her nose into my neck.

"I'm here," I agreed. "And I'm never going to let you leave again. Not without me, at least." Agreeing to this had been painful. I should have just gone, but then I would have had to explain why exactly my biggest project for work right now wasn't exactly *my* project anymore. And I thought I'd keep that explanation in my pocket for just a little longer.

"Good." Charlotte nodded against my skin. "Can you just... hold me for a bit?"

"Is everything okay?"

She shook her head as I picked her up and carried her to the king-sized bed, where I leaned against the propped pillows with her still in my arms, legs draped over my lap.

"Charlotte." I kept my voice low, tipping her head up to meet mine. "When your Mom called, she told me..." That she was bleeding. And sick. I'd immediately feared the worst. Especially with her passing out.

She winced. "I might have overreacted. It was just a bit of spotting. But that, combined with the dizziness... I thought..."

I frowned. "You passed out."

"I'm okay. But it turns out that more than just running after a two-year-old with very little water can make you feel a little faint." She paused. "And nauseous." She slid my hand over her stomach. "I was just ignoring all the signs because you weren't here."

The signs. I blinked. "You're..."

"It's still pretty early, and I haven't even taken a test yet, but... I missed my period."

"Charlotte..." I murmured, interlacing our hands. She hadn't even said the words yet, and my heart was already thrumming in my chest.

She nodded. "At least, I'm pretty sure I am. I hope I am, otherwise you came down here for nothing."

"It's not nothing, baby." I smoothed a hand over her hair as I held her. "No matter where you are, if you need me, I'll always come for you."

The woman who didn't even know how much I loved her. Something I would fix as soon as possible, because I was a fool. God, she was carrying our baby, and I'd foolishly told her to come here without me. To do what she needed to do for her family, and then come home to me.

"I didn't want to do it without you," she said, silent tears—happy tears—dripping down her cheeks, which I wiped away with my thumbs. "I couldn't do it without you."

"You don't have to," I said, kissing her hand softly. "I'm here now."

"Everyone kept telling me to take a test, but I said no, there's no way. I couldn't be... Not *now*. But I... Mom went and bought a few earlier, but I didn't want to find out alone."

"Do you want to take them now? Together?"

She nodded. "Yes."

My hand wrapped around the back of her neck, pulling her forehead to rest against mine. "No matter what happens, we're in this together, alright? And even if it's not what we want, it's okay."

Charlotte relaxed into my embrace, placing a kiss to the side of my cheek. "I know," she mumbled. Clambering out of my arms, she grabbed the plastic bag from her desk. "Guess it's time for me to go pee on some sticks now." She frowned down at the boxes.

"What? What's wrong?"

"Have you ever thought about how weird this is? About how one tiny box can hold the answers to your fate? I'm pretty sure I'm about to have stage fright over a test for the first time in my life."

I hummed in amusement, taking her free hand in mine, squeezing it. "Hey, breathe. We got this. I'm right here."

She nodded, cradling the bag to her chest. "Right. I'm just..." Charlotte squeezed her eyes shut. "I'm scared, Daniel."

Of all the people in the world, you don't have to explain yourself to me. You never have. "I know, baby."

Nodding her head, I squeezed her hand one more time before letting it go, and she left me sitting on her bed as she retreated into the bathroom.

I heard the toilet flush, and then she came back out, drying her freshly washed hands on her sweats.

"Now we wait," she murmured, curling back up in my lap. "I set an alarm," she mumbled, before burying her head in my chest, like she was trying to breathe me in.

Fuck, a week without her, and I felt the same. Like I needed to absorb her scent into my skin, to memorize every inch, every curve, because I missed her more than I would have ever thought was possible. But that was how it had always been with this girl. From the very first smile she'd flashed at me, I never wanted them to stop.

I wanted to keep being on the receiving end of her smiles for the rest of our lives.

While we sat in a comfortable silence, I absentmindedly played with her golden strands of hair that fanned out over my thighs until the alarm went off.

"Charlotte," I said, nudging her from her tiny cat nap.

"Mmm?"

"Should we go find out?"

Her big gray eyes blinked open, looking up at me. Even now, I thought she was the most beautiful girl in the world. And *mine*. My wife. All mine.

The corners of her lips tilted up in a small smile as she stretched her arms. She'd only been resting in my lap for three minutes, yet she seemed infinitely more peaceful than she had before she'd taken the tests.

"Yeah. Let's do it. Together."

"Together," I agreed, helping her off of the bed and keeping our hands interlaced as we walked into the bathroom, where the tests were laying face down on the counter.

"Ready?"

Charlotte nodded, worrying her lip through her teeth. "Yes."

We both reached for one of the sticks, our fingers brushing against each other, and flipped it over simultaneously.

Positive. Every single one was positive. She hadn't taken just one, but three, all different brands.

Pregnant.

Two pink lines.

A little plus sign.

Despite the tears still streaming down her face, she was smiling brightly with happiness.

"I'm pregnant," she said, not able to pull her gaze away from the sticks. She looked at them with amazement, like she couldn't quite believe this was happening. With so much reverence, because I knew this was something she'd always wanted. "We're having a baby."

The only reason I didn't fall to my knees was because I was holding on to her.

Charlotte—my lifeline. The love of my life.

"This is it. Everything you wanted." I let my forehead rest against hers.

Charlotte shook her head. "Not everything." She cupped my face in her hands, framing them as her eyes held mine captive. "Because everything—that includes you."

And I let go of all my fears, my doubts, my worries, and I kissed my wife.

Kissed her with everything I had—every ounce of love, care, and affection I'd carried for her all those years. The years of loving her quietly from the sidelines, being her best friend. Kissed her with every intention I had for the future. My heart was filled with the certainty that I would love her forever.

"You have me," I promised. "You have me."

Her arms slid around my neck, and I could feel the warmth of her body against mine. I was lost in the moment as our lips touched. Her kiss was intoxicating, and I knew that I could never resist her.

"Make love to me," she whispered, already a writhing, needy thing as she rocked against my thigh. "Please, I need you."

"But—" I ran my fingers over her head, tenderly. "Are you sure you're okay? After yesterday..."

"I'm sure." She took my hand in hers, placing it on her breast. "I want my husband to remind me who I belong to."

Fuck. "Baby—" I warned, my voice low, body trembling as her small hands tugged at my shirt, untucking it from my pants. Pulling it off, and I let her. Of course I let her. I did the same to her, pulling off her top, then unclasping her lacy bra, eager to have her bare in front of me.

Her hair fanned out on the light pink quilted comforter as she lay sprawled out in front of me on her childhood bed, both of us naked.

I kissed her flat stomach, knowing our baby was growing inside of there. A fact that I couldn't get over—that we'd created a *life.*

As I slid a finger inside of her, she gasped and arched her back, her body responding to my touch. No matter how badly both of us needed this connection, I didn't want to hurt her.

"*Daniel.*" She moaned my name, and fuck, I liked it. Too much.

I added another finger, feeling her growing wetter as I scissored them inside of her.

"That's it," I coaxed. "My good girl. You're so wet for me." I could feel her getting closer, the way her insides were squeezing my fingers, but I just kept up my slow pace, before pulling my fingers out and popping them into my mouth, groaning at her taste on my tongue.

Too long. It had been far too fucking long since I'd tasted her.

Our eyes connected, and it was like I was under a spell, because I couldn't look away. Not for a single second, even as I slid inside of her, soaking up her gasp as I thrust in deep.

"Oh." Her eyes rolled into the back of her head.

"Fuck, baby, I'm sorry. Did I hurt you?"

She shook her head. "No. You could never." Her eyes filled with tears, and I wiped them away with my thumb. "I've been waiting a long time for this, Daniel—and I care more about it being you than anything else. Nothing else matters but us."

It was like I had known all along, always—"You're mine." I captured her lips with mine as I slid inside her again, torturously slow.

"I'm yours. I've always been yours. And I'll always be yours. Always yours." She promised, and kissed me again, deeply, and I kissed her—my wife, my best friend of almost ten years—back with everything I had.

And when we came, it was together, her soft voice whispering into my ear as I detonated, her following seconds behind me, my name on her lips.

But we didn't say I love you. We didn't need to.

I'd give her the words, anyway.

Tomorrow.

I'd tell her I loved her tomorrow.

Because I had a plan.

CHAPTER 35
Charlotte

The scenery outside the window was a blur as we drove in silence, both lost in our own thoughts.

My head was filled with a jumble of thoughts. Namely, that we had hardly said anything to each other since we'd boarded the airplane. After we'd held the positive pregnancy test together, and tears of joy streamed down my face. I could still feel the way he'd slid inside of me and held me close, how my body had relaxed in his embrace. The night was a blur, but I remember him practically carrying me to the plane.

I loved him so much, my heart was practically bursting out of my chest.

My eyes drifted shut. When we'd gotten out of bed this morning, he'd pulled his sweatshirt over my head. It was so comfortable and warm that I couldn't bring myself to take it off. Right now, all I wanted to do was go home. To crawl into our bed and cuddle with our dog.

But—"Where are we going?" I asked him, watching as he pulled off the freeway. But it wasn't the exit to our house. It was —"To Benjamin and Angelina's?"

He gave me a little smile. "You'll see."

"Hm." I turned back to the window as the neighborhoods

passed by. Closer to the freeway, they were fairly small, but the farther in you got, moving uphill, the bigger the houses were.

We pulled on to the street, passing by the house our friends had built—but he didn't pull into their driveway. No, he pulled into a different one.

"Daniel." I looked up at the house in front of us. "What are we doing here?"

He said nothing. Just kissed my knuckles before getting out of the car. Daniel came around to my side and opened up the door before I could even move, helping me out of the seat.

Wordlessly, he took my hand and headed towards the door. It looked like it was in the final stages of construction, complete with a lockbox on the front.

It was *the* lot.

The one we'd both been in love with.

The one that had sold before I'd ever uttered a word.

And why would I have? Suggested we build a house together, when back then all we were was in a fake marriage? Definitely not. But I was still sad about what could have been. Gabbi and Hunter had bought a lot here. And Matthew and Noelle were heavily considering it, planning on using their current home as a rental.

"I don't think we should be here—" I started to say, before he pulled a key out of his pocket.

I swallowed roughly. What was going on? Did he want to buy it? I supposed it wasn't quite the same as a custom house, but...

Then the door was open, and we entered the grand foyer. The flooring was down, and it looked like there were only minor things left for them to finish. But after a paint of coat—this would be a beautiful house.

He led me through the rooms, not saying a word. But we passed through a beautiful master with a bathroom that would rival Angelina and Benjamin's. A walk-in closet where all of my dresses could hang in color order. Too bad it wasn't mine. Multiple bedrooms, because this was a family home. The most beautiful built-in library I'd ever seen, complete with a window seat reading nook.

Daniel still didn't explain as we went back downstairs, continuing to explore. I couldn't help but stop and stare at the kitchen. It was bright and light and absolutely amazing. Somewhere I'd love to spend hours and hours of time, sitting and watching my husband cook meals. To make cookies for our family. To celebrate birthdays with our friends.

In my fantasy, we lived here. We were the couple that occupied these walls. If only.

"This is nice." I ran my hands over the beautiful granite countertops in the kitchen. "But really, we shouldn't be in here. This is someone's house."

"Is it?" He raised an eyebrow at me as I moved towards the back set of French doors. Not sliding doors, but two beautiful glass doors that opened up to a deck.

The deck was transformed into a magical wonderland, thanks to the countless strings of lights. I was left in awe by the sight of it.

"Daniel." My hand rested over my heart. My next question came out quiet, my breath short. I wasn't sure I had enough words. "Who's house is this?"

"Ours, darling. It's ours."

"W-what?" I practically stammered out the words.

Our house? But we had a perfectly good house. Sure, he bought it for just him, but it was *home*, and therefore it was good enough for the two—soon to be three—of us. But... he looked so serious that I knew he wasn't kidding.

Our house.

He ran his fingers through his hair bashfully. Like this gesture wasn't *everything*. "I had it built and designed for you. All those late nights in the office, all the secret phone calls... I wanted to surprise you, Charlotte. To show you how serious I was about this. Us. And now..." He let his hands rest over my still-flat stomach, over our baby.

"Oh," I said simply. But he hadn't even known until yesterday that I was pregnant. And he'd gone and had a house built for me? "But the lot... I thought it had sold?" Months ago.

"I bought it."

I snorted. "Obviously. But you didn't tell me."

All my doubts about his love vanished in that moment. I couldn't believe he had done something like this for me.

"Charlotte... In case it wasn't obvious, I love you." His forehead rested against mine, and my breath caught. "I'm in love with you."

"You really love me?" I whispered, even though he'd already said it. Proved it, too. But I was selfish, and I just wanted to hear him say it again. "Not just as my best friend?"

"Yeah," he confirmed, "I really fucking love you, Char."

"Daniel—" I was blinking back the tears.

"I've been so in love with you—so desperately, *hopelessly* in love with you—since your freshman year of college, and I always hoped you'd see me like that too. That you'd wake up and realize I was right here, and I always had been. Watching you date other people broke my heart, and I tried so hard to move on. To not want you. But I couldn't. When we made that marriage pact my senior year, all I could think about was how much I wanted to tell you I had feelings for you. That I wanted to be with you, for real. But I didn't want to lose your friendship. The thought of not having you in my life was unbearable, so I decided it would be better to stay friends." With a shake of his head, Daniel paused and took a deep breath. "But this... this *is* real, darling. I've always longed to call you my wife. From the moment I met you, I knew you were the one I wanted to spend the rest of my life with. I want to walk through this life with you, hand in hand, and raise our children together. I want us to settle down and make a home here. Start our family here."

He dropped to one knee right there. In our future kitchen, where we would spend countless hours cooking and laughing, lay before me. There was no doubt about that in my mind. "Charlotte Alexandra Bradford, will you marry me?"

I couldn't suppress my giggle. "We're already married, silly."

"Then will you marry me again?" He ran his fingers over my ring, pressing a small kiss to it. "For real this time. If you'll have me."

"I don't know what to say." Because there were too *many* things to say. Not because I didn't know what my answer was. I'd always known what my answer was.

"Say yes. Because you're it. You're it for me. I took one look at you and I knew I was going to marry you one day. I have loved you since I first laid eyes on you, and I'll love you for the rest of our lives if you let me."

"Daniel..." My eyes were definitely full of tears. "I love you too. And I'd marry you a thousand times over, if that's what it took."

He pulled me into his arms, placing a light kiss to my lips before he started swaying us in our new kitchen.

"You know, I first bought that ring two years ago," he said, his voice rough. "I saw it sitting in a shop window, and I just... knew."

"You *did?*" He'd had a ring, all that time? At first, I'd thought our marriage was a spur-of-the-moment decision. But this was proof that he'd been planning this all along. That he'd always wanted me. My eyes filled with tears. Damn pregnancy hormones.

"I didn't even have a reason to back then. The marriage pact was in the back of my mind, always, but... It's yours. It's always been yours. Just like my heart."

"I'm yours," I said, sealing another kiss over his lips.

"Now, can I show you the rest of our house?" He asked, giving me the most dazzling smile as he pulled me towards the hallway.

"Lead the way, husband."

"Always, wife."

THE HOUSE WAS PERFECT. But for now, I just wanted to go home. Sleep in our bed. Adjust to all the news of the last forty-eight hours. Shower off all the airport gunk from my body.

Picking my duffel back out of the backseat, where it had sat ever since we'd left the airport, I trudged up the sidewalk towards the house.

I heard a bark, and a blur of brown flashed in my peripheral vision.

"Brownie!" Daniel shouted, as if that could keep him from jumping on my legs and practically pommeling me to the ground, showering me with kisses.

"Hello to you, too," I laughed once our puppy finally gave up on the relentless love of my face. I wiped off the slobber, scratching him between the ears and giving him lots of kisses.

"He missed you," Daniel said, grabbing hold of his collar.

"I missed you too, sweet pup."

It was the hardest part about leaving—not having both of my guys by my side. At almost six months old, he wasn't quite full grown, but he'd also been the runt of the litter, so he was still smaller than your typical German Shepherd. Still, he was already around 50 pounds.

"Good thing you're stuck with me, huh?"

Because I was never leaving, even for the most amazing job offer in the world. I loved dance, but I was happy with my local studio. I didn't need to go to guest teach classes, work intensives, or guest choreograph for dancers. They were things that made me happy, but the thing that made me happiest was here.

Home. With Daniel.

Giving Brownie another head scratch, I stood back up to grab my stuff, but Daniel stopped me. "I got it. You shouldn't be lifting a bunch of stuff, anyway."

I raised an eyebrow. "Daniel. Are you going to be all overprotective of me now that I'm—" I could barely say the word. It still didn't feel real.

"Pregnant?" He finished my sentence.

Following him in the house, Brownie at my feet, I hummed in response.

He dropped my bags, turning around to pin me against the door. "Yes."

"Yes?"

Daniel nodded. "I know how much you want this. So, yeah. I'm going to make sure you're both okay."

"Okay." I gave him a warm smile, wrapping my arms around his neck.

"What are you doing?"

I leaned my head against his shoulder. "Waiting for you to carry me to bed."

He laughed. "Oh, it's like that now, is it?"

"Mhm." Lifting me by the ass, I wrapped my legs around his back, and he trudged up the stairs with me in my koala hold.

"You know, I noticed the fireplace in the new house..." I said as he carried me up the stairs, burying my face in the crook of his neck. With every breath, I took in the spicy scent of him, feeling a rush of warmth spread through me.

"Mmm, you did, did you?"

I nodded. "Feeling a little reminiscent of our ski trip, husband?"

"Maybe I just wanted a do-over in our own house. Total privacy. No worrying about our friends catching us."

I let my mouth hover close to his ear. "But wasn't that half the fun?" I nibbled on his earlobe, bringing it into my mouth. "The rush of possibly getting caught?"

"Every time I think I know what you're going to say, you surprise me." He laughed.

"I mean, after the dance studio..." Tracking it back, I was pretty sure that was the night he'd gotten me pregnant. "And to think, less than a year ago, I was a virgin."

And for the rest of the night, he stayed by my side, neither one of us wanting to be apart for even a moment.

Even when he turned on the shower and stripped my clothes.

Even when he dried me off and pulled a clean t-shirt of his over my body.

Even when we curled up in our bed, Brownie laying at our feet and Daniel holding me tight.

Even when we whispered *I love you* in the darkness of our room.

It was everything I'd ever wished for—and more.

CHAPTER 36
Charlotte

MAY

"Charlotte Bradford?" A voice called. "You can come on back."

"You ready?" Daniel murmured to me as I stood up, weaving his fingers through mine.

Even with positive test results, the last two weeks of waiting for this appointment had been grueling, knowing that a million things could still go wrong.

"With you by my side... For anything," I agreed as we walked into the room.

The nurse got us settled in, took my blood pressure and asked a series of questions before letting me know the doctor would be in soon.

"Knock, knock," my OB said, opening the door. Her brown hair rested against her stark white coat, and she gave me a friendly smile. "Charlotte?"

"That's me."

"And this must be Dad?"

Daniel nodded, extending out his hand to shake hers. "I'm her husband, Daniel."

"It's great to meet you both. I'm Dr. Richardson, but you can call me Miranda."

"Hi."

"How have you been feeling?"

"Oh, you know, the usual…" Fatigue? Check. Sometimes I felt like all I wanted to do was sleep, but also I kept waking up in the middle of the night to pee, or tossing and turning in bed. Morning sickness that just wouldn't quit it? Check.

I quickly recounted my symptoms to her, leaning into Daniel's touch as he slowly rubbed up and down my back. But even if I was nauseous all day—I was happy. Because this was everything I'd wanted—dreamed of.

"If you want to lift your shirt, I'll take a look and see how you're measuring, plus we'll see if we can see anything, okay?"

I'd purposefully worn a flowy top for this reason, and I rolled it up, revealing my flat stomach.

"This might be cold," she warned before squirting the ultrasound gel on my abdomen and pressing the wand against my skin. Dr. Richardson focused on the screen as she moved the device around, looking at

"What are you doing now?" Daniel asked, watching her work.

"Taking a few measurements to get an idea of the gestational age," she answered, her eyes on the screen as she moved the wand over my stomach. "We measure from the top of the head to the bottom because that's the most accurate way to determine your due date."

"Baby's measuring at about 8 weeks and 3 days, so your due date should be somewhere around December 20th."

That seemed pretty in line with what I'd estimated based on my last period.

"And there's your baby." She turned around the screen, pointing at the small, almost-human like blob that had appeared.

Daniel's hand clutched mine as we looked at the image on the ultrasound screen, and suddenly everything felt so much more *real*.

"Ohmygod." My eyes filled with tears. "This is real. We're having a baby."

He squeezed my hand. "We're having a baby." Daniel kissed my forehead as we looked in awe at the screen. "Look at that." His voice was full of wonder.

"I'm assuming you want copies of the sonogram?"

"Yes," I nodded enthusiastically. "Please."

"And here's baby's heartbeat," she said, turning up the sound on the monitor.

And *whoosh*. Everything in my life changed in a single moment, with a single sound. All the pieces of my heart rearranged, fitting in this new life that I already loved so much.

"Oh." I choked back a happy sob. "I'm sorry, I'm just so happy and—" I shook my head, trying to get rid of some of the emotion. "I've wanted this for so long." Daniel squeezed my hand once again.

"It's alright." She laughed. "It's a perfectly normal reaction, especially with all of those hormones pumping through you. Do you have any questions for me?"

I shook my head. Knowing me, I'd probably have a thousand when we got home, but right now, my mind was focused on the screen, on the little thumping sound.

After removing the wand, I wiped the jelly off my skin, letting my shirt cover my bare stomach once again.

"What about you, dad?" She turned her attention to Daniel.

"Oh, um—" He scratched the back of his head, looking almost embarrassed.

"And just so you know, sex during pregnancy is totally safe for the baby. If you have any discomfort or bleeding, then stop, but otherwise, it's perfectly fine to satisfy all of her needs."

He practically choked, his cheeks bright red. "Right. Thanks."

"So, Charlotte, we'll see you about every four to six weeks for the next few months, and once you hit twenty-eight weeks, we'll have you come in a little more often. And you'll want to start thinking about your birth plan, where you want to give birth and all of those details. I'll have my nurse give you a packet."

"Okay."

"Any other questions?"

I shook my head, and she stood up, shaking both of our hands. "Again, it was so good to meet you. I'll see you next time."

We waited for the nurse to give us the rest of the information we needed, which I was pretty sure I already had in my pregnancy books, but I wasn't complaining. I'd take every crumb of knowledge I could get about growing our little one.

I stared at the little print out of the sonogram in my hand as we sat in the car. "That's our baby," I said, unable to tear my eyes away. "How is it possible that we've known for weeks, but it only now feels real?" At first, it was only a notion, a small glimmer of hope that could have been easily extinguished. But now, hearing the heartbeat, seeing it... "I can't believe it."

"I know," he murmured. "But it's real. This is real."

He slid his hand on top of mine, both of us resting them over my stomach.

"I love you," Daniel said, brushing his nose against mine. "And our baby."

"I didn't think it was possible to love something this much. So much that I want to do anything to keep it safe. To love it, cherish it. Make sure it knows how special it is."

"Oh, of course it is."

"How do you know?"

"Because that's what it's always been like for me—loving you."

I kissed him softly on the lips. "Let's go home, husband."

"Anything, wife."

"It's been *way* too long since we did this," Angelina called from the kitchen, carrying in a bottle of wine and four glasses.

She was right—we'd let our book club activities fall by the wayside these past few months, ever since Daniel and I had dropped our wedding bomb on them. Sure, we'd all still seen each other—a ton—but there was something about our book club that always felt a little like home.

We'd sent the guys off to the bar for a round of drinks so we could talk books in peace, and without judgement. Even if we'd probably all reenacted spicy scenes from books with our guys, they didn't need to hear us talking about it.

Not that I shared all of my tales with them. Some things were best left unsaid, like the details of our sexual encounter by the fireplace in the ski house we rented or what Daniel did to help me get pregnant.

Despite the passing years, it seemed like nothing had changed, and it transported us back to our college days.

"What's on the agenda, Gabs?"

We'd always liked to switch it up and take turns choosing books. It was fun, but it was also the way I'd (lovingly) forced them all to read a series about a bunch of humans getting stranded on an ice planet with blue aliens. I didn't care what anyone said—the world building was incredible, and they were enjoyable.

Gabbi was in charge of the pick for this upcoming month, and she had brought a few options—no surprise there.

Angelina started filling the glasses, and I quickly realized my error. Ever since we'd moved our once a week hangout from a coffee shop to one of our houses, we normally had a glass of wine or two. But now...

"Oh, I'm good," I said, covering the top of the glass before she could fill it. "I'm not drinking right now."

She shrugged. "That's fine. More for me."

But Noelle turned to me with a quirked eyebrow. "Why aren't you drinking?"

"I—" My cheeks flushed. It was still early but—they were my best friends. If anything happened, I wanted them to know. I slid my hand over my abdomen, biting back my smile.

Her eyes went wide. "You're—"

I nodded, my eyes filling with tears. Happy ones. "I'm pregnant. It's still early—we just went to the doctor this morning and had the first ultrasound, but... Daniel and I are having a baby."

"Oh, Charlotte. That's amazing." Angelina's voice was full of emotion. "I can't believe I'm going to be an aunt."

"Can we see?" Noelle asked. "The sonogram?"

I nodded, pulling it out of my purse. Maybe there was a part of me that expected this to happen tonight, and that was why I hadn't taken it out of there when we'd gotten home earlier. Or maybe it was the fact that I couldn't stop sliding it out and looking at it to confirm that this was, in fact, *real*.

Everyone slid closer to me, gathering around to look at the picture.

"Wow. Look at that tiny little bean. How far along are you?" Noelle gushed.

"Eight weeks. We were planning on keeping it a secret until I was out of the first trimester, but..."

"But we're your best friends, and keeping secrets from us is impossible?" Gabbi asked.

"Pretty much."

"Does anyone else know?" Angelina raised an eyebrow, and I'm sure she was thinking about her parents. Sometimes, it was still crazy to me she was actually my *sister-in-law*. I'd never once taken our friendship for granted, even when I'd been a shy freshman and she'd intimidated the hell out of me, but we'd been friends for so long that it was easy to forget who I'd married.

"My mom was there when I fainted, and when you combine that with the nausea and the morning sickness, I think it was pretty easy for her to figure it out. But other than that..." I shook my head. "We haven't told anyone else yet."

But somehow, this felt fitting—that these girls, the family that

I'd made, were the first that I got to *tell*. The ones who would grow up with my kid calling them Aunt, because even if we weren't all sisters by blood, that was what they were to me.

Noelle squeezed me tight from my side. "I'm so happy for you." Her eyes shined brightly, sparkling with unshed tears. "I know how long you've wanted this."

"Don't you cry," I groaned. "Or I'll cry too, and then I won't be able to stop."

She giggled. "You know, this is the kind of thing I always thought I'd miss out on not having any siblings. Being my sister's maid of honor, getting to be an aunt, all of that. But I guess I got exactly that, didn't I?"

"Thank the university gods for putting us right across the hall from each other, huh?" Gabbi said with a smile. "This is the best family I could have ever asked for."

Angelina raised her glass with a smile. "I'll toast to that."

We all laughed, clinking our glasses together—including mine, now full of regular grape juice.

"Well, on that note..." Gabbi said, picking up a book from her pile. "What do we think? Fantasy or..." She grabbed a different book, holding it up as well. "Contemporary?"

"Tropes?"

"Small town, single parent or... Fated Mates with a hearty heaping of *There's Only One Bed* and *who did this to you?*"

"Okay, I'm sold on the second one already." Angelina extended out her hands to the pile, stealing the book away from Gabbi.

"I've brought something else for you all as well," Noelle added, her rosy cheeks and smile lighting up her face as she bent down and reached into her bag. "My newest book."

"*Ooooh,*" I exclaimed, marveling over the cover. "This is so pretty. Ang, you did this one too, right?" It was the perfect team: Noelle wrote the books, I helped edit them, Angelina drew the cover art, and Gabbi created content for them on social media.

My redheaded best friend might not have been a New York

Times Bestselling Author *yet,* but we'd get here there. It was only a matter of time before the world discovered her.

"Yup." She traced her fingers over the art. "This never gets old, seeing my drawings like this."

Noelle nodded. "I could say the same about seeing my name on the cover. It's still so surreal."

She'd written her first book during her last semester of grad school, when she still hadn't known what she'd wanted to do next. After being a Hall Director, she'd ended up accepting a job as a Student Advisor for the School of Business, and while she absolutely loved working with her students, I knew this was what really sparked joy for her.

"You know, I'm actually thinking about opening up a bookstore at some point. For indie authors like me, and then we can add a little cafe on one side where writers could work, and book clubs could come and do what we do."

"That sounds *amazing.*"

"What about you?" Gabbi nudged me. "You thinking about opening up your own Dance Studio? Or taking your dress designs to the next level?"

I'd thought a lot about it over the last few months—ever since I'd said *I do*. I loved working, but I also had never had the same passion for my job as my friends did. "You know, I love teaching dance, and I don't think I'm quite ready to hang up my ballet slippers just yet, but… I really feel like this was what I was always meant to be." *A mom.*

"Feels like everything is changing, doesn't it?" Angelina reflected, looking around the room. "I'm married to a guy I used to hate. Charlotte *finally* married my brother. And you two are planning your weddings."

"Maybe everything is, but there's one thing I know. We've always got each other."

I leaned my head against Noelle's shoulder as we went back to our conversation about books, going from what we'd read in the last few weeks to theories about our favorite series and then to upcoming releases we were excited for.

When the front door opened, we realized that two hours had passed while we were chatting and the guys were back from the bar.

I'd curled up under a blanket awhile ago since I was cold, and I was practically half asleep on the couch after our book discussions and all the excitement of the day.

Growing a human was exhausting.

"Hi." Daniel placed a sweet kiss on my lips.

"Hi." I smiled, yawning sleepily. "Did you have fun with the guys?"

"Yeah." He ran his hand through his hair. "It was great. Hunter told me about how he and Gabbi have started planning their wedding, too."

"Don't forget the house," I said with a smile.

Three down, one to go, and somehow I would have achieved my ultimate dream: living on the same street as all of my best friends.

"Are you tired?" He asked as I yawned again.

I just nodded. "Your kid is sucking out all of my energy." I rubbed my hand over my stomach.

"Charlotte—" His eyes widened in surprise.

"I told them," I said with a smile.

"Oh?"

I nodded. "Turns out not drinking wine is very suspicious during book club."

Daniel laughed. "

"I'm glad they know," I murmured against his lips. "That we don't have to keep the baby a secret from them."

"Me too. Because I might have... Accidentally let it slip to the guys as well."

"Daniel!"

He gave me his best pout. "You know, I asked Matthew and Noelle to keep Brownie while I was gone. I'd told them what happened, so when they asked how you were doing, it kind of... All spilled out."

"It's okay." I kissed his cheek. "I forgive you." My mouth opened with another yawn. "But now it's time for bed because growing your baby is hard work."

"Mmm." He scooped me up into his arms, turning to the rest of the group. "Sorry, gang. It's time to take my pregnant wife home." Daniel beamed, the smile lighting up his entire face.

"Congratulations again, you two," Matthew said, with his arm wrapped around Noelle, pulling her close to his body.

All three pairs of our friends were standing close to their partner, holding hands or touching skin. I didn't know quite how we'd gotten so lucky, especially considering two and a half years ago we'd all been single, but I wouldn't complain.

Not when I was currently in the love of my life's arms.

"We're so happy for you both." Benjamin grinned, slinging his arm around Angelina. "And we can't wait to meet our little niece. Or nephew."

Gabbi laughed. "I'll tell you one thing. They're going to be so loved."

"Thank you," I said, looking up at Daniel's face as I kept my head resting on his shoulder.

And I knew the same would go for when any of them had children—they'd get that unequivocal love they deserved from all of us, their *family*. All eight of us.

Around midnight, I woke up, slipping downstairs to get a drink of water. Brownie followed me, and I wrapped a blanket around myself as I sat on the couch, looking out the darkened windows.

"Can't sleep?"

"No." I set my water down, scratching our dog's ears beside me. "Too much on my mind, I guess."

"It was an eventful day," he murmured, slipping in next to me. I laid my head down in his lap, giving a contented sigh when he ran his fingers through my hair.

"It was." Opening his eyes, I looked up at him, tracing his jaw with my fingertips.

"What are you thinking?"

"That this doesn't feel real. That I'm hoping it doesn't slip through my fingers and disappear on us. That everything feels too good to be true. That I love you."

"Well, the last one I can definitely agree with." Daniel pecked the tip of my nose. "Because I love you too." He let his hand settle on my abdomen, the weight surprisingly welcome. "Don't stress about the rest. Our little dancer is going to be just fine in there. They've already got such a great mom."

My eyes filled with tears. "Daniel..." He wiped one away with his thumb. "You're going to be such a great dad, too, you know?"

He kissed my forehead. "I'll be a better one once I get my wife to bed."

And then, just like earlier, he lifted me into his arms, this time carrying me bridal style up to our bedroom, and I'd fallen asleep before my head could even hit the pillow.

Happy. Loved. Life was *perfect*.

CHAPTER 37
Daniel

JUNE

"So... Where are we going?" She tilted her head, looking at me as I pulled out of the driveway.

"It's a surprise. We're going on a date."

"Oh. Okay."

I intertwined our hands like always, kissing her knuckles before letting them rest against her lap. My eyes landed on her ring, sparkling when the light landed on it. All these months, and there was something I hadn't fixed. A wrong I needed to make right.

If she paid attention as we drove, looking out the window, she'd be able to guess our end destination pretty quickly. But I was hoping she didn't, because I wanted tonight to be a surprise.

I put the car in park, looking over at her.

"What..." Her eyes scanned our old campus. "What are we doing here?" Charlotte asked, looking up at her old dorm building.

"I wanted to reminisce about where we first met. Where our friendship began." I chuckled. "Did you ever think we'd be here?" I slid my hand over her belly.

"Married?" She laughed. "Pregnant? Honestly, no."
"I did."
"What?"
"From the very first moment when I saw you in that hallway, I knew. That you were the girl for me."

Her eyes connected with mine. "You couldn't have known that. We hadn't even had a proper conversation yet. We'd just met."

"But somehow, I did. You're my perfect other half. We're opposites in so many ways, but we complement each other in all of the ways that matter. You're my *best friend*. Besides my sister, you always have been."

"Come on," I said, extending my hand out to her.

"What?" She looked at my hand. "It's not like we can go inside."

I smirked. "Why can't we?"

"Daniel." She frowned. "They're closed for the summer." Much like I had ten years ago, the seniors had graduated, and campus was now empty until summer classes started up.

But unlike ten years ago, I wasn't going to waste this opportunity. "I have my ways."

"You're crazy."

"For you, as it turns out." That one got a laugh from her. "Come on, let's go up."

Charlotte placed her hand in mine, like she always did—trusting me, letting me have a little piece of her to keep safe.

I had a friend I'd graduated with who worked for Campus Safety, and he'd agreed to help me out, unlocking the doors for our little trip down memory lane.

We waited in the elevator to go up to the floor they lived on, coming to a stop in between her freshman year dorm and my sister's.

"This is where it all happened," I said, brushing her cheek with the side of my hand. "This is where I fell in love with you."

"Daniel..." Her eyes filled with tears. "Damn pregnancy

hormones. Why am I crying?" She wiped them away, and I kissed the side of her cheek.

"You know I'd given up hope until you asked me to kiss you? And then I thought that maybe, maybe I had a chance..."

"I always thought *I* was the one who didn't have a chance with you," she murmured. "You were this cool, older guy. And tall. So much taller than me." She rested her forehead against my chest.

"Cool?" I laughed. "I wasn't cool. I was a shy, quiet nerd who liked music and engineering. I had three friends freshman year. It's a wonder I could even find anyone who wanted to date me."

Charlotte made a grumpy face. "Don't remind me. I don't enjoy thinking about you with anyone else."

"Good thing I married you and not them then, huh?"

"Shut up." She punched my shoulder playfully.

"I love you," I said instead, brushing my nose against hers.

Sighing, she closed her eyes. "I love you too."

Wandering back downstairs, we headed outside, as I guided her into the middle of the quad, where I'd written out the words in flower petals.

"Smile, baby," I said, brushing a piece of hair behind her ear.

"Is this..."

I couldn't stop my face as it split into a brilliant smile, even as I kneeled on one knee in front of her, taking her hand with my ring in mine.

She exhaled deeply, searching my eyes for whatever truths she needed.

But she already had all of mine.

"Yes." I squeezed her hand as she blinked up at me, like she couldn't believe the statement was true.

"What are you doing?" Charlotte asked, her voice barely detectable as I slid the ring off her finger.

"Giving you the proposal you deserved in the first place."

She deserved more than what I'd ever offered her, and now it was my turn to prove that. I'd been selfish before, proposing a marriage pact. Agreeing to a fake marriage had been selfish, and I knew it. But even so, it was worth it. It had all been worth it.

But I wanted to do it right now. The proposal—the way I should have the first time. Photos, so she could remember it and hopefully show them to our kid one day. The way she wanted it. A story to tell our friends. The story I would have chosen if we were madly in love and I was asking her to marry me.

Gabbi was in the bushes, snapping away on her Nikon. She'd been all too happy to say yes when I explained what I wanted to do.

And Angelina and Noelle were hiding with biodegradable glitter to shower us with when she said yes.

The flower petals behind me read: *Will you marry me?*

"Why should we wait until thirty when you're the only person I want by my side?" I cracked a grin. To think what might have happened if I'd waited another year. I was already twenty-nine. Thinking of going another year without loving Charlotte went against every fiber of my being.

Charlotte laughed. "I already told you I'd marry you again, silly."

"I know, but I wanted you to have everything you've ever wanted."

"This *is* everything I've ever wanted, Daniel. You *are* everything I have ever wanted."

"I was hoping you'd say that."

I slid the ring back onto her finger.

"I vow to love you, to cherish you, to protect you and feed you marshmallows and doughnuts whenever you want them—especially when you're pregnant—and I promise that no matter what happens, you'll always have me on your side. Because I'm not going anywhere, baby."

And I sealed my vows with a kiss.

JULY

The day had finally arrived. We were all moved into our new house. All the finishing touches had been completed, and while it was sad to leave our old place behind—the place where we'd fallen in love, had more movie nights than I could count, where we'd started our life together... I was happy to be here.

Home.

Our home. Together.

I liked to think that our house was flawless, from the built-in library she could fill to the fireplace in the living room and the giant sewing room with plenty of space for her creations above the garage. Charlotte certainly wasn't complaining about the extra-large closet or large tub in our room. She was in love.

And I was so, so very in love with her, a fact I reminded her of every day.

Even though I'd said the guys and I could move everything from our house, Charlotte insisted we hire movers instead. To be honest, we all needed a break from the constant moving. I was confident that once the other two couples settled into their new homes on our street, no one would be in a hurry to move again.

Charlotte wasn't showing yet, but that small bump was there all the same. We'd spent the last month practically holding our breaths, but she was officially out of the first trimester.

"I still can't get over this space," she said, running her fingers over the whitewashed wood table. "This is so perfect."

"I'm glad you like it." I might have been in charge of designing the structure, but I had handpicked each of the details inside also, down to the breakfast nook we were sitting in. From here, I could see Brownie running around in the big backyard through the framed windows.

"Daniel." Charlotte gasped, her hand going to her stomach.

"What?" Moving out of my seat, I kneeled in front of her. "Is everything okay? Is it—"

"The baby kicked." She laughed, grabbing my hand and placing it on top of her bump. "I could feel it—"

And there it was. A tiny bump against my palm.

"Oh!" I looked up at her, catching my wife with tears in her eyes. "That's... incredible."

"I know," she said, giggling as the tears dripped down her face. "Daniel..." She sucked in a breath. "You know, in five months, we're going to be parents."

I pressed a kiss against her bump. "I know. Everything we've wanted."

"I'm so glad it's you."

"Me too, baby."

There was no one else I could picture as the mother of my children, except for Charlotte. My best friend, now my partner in life.

"Thank you."

"You don't have to thank me."

"No, I do. This is the best gift. The greatest gift you could have given me. Not the house, but..." She sighed, rubbing her little belly. "You. The baby. Love. For a while, I didn't think I'd ever find it. That I'd settle, because at least it was something. But this... This is everything. You are my everything. And I wish I'd seen it sooner. In college, five years ago, but..."

"But you have me now." I stood up, pulling her into my arms. Swaying her back and forth in the middle of our brand new kitchen. "And I'm never going anywhere, darling."

"I know. And you're the best thing that's ever happened to me."

"No," I laughed. "That's *you*, for me."

"Mmm." She leaned against my chest, and I heaved her up into my arms.

"Should we go break in our new bedroom? Because I have plans for you, wife."

Charlotte laughed. "Oh, I can't wait to find out exactly what they are."

I smirked, and then I showed her exactly what I meant.

Over and over, until we fell asleep, exhausted, boneless, completely sated—and completely happy. Content. A feeling I hoped would never go away.

∽

AUGUST

"What do you want?" Charlotte asked me as I drew circles over her belly. At five months, she was showing, and it felt like her bump was getting bigger every day.

"For them to look just like you," I said with a smile.

She rolled her eyes. "I'm serious."

"So am I. Boy or girl, I'm happy."

My wife sighed, relaxing into my arms. We'd been having variations of this conversation for the last few months. I was almost certain that the walls of the nursery room we were in would be painted pink.

I just had a feeling.

We had our appointment later this week, and though we'd tossed around some names, we were waiting until we found out the gender to fully decorate.

"Besides, we can always try again, right?" I said, enjoying just sitting here like this. Holding my wife. "Have another one."

"It's not *Pokèmon*. We don't have to collect them all."

"Mmm. But you want more, right?"

She leaned her head back, tilting it up so she could look at me. "Yeah. I do. And that's... what you want still too, right?"

"Yes. As many as you want."

Because I knew they would grow up happy, loved, in a house where their parents were steady. Reliable. We had our occasional fights, but our ten-year-long friendship had taught us to understand each other better than anyone else. It made us strong enough to survive anything.

Even a whole brood of Bradfords.

A few days later, we were at the doctor's office. Charlotte was wearing a loose pink tank top and stretchy jean shorts, since it was a hot summer in Portland, and she was absolutely miserable with the heat. Luckily, our brand new house had AC, and Benjamin and Angelina's pool was coming along.

"You're still good to find out, right?" She asked, turning to face me. "No surprises?"

"No surprises," I agreed, kissing the top of her hand that I was holding.

"Charlotte?" the nurse called at the door. "You can come back."

We went through the routine questions and evaluations with the nurse, and then the doctor came in.

Charlotte pushed up her shirt to reveal her twenty-week bump. Dr. Richardson got started right away, squirting the gel on before pressing the wand up against Charlotte's belly.

After a few moments, with Charlotte's hand gripping mine, she turned to us. "You want to find out the gender, right?"

"Yes, please," Charlotte begged. "We couldn't tell at the last appointment and..."

"We want to paint the walls. And pick out a name." I finished for her.

"Well, congratulations, Mom and Dad. You're having a baby girl."

A girl. I kissed Charlotte's hand, still interwoven through mine as we watched our baby on the screen.

"It's a girl," I whispered, still in awe.

"A girl." Charlotte's lips tilted up into a smile as her eyes filled with happy tears.

"I knew she was. Our little dancer." I leaned over, kissing her forehead.

"If you two don't have questions for me, I'll go print out some photos and you can head home. I'll see you again in a few weeks. Congrats again."

"Thank you so much, Miranda. Truly. We're so happy."

I squeezed Charlotte's hand in response. *I love you*, it meant. "Come on, darling. Let's get you two home."

CHAPTER 38
Charlotte

OCTOBER

"God, look at you!" Noelle gushed, and I couldn't help but feel like the roles should be reversed.

"Babe, look at *you*. It's your wedding day." Her hair was perfectly curled, those red tendrils laying down her back. She'd done the top part in swooping braids, ready for her veil to be tucked underneath it. "You look so beautiful, Noelle."

We'd all spent the morning getting ready together, pampered by getting our hair and makeup done at the salon. After, we'd been chauffeured to the venue for Matthew and Noelle's wedding, the crisp autumn air swirling around us as we stepped out of the car. The pumpkin patch made for a charming wedding venue that perfectly reflected her personality. Her bridesmaids were us three, and Matthew's sister, Tessa. We were currently crowded in one bedroom at the little house on the venue, all trying to change at once.

"And you're *glowing*." Angelina smiled, squeezing my hand. "And just think, my niece or nephew is in there."

My dress was now zipped, my bump apparent even through the chiffon fabric that draped over it.

"I'm pretty sure we're supposed to be complimenting the bride, not the pregnant maid-of-honor," I said, attempting to crack a joke. Running my hands down my burnt orange bridesmaid dress, I took the time to inspect around me. The decorations were rustic, the colors perfectly fall toned, everything matching right down to Noelle's lace dress.

I'd had to get my dress hemmed when I realized I could no longer wear heels with my dress, but my very prominent bump stuck out far enough that I could no longer see my feet. Daniel had suggested I wear flats, and I couldn't argue with his logic.

Thirty-two weeks. I felt like I was massive, though I wasn't sure what else I expected at eight months pregnant. Somehow, my brain was finding it hard to believe I still had eight weeks to go. The whole nine months thing currently felt like a big fat *lie*. December felt like ages away.

On the bright side, we'd have two things to celebrate this year: our one-year anniversary, and a tiny little bundle of joy.

I slipped on my shimmery gold shoes, trying to ignore how big my ankles currently were. The thought of Daniel giving me a foot rub was the only thing getting me through the day. He'd already popped his head in twice to check in on me, and we'd had to shoo him out.

"I'm gonna go check on the guys," Tessa murmured, slipping out of the door.

We all exchanged looks. "I think she's crushing on my cousin," Noelle admitted. Her cousin Oliver had been hanging out with them a lot more since he met Tess. "It's kind of cute."

If there was anything I'd learned from all of us hanging out, it was that love was a little contagious. But I couldn't complain. I had my dream guy.

"Any advice from the two already married?" Noelle asked, suddenly looking nervous.

Angelina and I looked at each other, and she placed a hand on Noelle's shoulder. "Breathe. You love him, and he loves you. Nothing else matters."

Noelle nodded. "You're right." She looked at me.

I laughed, plopping down on a chair in the room. "You're asking the wrong girl, considering Daniel and I didn't fall in love until *after* we were married." I rubbed a hand over my stomach. They were already aware of all the details of the marriage pact, as I had confessed to them a while ago. "But she's right. You two are perfect together. I've known it from the very first moment you told us about him."

"Thank you." She pulled us all into a hug, squeezing tight.

Gabbi fiddled with the engagement ring on her finger. "Can you believe we only have one more of these before we're all married?" They were busy planning a small wedding on the Oregon Coast for the upcoming summer.

"No." *Where had the time gone?* "It feels like we just graduated from college."

"It feels like I just started dating Matthew." Noelle blinked, looking up at the ceiling like she was trying not to cry. "I can't believe it's been two and a half years."

We picked up our drinks, taking a sip, and Angelina held up hers in a toast. "To ten years of friendship."

"To best friends," Gabbi chimed in.

Everyone clinked their mimosa glasses together, even though mine was just orange juice.

"To sisters," I added.

A blush crept up Tessa's cheeks as she rejoined us, and she took a moment to look around at everyone. "Everyone ready?"

We nodded.

"Come on, bride to be," I said, holding my arm out for Noelle. "Let's go get you married."

I took a deep breath, hoping to keep my emotions in check during her vows. Knowing me, I probably *would* cry. I wondered if I could get away with blaming it on my pregnancy hormones. But it wasn't every day your best friend got married.

After a beautiful ceremony, we were ushered into the

converted barn for the reception, adorably decorated with tulle and pumpkins and everything that seemed to scream Noelle.

"Remember when it was us up there?" I murmured to Daniel as his hand rested on my bump at the reception, watching Noelle and Matthew sitting at the head table, him feeding her bites of red velvet cake. "I can't believe it's almost been a year already."

"How could I forget?" My husband put his lips near my ear. "I remember thinking I'd never seen a more beautiful woman in the world than you on our wedding day. Even if it was fake, I was so in love with you already." As he kissed the side of my head, I felt a warm rush of affection. "But I was wrong."

"What?"

"Because you, on our wedding day, isn't the most beautiful woman I've ever seen."

"Huh?" I scowled. "You're telling your *pregnant wife*—"

"Mm. Let me finish." His finger ran over my lips, swiping a bit of cream cheese frosting there, which I eagerly licked up. "You, like this, pregnant, practically glowing as you grow our child—that's the most beautiful sight I've ever seen."

"Daniel..." My mouth was dry, and if I was being honest with myself, desperately turned on by his words. People weren't kidding when they said it heightened your sex drive being pregnant.

I wanted him. I *needed* him. Later, I promised myself, wanting to enjoy my best friend's wedding. Wouldn't sneak away from one of the happiest days of her life. Even if I was seven months pregnant and had wobbled throughout most of it.

"I love you." He rubbed his nose against mine.

I sighed, letting my eyes fall shut as I rested our foreheads together. "I love you too." Snapping my fingers, I pointed at the cake. "Now feed me, husband."

He laughed, getting a forkful of cake and holding it up to my mouth. And just to torture him a little, I let out a moan as the rich flavor of the cake and the perfect cream cheese frosting illuminated my taste buds.

"Cake tastes *so* much better when you're pregnant," I groaned, closing my lips around the fork again to suck off the rest of the frosting. With a pop, I removed the utensil from my mouth and locked eyes with him.

"You're going to pay for that later," he practically growled in my ear.

"I'm counting on it," I whispered back into his.

Once we'd finished our cake, he stood up, extending out his hand for me. The dancing had already started, but I'd been trying to stay off my feet as much as possible.

"May I have this dance?" Daniel asked.

"Are you sure? There's no other beautiful women you'd rather dance with?" Looking around the room, I saw that Angelina and Benjamin had already started dancing, followed closely by Gabbi and Hunter.

He didn't give me a chance to respond before pulling me into his arms. "I'm sure. There's only you, darling. There's only ever been you."

I smiled, wrapping my arms around his neck. And then I kissed him softly on the lips as he rested his hands on either side of my bump, cradling our baby.

"I love you too, babe."

Daniel snorted. "Love you, baby."

"I know." I closed my eyes, resting my head against his chest.

~

MY PUMPKIN-ORANGE BRIDESMAID dress fluttered to the floor. "Ahhhhh," I sighed in relief. "That's better."

"Mmm, I agree," Daniel said, his hands skimming up my sides, over my bare skin. He'd already taken his suit coat off, leaving it on the chair in our bedroom.

"Hi," I giggled, turning around in his arms. Except—"Oh." My bump rested between us, keeping the two of us from touching completely.

"How are you feeling?"

I tugged on his tie to bring his torso closer to mine. "Mmm. Feet are a little sore from all the standing and dancing. But... Good. Happy."

"That's all I've ever wanted for you. To be happy." My husband rested his head against mine.

"You've made me the happiest woman alive, Daniel." I reached up, cupping his jaw with my hand. "I'm so glad we got married. That we fell in love. That..." I rubbed my belly. "We made her."

"Thank god for that marriage pact, huh?"

"Yeah."

Our lips were inches apart, and all I wanted—all I needed, was him.

"Charlotte..."

"Kiss me," I breathed, wrapping my arms around his neck. He gave me a brief and tender kiss on my lips. But I needed... "More. I need more." I moaned as his hands cupped my ass. "Daniel..."

He unclasped my bra, and I shrugged the straps down my shoulder, letting the garment fall to the floor.

"I know what you need, baby." He kissed my neck as his fingers worked deftly, pushing my panties down my hips, letting them fall to the floor before his hands skimming up the insides of my thighs.

But not where I wanted them.

"Are you..." His voice was rough. "Are you sure the baby's going to be okay?" Daniel asked, touching me so carefully. He ran his hands up my side, like he was cradling my bump.

I nodded. I'd bled after the last time, so we'd waited to have sex again until I got the all clear at my next appointment. It was just some spotting, but better to be safe than sorry. "The doctor said it won't hurt. *Please*. I need you."

If I thought I'd craved his body before I'd gotten pregnant, it was even more so now. The pregnancy hormones were driving me crazy, and all I wanted to do was have him inside of me.

"Just... Tell me if I hurt you, okay?" He leaned down, capturing my lips in another kiss as he slid his fingers inside of me.

I gasped at the feeling, holding back a moan at how good it felt.

"Fuck. You're so wet."

"*Yes,*" I agreed, and he kissed me harder, his fingers working me closer and closer as we kissed lazily, a bundle of lips, tongue and teeth.

He kept up his gentle, steady pace, working me closer and closer towards the orgasm I craved, desired, needed—

"Daniel, I'm so close—" I whimpered, holding onto him like a lifeline.

Like he was my lifeline.

But in a way, in every way, actually—he was.

"Come for me, darling," he whispered in my ear, rough in the deep, smooth voice of his that I always loved. And maybe it was the hormones, maybe it was just something about the night, but I did. I came on his hand, letting my head drop back as my eyes practically rolled into the back of my head.

He pulled his fingers out of me, laying me down on the bed on my side. Removing his clothes layer by layer, he gave me a full view of his body before dropping them next to mine on the floor.

Daniel slid in behind me, wrapping his arms around my belly, like he was protecting her—keeping our daughter safe in there. He kissed my shoulder, and I could feel him hardening against my back.

Skin to skin, he held me like that, my back pressed up against his front, until I was writhing, skin itching, desperate for him.

"Daniel," I moaned—practically begged. I didn't even have to say the words. He already knew what I was asking.

Grabbing my leg, he pushed into me from behind, one arm still wrapped around my belly as the other went to my hip. The angle was almost torturous, how tight I felt as he pushed into me, inch by inch, but I reveled in it.

It wasn't frantic, rushed sex, but slow, gentle lovemaking. And yet still, every touch, every kiss, every brush against my heavy, sensitive nipples made me almost come out of my mind with pleasure. If I hadn't already known that there was no one else in the world for me, no one else that could make me feel like this—I did now.

And when we both came, and he wrapped his arms around me, bringing our fronts together, I couldn't help the outpouring of love that I felt for him.

My best friend turned fake husband turned *real*. The only man who'd ever been for me. Who'd ever known me, inside and out, and made me feel like I was home.

It felt like the entire world faded away, leaving only the two of us in our bubble of happiness and love.

Breathing out, I looked at him, *really* looked at him. His structured jaw, those brown eyes, his dark, almost black hair, brushed away from his face—he was so handsome, always.

"Thank you," I murmured, resting my head against his chest.

"For what?"

"For this. For our happily ever after."

"Baby, our story's just beginning," he said, kissing my forehead.

CHAPTER 39
Daniel

DECEMBER

"Daniel." Her hand tightly gripped mine, jolting me awake from sleep. Not that I'd been sleeping much these days anyway, with Charlotte being so close to her due date. I was constantly on alert, ready to go at any moment.

My eyes popped open. "Everything okay?"

"I think my water just broke."

"You're sure?" I'd already started mentally preparing for what I needed to do.

"Unless I just peed myself, *pretty* sure." Her nose scrunched, and I flipped on the light.

"But you're not due till next week."

She laughed. "You try telling *her* that."

I leaned down to kiss her belly, trying not to freak out. The best thing to do was stay calm. That was what we'd practiced in all of those classes.

"Get dressed, and I'll grab the bags."

They'd been by the front door ever since she'd hit thirty-eight weeks. And they'd been packed for another week before that.

She waddled up to the door in a loose, flowy pink dress and a long chunky gray cardigan.

"Forgetting something?" I raised an eyebrow, looking down at her bare feet.

"Oh, shut up," she huffed, sitting in a chair by the front door. "You know I can't bend over to get them on."

She chucked a pair of socks at my face—pink ones, with little cats on them. Kneeling before her, I pulled on her socks, and then a pair of loose, fuzzy boots.

"How are you feeling, darling?" I kissed her belly, and then stood up, offering her my hand. Charlotte took it, clutching on tight as a contraction hit her.

Her knuckles were practically white as she held onto me, but I rubbed her back through it.

"Ready?"

"Uh-huh."

I pulled her into my arms, kissing her forehead. "Let's go have a baby, hm?"

Her face lit up, even as I tugged a puffball beanie over her head. "Yeah. I love you." Charlotte kissed my lips gently as I cupped her belly.

"I love you too."

~

TWELVE HOURS LATER, after a long night of tears and a hand I wasn't sure would ever fully have blood flow to it again, Abigail Hope Bradford was finally here.

Charlotte was sleeping peacefully in bed, a welcome retrieve after the night she'd had.

"Hi, little dancer," I murmured, running my finger over our newborn daughter's cheek. I couldn't believe how small she was. How much I'd loved her from the first moment they had placed her in my arms. Sitting in the recliner next to Charlotte's hospital bed, I'd been rocking her for the last thirty minutes. "I can't wait to watch you grow up, huh? Your mom and I already love you so much, you know that? Our sweet little girl."

Charlotte yawned, looking over at me, still rocking Abigail. "Mmm."

"You're awake."

She blinked, sleepily. "Yeah. How's our girl?"

"Perfect." I couldn't believe we'd made her.

Charlotte reached out her arms, and I got up, placing our baby into her arms, and then I slid in next to her on the bed.

"Hi." I leaned over, kissing her cheek.

"Hi."

"How are you feeling?"

She snuggled against my shoulder sleepily, her hair tickling my neck. "Good."

"Our friends came by to say hi."

"They did?"

"Of course they did. They've been asking for updates every hour since we got to the hospital. Everyone's been blowing up the group chat."

Charlotte sighed happily. "We got pretty lucky with them, didn't we?"

"Yeah." I looked between her and our daughter. "But I think I got the luckiest."

"Go get our family, Daniel."

∽

"I WANT ONE," Noelle whispered to Matthew, holding baby Abbi in her arms. She was so peaceful, sleeping happily as our friends passed her around. Charlotte had fed her one more time before everyone had come by to see Charlotte and the baby.

"We've been married for two months, sunshine," Matthew muttered back to his wife.

"So?" She raised an eyebrow. He just dipped his head with a smile, kissing her temple. "That's what I thought." She beamed. I knew Matthew loved her just as much as I loved my wife, and so I didn't think it would be long before they had some happy news to share.

Wiping the blonde strands from Charlotte's face, I took a moment to kiss my wife's forehead as our friends cooed over our newborn.

Angelina came over, slinging an arm around my shoulder. "You did good, bro."

"Thanks. I'm proud of you too, Lina." I looked over at Benjamin, standing in the corner. "Married, kicking ass at your job... Life turned out pretty great for the both of us, huh?"

She smirked. "I'm just glad you didn't break my best friend's heart."

"Never." I'd never have dreamed of that. I was going to keep her heart safe for the rest of our lives.

Pulling my sister into a hug, I pulled back. "Ready to hold your niece, Auntie Angelina?"

She laughed. "Yes. Definitely."

And my heart was so full—it was home.

CHAPTER 40
Daniel

TWO YEARS LATER...

We were all gathered at Matthew & Noelle's house, watching the snow fall in an unusually thick winter storm from the back deck. Luckily, we were all able to work from home, so we didn't have to worry about going into the office or driving in the snow.

The dogs were happily playing in the snow, all three chasing each other: Snowball, Brownie, and Rowan, Gabbi and Hunter's mini Aussie.

"So, what do you think?" Matthew looked out at the new fire pit they had built, admiring the string of lights that hung above it. The only reason we were outside in the cold weather was that it provided warmth. As the snow fell, we snuggled together under the overhang, watching the winter wonderland outside.

"It turned out great, man." I loved being a part of our friends' home-building journey, providing support and feedback. As a structural engineer, I had some knowledge from my years of work at the firm, even though it wasn't my specialty.

"It's perfect," my wife sighed, slipping in next to me with a mug tucked in between her hands. "I think we need one of these in *our* backyard, too."

I laughed. "The porch swing I built wasn't enough?"

She gave me a sly smile.

"How's our daughter?"

"Still napping. All of that playing in the snow earlier really wore her out. Noelle's got her eye on her."

"Her hands aren't too full, are they?"

Charlotte shook her head as Gabbi came out of the house, bundled up in a thick winter jacket. Hunter raised his eyebrows and slid his hand protectively over her belly as she sat next to him on the bench. He took the beanie off of his head and pulled it over the top of her head before settling back in, wrapping an arm around her. Hunter was always protective of his wife, but even more so now that she was pregnant.

"Thanks," she huffed, adjusting his hat on her head so it sat further back, and then cuddled into her husband. "I'm pregnant, not suffering from hypothermia."

Hunter grumbled in response.

The last two years had gone by in a flash for us ever since Abigail was born. We'd celebrated Gabbi and Hunter's wedding six months later, and sometimes it felt like time would never slow down.

Moments like this were rare, where everything felt calm and peaceful. Just all four of us couples hanging out at one of our houses. We practically had a rotating nursery of care, as someone was inevitably pregnant or breastfeeding.

Angelina came out of the house, carrying two chubby babies bundled up in snowsuits—one red and one blue—and Benjamin instantly reached out to take one of the twins.

It had been the shock of my sister's life when she found out she was pregnant with not one, but two babies. *Boys.* They were six months old now, happy, babbling boys.

"How's my little man doing?" Ben asked the twin in his lap, bouncing him on his leg.

Angelina ran her fingers through her hair. "Good. After almost pulling his mother's hair out." She rubbed a spot on her head. "But they're both fed, and diapers changed, so hopefully I can have a minute of peace now." She sighed.

Benjamin frowned at his son. "That's not very nice."

It was nice to see my sister—straight laced and always professional—like this. Her hair was down, not a lick of makeup on, high heels tucked away in a closet somewhere. The armor she'd used to protect herself for all those years until she met her husband. We'd always been close, but our relationship was better than ever these days.

It was just one more thing we bonded over.

Abigail loved her Aunt Angelina. I was pretty sure our little girl had no fiercer protector than my sister.

"I'm gonna go check on Noelle and our little man," Matthew said, standing up from his bench and leaving his beer on the side table. "Anyone need anything?"

I shook my head, but I was already standing up, too. Turning to Charlotte, I watched her sip on her hot chocolate as she cuddled under a blanket. "I'm gonna go grab Abs."

"Okay." She smiled, her eyes drifting shut as I leaned down to kiss her forehead. "Don't be long."

Following Matthew inside, I found Abbi still napping on their couch, Noelle sitting in the recliner next to him, rocking their son in her arms. Owen was almost a year old now, already resembling his dad with his mop of sandy blond hair.

"Daddy?" Abigail's eyes blinked open as I scooped her up off the couch.

"Hi, little dancer," I said, taking in her stormy blue-gray eyes. "Want to go see mommy?"

She nodded, giving me a toothy smile as I found her little pink coat discarded by the door, and pulled it onto her arms before carrying her outside.

"There's my girl," Charlotte said as I sat back down, Abbi

resting in between the two of us as Charlotte pulled the blanket over our little family.

"Hi, mommy," Abbi said, nuzzling into Charlotte.

"Did you have a good nap?"

She nodded. "More snow?" Our little girl looked out at the backyard with sparkling eyes.

Charlotte laughed. "Not right now, sweetie. Maybe later."

"Oh." She sighed, wistfully. I didn't know how a two-year-old could inject one word with so much longing, but she managed it.

Even if she looked just like me in so many ways, it was obvious she was just like her mom. Down to her love of pink and the way she insisted on copying mommy's dance moves when Charlotte was choreographing something in the living room.

That was another thing that had changed—Char had cut back at the studio, and even though I knew she missed some aspects of it, she assured me that this was her decision. She wanted to be a full-time mom, and not miss any part of Abbi growing up. Despite her busy schedule, she still found time to choreograph dances for the girls and attend their competitions when she could.

And watching our daughter's eyes light up when she got to tag along with her mom to the studio, well... It was magical. We'd gotten her a pair of ballet slippers for Christmas—little tiny toddler ones that had made Charlotte cry when they'd come in because they were so cute.

"No love for daddy, huh?"

Our daughter turned her head towards me, sprawling into my lap.

My heart was full.

Four years ago, the eight of us had been outside at a rooftop bar, celebrating New Year's Eve together. It wasn't the first time we'd all hung out, but that night had felt like the start of something.

And now, here we were. All married, with kids in our laps or coming into the world soon.

"What do you think, Angelina?" Gabbi asked, her voice drawing my attention away from the two-year-old in my lap.

"About what?" My sister asked, bouncing baby Wesley on her knee.

Gabbi rubbed a hand over her stomach. "Think you want to do this again for a girl?"

She snorted, glaring at Benjamin as if he'd purposefully knocked her up with twins. "I feel like the two-for-one special really says *one and done*."

"Yeah." Gabbi rested her head against Hunter's shoulder, then looked over at the other four of us. "What about you guys? Thinking about having more?"

I looked at Charlotte, who avoided my gaze. "We'd always said we wanted a big family. But we've had our hands full with this one, so…"

"We've been talking about it," Noelle chimed in, her cheeks flushed. I wasn't sure if it was just from the cold. "Being an only child was lonely for me. I think I'd like another one."

Matthew leaned down, kissing the top of his wife's ginger head. "Hopefully, the next one gets your hair."

I played with Abigail's hair in my lap, thinking the same thing. How much I'd love a little girl with Charlotte's blonde locks. I was perfectly happy being a girl dad, even if we had a whole brood of them. The little girl in my lap was everything I'd ever wanted.

The snow was coming down harder, and it was getting colder. "Think we should call it a night?" I asked the gang.

Gabbi nodded as she yawned, sleepily.

"I should get her to bed, anyway," Hunter laughed.

"It's not *that* early," Gabbi protested. "We still have time. We could watch another episode of our show." She fluttered her eyelashes, and I knew Hunter would cave.

Just like any of us would.

"This little one needs to go to sleep, too," I said, tickling my daughter, before looking up at Charlotte, who had a warm expression on her face.

WE'D PUT Abigail to bed in her big kid's bed, and then I planned on thoroughly showing my wife how much I loved her. And... maybe we could start on baby number two.

"She's asleep," Charlotte said, sliding into our bedroom and wrapping her arms around my waist from the back.

"Mmm. Good." She settled her chin on my shoulder. "So... What do you think if we gave her a sibling?"

I hadn't stopped thinking about it since everyone had mentioned it earlier. I turned to face her, my eyes roving over her body, wearing a t-shirt she'd stolen from my closet and a pair of leggings.

"Yes. One hundred percent, yes. You want to start right now?" I smirked, my hands coming to her waist as I pulled her closer to me.

"Actually..." Her cheeks pinked. "I took a test this morning." My throat choked up as Charlotte placed her hand—and mine—over her stomach.

"Are you?"

She nodded. "Surprise."

I laughed, lowering my forehead to hers. "And we didn't even have to try this time."

"I haven't exactly been very good at keeping track of my cycle. Blame it on the two-year-old I've been chasing all over this house." Charlotte leaned in close. "But I did miss that part, you know. *Trying.*"

My blood heated, thinking about all the cycle tracking and baby-making sex we'd had last time. When we'd gone from faking everything to being a real couple.

"Mmm. I think I'm willing to make a compromise."

"What?" She lowered her pretty little lashes, fluttering them as she looked up at me.

I put my lips to her ear. "We try again next time."

"Next time?" Charlotte giggled. "A little presumptuous there, Mr. Bradford."

"For you? Always, Mrs. Bradford."

I'd be happy to spend the next ten years with her barefoot and pregnant, if that was what she wanted. However many kids she wanted, that was what I wanted too. Two, three, five—it didn't matter to me. As long as she was happy. After all, she looked so gorgeous when she was pregnant, carrying our baby. I already couldn't wait for her to show again.

"How far along are you?" I asked, looking at her stomach. Pretending that if I squinted enough, I could see the faintest of swell to her belly.

"Five weeks." Her eyes trailed down to where I was looking. "I'm not showing yet."

Kneeling down in front of her, I pushed back her shirt.

"Hi, baby," I whispered to her stomach. Kissed the skin there, reverently. Then stood back up, taking her face in mine. "Darling?"

"Hmm?"

"I love you." I leaned down, brushing my lips against hers.

"Daniel?" It was my turn to hum in response. "I love you too."

And I kissed my wife. The love of my life. The only woman who ever owned my heart. I was glad she'd never given it back.

She could have it for the rest of our life, as far as I was concerned.

Picking her up in my arms, she squealed. "What are you doing?" Her laughter-filled voice echoed through the room.

"Taking my wife to bed." I leaned down, pressing a kiss to her neck. "Showing her how much I love her. How I want to worship her."

I dropped her on the bed, practically inhaling her giggles before I kissed her again.

"Mmm, I like the sound of that."

"Good. Because I never plan on stopping."

"If this is what forever looks like, I think I like it very much."

Forever with Charlotte? That was the dream I'd worked so hard to achieve. And it was everything I could have asked for. Everything I could have wanted.

Epilogue
CHARLOTTE

THREE YEARS LATER...

Puppy dog eyes. My weakness.

I quickly diverted my attention away, deeply inhaling the sweet smell of ice cream that surrounded me. My stomach rumbled, and a waffle cone sounded incredible right now.

"Please?" my daughter begged, and darn it—she was just too cute.

"Okay," my husband said with a sigh. "But only for a few minutes."

"Careful," I murmured, looking around us at the crowds. Family photo taken, we were standing off to the side waiting for our friends to join us. It was busy, and I didn't want her to end up kicking anyone in the back of the head.

I was regretting agreeing to meet outside as everyone else ran to the bathrooms. It was hot, and the Florida humidity was no joke. Wiping the back of my neck, I watched as tourists strolled by, balloons and churros in hand.

I might have been in my thirties, but this was still one of my favorite places in the world.

"Daddy!" Abigail squealed as Daniel lifted her up onto his shoulders, holding onto her legs so she couldn't fall off. "Look at the castle!"

He grinned. "It's beautiful, isn't it, sweetheart?"

She rested her head on the top of his, sighing dreamily. "I want to live in a castle like that someday." Abigail's dark curls mirrored her father's. The only sign of *me* was her adorable little button nose and her gray eyes.

"I'm sure you will, baby girl." He smiled, looking over at me.

I gave him a warm smile back as a little hand tugged at my skirt, and I looked down to the toddler looking up at me with wide brown eyes—Daniel's brown eyes.

"Mommy?" my son asked. I hadn't even realized he was awake.

"Yes, little bear?" I lifted him up on my hip, ruffling his dark hair. He was a carbon copy of Daniel, a fact that my husband was all too smug about. It was okay, though. My little mini-me was currently sleeping in the stroller.

"Can we get ice cream?" He pointed at the parlor that we were standing directly across.

I laughed. "Later, baby, I promise."

I'd had Beau two and a half years after Abigail—we knew we wanted more kids, but both of us had also wanted to enjoy our time with just one. My favorite part was I got to be pregnant with my best friends, and a little over a month after Beau was born, Penelope Elaine Harper came into the world.

Perched on Matthew's shoulders, she was wearing a Princess Anna costume. Thinking back to the first Halloween party we attended together, I can't help but smile at the memory.

That was the night Gabbi had met Hunter, and now they had a daughter of their own: Quinlan. She was a spunky three-year-old, with a wild and adventurous spirit that always left her covered in dirt.

We'd all brought our families to Disney World for vacation now that summer had arrived.

Owen, Matthew and Noelle's son, was currently keeping a close eye on my youngest, Ellie, as she slept in the stroller.

"Don't wake her up," I warned. "She's still little." Her second birthday was coming up in July, but it was still a few months away.

"I know," he said, whispering back at me.

At four years old, he was the spitting image of his dad—all that blond, messy hair—with just a splattering of Noelle's freckles. Unfortunately for him, he'd also inherited both of their abilities to burn. We were putting on sunscreen almost every hour on this trip. The Florida heat—even in May—was no joke.

"Did we miss anything?" Angelina asked, with one of her twins' hands clasped tightly in hers. Benjamin was right behind her, holding on to the others.

"Beau wants ice cream," I repeated, looking down at him.

Angelina's identical twins—Zachary and Wesley—were a little under a year older than Beau. The resemblance was almost uncanny, except for the twins' bright blue eyes. They all had the same thick, dark, beautiful hair.

"Oooh, ice cream?" Hunter asked, tickling the back of his daughter's legs. "I could go for ice cream. What do you think, princess?"

"Yes! Ice cream!" Quinlan agreed.

Gabbi rolled her eyes at her husband.

"It *is* hot," Angelina groaned. "That sounds like it would hit the spot."

Daniel flashed a grin at me. "What do you think, darling?"

"I think we need to feed the kids some actual food first."

"But mommy!" Abbi protested, still on Daniel's shoulders.

I shot her a look. "No ice cream until after we fill your tummy with *actual* food."

"Come on, spoilsport, we're on vacation." Daniel had let Abbi down, and even Noelle licked her lips, staring at the window display.

"*Fine,*" I agreed. "Let's get ice cream now."

"Lead the way, darling," Daniel said, and all of us, plus the kids, headed into the parlor.

"Why are my kids so obsessed with ice cream?" I muttered, looking at Daniel, who gave me a sheepish grin. He spoiled our kids, and we both knew it. We both did.

Everyone, except for Ellie, was holding a kid's cone with little chocolate ears on top, and us adults were enjoying own cones as well. I had to admit, it hit the spot.

"What's next?" Benjamin asked, his eyes looking at the map in his hands.

"The girls want to meet the princesses," Noelle said, looking at the group of our daughters, all dressed up in their princess gowns for the day at Magic Kingdom.

Our husbands all groaned, clearly not thrilled about the idea.

"Why don't you guys take the boys over to ride something while we wait?" With any luck, we'd make everyone happy and end the day without too many tears. The trick was frequent snack breaks and trips into the air-conditioning.

Daniel kissed my cheek. "Good call, darling. We'll meet you after?"

I bent down and kissed Beau's cheek. "Be good for daddy, okay?"

He wrapped his arms around my neck, hugging me tight. "Love you, mommy," he said, before running off, my husband wrapping a hand around Beau's chubby little fingers.

I might have been biased, but I thought he was the cutest little two and a half year old on the planet. And if he turned out just like his daddy, well—I knew he'd be okay.

My heart swelled with love and pride for my kids as I turned back to my girls.

"Who wants to go meet the Princesses?"

Daniel

The stroller was full of two sleeping kids, and Abbi was nestled in my arms. Her head rested against my neck as we made our way back to the hotel bus.

This wasn't our first trip to Disney, but it *was* the first time with all three kids. Like I'd promised her before we'd had Beau, we'd enjoyed the prospect of making Ellie a little *too* much. It didn't take long after her six-week checkup for her to become pregnant again.

After two back-to-back pregnancies, she was happy with our little brood. Three was perfect. Our family was complete.

"Do you think we let them have too much sugar today?" I asked her, thinking about that last churro we'd purchased.

"There's no such thing," she said with a gasp. "Besides, calories don't count at Disney."

I let out a chuckle while playfully poking her side. "If only that logic worked in the real world."

"I know a few ways you can work them off, if you want." She raised her eyebrows suggestively.

"That's what got us into this position in the first place," I said with a smirk, looking down at our sleeping toddler and her beautiful head of blonde hair.

"Worth it."

"They all were." I kissed her forehead, making sure not to squish our eldest daughter between us.

"When you first met me, did you ever think this was what our life would look like?" She echoed a question I'd asked her a few years back.

I looked down at the little platinum blonde and dark brunette heads that we'd created, and answered honestly. "Yes." I smoothed our oldest daughter's hair away from her face. "I wanted them to all look like you, but something like this, definitely."

"Oh." A contented smile spread over her face. "You knew, even then? That you wanted to marry me? Have kids with me?"

She smoothed down Abbi's dark hair, tugging on the pink princess dress she wore. The biggest lover of the color pink, just like her momma. She was in Ballet II now, and I loved going and seeing her dance. My little dancer had found her first love, and I hoped she would never lose it.

"Since the very first day. I told you. It's always been you. It'll always be you."

Charlotte sighed in contentment. "I want to come back every year."

"Done." *Anything for you.*

Our very first trip to Disney World had been for her babymoon—since I very much regretted that we'd never gone on a *real* honeymoon. She'd been a few months along, but a break in the Florida sunshine had been just what we'd both needed.

Our bus arrived, and we quickly gathered our two sleeping children and collapsed the stroller before boarding. Settling into the seats, Abbi nestled herself at my side, while Charlotte cradled little Ellie and I held Beau in my arms.

"I'm glad everyone came, but I like it when it's just like this. Our little family."

"Me too," I agreed. "Our *whole* family can be a little... much."

With eight kids between all of us, traveling anywhere in a group was almost impossible. It felt like almost everywhere we went, we were losing someone. At least it was usually an adult who did it, not one of our kids. They normally stayed where you told them to be. A lesson we'd learned quickly navigating the crowds here.

"Yeah. But I wouldn't trade them for the world."

Hearing Uncle Daniel was the best part of my day. We treated Noelle and Matthew's kids as if they were our own niece and nephew, despite not being biologically related.

It was our tribe. *It takes a village.* They were it. Our family. Our people.

My lips brushed against her cheek as I leaned over, and we laced our free hands together. "I love you."

She squeezed my hand. "I love you more."

"Impossible. But thanks for choosing me, darling."

"I never had a choice," she said with a smile. "You walked into my life and it was like I just knew that you were always going to be there. That I had you. Because you chose *me*."

This time, I squeezed hers back. Our little love language, the one we'd started a long time ago.

Long before we'd been in love. Before we'd been blessed with three children. Even before we'd gotten *fake* married, just to fulfill a marriage pact. Back when we were too scared to admit our true feelings.

It happened long before any of that, back when we were just two kids.

All my life, I had been searching for my path, but in truth, she had always been it. I realized that everything I had ever done had been leading up to her.

But she was mine. Truthfully, gracefully *mine.*

And I was hers.

Forever.

Extended Epilogue
CHARLOTTE

TWENTY YEARS LATER...

"Can you believe it?"

My eyes filled with unshed tears as I watched our youngest daughter cross the stage on her graduation day from college.

"We did it," Daniel whispered in my ear, eyes shining with pride. "We raised three kids."

I looked down the row, my gaze lingering on the two dark-haired adults that sat on the other side of Daniel. Both of her big siblings were both in the stands today, too. And we'd be celebrating at the house later tonight. Ellie had only gotten four tickets for the ceremony, but it didn't matter. I knew the rest of our family—the one we'd built—was watching her right now on the live stream.

"We did good," I murmured back, trying not to cry as they handed Ellie her diploma. She had earned an early elementary education degree, and I knew teaching was perfect for her.

We were all so proud of her. She'd been the littlest for the longest time until Angelina's daughter had been born. Lucy was an oops baby, almost ten years younger than her twin brothers, but all four of them doted on her like nothing I'd ever seen before. And Angelina had gotten her girl, finally.

Our kids had spent every important milestone together, and we'd celebrated each graduation the same way. Whoever was graduating, the parents would host at their house.

Not that it was very far. We all still lived on the same street. And when multiple kids graduated the same year—because we'd had all our kids close together—it'd always been a massive party. I didn't want it any other way.

I had the big, loving family I'd always wanted.

At twenty-five, twenty-three, and twenty-one, I couldn't believe I'd raised three kids from infancy to adulthood already. I still couldn't believe how fast they'd grown up in front of my eyes.

Abigail was running her own fashion line, jet setting between our home in Portland and all around the globe. She took after her aunt Angelina—a fierce fashionista, even sharing the same thick, dark curls. She'd gotten my eyes, though, those beautiful gray ones, and my love of pink. The hot pink sundress she wore was a bold choice, but it suited her well.

Beau had gone to Oregon State University on a football scholarship, and they had drafted him to the San Francisco 49ers after graduation. Daniel and I were so proud of him, even though he lived a state away.

When the time had come for Ellie to choose where she wanted to go to school, she'd chosen Daniel and I's alma mater. It felt right having her there, and the best part was she was so close to home. At least one of them came over for regular family dinners.

Part of me—a big part—wanted my babies back. There were no more nights spent cuddling with the five of us on the couch, or Disneyland trips coated in sugar just to see them smile or hug Mickey Mouse. The last time we'd all taken a trip to Disney World had been when Ellie was still in high school.

"Darling." Daniel ran his thumb over my cheek, catching

wetness I didn't even realize was there. When had I started crying?
"It's okay."

I gave him a smile, holding back the tears that threatened to spill over if I said anything more. My heart swelled with love for my kids. I was so proud of them. But it was time for them to go off and have their own adventures. Find their own love stories. Start their own families. Was it too soon to ask for grandchildren?

Abigail was almost the age I'd been when I'd married Daniel. Maybe I just missed having babies around. There'd been so many for years, with all of us growing our families together. I couldn't have imagined doing it any differently.

We filed out of the arena as the ceremony ended, following the graduates outside the building.

"Mom," Abbi whispered to me as we searched for a hint of blonde in the crowd. A sparkly blue cap. "Were you crying during the ceremony?"

"I think I've cried through every single one of your graduations, honestly." Even when they'd each graduated from kindergarten. But that might have been because they were so cute in their tiny hats. "I can't help it. When did you all get so grown up?" I pinched at her cheek, and she swatted me away, laughing.

"Mom," she groaned, swatting me away playfully. "We love you." My kids didn't hesitate to tell me every day. Even now, I hardly went a day without a call or texts from both daughters. Beau checked in weekly, even when he was on the road.

"Let's go find your sister," I said, resisting the urge to pull her in tight and not let go.

She squeezed my hand before pushing through the crowd, and by the time we found Ellie, our whole family gathered around her, showering her with love.

"Proud of you, sis," Beau said, handing her a bouquet.

Abigail pulled her into her arms and whispered something into her ear.

"Congratulations, El." Daniel wrapped his arms around our daughter. "I'm so proud of all you've accomplished."

"Thanks, Dad." She hugged him back, and I watched as Daniel held her tighter.

Just one more minute, he'd used to say. I didn't think he'd ever let his baby girl go, but eventually, she came over to me.

"Mom," Ellie breathed, running into my outstretched arms.

"Hi, sweetie pie. Look at you. My little graduate."

Her friend called her name, and she gave us a small smile. "Be right back, okay?"

"Remember when that was us?" Daniel wrapped his arms around me as we watched her hug her friends, take photos, and say goodbye.

I laughed. "How could I forget?" I'd been the one trying not to cry at his graduation, too. And he'd been there for mine. Sure, his sister had graduated with me, but I'd always been grateful to have all my best friends by my side that day.

Finally, when she came back over, Daniel looked at our family. "Everyone ready for the party?"

∽

My daughter scanned the room, gown now unzipped to show off her light blue dress that was cut to her knees, the scar there on display, for once. When she scanned the room, I knew she was looking for someone who wasn't there.

"Ellie." My voice was barely audible, a gentle whisper.

"He was supposed to be here, Mom."

"I know." We all knew who she meant.

The only member of our big extended family who wasn't here tonight. Noelle gave me a sad smile from across the room. She knew, too.

You know when you're growing up, how you dream about you and your best friend having daughters who are best friends? I'd never thought it would actually happen, but that was the funny thing about life.

Noelle's daughter, Penelope, had graduated today too. She

was nine months older, born in October to Ellie's July, but she'd missed the school cut-off, so they'd almost always been in the same class. And they'd been best friends since birth.

Penelope's red hair caught the light as she talked to Ellie. She'd inherited both her mother's looks and personality. Her love for reading and writing was evident since she was a little girl. She was fortunate enough to have her dad still teaching at the university, which allowed her to get her degree in English for free. Now, she'd started working on her own novel.

I suspected she'd learned to love romance novels with all of her time spent in Noelle's coffee shop, bakery and romance bookstore, *The Writer's Cup*. It had been her dream for years, and after having Penny, she'd finally done it. Our kids had practically all grown up there, using it as their hangout spot once they reached their teens, and hanging out at home was no longer considered *cool*.

"It doesn't get easier, does it?" Noelle murmured to me later as we watched our daughters take photos in the makeshift photo booth. She didn't have to say what she meant. We'd both watched our kids fall in love. And we'd nursed two broken hearts.

"No." I sighed. "We miss Owen. It's not the same without everyone here."

She sighed. "We miss him too."

"Look at us, with both of our kids in professional sports," I laughed. Beau had chosen football—Owen had picked hockey. "He's happy?" I turned back to Noelle, and I knew what she was thinking before she even said it.

"As happy as he can be, I think. He loves hockey. He loves his team. But he doesn't talk about it."

"El doesn't either."

About the breakup. Why everything had fallen apart. And despite how much I wanted to, I wouldn't be that meddling parent. Some things just took time to heal.

Even if it had been four years.

"I know he misses her." I felt Noelle's reassuring touch as her fingers brushed over my arm.

"Yeah." I knew Ellie did too.

Huddled in the corner, Angelina's twins were engrossed in conversation with Quinlan, who had landed a job as a Zoologist at the Oregon Zoo. Zach was currently getting his masters degree in History, while Wes worked for Nicolas's company—the same as his parents had.

Meanwhile, my oldest two were thick as thieves in the corner, as always. Abbi had loved her little brother from the moment he was born. I was glad the two were so close, even now. It reminded me of Angelina and Benjamin's relationship in college.

"They'll be okay," I murmured. *All of them.*

Because we'd lucked out and gotten the best kids in the world. The four of us girls, who'd walked into our dorms freshman year and left college with lifelong best friends, my sisters by choice. Each of us was affectionately referred to as "aunt" or "uncle" by each other's children.

Matthew wrapped his arms around his wife, who still had her signature red hair. I hoped it never faded. "Hi, sweetheart."

"Hi, babe," she murmured back.

"What's with the somber mood over here? You two are really putting a damper on the party," he chuckled.

I still remembered the day she'd told us about her crush on the professor she kept bumping into across campus. Selfishly, I'd hoped I found someone who made me light up the way he did. And I had.

I'd married my best friend, and we'd built a life together, and every day, I fell more in love with him. He'd driven our oldest daughter to countless ballet classes, and then competitions. Her choice—because we let our kids choose their activities. There wasn't a single one of Beau's high school football games that he hadn't been at.

And when our six-year-old had announced that she wanted to be an Olympic Figure Skater one day, he'd promised to be there every step of the way. And he had been. But some dreams didn't pan out. My eyes glanced over the scar on my daughter's knee once again. The career ending scar. The one that had led her to become a teacher.

But at least tonight, she seemed happy.

"We were just talking about Owen," Noelle said to her husband, rubbing at his beard.

"Ah. Living his best life in Seattle. I should be happy that he ended up on an NHL team on the west coast, but..."

With a simple nod, I conveyed my understanding. "But it's so far away, and you wish he was here." He was supposed to be. It felt like there was a missing hole in our family without him here.

Daniel came up behind me, resting his head on the top of mine. I still liked it when he did that—wrapped me up and reminded me he had me, no matter what happened.

Wordlessly, all of us ended up in the kitchen, watching our kids interact in the living room.

Noelle and Matthew.

Angelina and Benjamin.

Gabbi and Hunter.

Me and Daniel.

The eight of us, back where we first started.

"Did you ever think this would be our lives?" Angelina asked.

Gabbi shook her head. "I definitely didn't." She looked up at Hunter, whose green eyes were shining down at his wife. He still looked at her with so much love and affection that my heart swelled sometimes. "But I wouldn't change a thing."

"Me either," Hunter murmured.

Angelina looked at Benjamin with a smirk. "Well, maybe *some* things."

"Nope, Angel," Benjamin said, practically pinning her up against the countertop. "Not a single thing."

She laughed. "Not even me hating you?"

"Never."

Daniel squeezed my hand. "What about you?" He asked into my ear. "Would you change anything?"

We'd had this conversation before—about the years we could have had if we'd realized how much we loved each other earlier. But my answer was still the same. "Every day, I wake up grateful for the life we've built together. For our kids." I twiddled with my ring, feeling the smooth metal beneath my fingers. "I love our story."

Unconventional, sure, but how many people could say they'd made a marriage pact with their best friend and ended up with the love of their life? Even after three kids together, it had never diminished that spark between us. The need for each other's presence. If Daniel Bradford was like a drug, I was well and truly addicted.

"Good." He inhaled the side of my neck. "I do too."

"What do you think?" Noelle asked. "Better than the books?"

Our love stories. We'd spent so many years reading romance novels, and somehow we'd all ended up with a man straight off the page. Or better—because they were real, and they were ours. That was something we would never take for granted.

"So much better than books," I agreed, with a grin. I could only wish that for our kids, and our friends kids. That they'd find happiness and love, the person who made every single day, every individual moment that much better.

"And I think that I'm very glad we only have one more of these parties to throw before everyone's kids are out of college."

Angelina's cheeks flushed. "It wasn't like I intentionally had her at almost 40 years old, guys. Blame this one." She jabbed her finger towards Benjamin. "It was his sperm that found my egg." Her eyes danced with playful laughter, even as she scowled at her husband of almost twenty-seven years.

Little Lucy was a teenager now, the last of the kids to enter high school, but Angelina doted on that blue-eyed, dark-haired little girl. Hunter might have called his daughter Princess, but

Lucy truly was one. In every way that mattered, she was the littlest princess of the Bradford-Sullivan clan.

Gabbi laughed. "And that was why I'd had a hysterectomy after Quin." She and Hunter had momentarily thought about having a second, but it hadn't been in the cards for them, and they'd decided it was the right move.

Sometimes, when Angelina's daughter Lucy had been a baby, I'd thought about having another one, too. One more little baby to snuggle. But three was more than enough, and by the time they were old enough to walk, I didn't have the energy to chase around one more toddler.

My family turned out to be bigger than I had imagined. There was so much love surrounding us, always.

A blur moved outside the window, and suddenly, my daughter was outside the door, hurtling for the blonde boy who'd stolen her heart. Maybe he'd never given it back. I wasn't sure she'd ever given his back, either.

"Now everyone's home." Noelle's eyes filled with tears as her oldest entered the house, wrapping his arms around his little sister.

Although Ellie was quiet, I noticed she stayed by his side all night, occasionally stealing glances in his direction.

∽

Daniel's arms enveloped me as he spoke in a low, soothing voice. "How'd we do?" It was clear that he wasn't referring to the party. That, thankfully, had been a success.

"They're all grown up." I sighed contentedly and leaned against him, feeling the cool metal of the railing against my back.

"We're officially empty nesters. No kids left in the house. What do you want to do?"

In his embrace, I spun around, looking up into his familiar brown eyes that had become synonymous with home over the years. My best friend since eighteen. My soulmate. The love of my life.

"Spend the rest of my life loving you." I leaned in and pressed a gentle kiss on his lips.

"That, my wife, is something I can agree with."

"I thought so," I murmured, as he cupped my cheeks and looked at me so reverently.

A feeling of warmth spread through my chest, and my heart felt full of love.

Wherever Daniel Bradford was, that was home. Right here in his arms.

I couldn't think of anywhere else I'd rather be.

I felt a comforting squeeze on my palm as our hands entwined. With my head resting against his shoulder, we turned our gaze towards the stars, contemplating what the future might hold.

Whatever we'd face, we'd do it together.

The End.

THE BEST FRIENDS Book Club story will continue in Uniquely Yours—Ellie and Owen's story, coming 2024.

Acknowledgements

Acknowledgements

Writing a book is always a daunting task, and I'd be remiss if I didn't thank the people who cheered me on through this one. When I started writing Academically Yours last year, I had no idea how much these characters would come to mean to me. It's been an incredible journey, and one I'm so glad to have taken with all of you.

To my readers, thank you! Your edits never fail to bring a smile to my face, and every positive review is so appreciated. Truly, I couldn't do it without you.

To Katie W, my sister in heart, thank you for always telling me nice things about this book (even when it was a mess and made no sense). Your words of encouragement always got me through the day, and I am so very glad that a dancing alligator brought us together on that fateful day in 2016. I love you!

To Arzum, my endless hype girl. What would I do without you? Thank you for always listening to me ramble about my characters, and for your support and love since day one. I hope you liked your little cameo as one of Charlotte's dancers. I am so grateful for your friendship and your help to promote my books!

To Taryn, my Barnes bestie: where do I even begin?? You came into my life last December and it was instant friendship. I'm so grateful you gave my books a chance, and thank you for being my social media manager. I can't wait for many more bookstore runs and Panera dates.

To Al, my cover designer. Truly, you've done it again! This

cover is GORGEOUS, and it's so amazing to finally have all four four covers completed. THANK YOU. I could say it a thousand times, but truly, it will not be enough.

To Meg—thanks for being my author bestie. If you're reading this, you should probably go finish your book. We should also probably stop being the worst distractions for each other. Here's to ice cream breaks!

To my Faithlynn, Autumn, and Gwen: you all are the best. Thank you for helping me make sure this book was perfect before placing it in the hands of readers.

To my Parents, who I love very much: thank you for supporting my dreams, always. Thank you for always posting about my books on Facebook, and telling people your daughter has published books. And, as always, please don't read this. Thanks.

About the Author

Originally from the Portland area, Jennifer now lives in Orlando with her dog, Walter and cat, Max. She always has her nose in a book and loves going to the Disney Parks in her free time.

Website: www.jennchipman.com

- amazon.com/author/jenniferchipman
- goodreads.com/jennchipman
- instagram.com/jennchipmanauthor
- x.com/jennchipman
- facebook.com/jennchipmanauthor
- tiktok.com/@jennchipman
- pinterest.com/jennchipmanauthor

Also by Jennifer Chipman

Best Friends Book Club
Academically Yours - Noelle & Matthew
Disrespectfully Yours - Angelina & Benjamin
Fearlessly Yours - Gabrielle & Hunter
Gracefully Yours - Charlotte & Daniel
Contractually Yours - Nicolas & Zofia (coming soon)

Castleton University
A Not-So Prince Charming - Ella & Cameron
Once Upon A Fake Date - Audrey & Parker (late 2024)

Witches of Pleasant Grove
Spookily Yours - Willow & Damien
Wickedly Yours - Luna & Zain (coming Fall 2024)